A QU

Allan Johnstone Massie was born in Singapore in 1938, brought up in Aberdeenshire and educated at Drumtochty Castle, at Glenalmond and then at Trinity College, Cambridge, where he read History 'not very industriously'. He was a schoolmaster at Drumtochty Castle in Scotland for ten years and then taught English as a foreign language for three years in Rome. Since the middle 1970s he has worked as a journalist and author. His first novel, *Change and Decay in All Around I See*, was published in 1978. In the years since then he has written seventeen novels including a historical series set in ancient Rome: *Augustus* (1986), *Tiberius* (1990), *Caesar* (1993) and *Antony* (1997). These widely successful works have been translated into fourteen languages. His novel *The Ragged Lion* (1994) was on the life of Sir Walter Scott, while *King David* (1995) took its subject from the Old Testament. Massie's non-fiction work includes *The Caesars* (1983) on the twelve emperors of ancient Rome, *Byron's Travels* (1988), and *Glasgow: Portraits of a City* (1989). He has written critical biographies of *Muriel Spark* (1979) and *Colette* (1986).

Massie's second novel, *The Last Peacock* (1980), won the Frederick Niven Award in 1981, *The Death of Men* (1981) won a Scottish Arts Council Book Award, and *A Question of Loyalties* (1989) won the Saltire Society / *Scotsman* Book of the Year Award. *A Question of Loyalties* (to be published in France in 2003) belongs to what the author has described as 'a loose trilogy of novels dealing with the European crisis of the mid-twentieth century', the others being *The Sins of the Father* (1991) and *Shadows of Empire* (1997). These books have been widely praised for their engagement with the sometimes still-unresolved issues of morality and culpability in the Second World War.

Allan Massie was a Creative Writing fellow at Edinburgh University from 1982–84 and at the Universities of Glasgow and Strathclyde from 1985–86. He was editor of *The New Edinburgh Review* from 1982–84, and has worked as a television critic (Fraser of Allander award for Critic of the Year, 1982), and a sports columnist. He has also been the principal fiction reviewer for *The Scotsman* for over twenty-five years, and a columnist and reviewer for the *Daily Telegraph* and the *Sunday Times*. He is a Fellow of the Royal Society of Literature. He and his wife Alison have three children, now grown up, and live in the Socttish Borders with 'a number of spaniels'.

Alan Taylor is Associate Editor and Literary Editor of *The Sunday Herald*. He was formerly Deputy Editor and Managing Editor of *The Scotsman*. With his wife Irene, he co-edited *The Assassin's Cloak: An Anthology of the World's Greatest Diarists*. In 1994, he was a Booker prize judge. He is half of the Scottish team on Radio Four's Round Britain Quiz.

ALLAN MASSIE

A Question of Loyalties

Introduced by Alan Taylor

CANONGATE

CLASSICS

108

This edition first published as a Canongate Classic in 2002 by
Canongate Books, 14 High Street, Edinburgh EH1 1TE. First
published in 1989 by Hutchinson, an imprint of Century Hutchinson Ltd. Copyright © Allan Massie 1989. Introduction copyright © Alan Taylor 2002.

The publishers gratefully acknowledge general subsidy from the
Scottish Arts Council towards the Canongate Classics series and
a specific grant towards the publication of this title.

Set in 10 pt Plantin by Hewer Text Ltd, Edinburgh
Printed and bound in Denmark
by Nørhaven Paperback A/S, Viborg

10 9 8 7 6 5 4 3 2 1

CANONGATE CLASSICS
Series Editor: Roderick Watson
Editorial Board: J. B. Pick, Cairns Craig,
Dorothy McMillan

British Library Cataloguing-in-Publication Data
A catalogue record for this book is
available from the British Library

ISBN 1 84195 229 0

www.canongate.net

First, for Alison:
then, for Euan and Jane

AUTHOR'S NOTE

Any novel written from more than the author's immediate experience is likely to owe much to his reading. My debts in this respect are too numerous to list here, but I would like to acknowledge my especial indebtedness to the writings of Herbert R. Lottman and Richard Cobb.

All we have gained then by our unbelief
Is a life of doubt diversified by faith,
For one of faith diversified by doubt:
We called the chessboard white, – we call it black.

Browning – 'Bishop Blougram's Apology'

Introduction

For France, perhaps more so than for any other country, the Second World War was a humiliating affair. After eight enervating months of the *drôle de guerre*, the phoney war, the Germans invaded on 10 May, 1940. Within six short, traumatic weeks France was overwhelmed. For a population still reeling from the monstrous losses suffered during the First World War, it was without doubt the worst of times.

Though national pride in the victory of 1918 was high, the French public was not keen to rush into another conflict. Indeed, in the months before the declaration of war against Germany in September 1939, there were many in France who enthusiastically espoused pacifism. Thus they were ill-prepared to confront Hitler and his brutish regime which had been sabre-rattling and re-arming for the best part of a decade. In the French forces, the emphasis – if such it can be called – was on defence. But in the words of one British eyewitness, 'the French perceptibly froze'.

Bullishly, Churchill urged them to make a last stand in Paris, but the stuffing had been knocked out of them. Divided about what they were meant to be fighting for, and desperate to avoid ruination, the French capitulated. It was left to 84-year-old Marshall Phillipe Pétain to call on his countrymen to lay down their arms and negotiate an armistice, first with Germany and then with Italy. Thus from June 1940 to the Allied invasions of 1944, France was subject to German occupation.

Until November 1942, however, there was an unoccupied zone in the south, centred on the spa town of Vichy. From there, Pétain led a government which, as the war wore on, became increasingly identified with collaboration. When the Germans were finally evicted, many of those associated with the authoritarian Vichy State suffered retribution and were labelled traitors. Their legacy – known as the 'Vichy syndrome' – is one of shame and guilt, and ambiguity laced with controversy.

The questions persist to this day. To what extent were the supporters of Vichy complicit with the conquerors? Did they have any inkling of the atrocities carried out in Hitler's name, given that the Vichy government was responsible for sending back to Germany thousands of Jewish families who had fled to France for refuge? Or was the prime concern the preservation of France whatever the cost, a pragmatic decision taken in the hope of salvaging as much as possible from the débâcle of defeat?

All of which is grist to the mill of a novelist such as Allan Massie, whose favourite stomping ground is the no man's land where bald 'facts' leave chasmic holes in the historical narrative. For Massie, history is full of unlit corners and unwritten characters. It is not so much about events as individuals. In his author's note to *A Question of Loyalties*, he pays tribute to Richard Cobb, the maverick historian of the French Revolution, who wrote: 'I have never understood history other than in terms of human relationships.' Massie *aussi*. For him, as for Cobb, history is human. It is not empirical or predictable or manageable but chaotic and inchoate, affecting people as individuals, each of whom is happy or unhappy in his or her own way.

This is particularly true in a time of war, when none of us knows how we will behave. Circumstances differ. Old hierarchies are swept aside. Temperaments alter and past enmities re-surface. Fear is the great leveller, blighting everything in its path. Living constantly with its spectre can turn peacetime heroes into villains and vice versa. War complicates an already complex existence, turning things on their head; undermining definitions, demanding decisions, determining on which side we stand. Lucien de Balafré, the central character in *A Question of Loyalties*, a well-read man of refined tastes and sensitive disposition, understands better than most the dilemmas thrust upon us by war. 'We live,' he says, 'unfortunately, in a time of categories.'

Lucien is a good man in a dire situation. An idealist with an ingrained sense of civic duty, he is the kind of character who appears often in the novels of Allan Massie. His avowed aim is to serve his country, which seems on the surface to be relatively straightforward. But in a war in which one's country has been subjugated, how best to achieve this? Unlike de Gaulle, who spearheaded the resistance movement from London, Lucien chooses to remain in France. Like so many of his countrymen, he remembers the First World War, in which he served at the Front albeit for only a couple of months. 'There's no denying it,' he says, 'war today, modern war, is simply an atrocity, an offence against God and a surrender to whatever is infernal in our nature.'

As a young man, maturing between the wars, he is determined to throw himself into a public life – 'because after all it is my duty, it is the duty of people like myself' – in order to ensure there will be no more war in Europe. He studies at the Sorbonne then enters the Foreign Office and ends up in the embassy in Berlin, where he connects with a young German of noble birth and similarly high ideals, with whom he drinks 'to the fundamental integrity of Europe'. Lucien is blind to the significance of the rise of Nazism. In hindsight, however, he realises that the 1918 Treaty of Versailles, which was designed to prevent future wars by redrawing Germany's boundaries and restricting her armaments, had actually 'spawned' Hitler, who demanded that the Treaty be repudiated. His German friend tells him he 'all but joined the Party'. Later he plots in vain Hitler's assassination with dire consequences for all concerned.

It is an example of the cruel way in which war makes a mockery of individuals. The machine has no respect for doubters or prevaricators; it has no patience for those uncertain of their position. Decisions which in normal circumstances would be insignificant are exaggerated and become life threatening. The same is true of friendships and family background. In a world turned upside down Lucien flounders, serving in the Vichy government because he thinks he is a patriot. He loves the boulevard cafes of St Germain. He reads Balzac, Gide and Colette, André Malraux, Henri de Montherlant and Louis Aragon. In Provence, he even appreciates the icy gusts of the *mistral* rattling the naked olive trees. He is *au fond* an aesthete with dilettantish tastes. Before the war he edited *L'Echo de l'Avenir*, a literary magazine, which was his true métier.

Some forty years after Lucien's mysterious death, his son, Etienne de Balafré, tries to reconstruct his father's life, using journals, letters, official documents and personal memories. Now 55 years old and washed up in Switzerland, Etienne dovetails the account of his own pallid lifestyle with that of his father, talk of whom 'was forbidden territory for many years'. As he delves, he discovers to his surprise that he rather liked him. 'I traced in my father a desire to succeed, but on his own terms. He returned time and again to the consequences for France of what he described as the abdication of the *gens du bien* – the well-born men of property. According to him, all the ills of the country – socialism, irreligion, the dominance of the Jewish interest and high finance – stemmed from the disinclination of men from families like ours to involve themselves in public life.'

In part, *A Question of Loyalties* is an exploration of the limitations and the possibilities of genres – fiction, biography and

history. The plural in the title is profoundly significant. Massie
has always been interested in ideas and in this book – arguably his
best, certainly his most ambitious – he challenges many common
perceptions and received opinions. It is a novel, like others in his
oeuvre, which argues against rhetoric. Above all, he asks the
reader to put himself in the shoes of a fallible, honourable man
like Lucien, who desires to do his best in a world without
absolutes, and imagine what it must have been like in those dark
and desperate days. Doubt, for which war allows no room, is
Massie's governing emotion, as underlined in the novel's epi-
graph, which is taken from Robert Browning's 'Bishop Blougram's Apology':

> All we have gained then by our unbelief
> Is a life of doubt diversified by faith,
> For one of faith diversified by doubt:
> We called the chessboard white, – we call it black.

Eventually Lucien, a nervy man of 'fluctuating will and some
imagination', realises that he is impotent in the face of fate. He is a
pawn pulled every which way and is dragged reluctantly into
politics. His instincts, like Massie's, are literary, and *A Question of
Loyalties* is a very literary book. To Lucien, thinking and dream-
ing are preferable to doing. He is one of life's observers. 'Only one
thing depressed him that first winter of the war,' we're told. 'This
was the stream of people approaching him to beg that he should
intervene on their behalf with the authorities, to procure a licence
for this, a post for a son, a special concession of some sort. He did
not yet admit that their importunity defined the regime to which
he had given his heart and mind, but he was embarrassed to be
seen as the fount of favour.'

To Lucien, loyalty to France is non-negotiable. But how to
interpret that loyalty? How to respond to it practically in a war
that does not respect borders? Questions like these hover over
Massie's novel like an albatross. Lucien, whose fallibility is almost
painful, is a man overburdened by loyalty, to his wife, his family,
friends, France, to himself. His journals, like Gide's, are not
concerned with his private life but the discussion of 'abstract,
quasi-philosophical political matters'. Etienne wonders if his
father was a bore and concludes, perhaps correctly, that he
was to some people. To others, however, including his meretri-
cious wife Polly, he had charm. It is the curse of the diplomat
who, in attempting to please everyone, ends up pleasing no one.
Therein lies the tragedy at the heart of this engrossing, pro-

vocative novel. With a surefooted grasp of the period and ranging across England, Germany, Switzerland and South Africa, as well as France, it is epic in its embrace, encompassing almost the whole of the twentieth century. It is a learned book but imaginatively so. Indeed, Lucien's lack of imagination may partly account for his inability to see the Vichy regime as others saw it. For all his agonising, he is no visionary. He is locked in a way of thinking that is suffocating.

This is Allan Massie's sixth novel in what has proved to be a remarkable and prolific career. In his earlier books, including *Change and Decay in All Around I See* and *The Death of Men*, the influence of Evelyn Waugh and Graham Greene was apparent. *A Question of Loyalties*, however, has more in common with its immediate predecessor, *Augustus*, the first in his celebrated series of 'Roman' novels, in which he reconstructs the lives of the emperors. Like Augustus, Lucien is a man at the centre of events. But unlike Augustus, he is unable to exercise any control over them. He is an ordinary man grappling with extraordinary circumstances, his sins – if such they be – magnified until they are blurred because of the context in which they are revealed. In war, Massie suggests, everyone is a loser, though some, like Lucien, have more to lose than others.

Alan Taylor

PART ONE
1986

CHAPTER ONE

THE OTHER EVENING, for the first time since I came to live here two months ago, I crossed over into France. I took the little suburban train at the Gare des Eaux-Vives. I smoked a cigar as we clanked up the mountainside and then I descended at Monnetier, and strolled, still smoking, to the restaurant which the Baroness had recommended. It was, she said, 'in the country style, which has become ubiquitous, of course, but nevertheless this one is, I assure you, authentic'. I didn't really care about that; I was interested rather in my own sentiments; what it would feel like to be again in France.

I live in Geneva now, because Switzerland is comfortable; you are valued simply according to the promptitude with which you settle your bills. And I am always prompt.

The restaurant was quiet. Only two other tables were occupied. There was an American couple and a stout Frenchman who exuded bourgeois respectability. He wore the ribbon of the Légion d'Honneur in his buttonhole. It was absurd that in that ribbon, which is awarded to every postmaster and to every clerk who has shuffled papers for thirty years in the Ministry of This or That, I should see something denied me. Yet I did.

The dinner was equally unremarkable. What they call 'mountain trout' – justifiably since the fish-farm will be situated on the mountainside – a *tranche d'agneau* in a sauce too sharp with too many peppers – which passes for peasant style – and then the choice between the inevitable flan, the peach or cheese which you can always buy in better condition in the market-place. The coffee was burned, and I sighed to think of the coffee, without chicory, which Hilda used to prepare for me at what I still think of as home.

Then, I asked the bored proprietor if he had a *marc de Provence*. Provence not Burgundy, I insisted, knowing that he would prefer to give me the supposedly superior and more expensive variety, and, when I tasted its harsh and fiery corruption, I knew my little excursion had been a failure, and went out into the night.

Of course it was ridiculous to imagine that I might exorcise ghosts in such a perfunctory manner. There was a wind coming off the lake as I walked from the station to my hotel, that nipping wind which never quite leaves Geneva, and which is nevertheless for me one of its attractions.

When I am asked my nationality nowadays I generally say I am South African. It is true I carry a South African passport, but I would not have any difficulty in replacing it with another. And I think I may have to do so, for it has become tiresome and even embarrassing to be marked South African. People are so often sympathetic. They assume that I have left the Republic because I disapprove of its policies. In fact I am indifferent to them. Apartheid is evil but I have no reason to think any politics other than evil; they are the clearest expression of the truth of the doctrine of Original Sin. That's all. I detest all politics and all politicians. How could I do otherwise, being what I am?

And actually my heart is in South Africa. 'Whoever has once drunk Vaal water will always return', says a proverb which I take to be Bantu originally. It is an enchanted land, which, doubtless, is the reason it has been given over to its infernal politics. We can live only a brief season in Eden. Yet when I dream it is generally of the infinite spaces of the high veld or those rocky sun-baked hills of Cape Province which rise from vineyards, orchards, water-meadows and cool woods of chestnut. They are closer to Arcady than anything Europe has known since the Ancient World, and yet, spared Europe's history which hammers on us its relentless message of man's cruelty, violence, fear and lust for power, there remains, even today in South Africa, an indefinable and empty remoteness. The land lives aloof from man. Nowhere that I know so firmly insists that man is and is not, while the land remains. It is splendidly and proudly impersonal, that landscape. It eats into my dreams and fills my heart.

I spent much of my youth there, important years, and were I to choose a moment of well-being I would place it there: I would take a summer morning when, rising before dawn at an hour in which the cold still nips the empty veld and mist hangs around the fringes of the sky, I would saddle my pony Ben, and with the boy Joshua mounted on his beside me, gallop, it seemed for ever, towards the sunrise. Oh, the sharp beauty of the air, the tang of the reek of dung fires rising from the kraals, the sour-sweet scent of mimosa, and then, the ride home, as mules and oxen cough in the dust, but the dew – and there is no dew like it, not even the Alpine dew that sparkles on the gentian – still shines iridescent. Joshua slips off to the kitchen quarters to chew biltong, or for his bowl of mealies, and I stand by the pony's heaving side, smelling its sweet flesh, before turning to breakfast on the terrace. Do you wonder that I rhapsodise? Do you wonder that it comes back to me in dreams as by the waters of Babylon the children of Israel longed for Sion?

But my mother and stepfather are already on the terrace, and, seeing them, I am at once dragged from my idyll into the all-too-personal. Who was it said 'When you go to heaven you can choose to be exactly what you like, and I shall be a child'? He must have forgotten the grown-ups.

I have just remembered. It was Lord Alfred Douglas. How could he, of all men, have forgotten his father?

So, back to my hotel, through the old town, where, despite the immigrant workers, it is still safe to walk the streets. People tell me this is the great recommendation of Geneva and other Swiss cities, that you can still walk at night without fear of attack. In fact, when I have lived in cities, I have always enjoyed walking when the traffic is still and ghosts murmur at street corners, and have never been assaulted, or even experienced fear. Of course I am very solid, and that may act as a deterrent. On the other hand, I don't trouble to disguise my prosperity. I look what I am and am not, a fat burgher with an easy conscience and the fixed belief that the world is ordered for my convenience.

We went to South Africa in 1945 when I was fourteen. Polly, my mother, was only too happy to leave Europe at the earliest opportunity: she craved the sun and had no taste for the austerity promised post-war Britain. Besides, my stepfather, Roddy, was eager to be home. He was only a dozen years older than me, and so some ten years younger than his wife, and I think perhaps a little anxious as to how she would be received by his family. Being brave, in short bursts anyway, he wanted to get the meeting over. I don't mean to disparage Roddy, he had plenty of physical courage, as he had shown as a fighter pilot, but he hated rows; which was unfortunate for him, married to my mother.

I was pleased enough to go. England meant the thin cocoa and cold corridors of the preparatory school to which I had been consigned, and where I had been mocked for my French accent. Everyone knew that 'France has let us down.' 'My Daddy says the Frogs were windy as anything.' 'They jolly nearly lost us the war.' 'I bet they're as windy as the Italians.' 'De Balafré's a windy Frog.' Etienne de Balafré; what would I have given to be Stephen Scarface?

There was one master who tried to befriend me. He was a

weedy young man, only nineteen or twenty, but debarred from
military service because he was asthmatic or consumptive, something to do with his lungs; I can't remember. Despite his condition his fingers were stained yellow by the Goldflake cigarettes
he smoked to the very tip. He was due to go to Oxford, but was
'doing his bit' by teaching us seventy young savages English
language and literature. How cruel we were to him! There was
one boy, Tomkins, who could reduce Mr Fielding almost to tears
by the contemptuous response he offered to the poems the poor
man read us. Well, Mr Fielding was a Francophile, who used to
carry copies of novels by Gide and de Montherlant around with
him. I didn't know then that my father had been acquainted with
both men. Mr Fielding had developed a cult for General de
Gaulle, which, out of kindness, I suppose, he was ready to extend
to me. Poor man; I wonder what became of him.

I hated England, and hungered for the sharp outlines of
Provence. Its smell came back to me . . . when? In dreams?
surely not . . . till it was stifled by the wet laurels and lush grass of
the Home Counties. My father once said that the South of
England was 'like a salad, without oil, vinegar or garlic, of course',
and I repeated that line which was one of the few things I could
positively recall that he had ever said, and held it to my heart as a
talisman.

Then it was discovered that my Aunt Aurora had been in
prison. I don't know how that came out. I can't imagine any of the
boys had ever heard of Mosley. One of the parents, a mother most
likely, must have said something. 'De Balafré's aunt used to
dance with Hitler' . . . 'Did you call him Uncle Adolf?' they cried.

They never found out about my father. I wonder what Mr
Fielding would have said. I feel sure he would have found
something sympathetic. That certainly is a measure of my misery
in those years. Of course you will say, rightly, that my sufferings
were as nothing in comparison with what was happening to
children in Germany, Russia and indeed France. They were
trivial. Boys however have no objective standards, no means of
measuring their pain against anyone else's. The life of youth is a
sort of solipsism, and I was wretched. We are too fond perhaps of
objective standards now, it is part of our obsession with statistics:
Hamlet was a prince in Denmark, which didn't prevent him from
self-torture.

I have often wondered, though not then, why they left me my
name. Was it because, thanks to Aurora, my mother's name,
Lamancha, was itself notorious? It had a foreign ring too, though

in fact it is the name of a Border Parish whence my great-grandfather came south, to make a fortune in the China trade and then establish himself as a landowner in Northamptonshire.

When I was recently in England, after my Lamancha grand-mother's funeral, I was approached by a young man who was writing a book about Aurora.

'A thin subject,' I said, 'surely.'

He waved pale fingers at me, and smoothed the waistcoat he affected.

'Fascinating,' he said, 'a period piece. And a woman of rare quality.'

'You're too young to have met her,' I said.

'Oh indeed yes, though she would only be seventy-two now, you know.'

'Yes,' I said, 'I've just buried her mother.'

'All that period,' he said, 'and that set mean a lot to me. I would have chosen Unity, but she's been done, and Lady Mosley' – is it my imagination, or did his slim fingers inscribe the sign of the cross over his dove-coloured waistcoat? – 'is still out of court, as it were. Though I've had such a charming letter fiom her.'

Perhaps I do him wrong; perhaps he was only brushing the crumbs from the cloth – he had constrained me to offer him tea in the hotel where he had run me to earth.

Roddy was, I am sure, eager to be back in South Africa, eager but anxious too: anxiety was at the heart of his character. Perhaps that was caused by the head wound which had ended his career as a pilot, I don't know, but I fancy it had always been there. There was something vulnerable about his beauty: so slim, so blond, so tawny-skinned, with deep blue eyes; had he married Polly, I came to wonder, to protect him from himself? Even approaching forty Polly retained that androgynous appearance so characteristic of her decade. Roddy was quick to be wounded, and Polly, I soon saw, now that I was released from my boarding school, and from holidays passed at my grandmother's, was discontented. With her this has always taken the form of an increased, a desperate sociability: and Roddy, who was in full retreat, even then, was anxious to cut himself and the wife and child he had acquired off from the surrounding life of those who would have to be regarded as equals. Then there was his mother, brisk, dominating, out of key: how she brooded on Polly, how she suspected her. So when Roddy, with that silent obstinacy which had in the first place taken him across the sea to fight for an England to which he had

surely little reason to feel attached, now removed us after only a
few months from Cape Town, where Polly was already, with her
nose for society, acquiring as interesting a 'set' – her own word,
always – as might be found there, and settled us on the farm he
had inherited from his grandfather, which lay some three hundred
miles out of town, you might have guessed that the marriage was
heading for the rocks: to the satisfaction of course of Roddy's
mother.

Yet it never quite arrived at that destination. Perhaps my own
happiness on the farm helped to reconcile Polly. I used to believe
that, but the illusion has faded. How could that have been the
case? The truth, as I now see it, was that Polly herself, beneath the
brisk carapace, was alarmed. Heaven knows, she had cause
enough; she had looked into deep whirlpools; she had seen
how even the most confident and the strongest could be broken,
she had lived, after all, among those who never questioned their
own immense superiority, who gloried in it indeed; and where
were they now? Polly herself had never of course quite tempted
fate in the same way. She had an English scepticism which served
as a substitute for the Greek sense of hubris, something which had
been denied to Aurora; she accepted that she was one of the
fortunate ones in so many ways, and she knew that when you spin
a coin it may fall either side. So now, instead of making scenes,
she sat on the terrace, smoking her imported American cigarettes,
those long Pall Malls from the pre-filter age, with the bottle of
Cape gin to hand, gazed across the golden and green expanse of
Roddy's farming enterprise, and watched the lines creep down
from the corners of his mouth and eyes, and watched his hand
stray ever earlier in the day to the bottle of Cape brandy, which
was set out on the wickerwork table beside her gin an hour after
breakfast every day, and said little that was pleasant to him, but
nothing that crossed the verge of disaster. Once bitten, twice shy.

We never talked of my father; that was forbidden territory for
years. And we never, Polly and I, in those days discussed Roddy
either. It wasn't until my last visit that, holding a photograph of
him in his Air Force uniform, so young-looking, so afraid and so
nerving himself to overcome his fear, she said, with a flicker of
contempt, 'Strange the taste for men who are not quite strong
enough.' She took a sip of gin. 'And, when you can see so clearly
just what they are, why do you prefer to pretend they are
different?' She has never thought, it has not perhaps even occurred to her, that she might have let them both down.

How extraordinary, in my fifty-fifth year, to be mulling over this dead stuff in this wayward journal. It is like a compulsion to turn out an attic room. Polly hated lumber. She would have thrown everything out. Yet now she finds herself turning back, with cool resentment. Life has not been as it was sold to her. I had a letter the other day: '. . . it's so murky, darling. Of course everything is going to pot here, and that's maybe why I find myself remembering what it was like then. Not happily, I assure you. Oh it was great fun when we were all young, but let's face it, your poor father was no good. And yet, except in the hunting-season when I was a girl, or on hunting mornings anyway, I don't suppose I have ever been really happy except in our years together when we lived in that little apartment off the Palais-Royal, and we still made love, and he still laughed at my jokes. That's the really important thing in a marriage or an affair, and of course poor Roddy has no sense of humour at all. Perhaps if he had, I could have stood the fact that he doesn't really like women. But what on earth are you doing in Geneva? Dismal town I should have thought. Switzerland's all right for operations and for keeping money in, I suppose, if you have any, but then you do, don't you? Sarah came to see me the other day, and I was so sad, such a waste, silly girl. I'd like to see you again, darling, before I pop off.'

Which she is not going to do for years. There's tenacity there, which Sarah, my only child, inherited.

She is wrong about Geneva and it is interesting that she is so mistaken. But then almost everybody misunderstands the Swiss – when they can be bothered to take an interest in them; which isn't often. I find this curious. Here after all we have possibly the only case of a successful political and economic system in the world, and we're told it's a bore. I daresay there are dark corners of Swiss life that I have not penetrated, reasons for shame – they are human, so there must be reason for shame; nevertheless, Switzerland, which used to be regarded as a bastion of liberty, and quite right too, is now viewed with a mixture of envy and contempt; very rum. Can it be that humankind cannot bear too much peace and prosperity? Do we dislike the Swiss because of the complacency with which they refuse the temptation of the abyss?

Certainly I think Sarah would say so. How I long for her, and how certainly I know that she would quickly make me miserable with her disapproval of me. For Sarah is everything that I have never been and could not be; she is a rebel with a cause. She believes in human rights, and I . . . well, inasmuch as I suppose that I am writing this for her, I am still trawling the past in search of any reason to believe in anything.

That is not quite true. Last week I went fishing. I took a little train which climbed up into the mountains and debouched me in a village which has somehow contrived to escape any tourist development. Then, in what was still the cool of a crisp mountain morning, I bought rolls at the bakery, cheese and wine at a grocer's and tramped up a narrow hill path to cross the neck of the valley, and descended to a brisk stream. I put my bottle of wine in a pool under the shadow of a rock, and fished half a mile upstream and down the other bank. Larks cried overhead, and in the distance cowbells tinkled, and the air was rich with the scent of meadow flowers. The trout were eager and nimble, but I returned the first three I caught. I kept the fourth, which weighed three-quarters of a pound, and made a little fire, sprinkled the fish with rosemary, and when the fire died down cooked it in the ash: as I did so, I saw Joshua squatting by just such a fire beside the stream that rose in the hills behind Roddy's farm, and I heard the muttered humming with which he accompanied all tasks that demanded care and precision. The two scenes came together; it was as if Joshua were there, a numinous and innocent presence. Tears pricked my eyes; but it may have been the smoke. Yet of course it wasn't. I knew that very well. It was an assurance of some sort of immortality, of our ability at the same moment to live in a delightful present, and to slip time's halter; and what is such an experience but a confirmation of the goodness and reality of God?

Today it is raining. Mist obscures the lake, and I have been reading. Gide's *Journal*. One keeps coming back to Gide; there is such a splendid mendacity, such an ignoble truth to his writing. I have been reading that section which deals with his time in Tunisia in 1942-3, when he was persecuted by the son of his hosts, a boy whom he calls Victor. I don't think many of the writer's admirers can have read about this appalling young man without having had a strong impulse to kick his behind. His persecution of the distinguished and elderly writer seems merely malicious. At table he would grab the choicest cuts simply so that Gide wouldn't get them. He claimed to be a Communist, and Gide was convinced that this was only to emphasise his bullying, boastful and anarchic character. Of course some may have wondered why the boy – he was no more than fourteen or fifteen – should have behaved in this way, and concluded, naturally enough in view of what is known of Gide's tastes, that the writer had probably made advances to him which the boy resented. (And indeed, years later, when the boy had grown up, he wrote and published his own memoir in which he confirmed such a suspicion, while nevertheless presenting himself as being at least as disagreeable a young man as the one Gide had portrayed.) Yet, without having any such suspicion myself when I first read Gide's *Journal*, I recall how all my sympathy went to the wretched and in many ways despicable Victor. Why shouldn't he, I thought then, put this pretentious and sanctimonious old thing, this canting proser, so firmly and painfully in his place; if there was something malicious about it, well then, I thought, the old booby asked for it. What right had he to assume the airs of superiority he had; to insist that his standards were so much more admirable than poor Victor's, who had after all his own life to live, his own way to make, in his own manner? My youthful sympathies went out to Victor, and the more evidence Gide accumulated of the boy's vileness, the closer I felt to him. Wasn't he, even, in his assertion of a ridiculous and insincere Communism, making a very apt criticism of all ideologies, of all high-minded self-justification? So I thought then, and I wonder now if the strength of my partisanship wasn't occasioned by a memory, buried then, of that poor Mr Fielding who had tried to befriend me, and who had carried copies of *Les Faux-Monnayeurs* and other novels by Gide so ostentatiously about with him?

And reading it all again now, I find that my sympathies are absolutely and ridiculously divided. Victor's vileness is very apparent, and yet I still find myself attracted by his farouche refusal to be anything less than himself. The cause of the estrangement, the occasion of the boy's compulsion – for it was certainly that – to persecute the distinguished writer is unimportant. There is something fine as well as malicious in Victor's behaviour. Why should he have accepted Gide at his own valuation?

We cannot be really damaged while our personal myth remains unimpaired. Who said that?

The last time I saw Sarah was in London six months ago, when she told me she was returning to South Africa 'to continue the struggle'.

'By the word or the gun?' I asked.

'I'm not much good with guns,' she said. 'All the same it will come to that in the end, there's no real question of that, I'm afraid.'

As she spoke she looked at me with candid eyes in which I could see no fear at all. We were sitting in the lounge of my hotel, and at one time she would have looked out of place there, in her dirty jeans, blouson jacket and sloganned T-shirt. But things have changed, and now it seemed to me that it was I myself in my herringbone tweed suit who did not belong.

'Well,' I tried to make a joke of it, 'at least you disdain revolutionary chic.'

She paid no attention.

'By all the rules,' she said biting into a cheese sandwich, 'I ought to have no time for you. Fathers, some of my friends say, are always the enemy.'

'Isn't that rather old-fashioned?'

'Well, you are too, aren't you?'

'Oh, I don't know,' I said. 'In certain respects I seem to myself to be terribly, deplorably, modern. I don't believe in anything, and isn't that a characteristic of the coming age? It may be you who is old-fashioned. When I look around me, I can sometimes feel quite in tune with 99 per cent of humanity. Even those for whom you are ready to fight. Doesn't it ever occur to you that the age of ideology is dead, and very properly dead, and that we all ought to be grateful for that? What cause has ideology ever served but its own?'

'You don't understand,' she said. 'I'm not interested in ideology, only in people's natural rights. Which they are denied.' She stopped speaking and looked at me with exasperation. I would have liked to have been able to read love in that glance . . . and yet she had come to see me, making a point of doing so. There must be something there, I told myself. After all, innumerable girls do cut off their fathers.

Her name appeared in the press today – in *The Times* in fact – among the signatories of a letter demanding . . . do you know, I can't now recall just what they were asking for, though I am sure that I read the letter. Indeed yes, for I remember thinking how leaden and yet empty it sounded; how shop-soiled and ready-made the language; politics as Nescafé.

It was the Baroness who drew my attention to it.

'I'm surprised,' I said, 'that you read the English newspapers.'

'Oh,' she replied, 'one must keep in touch.'

She is forty, with a metallic glitter, and an allowance from her estranged husband, and she has taken a fancy to me.

'She must be a trouble to you, that girl,' she smiled.

'Ah well,' I said, 'she does what she thinks is right.'

'So foolish. These people will not thank her. Why, it is like cutting your own throat. We know that, you and I, we old Europeans,' and she shook her head as if measuring the imbecility of optimism.

'Oh come,' I said, 'you're post-war, you can't claim to be an old European any more than I am. And if we were we should have little cause for pride, don't you think? Old Europeans made rather a mess of old Europe, wouldn't you say?'

I knew she wouldn't, for she makes a cult of the idea of Old Europe. Perhaps it is natural enough that she should. She is one of the dispossessed, the child of a Pomeranian Junker family which scuttled from its sandy Baltic estates before the Red Army. And yet she has done well enough for herself: a career as a model, and then marriage to the Baron von Ochsdorf, who has made a fortune as a magazine publisher catering admittedly for a fairly low common denominator. She accepts none of this however, though for some years she tolerated her husband's annual infatuation (her word) with some teenage girl willing to remove her clothes for his cameraman and her own future. But for all that Reineke (the Baroness) didn't leave him; he gave her her *congé*, I don't know precisely why.

Was it because he finally couldn't endure her sighs for a time lost that was in her case purely imaginary? The Baron, as far as I can see, wallows in the present like a pig in shit. But her nostalgia is even more self-indulgent, and perhaps disgusting. She wants me to make love to her, and the thought horrifies me. Even after a brief conversation I feel as if she had been biting my shoulder.

I looked at the rain mingling with the lake, and said, 'You will make yourself unhappy if you go on thinking like that.'

She said: 'You can't draw a line under the past. You of all men ought to know that.'

'But it is not our past,' I said.

I have formed the habit of going to bed after lunch. I generally sleep straight away and wake in a melancholy yellow light to the sound of car-horns. Then I turn over and read, to shut away the thoughts that come. Just now, Balzac is my narcotic: the enormous energy and gusto that do not exclude despair.

It was my wife Rose who said to me: 'If I didn't know you were half French your love of abstract nouns would still give you away.' And it is true: abstract nouns are a sort of betrayal. But they are also a guard, they objectify feeling.

As the light dies, I take a shower and dress and go out. Usually I walk in the old town on the other side of the river, where the streets are shabby and the wind disturbs the complacency of the city. It kills time, and then I sit in a café where I watch the coming and going, and can eye the girl behind the bar whenever she is occupied. She has a pale face and an ample throat – thyroid trouble, I suspect – and her movements are slow and heavy as her mane of auburn hair. She looks soft and lazy and pliable, and it is all I can do to take my eyes off her. But I have never spoken beyond asking for a *café crème* or a third of a litre of white wine. What would be the point? I have no desire for an affair, and she is the sort of girl who would expect one. Or so I tell myself. For all I know she may go back to a husband and three children. But I don't think so. There is something about the hopelessness of her movement that suggests she is the type to find her approximation to fulfilment in a doomed affair.

To stop myself thinking about her – I have discovered that her name is Elise – I picked up a whore this evening. She beckoned from a doorway and without thinking I responded and followed her upstairs. There were posters of pop stars on the walls and the girl straightaway took off her cotton skirt, which was short and bright with poppies on a blue backcloth, and invited me to put my hands under the belt of her tights and slip them off. She smelled of almonds. She feigned eagerness but when I pushed my hands under her jersey to fondle her breasts, she thrust them away and said, 'Not that, I don't like that.' I thought to myself, 'Who's paying?' and let my hands drop. She sat on the narrow bed, her legs apart. She licked her finger and laid her hand on her pubic hair, curling the damp finger round. Her legs were thin and I looked at her smudged face and saw she was hardly more than a child, and, though I felt an enormous lust rise in me, I also felt disgusted. 'No,' I said, and put my hand in my pocket and found a handful of fifty-franc notes and tossed them to her. 'No,' I said again, 'I've made a mistake, I'm sorry,' and I left her and descended the dark and rickety stair.

Outside in the street I found that I was quivering. I turned two corners and went into a bar and ordered a large brandy. All round me were people sitting in silence, and the only noise came from billiard balls being struck in the room beyond.

'Is she still lying there,' I wondered, 'letting her finger do what I did not dare? A novice,' I thought. 'She really wanted it, poor girl, even from me.' And I felt doubly ashamed, as if I had indeed provoked her lust and then insulted her.

I had a letter this morning from an American called, or calling himself, Hugh Challefray. I put it like that because it seems an

improbable name, even for an American. I had never heard of
him before, but he describes himself as a historian. I am slightly
suspicious because he tells me of nothing which he has written,
and such reticence is in my experience untypical of American
academics. But I confess that I really know very little about such
things and my impressions are probably drawn from lazily con-
structed stereotypes.

Anyway, young Mr Challefray would like to meet me. He is
writing a book 'about the ideological ethos of Vichy', and would
value my 'assistance and co-operation'. I can't imagine how he
has tracked me down, but the letter is addressed directly to me
here in Geneva. He 'purposes to be in Geneva next week and',
etc., etc.

I have no reason to call him 'young Mr Challefray', but I would
wager he is not yet thirty. Only a young man could be interested
in such cobwebby stuff.

There is a mist hanging about the lake obscuring the mountains.
The cold penetrates even my overcoat of Donegal tweed, and
when I returned from my walk I discovered that the cloth was
damp, flecked with drops of liquid, though it had not been
raining. The mist thickened all the time I was walking and as I
crossed the bridge it was impossible to see the water below. In
such moments the city feels like a prison where one is the only
inmate. I stopped off in a café and played chess with an opponent
whose name I do not know. I came on him first a couple of weeks
ago. He was sitting in the back room of the Café de la Banque,
with the chessboard in front of him, and a newspaper written in
some language which I could not identify on the bench beside
him. Seeing me look at him, he asked if I would like a game. I
nodded and we played in an agreeable silence, while he drank tea
and I smoked a cigar and had a glass of marc and a bottle of Evian.
It was very still in the café. There was only an old woman there,
dressed in black with a pink flower in her black felt hat. She had a
little dog on a pink lead and fed it the corners of her croissant.
That day, I mated him on the twenty-fifth move after sacrificing
my queen. But since then we have played five times, and the best I
have achieved is a draw. The game is in danger of becoming a
ritual. I think his newspaper may be Ukrainian, and am obscurely
glad to have concluded this. He has three scars on his left cheek,
and it might therefore amuse him to know my name. What would
I have given to be Stephen Scarface? But we have not exchanged
names, only pawns and other pieces. Today he produced a move

with his king's bishop which took me by surprise. He is a man perhaps ten years older than myself, and the fingers of his left hand, with which he moves his pieces, are twisted as if they have been broken and badly set.

I spend less and less time in my hotel because whenever I am in the bar or one of the public rooms, the Baroness seems to have been lying in wait.

'It was absurd,' she said to me today, 'the life we used to lead. Truthfully it was absurd, don't think, my friend, I don't realise that. You would not believe the extravagances my grandfather used to commit. He would hire all the ladies of the chorus to dance at the supper-parties he gave his brother officers, to dance on the table, you understand. Then the officers and my grand-father would drink champagne from their slippers. I think they were mostly gypsies of course. That would explain why they were willing to do it.'

And she smiled as if she had arranged the entertainment. It may be that she is going mad, because this conversation would have seemed – what? – more in keeping, more suitable, shall I say? – if she had been twice the age she is, and in reality a refugee from the Bolsheviks. I don't know if she expects me to believe her stories, which are palpably absurd, or if she just talks for her own amusement.

Today she also said: 'My husband used to say I fantasised, and he hoped I would go into a clinic for treatment when I came to Switzerland, but you and I, my friend, know differently. It is his life which is fantasy,' and she pulled out a copy of a magazine, presumably one of her husband's, and showed me a young girl lying on the beach in the scantiest bikini looking over her shoulder at the camera.

'You see,' she said, 'and it's not as if he takes them to bed. I could have stood that.'

'Well,' I said, 'we must all find our reasons for living.'

'But why?'

But why?

To have reached my age and be without achievement; to have reached my age and be without hope; to have passed fifty and never have known content; to be in sight of death, and still without faith. Waiting perhaps for that *vecchio bianco per antico pelo* who will cry out: *I' vegno per menarvi all' altra riva, Nelle tenebre, in caldo e in gelo* . . .

But I could not have spoken of that to the Baroness, so I left my question dangling in the air, like a noose. There are those in our time who have said, speaking with the assurance and succulence of a rose: 'I choose evil.' But if we deny evil, if we explain and excuse choices, if we can always find some reason why the cork, that particular cork, should be drawn from the bottle, do we become accomplices? Or is that nothing but rhetoric? Isn't it rather our problem that evil presents itself as good? And that we are so easily deceived?

I turn these thoughts round in my mind, or my mind somersaults in these thoughts, and the *jet d'eau* rises from the lake, and loses itself in the mist.

When Arthur ordered Bedivere to throw the sword into the lake, and the hand rose to seize it and draw Excalibur under the dark waters, was that arm good or evil? Was it preserving justice – for Excalibur was the sword of righteousness and justice – or was it drowning it?

It is autumn turning to winter in the gardens that march by the lake where the steamer plies to and fro, to and fro, and I walk up and down, and draw on my cigar, and wait.

I am becoming a popular man. Three letters this morning, apart from another from my broker, and none except his pleasing. The first is from Mr Challefray, announcing that he will be in Geneva on Friday and proposing to wait on me at my hotel at eleven o'clock on Saturday morning . . . perhaps if I am unavailable, I could appoint another time. Well, I am in the deepest sense unavailable, but Mr Challefray (who must, I think again, by the pomposity of his prose, be very young) is evidently determined in pursuit. I remember talking once with a friend who had spent two years in prison; he described the relief he had felt when he knew his arrest was certain. All that had been years before, but he still rediscovered the note of wonder when he told me of it; 'It was like being free of living,' he said, 'and simply watching a movie of one's own life.' And immediately he said that, I could feel the velour under my hands and sense the dimming of the light. One has no responsibility for an auto-movie. Such surrender of control is a way of escape, yet it may also be a trap, flight up a one-way street. For I find, like Flaubert, that 'as my body continues on its journey, my thoughts keep turning back and burying themselves in days past'. Involuntarily; indeed with reluctance, and without hope.

I didn't recognise the name scribbled with the sender's address on my second letter: Bendico Perceval, unconvincing surely. And then I remembered it was the rather too exquisite young man who had expressed his intention of writing about Aurora, and I tore the envelope across without opening it. I had only seen Aurora once since the war and then she had said, 'Well, I was silly, darling, but you can't imagine what awfully good sense it seemed then. And of course they made such a heavenly fuss of me in Berlin that any girl could be excused . . . but now you know I just run the village, and grow azaleas, much more satisfying, don't you think?'

The third letter was from Sarah, and I had to read that. All the same I stuffed it in my pocket and kept it there till the middle of the afternoon; and I got myself a glass of brandy before opening it.

'Dear Daddy,
    I'm going back, and I had to write to you first, because I don't know what will happen when I get there, and anyway I'm fairly certain that my letters will be opened.

    I would like you to understand me, and I know Mummy can't. But that doesn't mean much, and you two haven't ever really been on the same wavelength, have you?

    I was so depressed by our last talk in London, I even came away from it wondering if you were right when you said that 99 per cent of people don't believe in anything, so why bother? But it's not true, and I have been trying to work out why you should say anything so untrue and awful. It's something to do with my grandfather, I know that, and then I realise that I really know nothing about him. You've never talked of him to me. I did ask Mummy once, but – you know her way – she just waved her hand and said something about it all being so long ago. So I tried Granny because I'm persistent by nature, I suppose, even though I knew she never talked about him either, and I realised I've never even seen a photograph of him, but I put that down to Roddy's being jealous of his memory, which makes sense. Anyway, I did ask her, and, to give her credit, she looked me straight in the eye, and do you know what she said, "Kind of you to ask, child. He was killed in France, during the war. I'd rather not talk about it if you don't mind. Pains me still you know." Oh, I'm no good with words and I can't catch the way she speaks, but it was so offhand it made me ache. I mean I realised how much it did hurt and felt a brute for asking. Still, that makes it clear enough to me, and I suppose he was tortured by them, poor man. And that's why you flinch from commitment. But don't you see he was right? I mean, I do, and don't you see that it's exactly the same Fascist mentality that I'm fighting against? The people with power always believe and you have to have a belief to fight them. Now you have spent your life running away from this, and that is why you are unhappy. Because you are, and it's no use pretending it's just because of Mummy. I think actually she's done as much for you as any woman could for a man who is fundamentally unhappy because he keeps running away from the truth and shirking things. I daresay you will laugh and call this very pompous talking from a chit like me; pompous is one of your favourite words, isn't it, and I've noticed that you use it when you want to escape having to take things seriously. But the trouble about refusing to do that is that you end by taking yourself too seriously, and I daresay that's why you're sitting in Geneva now – what a bloody awful city to choose – drinking too much brandy and feeling sorry for yourself. Oh dear, this seems to have turned into an angry letter, and it was meant to be a loving one, saying that I understand you better than you think. And still love you. Because I do, though you drive me nearly mad with your refusal to face up to things . . .'

I have rarely read a more masterly analysis based on a false premise.

A vile dream last night which has made it impossible for me to eat any breakfast.

It began as an idyll. I was lying with Rose under an oak tree. It was a glorious summer afternoon, and a picnic was laid out on a white cloth before us. We had made love, though that was not part of the dream, only the consciousness that we had done so, and there was no sadness. It was as in the first weeks of our marriage. She spread herself on the grass and I leant over and popped a strawberry in her mouth. A little juice trickled from the corner of her lips, and she drew me down towards her and its sweetness delighted my tongue. So we lay for a long time in a happiness that seemed everlasting while doves cooed and in the distance I could hear a woodpecker hammer at a tree. Then 'Look,' Rose said and pointed towards a clearing in the wood, and I saw that a ruined temple – three or four broken columns and a fragment of pediment – stood there, but it was not to the temple that she pointed, but beyond it to a vine-wreathed arch under which two boys stood with their arms around each other. One was blond with hair that curled into his nape like a Greek statue, and long honey-coloured legs, the other dark, with the sharp face of a fawn and a wide mouth; the blond boy wore a short white tunic, and the dark one, whose fingers now moved to the belt that encircled his friend's garment, was naked to the waist and clothed in goatskin breeches cut off at the knee. They stood still a moment as if posing for a photograph that required a long exposure or waiting for time to stop, and then, wordlessly, embraced each other. A little wind blew up from the east, and all at once the blond boy was alone and I saw him shiver. A white peacock shrieked from the broken temple and a voice called, 'Bubi, Bubi.' The boy dropped to his knees, and the glade was transformed into a court full of men in uniform. At a word of command two of them seized the boy, and threw him across a bench. He screamed, and his legs twitched as he sank his head, and the bird answered his cry, as if in mockery. I thrust out my hand for Rose, but she was not there. My mouth was dry, and the wind blew hot and gusty from the east.

I was sweating, and switched on the lamp by my bedside. Three o'clock and a well-mannered Swiss silence in the street without, and in the depths of my hotel. I was brought up to believe that dreams had a meaning. Any African will tell you that, and without believing that they crudely reveal the future, I have never doubted that they disclose a parallel world. One's secret self forces itself through the veil of consciousness. The world of night is the same as the world of day; the same objects stand in the same relation to each other. Space is not altered by dark, and yet who in man's history has ever felt night not to be different?

The boy's fear had excited me. Was that why Rose had slipped from my side?

I rose and put on a dressing-gown and opened the window, and stared through the wet street-lamps of Geneva. It had begun to rain and the drops leapt from the purple puddles. The setting of the dream was nowhere I knew, except in imagination. And Rose had not left me for that reason or for any cause that was equally serious. She had been bored and she had fallen in love, to speak loosely, and that was that. But I heard the boy scream and saw the shiver of his flesh and the peacock strut.

I have written nothing in this journal for three days, not since I recorded that dream (which, I think, if I ever come to showing

this little school exercise book to anyone – or leave it behind me –
I shall destroy), and in these three days I have felt myself more
nervous and have experienced a certain horror of my own nature.
Yet my nature is only human – the most pathetic of standard
excuses – and humanity has shown such a relish for cruelty as
exists in no other species. It is ironic that we also use the word
'humanity' to describe a moral quality of which we approve. At
this very moment a trial for war crimes is being held in Israel, and
we read, over our croissants and apricot jam, of how the guards in
the death camps would select prisoners for execution; any prisoner marked by a blow from the guards would be executed the same
day.

And what is also horrifying: if I told my dream to the Baroness,
she would seize my hand and cover it with eager kisses.

Young Mr Challefray will be here tomorrow. One thing is certain,
and I suppose, some relief. Mr Challefray's book will never be
written.

My certainty would surprise some, for he is a young man of very
obvious energy and enthusiasm, with brush-like reddish hair, a
pale freckled face, and a warmth of manner. He leapt to his feet as
soon as he saw me, and bounded forward with a wide and, I think,
genuine smile of welcome on his face. He at once transformed
himself into the host, solicitous for my welfare.

'I don't think I can help you,' I said, 'if I read your letter right. I
know next to nothing of these matters.'

'It's something in the way of a general discussion I want,' he
said. 'I'm still at a preliminary stage.'

'And yet you have reached me – surely the most remote
sources . . .'

'The preliminaries are taking a long time,' he said, snapping his
fingers for a waiter and ordering coffee when he obtained one.
This took him a long time also, despite his energy. Perhaps it was
then that I concluded that the book would be beyond him.

He began to outline the origins of his interest, giving me first of
all a canter over his qualifications. I barely listened. His American
accent was slight, as if it had been acquired late, and his voice
pleasant. He came to an end just as the coffee arrived and then
busied himself seeing that I had just what I wanted.

'Your name suggests that your own family is French,' I said.

'Sure,' he said, 'but not for a while back. We're French-
Canadians in fact, but I've never lived in Canada: or not much.

My father was a diplomat, worked for the UN, I've moved around
a lot, and went to university first in England, Oxford actually. But
you were Cambridge, weren't you?

'So,' he said, 'I came to you this way. Your father's essays
interested me. One in the *Nouvelle Revue Française* in 1942,
particularly.'

'Ah,' I said, 'I doubt if I've read it.'

'It was remarkable,' he said. 'Remarkably logical and cogent.
He argued that while there might have been a patriotic case for de
Gaulle, or for opposing Pétain, in 1940, there was none in 1942,
since by then a German defeat must result in a Russian victory.
Communism, he argued, offered a more serious threat to France
than Germany did, because it threatened the national identity.'

'History,' I said, 'hardly suggests that his judgement is to be
applauded. Where is Communism today?'

Mr Challefray sighed. 'I take your point, of course, but you
miss mine,' he said. 'You have to consider the intellectual atmosphere in which I grew up to understand it perhaps. And I was
struck also by what he called "the morality of Macchiavelli",
which really startled me. He said, more or less, I'm awfully bad at
quoting from memory, though I've got it all on disc of course, that
the only true difference between the Macchiavellian governor or
statesman and the common run was that he understood that no
politician could really be in sympathy with the people, and this
realisation gave him a degree of consciousness that they lacked; he
was the point of intelligence in the system of force. I found that
persuasive. So straight away Lucien de Balafré seemed to me one
of the more interesting minds I was dealing with. What sort of
man was he?'

'Oh,' I said, 'I'd forgotten that he was to be taken seriously.'

Mr Challefray's face assumed an air of incomprehension. I
stretched out my hand for the coffee-cup.

'Well,' I said, 'I can't imagine that I can be of any help to you.
I've never been interested in my father's ideas. All this stuff about
Macchiavelli is way above my head. I don't suppose I have
opened a book of philosophy since Cambridge. I'm a businessman and wine-grower. Or was, till I retired last year. I'm sorry to
disappoint you.'

'Oh no,' he said, 'I checked you out. I wasn't looking for this
sort of co-operation from you. Like I say, I've got all that on disc
and I have a computer system to run it through which lets me
evaluate it. It was something quite different I was looking for.
Look, I don't know how much time you can give me, sir, but I

observe that the sun's coming out. Can we take a walk? I'd like to
see something of the city, and then you would perhaps allow me
to buy you lunch.'

'That's the Palais de Justice,' I said, as we walked along. 'It ought
to interest you.'

'You're laughing at me, sir, but do you know that epigram, I
can't remember whose . . .'

('But you've got it on disc,' I thought; will computers destroy
memory? Is that the future? Does that way happiness lie? But then
memory has charms too . . .)

' "Treason doth never prosper: What the reason? For if it
prosper, None dare call it treason." Don't you think that might
be held to apply to recent French history?'

'And those who fail are traitors? Look,' I said, 'Servetus was
burned here.'

'Servetus? I can't recall who he was I'm afraid. Was he
significant?'

'Well,' I said, 'it all depends on what you mean by significant.
But you might rather call his history ironical. He was burned by a
heretic, Calvin, on account of heresy. It should be rather to your
taste.'

He digested the matter and then said, 'It's not like that,
exactly.'

We walked for perhaps five minutes in silence. The sun had
indeed emerged after days of concealment and now shone with a
shy wonder, like a refugee who has passed a frontier post. Trams
clanked by us. There was snow on the mountains, and a blonde
girl at a café table threw her coat open and leaned back, gazing at
the peaks and imbibing the sunshine.

'I like this city,' Mr Challefray said, 'it has a good feel.'

'All you have to do,' I said, 'to be comfortable here is pay your
way. And the nice thing about modern Europe is that it seems to
be tending to the condition of Switzerland. There's a lot to be said
for that.'

We settled ourselves in a restaurant, and Mr Challefray quickly
asked if they had lobster, to put me at my ease perhaps, and let me
see that expense or expense account was no object. When I said
that all I wanted was a sausage and a hot potato salad, he looked
disappointed.

'And how do you remember him?' he asked, unfolding his
napkin.

'I never saw him after I was nine.'

'Tell me about him. What happened then?'

'Isn't this,' I said, 'some way from – what is it? – the ideological ethos of Vichy sympathisers?'

'It's background,' he said.

'Well,' I said, 'there would be no mileage in a book about him. I warn you of that. Nobody remembers him, and, as far as I know, there are no papers of especial interest. He wasn't of any great importance, you know.'

'But you must remember something?'

You must remember something. Of course, yes: a thin and gentle man who was very anxious that I should speak correct French. 'It's all we have left,' he said to my mother once as he corrected some inelegance. 'It's almost the only thing that holds France together. Even a Communist like Louis speaks and writes beautiful French.' My mother of course, like many foreigners – but it was also natural for her – was in love with slang. That pained my father. But he also spoke and wrote Provençal. 'The strength of France is in the provinces; it was the heresy of the Revolution to try to impose uniformity on the nation. Of course, with a democracy, what can you expect?'

'It must have been a peculiar and unexpected marriage.'

No doubt: but they fell in love. I have never had reason to question that. So many other things, but not that . . .

PART TWO

1951

CHAPTER ONE

IN THOSE DAYS the Golden Arrow still had some style, but we didn't realise it. Indeed, quite the reverse. All the way to Dover we sighed for the lost graces of pre-war Europe. Were we unfashionable young men? I can't say. I am inclined to think we must have been, for I have never felt in tune with my generation. Perhaps that is why I drift round Geneva like a stateless person.

The engine hissed steam, and when I look back now, I see Victoria Station like an old black-and-white movie. We had porters, two of them for three undergraduates. It would be only a few years before denim became the uniform of a student generation, but all three of us wore suits. Did we travel first-class? We may well have done.

We aspired to nonchalance, as the approved mode in which to face life, but only Jamie Fernie at that moment achieved it. His father was on the staff of SHAEF and he had made this journey in the last two vacations, but both Eddie Scrope-Smith and I were lively with excitement. Eddie was nineteen and it was his first time out of England, and as for me I had not been in France since we decamped in 1939.

'Do you know what Wilkie Collins said to Dickens?' Eddie asked. And without waiting to hear if we did, said, ' "The morality of England is firmly based on the immorality of Paris." I must say, I do hope so,' and he rolled mischievous dark eyes and pushed a lock of hair off his left eye.

Jamie busied himself giving instructions to the porters. Our luggage was at last stowed aboard, and we settled ourselves in a carriage.

'Do you think we should have some champagne?' Eddie asked.

'I wish you weren't always so flash, Eddie,' Jamie said.

'Me flash? I'm a perfect beau.'

When Eddie used that word, which had become one of his favourites that summer term, he recalled not only the Regency, in which he delighted, but also the fiction of the Old South, and Tennessee Williams' plays, the first of which had been staged in

London. They enthralled him, and for several weeks the long vowels of the South invaded his speech.

The conversation of undergraduates can hardly seem other than banal in recollection. It may also appear impenetrable. So much of our talk was based on jokes that depended on secret allusions. You can find the same sort of thing in Byron's correspondence, and it requires footnotes to elucidate the meaning. But in our case the passage of time has effaced even the content of our talk, let alone its form. I cannot remember another word of that journey, and yet, as I sit in my hotel room, its mood enfolds me, sweet and momentary as evening honeysuckle in the summer garden.

We were all at the point of splendid and irresponsible possibility, when life seems a toy, fluid as mercury, malleable as plasticine. We could be whatever we chose, and what we chose first was to be in love, with ourselves, with each other, with existence and the immediate moment which we enriched by our absorption in a wholly, or almost completely, imaginary past. Our love was tender, nervous and evanescent; it survives as the most distant and faint of woodland melodies. This is why it is possible to gaze back on youth with longing, even while particular instances may remind us that in those days we were just as ready to weep and despair as to laugh and rejoice. All our emotions were merely garments in which the whim of a moment clothed us, and we shed them as easily as we hopped into a bath before preening in front of the glass in a new suit.

> *Quand il me prend dans ses bras*
> *Alors je sens en moi*
> *Mon coeur qui bat . . .*

La Vie en Rose is the tune that sighs through those first days in Paris. And yet I cannot even remember where Jamie's parents had their apartment. He was nervous before we met them, and they seemed an ill-matched pair. His father gave a good performance as the professional soldier, so good that I had no notion it was a performance. Eddie was more alert: 'the Poona Pathan', he called him. But I didn't see beyond the caustic teasing which he adopted towards Eddie; I saw only the Colonel. As for his mother, there I felt myself on firmer ground. Mrs Fernie looked like an exceedingly well-bred horse, and this struck me as quite suitable because I knew she had some reputation as a novelist. It's gone now of course, and when out of curiosity I got a couple of her novels from the London Library, they gave off an authentic, yet dead, smell of the forties. Her talent, I realised, lay in her ability to write like Elizabeth Bowen, so like Elizabeth Bowen that you were first surprised, checking back on the book's spine, to see the name Laura Maudsley there. But that's all there was, this echo of a stronger writer. Yet with what admiration, amounting even to reverence on the part of some, her books were received then. She doted on Jamie. He was her only child, and she saw him both as an ally in the cold war she conducted with Colonel Fernie, and as someone who had to be protected from her husband's values; yet these were precisely the civilised standards she upheld in her writing, and in truth he embodied them in action far better than she did. All marriages have something of mystery in them to outsiders.

'Terribly Oedipal, isn't it,' Eddie said, lolling on my bed wrapped in a huge deep-piled yellow bath towel, and admiring his reflection in the glass. 'No wonder Jamie acts cold. As for the Colonel, it's a case of "he loves me," – he puffed out his lips and blew a kiss – "he loves me not." '

'How vain you are. You think every Colonel loves you.'

'Well I do see I am rather a Colonel's boy. I expect my National Service to be scrumptious.'

'Oh shut up,' I said, and threw a pillow at him.

'Don't fancy this dinner tonight,' he said. 'My lousy Frog will be revealed. It's all right for you, ducky, speaking Frog like a native.'

'Don't let Cyril Connolly hear you call the language Frog.'

'Why not? My mama tells me his own Frog is something dreadful.'

I began to shave.

'I think I'll tell the Colonel my own papa was the wrong sort of CO. That might choke him off. He won't get it at first probably, like Hannay when he is just about to ask Mary's aunts what regiment Lancelot Wake commanded, and then remembers what, in their language, the initials stand for. But if he says, "And what did your dad do in the war, young fellow?" what do I tell him? You must see my dilemma. He might after all find it exciting to think I am a conchy's son. Perhaps' – he examined his fingernails – 'perhaps I'll just say he was in the RASC. Nobody could find the RASC sexy, could they?'

'So you want to choke him off then, do you?'

'Oh, I think so, I ever so truly and really and sincerely think so.'

*

'And what did your dad do in the war, young fellow?'

I had been embarrassed to find myself alone in the drawing room with Colonel Fernie, whom I had surprised mixing a Martini. He hesitated, uncertain whether he should offer me one, and posed this question instead.

I looked round the gilt and heavy mahogany furniture of the Second Empire room and said,

'He was killed, sir.'

'Oh,' he said, 'rotten luck for you. And your Ma lives in South Africa, Jamie tells me.'

'That's right, sir. She married a South African pilot, and we went out there after the war.'

'Marvellous country. We called in there on our way to the desert in '42, and I went down with fever and spent three months convalescing. Marvellous country, I thought, and a great future. To tell you the truth I've thought of settling there myself some time, but Laura wouldn't like it. She's very cultured, moves in a narrow triangle.'

He jerked his head backward, so that it passed into the shadow of the table lamp beside which he had been mixing his drink, and the movement, of which he was probably quite unconscious himself, suggested a rejection of his wife's standards, even a revulsion from them.

'Martini?' he now said, perhaps concluding that my assurance of a dead father and a mother domiciled in remote, if marvellous, South Africa made it proper for him to offer me one.

'I warn you,' he said, 'I make them strong. What our American friends irreverently and unfairly call Montgomeries, thirteen parts of gin to one of vermouth, that is. The Field-Marshal's teetotal himself of course, which makes the description irreverent, and though he was reluctant to engage in battle till the odds were in his favour, he didn't demand that sort of superiority, which makes it unfair. In fact, it's practically unattainable in war, and when it comes to superiority in material, well, I have to say that our American friends can give points to anyone. They've never in the history of American conflict fought a battle where they suffered material inferiority, not since Robert E. Lee handed over his sword to General Grant. Laura doesn't like me talking of military matters, no more does Jamie. Do you know what a soldier is, young man? He's the chap who makes it possible for civilised folk to despise war.'

I sipped my Martini. It was certainly strong, though it might have surprised him to learn that Jamie made them even stronger. The Colonel downed his, and poured another from the shaker.

'Sorry about your dad,' he said. 'I won't ask you about it, because I've learned it doesn't always do to nose into these matters, here in France. There's a very natural sensitivity. I don't know your politics either, or your family's. But just remember this. In a civil war, and it was just that in France, there is always right on both sides. And a soldier has to obey orders, which – some folk forget – in 1940 emanated from the Marshal, emanated lawfully. His trial stank. Was your dad a professional soldier?'

'No, sir. His father was. He was killed at Verdun. He was a regular Army officer and, I believe, was convinced till the day of his death that Dreyfus had been guilty. That sort of professional soldier.'

'We hardly have that sort in England – not that I'm English – my family's Scots, but on my mother's side we're Ulstermen, and that's the nearest to a military caste we have produced. Don't know if you're interested in these things. I am. Jamie tells me he wants to go into the Diplomatic. His mother's idea. Talk him out of it, if you get the chance, old man. No life for a chap, just a career.'

He inclined the shaker towards me.

'Jolly good Martini, sir.'

'Glad you like it. Sure you should be drinking it, are you? My Dad forbade me spirits till I was twenty-five, but when I came out of Sandhurst, my first Colonel said he wasn't going to have an officer in his mess who wouldn't down a glass of brandy in the evening. He'd spent his early service in the Indian Army, you see. I suppose, with a French father, your own French is pretty good, eh?'

'Well, my first language, sir.'

'And you've kept it up? Good. I spoke nothing but Hindustani till I was five. Or so they tell me. Can't put ten words together in the language now. Always regretted it. But at least that means that this evening won't be a trial to you linguistically. We'll only be 50 per cent French at dinner, but Laura likes general conversation to be conducted in French. Out of courtesy, she says. God knows what she'd demand if I was posted to Constantinople.'

'You might not invite Turks to dinner, sir.'

'Hadn't thought of that. You may be right. Are there any Turk novelists? What's Jamie's French like?'

'Good enough for the Diplomatic, sir, I'm afraid.'

'Hell's bells, all grammar and no idiom, eh? The only way to learn a language after you're a child is to get yourself a mistress, a girl from the streets, or what they call here the *demi-monde*. A little milliner. That's what Puggsy Baker used to say. Wouldn't know myself.' He laid his finger along the side of his nose. 'My own French is wooden.'

In fact, it was more fluent, and far more racy, than his wife's. But the Colonel, as I began to see, was more than a bit of an actor.

'This shaker's getting dull. We'd better liven it up,' he said. 'Glad you came down early. A man ought to get to know his son's friends. It's probably the nearest he can come to knowing his son.'

And he smiled, looking like Mr Punch.

'All fathers worry about their sons, I suppose,' he said. 'That they can't talk to them. That they will grow up not to resemble them, that they will grow up to do so. Either prospect seems alarming, if we are honest. But it's hard to be honest about family affairs.'

As he spoke I saw how absurd Eddie's fantasies were; how, even more than I, he lived in a world of make-believe. We were still in the nursery, playing at grown-ups.

'But of course, you know what sons want to do,' the Colonel said. 'There's a German proverb I believe: "Happy as the boy who killed his father". Sums up a lot, I've always thought. I hear the bell. Gird up your French, oil your idioms.'

And, very quickly, to assist me, he tipped the cocktail shaker in the direction of my glass.

I soon saw that Jamie was sulking. He had been placed opposite me, at a slight angle, between two Frenchwomen, one blonde and statuesque, as if she had risen from a marble plinth in the Louvre where she had been reclining since Canova gave her form, and the other slim, dark, bread-crumbling, and quicker to lift her glass of champagne than her fork. It was clear that Jamie's diplomatic French wasn't up to dinner-table conversation. As for Eddie, his lousy Frog was proving no handicap, though it was a plump yellowish man sitting opposite him in a ruffled shirt, looking as far as features went in fact extremely like a frog, who had engaged him in conversation, rather than either of the unremarkable ladies who flanked him. I could see Eddie sparkle, as he did when people chaffed him, and three or four times the yellowish frog broke out in laughter. There wasn't in fact much laughter at the table, and this made Eddie's success all the more remarkable.

The champagne and the *foie gras* were succeeded by a fish and some white burgundy. The fish – a sole – was cooked with a simplicity that I ignorantly thought of being defiantly English, but which was actually of the purest French. Situated as I was, near Mrs Fernie's end of the table – we were, I think, sixteen – I found myself envying those at the other end where the Colonel presided and the frog laughed and Eddie displayed his naivety and charm. For Mrs Fernie kept things serious. Her conception of dinner-party conversation was lofty and old-fashioned. She had an elderly man with a goatee beard on her right, whom I identified to my own satisfaction as an Academician, and a very dark, very thin man with a pencil moustache on her left, who was laying down the law in precise terms about the relation of art to experience. It was not awfully exhilarating, and yet one couldn't help but listen. He was making it clear that though France might be in dire straits politically and economically, the French nation had already resumed the cultural dictatorship that was its due. I was bored, but most awfully impressed. It seemed to me that this was the authentic voice of France that had been buried under failure, defeat and recrimination; and I could see that Mrs Fernie thought so too. She was indeed lapping it up, while at the same time, every now and then at least, she stuck in a delicate and even fragile oar of her own; her line was that, although she came from a nation that could only be considered barbarian by those fortunate enough to be French, she had nevertheless somehow escaped contagion, and even, by her own efforts and the gift of her serene intellect and fine sensibilities, contrived to aspire to be treated as an honorary Frenchwoman. The thin man declined to admit that such a being was possible – not of course in so many words, but by his terse dismissal of her proffered wares; while, from the depths of his vast civility, conceding that, if the unthinkable could indeed have been thought, then, in that case – *mutatis mutandis*, as you, or rather he, might say – she would be wearing the white robe of a candidate.

If my language seems mandarin – and absurd – it is because I am trying exactly to reflect my sensations.

Their conversation was a little comedy, and these impressions of it which have remained with me could not have found just this verbal expression at the time. I was only conscious of the falsity of the conversation, and of its fundamental absurdity.

I had however plenty of occasion to observe, for I had, despite my proclaimed mastery of the demotic, had no more success than Jamie in arousing the interest of the ladies on either side. To my left, a woman with short spiky grey hair had first resolutely tried to engage the Academician in talk – a task in which she failed because he was fretting to supplant the thin man and capture Mrs Fernie's attention. While on my other side I had been landed with a very tall woman wearing a monocle who told me only that her father had been the ambassador of the Austro-Hungarian Emperor to France and that she bred and showed Arab horses, an activity which the war had seriously and unforgivably disturbed. There wasn't much I could say to that. It would have been ridiculous to commiserate with her grievance; at the same time I didn't see how, at Mrs Fernie's table, at which the sole had been succeeded by duckling so tender and tasty that it seemed an insult deliberately levelled at the starving people of Europe – which thought I do remember as a measure of my boredom and disaffection – how, as I say, at Mrs Fernie's table, I could have told her that her complaint disgusted me. So I sat silent, and ate the duckling, which despite my moment of priggish repulsion was so delicious as to disarm any criticism, and drank the claret which accompanied it, and listened with rather more than half an ear to the thin man telling Mrs Fernie that the novel was finished, superseded by criticism and the journal; fiction had become impossible because the artificiality of the construct was now inescapable; reality had rendered the imagination superfluous, just as psychology had made the whole Victorian concept of characterisation an activity suited only to moral imbeciles and mental defectives.

'But what is reality?' Mrs Fernie advanced. Her eyes shone very blue, as Jamie's did when he felt that he was not appreciated.

'It is because you can still ask such a question,' the thin man flung his hand out, perilously close to the rim of his wine glass, 'because you do not see that it is itself quite superfluous, . . .'

'And yet,' Mrs Fernie pursued, 'we must surely have some framework within which . . .'

'My dear lady,' the thin man said, 'all we have is experience. We are that, and nothing else. Our only knowledge is what happens to us, and what we feel . . .'

The lady on my left sighed, and abandoned her attempt on the Academician.

'I always think,' she commanded my attention, 'that there is something sad about a mixing of generations. I like the seasons to be distinct.'

'In South Africa,' I said, 'where I have been living . . .'

'But you live in England,' she said, 'you are a friend of Jamie's at Cambridge.'

It was at that moment, more from a peculiar note of regret in her voice than from her accent, that I realised she was English herself; and it seemed to add to the absurdity of the evening that we should be engaged in French conversation, while a debate on the nature of reality went on around us. I asked her if she had lived long in France.

'Oh dear me yes,' she said, in English. Then, reverting to the house rules, she returned to French and told me she was a sculptor who had come to Paris in the 1920s to study under a pupil of Rodin and remained here ever since.

'Even under the Occupation?'

'There were difficulties, but yes.'

'But they must have been enormous.'

'Well,' she said, 'I had a brief marriage to a Frenchman. A mistake, but I was grateful. It meant I could get the right sort of papers. But yes, it was difficult, and yet, you know, what they are saying about experience being the only reality, well, we learned something of that. Do you know what I missed most during the Occupation: fish. It was impossible to get a sole or halibut. But you know people did the most surprising things, people really did surprise you, and that's why Philippe there is quite right about character. Helena, you know – the lady on your other side' – she lowered her voice – 'she hates me to talk about it, and herself will speak of nothing now but her Arab horses, so that I could see, for I was listening with half an ear, that you thought her a tiresome and empty woman, she was a heroine of the Resistance, yes, a real heroine. Oh, I know' – she leaned across me raising her voice – 'that you don't care for me to say so, but it's quite true, you were a heroine.'

'And you, Judith, are a tiresome gossip. It is over and done with.'

All this was embarrassing in a surprising fashion. We are of course usually wrong about other people. I knew that even then. All the same it is disconcerting when one's errors are so quickly and publicly exposed. I saw I could only make things worse if I admitted that I had indeed dismissed Helena as tiresome and empty. And yet why shouldn't I have done so? It was after all the impression that she sought to convey. I might have made things worse and added that I had been quite convinced that she was herself a Vichyiste, even a Fascist. So I muttered something and hoped the subject would pass away. I glanced across the table at Eddie, who, attracted by my attention, whisked up an eyebrow, before leaning over the table and addressing the yellowish frog again, intensifying his performance for my pleasure and amusement. I wondered when this appalling dinner-party would end, and thought with longing of escaping with him – and, yes, I supposed, Jamie too – on a round of the bars and night spots.

There was a momentary silence: twenty to ten on the Louis Quinze ormolu clock, an angel was passing. Then from the void a harsh voice:

'Helena is quite right. Her Arab horses are a great deal more important than her experience in the Resistance.'

It was Jamie's dark companion.

'How can you say such a thing?'

'Because the war was odious.'

'Oh, how glad I am to hear someone say that.'

It was Mrs Fernie who spoke, and for a moment the air seemed to hold those two voices, still and simultaneous, the one harsh and awkward, the double r of '*guerre*' rasped out, the other mellifluously low, and then the spell was broken.

'If only we could forget it,' Mrs Fernie said, her Englishness exposed.

'Oh, my dear, but that is of course absolutely impossible, I find that sentimental,' the thin man, Philippe's, hand again flashed over the rim of his wine glass. 'We suffered of course, how we suffered is inconceivable for anyone with the innocence of islanders, we suffered treachery, which was worst of all.'

'And some of us, Philippe, benefited,' the dark woman said. 'And we all know that what was destroyed in the war, in the Occupation, in the Resistance and in the *épuration*' – a word I must leave untranslated, because 'purge', which is its dictionary meaning, lacks the connotations with which history has now encrusted the French – 'what . . . what was destroyed was a trust in human goodness.'

'Oh, but this is naive, my dear. I'm almost ashamed to listen to it. What after all is goodness?'

'Very well, Philippe,' the woman lifted her glass and gestured to the butler, who proffered the bottle, but not before – I noticed – exchanging a quick glance with Mrs Fernie, whose nod seemed to suggest that the scene would be worse if he failed to comply with the woman's request, 'Very well, Philippe' – she knocked back the claret as if it had been the roughest *pinard*, and she in a low bistro – 'I don't expect you to know. After all, we are what we experience, that's right, isn't it, and so doubtless we are not what we would prefer to forget. But I don't forget that you were only a provincial schoolmaster back in '37, and would probably have remained that and nothing more, if Lucien hadn't seen a vestige of talent in a journal you submitted to him, and, with infinite care, brought it to some sort of birth. It was a thin thing even then in the end, but it offered you your escape and beginning . . .'

'No, but this is . . .'

'Be quiet . . .'

'Monstrous . . .'

'A good word. And he published my first poems too, or the first to be published, and encouraged us both. And everything you said, your whole tone of voice, was antipathetic to him, but he discerned talent. That was goodness. To put art above his own ideas of what was moral in ordinary life. Just as it was when . . . I never knew him other than good, a man of the highest and most generous sentiments, and now you trample on his reputation and spit on his memory and that is why I say war is odious.'

'Oh, but this is too ridiculous,' he said; and if it wasn't just that, we all felt that it was inappropriate. Mrs Fernie's eyes were opened to her own maladroit social behaviour, and I saw a flicker of pleasure cross Jamie's face at the revelation. Then she, who was engaged in a long war with her husband, turned to him in appeal, and he rose; putting his arm round the dark woman, he escorted her from the room, as he might on another occasion – and I saw he always would – lead a mourning widow or deprived daughter from a graveside. And the door closed behind them, white, with gold embossed.

'I am so sorry, Laura,' said Philippe. 'That was painful and ridiculous. I did warn you about poor Mathilde. Her talent has quite gone, you see, that is why she is now unbalanced. It is sad, but we have to accept it. And as for the man of whom she spoke, Lucien de Balafré, he was of no account. It is true he published my first things, but to say he helped me is otherwise absurd. We had nothing, I am pleased to say, in common. No, I assure you, a madwoman would now conjure with his name as Mathilde does . . .'

'I think you should know, Monsieur,' Jamie's careful diplomatic French sounded from the doorway, 'that his son is my friend, and with us tonight. That's right, Etienne,' he said, in English, 'your father was Lucien wasn't he?'

'Yes, Monsieur,' I said, 'my father was certainly Lucien de Balafré.'

Eddie put his arm round me and squeezed.

'That was brave of Jamie,' he said. 'You know how he hates a scene. And he puked after, he really did. As for you, ducky, what you could do with is a stinger.'

He snapped his fingers at the waiter and instructed him in the proper proportions of brandy and *crème de menthe*. Eddie's French might be as lousy as he promised, but at this stage of life he could usually get what he wanted.

'And I think I'll have one too, my dear,' he said to the waiter.

'Oh yes,' I said, 'I'm grateful to Jamie, it was brave of him. Sort of Jacobite. All the same I'd rather he hadn't.'

'Jacobite?'

'Yes, a splendid and useless gesture.'

We were in a bar in Montmartre. Jamie had declined to come with us. The dinner-party had ended, not exactly in confusion, but in some embarrassment. Mrs Fernie, I felt, regarded me with disfavour and suspicion. I had been transformed from a harmless, possibly even helpful, friend of Jamie into a disagreeable object. The Sicilians have an admirable expression: 'to swallow a toad'. It means to accept an unwelcome fact. I rather felt that I was a toad in Mrs Fernie's gullet, and that it wasn't at all certain that she could get it down. She hadn't known anything about my father, and she was not the sort of person who could bear with equanimity the finding of herself at a disadvantage at her own table. It was in one sense as simple as that.

But it was also much more, as indeed it was for me. We like, to put it at its simplest, to be judged for ourselves, as we would like, or think we would. Yet it never of course happens. Our reception is always coloured and distorted by associations, which we are – so often – powerless to protect ourselves against. I used, some twenty years ago, to be friendly with the widow of a famous poet, celebrated as much for his wild and self-destructive behaviour as for his verses. She was proud of him, and in memory had made their marriage perhaps into a finer thing than she had known at the time; and she was jealous to defend him. Yet at the same time she knew that she was diminished by it all too. People came to see her because of the man to whom she had been married. And it was a long time ago; in another country. All the recognition she got was a denial of her own reality. It was as if for so many people her own life had also ended in that New York hospital. Reflected fame subtracts from the identity of the person on whom the reflection falls.

I couldn't have elaborated this, as I sipped my stinger with Eddie and watched his eyes rove the little bar, but, looking back, these were the sentiments which disturbed me. And yet I was at the same time awfully curious.

'It's not working for Jamie,' Eddie said.

'What?'

'Our being here. It's not working. He thought it would help, but it doesn't.'

'Did he actually say so?'

'He doesn't have to. I think we should go.'

'Because of this evening?'

'Not just that.'

'How do you know?'

'I just do.'

'Well, I don't understand. I don't mind going. In fact, I would like to, and anyway, as you know, I have my other plans. All the same, why?'

Eddie picked up his glass.

'The compartments have got mixed,' he said. 'That gets on his nerves. He's far more nervous and high-strung than you think.'

'You know him better. You probably know him better than he knows himself.'

'Oh yes. Much better. So shall we?'

'Yes,' I said, and hesitated. 'I'm going to my grandmother's. In Provence. I haven't seen her in . . . well, since I was a child, before the war. But you know that.'

'It's all right,' Eddie said, 'I'm not suggesting that I should come with you. Compartments are important. Nobody knows that better than me. But I think we should get out soon. If you've got a definite date to go there, we could drift about first. That might be fun.'

'This evening,' I said.

'You don't have to talk about it. You don't have to at all.'

'No,' I said, 'I don't, do I?'

'So now,' he said, 'let us resume the having of the fun. There's a bar Toby told me about I want to take a look at . . .'

But we didn't go off together, though not because of anything that happened that evening, which led us through a succession of bars till we came to one where Eddie disappeared upstairs with a mulatto sailor, while I sat drinking *pinard* with his dancing-partner and declining more and more laconically the repeated, but half-hearted, suggestions that perhaps we should go upstairs too. It wasn't anything to do with that, and I was grateful to Eddie for his lack of curiosity or his self-restraint. But I wondered at my decision even as I boarded the train to the south, and sat back on the hard shiny green leather, and watched the suburbs of Paris slip by. Tears pricked my eyes, tears of loneliness and apprehension.

Compartments are important. I had locked one door behind me, and I have often wondered since how different my life would have been if I had not done so.

There were fewer suburbs then, and no high-rise apartment blocks on the fringe of the city. The train was soon passing through a miniature and scruffy landscape of canals and rivers, cottages crouching by the lines which were flanked with poplars under a heavy grey sky. It started to rain. The occasional clumsy lorry or chugging little car waited at level-crossings, a curé bicycling in his long cassock hung for a moment motionless on the hump of a bridge, a girl drove black-and-white cattle from a water-meadow. It was the landscape of the Impressionists, but diminished and meaner, with a suggestion of attenuation which is absent from their paintings. The rain streamed down the pale green willow that overhung the waters. I looked out of the window and avoided the gaze of my fellow-passengers, and when the call for dinner came made my way to the restaurant car.

I WASN'T EXPECTED yet, for the change of plan had been sudden, and I had not been able to bring myself to telephone my grandmother. I wasn't in fact sure that she had a telephone – certainly I had no number for her. But of course I could have wired; and hadn't. I was, I suppose, reluctant to commit myself, and I may also have felt that it really couldn't matter to her just when I did in fact arrive. It wouldn't have occurred to me then that the old value precision in arrangements. But I don't think I had any intention to take her by surprise. Which is of course just what I did; and it disconcerted her. And that surprised me for, immediately on disembarking from the express – or what passed for an express in those days – at Avignon, I had felt I was home, as I had not felt in Paris. One symptom was that my English clothes seemed all at once not to belong to me. It was absurd to look like a public schoolboy – as undergraduates still did in the fifties – in Provence. I drank a *café crème* in the station buffet and left my bags in the station and walked up to the Palace of the Popes to look at the wide valley of the Rhone. The sun was high, the streets smelled of bread and melons and black tobacco, the sweet scent of the drains was growing warmer, and there were flowers everywhere. I was in no hurry to move.

So it wasn't in fact till late afternoon that I reached Carpentras and found a car that would take me to my grandmother's house.

If I wasn't the Prodigal Son, I don't suppose my feelings were so very different from his. Everything was as I remembered it from childhood, but I was not a child: the vineyards, olive-groves and, in the distance, the mountains, the earth red-gold under the hot sun of June. It was a different and more lucid world; Africa with a past.

My driver smoked incessantly, but was uncommunicative. When I had asked him to take me to the château, he had given me a long look, shrugged his shoulders and asked whether I minded waiting till he had finished his game of *boules*. I sat by an oleander aware that I was the subject of glances, and drank a glass of beer. Then he crossed over, opened the back door of his car and himself climbed into the driving-seat, waiting for me to put my bags in. Smoke curled over his left shoulder; the back of his neck shone like burnished copper. When we reached the château, he didn't move to help me with the luggage, but took the money and drove off with a jarring of his gears. I was left standing in front of the house; dogs pursued the car with sound. A cock crew, and then there was silence, except for the crickets.

It is called a château, but the English would think it no more than a manor house, a long two-storeyed yellow building with a single diminutive tower at its east end. The shutters, grey, the paint peeling, were closed. It rested like a mangy lion in the sun, as if it had always been there and was insensible to time and fashion. The main part of the house dates from 1687 when the estate was obtained by my ancestor after the Revocation of the Edict of Nantes. There is a date under the coat of arms above the main door.

I pushed against that door but it was locked or barred. There was no bell and I was disinclined to make my presence known by banging my fist on the wood. I called out instead and my voice seemed lost in a silence that was suddenly as eerie as it was profound. I had been a fool not to alert them to my arrival. And yet I knew, even as that thought came to me, that I couldn't have done so, couldn't, that is, have brought myself to it. So leaving my bags there I walked round the end of the house to the little yard which gave off the kitchen. As a child I had long been wary of it for there was a mastiff chained there, and a white cockerel that would attack anyone who moved at anything more than the slowest pace. You had to deceive him into thinking you were hardly moving. Well, both must be dead long since.

But in the yard it seemed as if it were the house that was dead. There was not only neither dog nor cock, but no poultry at all, no cats, such as had been used to sun themselves there, while the door to the kitchen was also shut. Weeds grew where none had been permitted once, and the appearance of the yard suggested that life had departed. Yet I knew that this could not be. I had after all exchanged letters with my grandmother, had deciphered her handwriting, and knew that she expected me, even if not for another ten days or so. But she had said: 'You need have no fear of not finding me. There is nothing now that tempts me to go far beyond the gates of our property.'

I knocked on the door and fancied I could hear the sound bounce through the house, as in a fairy-tale. Wasn't it to just such a house – though in Normandy rather than Provence – that

Beauty's father had come, having lost his way, and there encountered the Beast? The swirling mists of Cocteau's film seemed to hang round me, though the light was lucid and the sun still shone on a quarter of the yard.

'Who are you? And what do you want?'

The voice came from behind me, and, turning, I saw an old woman, dressed all in black with a shawl round her head. She was carrying a basket containing eggs.

'I have come too soon,' I said.

'No,' she said, 'you are late. You are several years late.'

'What do you mean? I don't understand.'

'You should have been here all the time.'

She pushed past me and opened the door.

'The hens lay very badly,' she said, 'and it takes a long time to find all the eggs. Your grandmother needs you, poor woman, that's what I mean. You are very like Monsieur Lucien, that's a relief.'

She led me into a large dark kitchen. There were stone flags on the floor and the roof was curved. She placed the basket of eggs on a large table in the middle of the room, and wiped her hands on her apron.

'I am Marthe,' she said. 'Do you remember me?'

'Marthe? But you were . . .'

'Yes, I was young, and now I am not. We are none of us young here. You must not wonder at that. Sit down, and I will prepare your grandmother. She has talked of nothing but your coming . . . when she has talked, that is.'

She left me alone. Did I indeed remember her? There had been a Marthe, certainly, a peasant girl who swabbed floors, and was permitted to help the cook with the preparation of the vegetables. She had been the cause of scandal – at least two illegitimate children. Though how had that fact come to my knowledge? Or to my memory? Had the babies been brought to the house? But that Marthe had only been a girl a dozen years ago.

'The *marc* is our own,' my grandmother said. 'We no longer make it, of course, but there are some bottles left.'

She poured two glasses and held one out to me.

'You have been a long time in coming,' she said.

Throughout dinner – a *saucisson d'Arles*, followed by an anchovy tart and a basket of strawberries – she had said little, though I was all the time aware of her scrutiny. She picked at her food, made a couple of approving comments on my appetite, once said,

'It's fortunate that Marthe had prepared this tart. I'm pleased you like it.' It was as if the tart had been a sort of test. 'Your mother dislikes anchovies, I remember. I suppose most English do.'

'There's a sort of anchovy paste called Gentleman's Relish, which a lot of Englishmen dote on.'

'Do they?'

The dining room was at the side of the house. The windows gave on to distant mountains which turned to a dusky grape-purple as we ate. The room was full of heavy sharp-edged furniture, stained a dull shadowy colour. Tapestries depicting hunting scenes hung on the wall to the right of the window; they were faded and the ends frayed.

'You have been a long time in coming,' she said again. She crooked a twisted finger round her coffee-cup. Her hands were heavy with rings.

'What sort of place is South Africa?'

'My stepfather has a farm there.'

'And you live on it? Your mother hated it here. Paris, it must always be Paris. Now you are the head of the family. All this will be yours one day, except for Armand's share of course. And he won't want the land. He prefers to make money.'

I sipped the *marc*. Journalists who write about these things use all sorts of adjectives to describe drink. Most are absurd. Really the only epithets that have any meaning identify its effect. The *marc* made me feel strong, defiant, knowledgeable, bitter, older than my years. Looked at from this distance, the sensation was ridiculous, like smoking a cigarette in the manner of Bogart.

'You know who I'm talking about?'

'My uncle. I remember him well. On a beach and coming to our apartment. He used to lift me on to his shoulders . . .'

A snapshot: crinkly dark hair and a smile full of teeth, a laughing face. I saw him more clearly than I saw my father.

'I'm tired.' She threw down a napkin with which she had been wiping her mouth. 'There are too many things to talk about, and too much that is too painful. It is good that you have come home.'

Her back was very straight as she left the room.

But if there were too many things to talk about, there was too much that was hard to say. I soon realised this. It was not that we had no common ground, but that the ground was a minefield. My grandmother treated me as carefully as if I had been a rare and precious piece of china which, by a moment's inadvertence, she might let slip from her fingers and shatter on the parquet floor. As for me, I became aware, for the first time in my life, of the power,

my power, to wound. There was some pleasure in that knowledge, which even then disgusted me. A few years ago I found it
exactly described in a biography of T. H. White, who, brooding
on his Arthurian novels, had noted of Lancelot: 'probably sadis-
tic, or he would not have taken such frightful care to be gentle'. I
scribbled in the margin: 'this is me; *facilis descensus Averni*'.

So for two weeks, possibly more, we circled round each other,
endlessly polite and reticent. She was disappointed – she must
have been – and yet Marthe, whom I tried to question, would only
say, 'No, she has you here, that's what is important to her.'

In the mornings I walked round the estate before the soaring
sun made such exercise disagreeable. I had learned enough from
Roddy, poor farmer though he was, to realise that its condition
was wretched. The vines were ill-tended, the olive-groves neglected, and some fields which had once borne crops had reverted
to the wild; they were no more, or would soon be no more, than
maquis. An old man with his son, who was near to being an
imbecile, was supposed to care for the land, but it was clear that it
had escaped him. Yet at the same time the outlines of the country
were so stark and uncompromising that I felt abundantly well. We
were quite high up the hill, the soil was parsimonious, everything
had to be worked for, there was no lush English deception
possible. It was a land to cherish, even in its neglect, and one
which stimulated.

One day, going into the kitchen in the late afternoon to ask
Marthe if she would make me a pot of coffee, I found a young
man there. He was about my age, wearing Army uniform, and he
sat with his back against the wall and his feet, in Army boots,
resting on another chair. He made no move when I entered but
looked at me from dark eyes under heavy lids. He was chewing a
matchstick. There was no sign of Marthe. I asked where she was.
He gnawed the matchstick as if pondering his reply.

'Don't know.'

'We haven't met.'

'She told me you were here.'

I sat down and waited.

'Why have you come?' he said.

'What's that to you?'

'They're both mad. You know that? Both the old women. They
say it's because of what they've gone through – at least she does' –
he jerked his finger towards the stove – 'the other won't talk to me,
but I reckon they were always mad.'

I lit a cigarette.

'I don't understand you,' I said. 'Who are you anyway?'

He removed the match from his mouth and rubbed what was left of it between his fingers.

'Oh,' he said, 'sorry I'm sure. I'm one of her brats. As you can see I'm in the Army, National Service, which they don't approve of, you understand. I've come to see her and I've brought one of my brothers, my half-brothers that is, one of the German ones, home for his holidays. They go to a church school, a church boarding school down in the city, which the other one pays for, you understand, and all because they won't have anything to do with the village, as the appearance of the place will have told you. And now tell me they're not mad.'

He kicked his chair away so that it fell over backwards, and was on his feet, emitting a wave of energy which seemed foreign to that silent kitchen, where even the clock was broken.

'I don't know why you have come here, but there's nothing left. I tell you that, understand it well. They are diseased, both of them, riddled with the plague.'

'I don't know what you are talking about.'

' "I don't know what you are talking about." How very English. I am talking about France and madness. I am talking about what I have suffered. Nobody will have told you about my sufferings, they pretend they don't exist. As if it's not something to be imprisoned by two minds that are in prison themselves, as if it's not something to have been scorned as a child because of them, as if it's not something to have seen my mother sitting here, in this chair, in the lap of a German soldier, while the other one entertained his officers in the drawing room. Now do you understand or do you still refuse to know what I am talking about?'

I was rescued by the return of Marthe to the kitchen. She was holding a small blond boy by the hand. She must have heard her son shrieking at me, and probably his precise words, for she at once told him to be quiet. That was no way to speak to Monsieur Etienne.

'No, of course not,' he said, 'not to Monsieur Etienne. I was forgetting he is the son of a saint and hero. You must forgive me, Monsieur Etienne, for addressing you as if my words might mean anything to you. You will have to learn, Kurt,' he seized the small boy by the hair, 'that most things which ought to be said must not be said. It is a very difficult lesson, little brother, but if you attend to your Maman as I have not, then you will learn it. And grow up an imbecile.'

He shook the boy's head, till I saw the child's eyes water, and then released it, uttered a theatrical laugh and stamped out of the kitchen.

'I am sorry for that,' Marthe said. 'He should not have spoken so. And he has been drinking. Now I expect you want some coffee.'

Well, yes, I did, I still did.

It is not often you encounter what seems like hatred, and it is unnerving. I think this is what makes expressions of racial antipathy so disturbing: the loosing of the irrational. Yet that cannot be enough in itself. What else, after all, is love?

That evening I nerved myself to ask my grandmother about the young man.

'He is *canaille*. There is no more to be said.'

'But why do you let him come here?'

'It is not for me to keep a son from his mother. You may wonder why I keep Marthe. Well, there are worse sins than fornication, and she is loyal. She has suffered, herself, like me, with me. That is a bond. Are you bored here, Etienne?'

'Bored? No, I'm not easily bored. But this afternoon I was disturbed. I didn't like that young man . . .'

'Of course not, he is *canaille*, I tell you . . .'

'But I found him alarming . . .'

'Come,' she said, 'I have something to show you, something for you. It is time you had it.'

She led me out of the room and upstairs. It was painful for her to mount the stairs. She had to grip the banister hard and use her arm to help her legs. When we reached the landing she led me along a corridor to the right. It was a part of the house I hadn't been in before, for I had been careful to regard myself as being there on sufferance. She drew a key from a pocket in the front of her dress and unlocked the door that faced us at the end of the passage.

'It is not,' she said, 'I assure you, Bluebeard's Chamber.'

It was the first joke I had heard her make, and it didn't seem like a good one, because I had a nervous feeling that the room would reveal something equally awful. That was silly of course, and it was just an ordinary room: evidently a study, the walls lined with book cases, the shutters closed, a couple of Oriental-looking rugs on the polished floor. Everything was clean and polished, even to a row of pipes that hung alongside a plaster statuette of the Madonna. There were photographs in silver frames on a table to the right of the desk, and I was surprised to see that the largest was of my mother and myself. It was a photograph she kept on her dressing table: I was perhaps five years old and we were on a beach.

'Yes,' she said, 'this is your father's study. Nothing is changed, but of course it is yours now, Etienne.'

A small pile of letters had been placed beside a pad of blotting paper, just below the inkstand. I picked up the top letter. The seal was unbroken.

My grandmother lowered herself into a high-backed chair beside the table with the photographs. She indicated that I should sit at the desk. As I did so, I saw the room as in a mirror. Only, the figure behind the desk was my father; he had pushed the spectacles back on his forehead and was lighting a pipe and watching me over the flame. I didn't know what I had done wrong.

'It is time we talked,' she said. 'I have been waiting for this moment for six years, to see you in that chair. When you told me of that appalling young man, I knew it had come.'

'Do you know why I came here before I said I would? I mean, I know you don't because I haven't told you.'

'It doesn't matter. I am just glad that you did.'

'But it does,' and I recounted the conversation at Mrs Fernie's dinner table.

She shook her head.

'I knew none of his literary friends, though he would speak of them. I cannot recall the man of whom you speak. Obviously, he had talent, or Lucien would not have published him. Obviously, he is *canaille*, like the wretched Yves. Your father was too generous.' She picked up the photograph of my mother and myself. 'He was deceived by his generosity. Your mother was very beautiful, of course. Is she still?'

'I think so. I think most people do.'

'Does she speak of your father?'

'Sometimes, of the days before the war.'

'She abandoned him. I told him she would. When the war comes, I said, she will belong to England, not to France. He could not see that.'

It was not a view of my mother that was familiar to me.

'He was a hero,' she said, 'and a patriot. You are very like him sitting at his desk. He used to wear just that same frown.'

'Oh,' I said, 'I don't think I can claim to be like him. He was obviously very clever, I'm just . . . ordinary, I only scraped into Cambridge, you know, and my supervisors don't think much of my essays.'

'None of that is important. You are very like him, even to some of your gestures. I see him in you, very often.'

A little gust of wind rattled thin branches against the shutters. The lights flickered. Far down the valley a dog barked; further off another answered; then another. The fringes of the lampshade fluttered and the light's reflection danced on the row of my father's pipes.

'How did he die? My mother never told me.'

'Like a hero. He had an idea of France, and Frenchmen failed him. As they have failed heroes since the Revolution.'

She smoothed her hands over her dress.

'I like seeing you there. I hope you will regard this room as your own. Now that you have come home.'

The word was like the turning of a key; but which side of the door was I? She rose and, for the first time, brushed my brow with her lips, and I listened to the sound of her footsteps die away. I was left to myself and the murmur of the branches against the shutter.

I was left with the ghost of my father. Could personality still inhabit a room? After so many years? And what sort of personality was it here? I pulled open the top drawer of the desk. It was full of papers, all arranged in order, held together in neat piles by red ribbon. I fingered them without untying the ribbons. There was too much here: letters, receipts, anything; no place to start. I tried another drawer, and found a stack of leather-bound volumes each stamped with the date of a year. They were reflective journals, notebooks rather than strict diaries, but burrowing through them I came to the year of my birth, the month, the date:

'It is a boy as Polly assured me it would be, and now that it is born I wonder if I really wanted a daughter. How strange to be a father . . .'

And how strange, if it came to that, to be a son finding himself in this sort of relationship to an unknown parent.

'It is such an involuntary relationship. When I held the baby in my arms, he seemed to have no connection with me or even – and this is strange – with his mother. It was as if God himself had breathed life into the little body . . .'

I put the book down, hearing my mother's derisive laugh; and yet this same man had smoked these pipes that hung there and which were still polished. And had he prayed to that Madonna? The room oppressed me, overladen with the being of another from whom personality had departed. Yet wasn't it precisely to discover that personality that I had come here? On the other hand

– I picked up the photograph that showed me with my mother –
since I could sense no correspondence between myself and the
child pictured there, who had nevertheless indubitably been me
myself, what chance did I have of achieving reconciliation with a
dead father I had scarcely known?

On an impulse, I fished in the desk and found writing-paper.
There was a pen there too and the inkstand was full of new ink, as
if my grandmother had kept everything ready for me, as if the
turning of the key in the lock had been like that moment when the
prince cuts through the cobwebs to release the Sleeping Beauty
from her trance. To break out of mine, I would write to Eddie. I
paused, pen suspended, conscious of the enormity of the attempt
to open one life to another.

I spent much of the next fortnight in that study. We were in high
summer now – July – and from the middle of the morning the
heat, rarely disturbed by a little breeze, baked the earth. I would
rise early, usually to find Marthe in her bare feet in the kitchen
swabbing the stone flags. She would give me a bowl of coffee and
a cut of yesterday's bread to dunk in it, and then I would stride up
the hillside to a grove of chestnut trees, from where one could see
right down our valley to the yellowish stretch of flat country which
marked the point at which it entered the wider vale of the next
river. The mountains backed up behind me as I sat against the
trunk of a tree and smoked. The air was keen with the morning
and the scent of thyme and marjoram. Sometimes sheep bleated
from higher up the hill, and one morning I heard their shepherd
play a little tune on a reedy pipe which carried the imagination
back to Arcady. Stretched out on the rough ground below the
tree, listening to the myriad of little sounds, which only deepened
the silence that was the background to their music, it was possible
to imagine that there was no such thing as History.

But in my father's study History was all too present. I set about
things methodically, reading his journals in order. They by no
means offered a complete record of his life, for there were many
blank periods, and I soon realised that my father, whatever his
literary talents might have been, was no Boswell. His capacity for
introspection was limited. He lacked the shamelessness of the
born journaliser. Many of his views seemed to me to be no more
than the reflections of what he heard others say, so that someone
unconcerned with Lucien de Balafré would have found him of
interest only as a specimen, hardly at all as an individual. When he
wrote of his courtship – and it was a courtship – of my mother, his

language was quite without any individuality: a display of conventional ineptitude, in which I could not recognise my mother. He seemed humourless, unless there was a certain deadpan humour in his description of his first visit to Gore Court, my mother's father's house in Northamptonshire.

And yet I found myself liking him – he was so sorely troubled in a priggish way, and so surprised by his feeling for my mother, whom he knew from the first to belong to an alien species, not because of her nationality, but because of her temperament.

As I read I became aware of the depths of my ignorance. My study of French History at Cambridge had so far taken me no further than the July Revolution of 1830. I had read Voltaire and doted on Saint-Simon. I knew something of the Dreyfus case and more about France's appalling losses in the First War. I had read a little Gide – *La Symphonie Pastorale* and *Les Faux-Monnayeurs* – and some Balzac, but when it came to other French novels, the only writer with whom I could claim much acquaintance was Simenon. I had as a child revered General de Gaulle, who seemed to me to represent the honour of France in a profoundly satisfactory manner, and it still amused me to proclaim his moral and intellectual superiority to Winston Churchill, whom I liked to describe in Belloc's admirable and ridiculous phrase as 'that Yankee careerist'; but really I knew very little about him, and nothing that hadn't appeared in the newspapers I read. He had been engaged for the past three years in the movement which he called *Le Rassemblement du Peuple Français*, which had struck me, from a distance, as admirably exciting, but I had so far found no one in France with whom I felt I could discuss this phenomenon, and I was obscurely certain that my grandmother would not be that person.

Now, reading my father's journals, which were far more concerned with the discussion of abstract, quasi-philosophical political matters than with the details of his private life – if he had one, beyond his mother and his marriage – I found myself bumping against names which had either only a shadowy significance to me, or none at all. There was André Malraux of whom I had heard; hadn't he written about China and done something in the Spanish War – but for which side? There was Henri de Montherlant whose novels poor Mr Fielding used so conspicuously and proudly to carry about with him. But who, for instance, were Drieu and Robert Brasillach and Louis (? Aragon, it seemed from references) with whom he held such animated discussions and whom he seemed to regard as of public importance? Evidently

there was much background reading that would be necessary if I
was to make any sense of my father at all. Which was disheart-
ening, and I wondered, being intellectually lazy, if there was any
point to it.

Yet I felt, obscurely, committed, all the more so because my
memories of him were so sparse and unsatisfactory. And also
because I found that I rather liked him. He was so different from
me. I couldn't imagine him cavorting with Eddie and laughing at
the way he eyed up mulatto sailors or making a cult of Flannagan
and Allen and taking every opportunity to see the Crazy Gang
Show at the Victoria Palace – Eddie and I had seen the latest one
three times in one week of the Easter vacation. And this wasn't
simply a difference between England and France – there existed
after all French music hall, I had heard of Chevalier and Piaf, but
the man about whom I was learning was evidently foreign to that
side of French culture; which indeed he might not, I thought,
have been prepared to accept as culture.

Was he a bore? I wondered. I could see that in some respects,
and for some people, he might have been. But he must have had
charm, which he could hardly convey in writing. Polly would not
have married him otherwise, would not have fallen for him.
Charm was something she needed and responded to. Roddy,
for all his faults, had charm.

I traced in my father a desire to succeed, but on his own terms.
He returned time and again to the consequences for France of
what he described as the abdication of the *gens du bien* – the well-
born men of property. According to him, all the ills of the country
– Socialism, irreligion, the dominance of the Jewish interest and
high finance – stemmed from the disinclination of men from
families like ours to involve themselves in public life.

I was puzzled by his list of enemies. According to my English
education, Socialists and financiers were in natural opposition to
each other. Lucien seemed to lump them together. How could
this be? I wished there was someone to explain.

Then there were his essays. They had titles like 'The Corruption
of Power', 'The Inevitable Decadence of Republics', 'The Cult of
the Individual', 'The Failure of our Institutions', 'The Latinity of
France', 'Towards a New Social Dimension'; and they were full of
abstract nouns and abstract reasoning. No doubt they would help
me to understand him – or his mind at least, by no means the same
thing, I now realised. Unfortunately I couldn't bring myself to read
them. They were dead as mutton. I felt I was wasting my time.

And yet, despite this, every morning I took myself to the study and delved in his desk, and returned there in the evening for another session. It was like a drug, and it had the same isolating effect. Often I simply sat in the window-seat watching the light die over the Midi, and it was perhaps in those half hours of twilight that I began to come to experience some sense of communion with him. He too must have watched the gold slip away from the trunks of the olive trees, seen them turn silvery-grey, then lose themselves in a thick obscurity.

One morning, having the night before read a poem he had written on Roman Provence, I took a car, an old Citroën, which I had found in a stable and had overhauled in the village – and drove to St-Rémy, and then up the hill, past the hospital where Van Gogh was confined, to the Roman ruins of Glanum. They were deserted, vineyards surrounded them, and fields of maize, the arch that had been the gateway of the town rose like an outcrop of nature, as much part of the land as the rocky hills, *les Alpilles*, which broke the azure of the sky with their jagged fringe. There were sheep bleating in the distance and, for me, it was no more than agreeable pastoral given a certain edge by the antiquity of the setting. But for Lucien it had been more. This represented the City, that ordered Roman world of intelligence and significant form. That there had been subversive undercurrents in Rome I knew even then – I had read enough Virgil to be aware of that – conscious that even the celebrant of imperial virtue and the imperial mission heard discordant other-worldly strains of music, that a disturbing knowledge underlay the abstract nouns. And yet there was something disturbing in my father's vision too. A line, which I took to be a quotation, appeared several times in his pages: '*la beauté véritable est au terme des choses*' – 'true beauty is found at the limit of things' – I translate for the benefit of my purely hypothetical grandchildren, if they should ever read this document, as I pored over my father's notebooks – for it seems unlikely that they will read French. And if they don't, does that mean that my father's forebodings are justified? Are we really approaching the end of that historic civilisation of Europe, which – I was beginning to see – he had devoted his life to sustaining? And if we are, will they find '*la beauté véritable*' there?

I lay in the sun listening to the crickets for a long morning, and then, suddenly, aware of the demanding hunger of youth, drove over the little hills to Les Baux.

Was it that evening that the curé visited? I think it was. At any rate, when I entered the drawing room for the aperitif I had become accustomed to share with my grandmother, I found him there: a small man, with a strangely pink face – a complexion that is rare in Provence – and very pale blue eyes.

'Do you play chess?' he asked, after the conventional preliminaries, and when I said yes, invited me to visit him that evening after dinner.

'I am starved for a game,' he said. 'The schoolmaster is the only other chess-player in the village, and of course we are not on speaking terms.'

'Why "of course"?' I asked my grandmother when he had gone.

'Oh,' she said, 'the schoolmaster is a terrible man, an atheist and a red. Our masters in Paris think that type suitable for the instruction of young French men and women, for the formation of their intellects and characters. But the curé is a good man, though timid.'

He was certainly a good chess-player, far too good for me, and there was no timidity evident in the way he brought his queen into play early in the game. He beat me three times within the hour. I apologised for not being able to give him a better game.

'It's no matter,' he said. 'It is a pleasure simply to move the pieces, and a change from playing over the games of the masters. Besides, I am pleased to meet you. I would have done so before, but I have been away. Perhaps your grandmother told you. Besides, I knew you as a child.'

'You've been here a long time then.'

'Twenty-five years, and I hope, God willing, to die here, despite everything. I was a protégé of your great-uncle, the Bishop. He took me from the village school – not here, but only a dozen miles away. I owe everything to him. My mother was poor and a widow. We were poor in a way that nobody is now.'

He filled his pipe and then produced a bottle of *marc* and two stubby glasses.

'I'm afraid that I didn't even know that I had a Bishop among my relations,' I said, 'but then I know very little – shamefully little, I suppose, about my family.'

'But you have come here to find out,' he said, puffing away. The tobacco was cheap shag with a pungent aroma . . .

'I suppose so,' I said, 'but it is all very strange, and I am not making much progress.'

'No.'

He fell silent. There was no electricity in his house and the oil lamp was smoking. The remains of his supper stood on a table in the middle of the room, giving off a smell of sour cheese. He sucked on his pipe and lifted his chin and I could see a watermark on his neck. The skin was grimy below it, and his nails were black.

'It is a great pleasure for your grandmother to have you here. She has been waiting a long time. She has often said so to me.'

He puffed out smoke. I could think of no reply to make.

'Are you a good Catholic?'

'I'm afraid not. That's to say . . .'

'But then,' he pursued his thought, apparently paying little heed to my answer, 'what after all is a good Catholic? One who keeps the observances of course, but then? Your grandmother is a great woman, and I revere her. She has shown fortitude and few of my parishioners would be as charitable to poor Marthe as she has been, and yet . . . you understand that I say nothing against her, I owe everything to your family, even, I sometimes think, my faith, and yet there are times, I must confess, when I think there can be too much faith. Faith excludes humanity. Of course you know that "Humanity" is the name of our Communist news-paper, and that is not what I mean, but I have seen faith elevated and distorted, so that only the Church was remembered and Christ forgotten. Do you follow what I am saying? I am only a simple country priest, who has forgotten all the philosophy and most of the theology he learned at college, and no doubt I often stray from what is true, but . . . do you know that General de Gaulle calls the Holy Father the "Nazi Pope"?'

'No,' I said, 'I didn't.'

'And that distresses me, because I fear the truth in the charge . . .'

'You must have known my father.'

'Did anyone?'

'I'm sorry. What do you mean?'

He was silent. His pipe had gone out, and he made great play with the business of relighting it. Then he swallowed his *marc*, in one gulp, without a grimace, and filled his glass and topped up mine.

'What happened to him?' I asked. 'How did he die?'

'She hasn't told you?'

'That he was a hero. Nothing else. She has encouraged me to read his papers.'

'Ah, his book?'

'Which book?'

'His confessions. The last time I spoke to him he told me he had been writing his confessions. I have always wondered how much he had done.'

'There's no book that I have come upon yet. And you haven't answered my question, Father.'

'Because I can't.'

'You don't know?'

'It is not precisely that, though I don't know precisely. I speak awkwardly. But it is not for me to say, not for me to tell you. But I will say one thing. There were no simple deaths in France at that time, none. There was not even tragedy. There was no dignity, you see. That is the thing. There was no dignity in France and perhaps there never will be again, and without dignity there can neither be a good death nor a simple one. And perhaps the two are the same thing.'

I played chess with him again, more than once, in the next few days. But I learned nothing.

'If you come on his confessions,' he said, 'then, when you have read them, promise that you will speak to me before you form a judgement.'

Yves had disappeared after staying only one night. Marthe had made no mention of him, but I was aware from the day of our encounter in the kitchen that she regarded me with a certain suspicion. Or perhaps suspicion was not the right word. Perhaps it was shame. When I met her she would lower her eyes, and whenever I tried to engage her in conversation on any subject other than the making of a pot of coffee or a sandwich, she would mutter, 'It's not for the likes of me to talk about that, Monsieur Etienne.' It annoyed me that she addressed me in this way, though I was accustomed to having our college porters call me 'Mr de Balafré'. But that was different, and back home on the farm Hilda, who was probably younger than Marthe, would call me simply 'Ettenne' – the nearest she ever got to the correct pronunciation. It was Yves who had interrupted the progress I had been making with his mother, and I thought of him with resentment.

Then one day there was another boy in the kitchen. He was younger than Yves and not, it seemed, 'one of the Germans' for, unlike the small boy she had led in that afternoon, he was dark-haired and dark-complexioned. He was very thin and looked undernourished, but he greeted me with a smile and lively eyes.

For a moment we stood and said nothing.

'I'm called Jacques,' he said. 'You must be Monsieur Etienne.'

'You don't need to call me Monsieur.'

'My mother does. She told me to. "Be sure to remember to call him Monsieur," she said.' He laughed. 'But if you don't like it I won't.'

'I'm losing count,' I said. 'You're the third I've met. How many of you are there?'

'Five altogether. I know you've met Yves. Maman said he behaved awfully. But then he does, he is awful. When I see him he pulls my hair, but he can't now' – he pointed to his cropped head – 'the Fathers shaved me, because of lice. Not that I had them. But the others did. It'll grow again and then I'll look human, I can't stand looking like this . . .'

'You're home for your holidays. Where do you go to school?'

'With the Fathers. In Avignon. I would have been home three weeks ago, but we went to camp. A praying camp of course. They called it a retreat. I'm glad it's over. Being woken for prayers in the middle of the night isn't my idea of a joke.'

He leapt off the table.

'How old are you, Jacques?' I asked.

'I'm eleven,' he said, 'nearly twelve. And you're nineteen.'

'Nearly twenty,' I said, and we both giggled.

'Will you teach me how to shoot?'

I did, of course. Shooting happened to be one of the few things I was rather good at, but even if I hadn't been proud of my skill, I would have done what I could to teach him. He had that sort of effect on me, it was a pleasure to please him. In the next fortnight I found myself shedding years, becoming fourteen or fifteen perhaps. We wandered over the hills with a gun, Jacques popping off at any small bird that dared to show itself. Fortunately, despite my instruction, he was a terrible shot. He was an impulsive child, changing direction every few minutes. This characteristic was both physical and mental. He darted and zigzagged up the hillsides and throughout the stories he would tell me of the Fathers who taught him. Every one was a grotesque, he could do all their voices. This one swore by St Antony's bones – 'St Antony of Padua, you understand, Etienne, you pray to him when you've lost something, you know, but where the bones come into it, I can't tell you' – that one sipped cognac in class and would fondle the boys' necks in the afternoon – 'But only if they are pretty and have no spots, you understand, I'm quite safe' – the next was in love with his motor-bicycle – 'He strokes it when he puts it to bed' – another spoke to himself – 'Terrible things he says, you can't imagine, bring a blush to even my cheeks.' He lay back on the grass and kicked his legs in the air, and laughed, then sat up and looked at me, his face straight and his eyes gleaming black.

'Etienne, do you think everyone's mad? I do. Except women maybe. And us of course.'

'What makes you think we're not mad?'

'We couldn't be, we're too sane, it would make no sense if we were mad too.'

'Maybe it does make no sense.'

'Oh no, that couldn't be. You see, everything makes sense, except people. The world's not mad, nature's not mad, these olive trees aren't mad. Only people.'

'What about rabies and mad dogs.'

'That's different. That's a sickness.'

'I see. And why aren't women mad?'

'Because they aren't. Give me a cigarette and I'll think why.'

'You're too young to smoke,' I said, passing the packet.

To prove me wrong, he drew the smoke into his lungs, held it there – I was sure he was counting to ten – and puffed it out through his nose. It hung, blue, in the golden air of the afternoon.

'Because they're good,' he said. 'That's the difference between men and women. They can live for others. That's why they're not mad.'

'Oh,' I said, 'you only know my grandmother and your own mother. You don't know any other women. You don't have the material to judge.'

'No,' he said, and put his hand on my knee, 'don't speak like that. I know enough, and I'm right.'

It was as if a cloud had crossed over the sun.

'What do you remember about the war, Jacques?' I asked.

Then he smiled.

'I knew you were all right,' he said. 'Not mad. Like me. That's the whole point. Can you imagine a women's army?'

'You're a very remarkable child.'

'Don't call me a child.'

'But some women did terrible things during the war. There was, what's her name, at Belsen, the one who made lampshades out of human skin, you've heard of her, haven't you? And during the *épuration*' – I stopped, feeling the ice crack.

'Yes,' he said, 'I don't know how much you know, but I remember. You've seen Kurt, my half-brother, the German's son, and you've heard stories. They came here, you know, the heroes of the Liberation, and they shaved Maman's head, because of Kurt and his father. I was five. They did it in front of me. There were women among them, but the leader was Simon, the *garagiste*. Oh, he was brave, a real hero. I'm glad you taught me to shoot. Do you see why? They tied her to a chair in the kitchen and they shaved her head. Then they drove her down to the village and made her walk through the street. I didn't see that. I was left in the kitchen, crying my eyes out.'

He threw himself, face down, on the harsh grass and shook with sobs. I didn't know what to say or do. I put my hand on his shoulder and felt him heave and squirm and shudder, as if in a fit, trying to expel devils.

When Marthe brought in the coffee that evening, I watched her, as though in some way she could be marked by the knowledge I had been given. It was ridiculous. She had accommodated herself to experience years ago. The fact that I now knew was only a fact. Of no significance. It was like meeting someone released from prison and supposing that he would be changed by my knowing that. But other people's knowledge is trivial compared to the fact of what happened. It is only peripheral. The last sunlight fell on the table and my grandmother wiped her lips with her white linen napkin and laid it beside her plate. Marthe closed the door behind her. She was wearing carpet slippers and her retreat was silent.

Jacques said: 'I've never told anyone what I told you yesterday. That they made me watch it.'

We were in the car going to the cinema, in the late afternoon. Jacques sat with his arms hugging his knees, his feet on the dashboard.

'I had to tell someone,' he said. 'I never thought I would be able to.'

We ran through the village. The *garagiste*, Simon, was standing by his pumps. He waved as we passed. I saw him in the rear mirror, standing gazing after us, his hands on his hips, cigarette in the corner of his mouth, beret pulled down over his eyes.

'He's my mother's cousin, you know,' Jacques said, 'and he used to sell petrol to the German officers on the Black Market. I know a lot about him. He likes to talk of the war, he was a big shot then. Like a lot who were in the *Maquis*, he played both sides.

'The Germans can't have been here long though,' I said. 'This was the unoccupied zone after all.'

'Oh yes, and the *Milice* – they were the Vichy police, you know – were worse even than the Gestapo, some people say. But you see, Etienne, it was all mad, I don't really understand what happened then, except that people were hateful, at their worst, like school bullies. I suppose Simon was a school bully.'

'Do you speak to him ever?'

'No, of course not. We don't forget things, we southerners. I told you I was glad you had taught me to shoot. That's my duty, you see.'

And he began to whistle a little tune which I couldn't identify, and then he talked about the movie we were off to see. He knew a lot about movies, Jacques, and I couldn't understand how, for I was sure that the Fathers wouldn't let their charges be exposed to the corrupting influence of the cinema. But it was the least of the things I didn't understand.

Now, looking back over more than thirty years, I wonder at my naivety and lack of curiosity, my failure to try to understand Jacques. Of course we all have an ability, perhaps innate, to hide from whatever is unwelcome. Sarah, I reflect, thinking of what she may be up to in South Africa, chooses not to see how injustice succeeds injustice or to admit that revolutions always destroy what is good in people as well as whatever may be evil in social structures.

What I couldn't believe that evening, and then easily forgot, in fact happened. Jacques shot Simon through the back of the head, stepping out from behind his petrol pumps. He did this the day before his own eighteenth birthday, choosing the date exactly so that he would escape the guillotine.

So, when I think of Jacques, the first image is something I never actually saw: not the boy who lazed chattering on the hillside or with his knees drawn up beside me in the front of that old Citroën, but instead a thin figure slipping into the dark blanket of the evening shadows.

For years that sharp act shone across the wasteland of my own indifference, incomprehensible because beyond my range of sympathy, belonging, it seemed to me, more to the clear imperatives of the Trojan War than to the hesitating morality by which I lived myself.

I HAD BEEN there five weeks, perhaps six. Jacques had left, though it can't have been time for him to return to school; yet I cannot now recall why he had gone.

One evening my grandmother said: 'I think you feel you belong here.'

I couldn't reply, for it would have been brutal to tell her she was wrong.

'It will be yours,' she reminded me again. 'Indeed it is rightfully yours now.'

She poured me a glass of *marc* and took one for herself.

'I am glad,' she said, 'that you were so ready to take care of the little boy. I hope it didn't bore you.'

'Not at all,' I said, 'he is charming.'

It was a word I couldn't have brought myself to utter in English, even though charm is, I suppose, an English characteristic rather than a French one. Eddie, after all, was the epitome of charm; he used charm as he had done all his life to evade the demands of the intellect, and the charm of others.

Aware of this perhaps, I said again: 'He is charming.'

'Ah,' she said, 'I have been wondering if I should explain him to you. Had you not liked him I don't think I would have done so. He doesn't know himself, of course.'

'I don't understand you,' I said, when she fell silent.

'I am sorry,' she said. She smiled. She hardly ever smiled, and, when she did so, you could see that she must have been beautiful as a girl.

'I have fallen,' she said, 'into the way of speaking so as not to be understood. An elliptical manner, the use of irony. Your Uncle Armand chides me for it. He says it is arrogant. Perhaps I am arrogant. But it comes perhaps from living alone and talking only to fools. And not even many of them, for I have never been able to abide fools around me. It is a great relief, Etienne, that you are not a fool. Armand himself is a fool of course, though a clever one. He is only interested in making money.'

She paused and looked out of the window at the hills, which

were now purple. The trees below the terrace were swathed in black. The shadows cast by the fringed shade of the lamp over the table made her face look like an ancient and ravaged landscape; one where seams of some mineral had been exhausted and which the exploiters had abandoned. How, I wondered, did she get through the day? What drove her to rise in the morning? The tenacity, even the heroism, of the old, of this particular old woman, appalled me. I couldn't imagine, then, how anyone acquired the ability simply to go on. It didn't occur to me that it is the young who kill themselves.

'Jacques,' she said . . . and paused. 'To cure myself of this habit of irony, or at least to set it aside for a moment, let me tell you straight out, this little Jacques is your half-brother. He doesn't know it himself of course, and you, I think, are the only person who has the right to tell him.'

'Surely, his mother . . .'

'Marthe has no rights . . . it will be a question of property of course . . . you may wish . . . but no one will exercise any persuasion on you, rest assured of that.'

Having read over my reconstruction of these first weeks in Provence I realise not only that there is no narrative – and yet what is life but narrative? – but that I have signally failed to bring my grandmother to life. That is inescapable; could hardly be otherwise. I couldn't understand the spark of life persisting there. Even when she dropped this monstrous revelation on the dinner table between us – and it was, it seemed, only at the table that we met, so that I am driven to wonder how in fact she passed the days – even then, she did it without animation, without any sense that what she was saying was actually staggering, that it is not every day that one is suddenly presented with a brother; even a half-brother. And yet I couldn't question her either, I couldn't ask for the circumstances.

I could look at Marthe in a new way, could summon up the imagined picture of her in my mother's bed, or in a dusty corner of the hayloft, or had my father crept like a thief up the back stairs to the garret where Marthe lodged? – if she did indeed lodge in a garret; could ask myself how he had felt at taking his place in that long line of men, whom, in the circumstances as I apprehended them, I could not really bring myself to think of as lovers. I visioned instead Marthe's copulations as things of the field, mere brute necessity – without joy, for I could not in any way associate Marthe with joy. (And yet there had been nothing but joy, and perhaps surprise, in the actual moments of my own sexual cavortings.)

And there is too much 'I' in this motionless narrative, and yet 'I' is the essence of autobiography if that is what I am struggling, like a rough beast, to bring forth.

Yet the next morning I confronted Marthe with my knowledge, straight out, like a newspaper revelation in the headlines.

'My grandmother told me last night about Jacques.'

'She said she would.'

'I wish I had known while he was here.'

'Understand, Monsieur Etienne, we ask for nothing. Jacques doesn't know who his father was. There's no reason why he should, unless some day you choose to tell him. But that's not necessary. He's a clever boy who can make his way in the world, and may do so more easily without the burden of such knowledge.'

She didn't look at me while she spoke, but kept her face lowered over the basin in which she was scrubbing at a pan, and I had to strain to hear what she was saying.

'Indeed, Monsieur Etienne, I would rather he remained ignorant, and I told your grandmother so. "Better they both remain ignorant," I said to her, "it will only fill their heads with nonsense if you tell them." But she would have it that you should know.'

'Why do you call it a burden, Marthe?'

'It was when war was coming, your father was at home. He was desperate and unhappy and I thought to comfort him. But it brought no comfort, and I can't see that the knowledge of his birth would do anything for Jacques . . .'

She straightened her back and began to dry the pan she had been washing.

'I've watched you since you arrived, Monsieur Etienne, and I know that you have been burrowing into the past, wondering about what is over – in your father's manner – and it did him no good and can do you none. I'm an ignorant woman, but I know that. You're like your father, and that is not good. He was a man marked for sorrow. That's all I have to say on the matter except that I'll thank you, if you have a care for the boy, and I think you have, not to burden him with knowledge that can only be useless and painful.'

What could I say to that?

'I wish you would tell me more about my father.'

'It's not for me to do so. Besides, if you think I know anything simply because I happened to let him into my bed one night, you're mistaken. He thought too much, that's all I can tell you, and you know that already. It's not the way to get through life. We must take what comes, and he never knew that.'

It was the sort of remark which passes for peasant wisdom, useless unless you happen to be a peasant. The Bible tells us that no one can add cubits to his stature by taking thought, and Jesus tells us to consider the lilies of the field, but the habit of thought cannot be broken by such advice.

So both women left me more disturbed. It was as if contact with them had only given me an itch. I wrote to Eddie about my brother. 'Lucky you,' he sighed when we met in the autumn mists of the Fens. He didn't mean anything except the absurdity of fancy.

My Uncle Armand arrived in a flash of shiny Citroën, that long-nosed car which in old gangster movies sets off a throb of nostalgia for a vanished France. He withdrew himself from it, tall, beaky, crinkling with suppressed laughter; embraced his mother and held me off a moment, his eyes dancing, enfolded me in his arms, and said,

'It's not possible, the resemblance. As soon as I learned from Maman that you were indeed here – I have been away from home, you understand – I leapt into my car and sped south. It's remarkable,' he repeated, 'I could never have mistaken you, it's like seeing Lucien again, like wiping off the years.'

Armand changed everything. The silent house was full of chatter and movement. All the shutters which enclosed it were thrown open. He talked a faster French than I had ever heard, from the corner of a twisted mouth, which, all the time, even while he spoke, retained a Gauloise. He was a frenetic smoker. As soon as he sat at the dining table, he would lay the packet and an onyx lighter at his left side, and he would continue smoking until Marthe had placed his food before him. It wasn't exactly with reluctance that he then stubbed out a cigarette in the capacious ash-tray which he had himself brought to the table, but that was only because it was inconceivable that Armand could ever be brought to do anything with reluctance.

And he talked all the time, mostly about people of whom I was naturally quite ignorant. His conversation was laced with jokes which I couldn't understand, and which his mother only rarely acknowledged with a slight slow movement of the lip. This didn't disconcert him, he was always ready to laugh at his own humour, though, unlike many who have this habit, he never did so uproariously; it was as if he couldn't spare the time to give vent to a thoroughgoing laugh – it was more a light trill which was scarcely allowed to break the flow of his sentence, and then he was off again. I had never encountered such a stream of perpetual gaiety.

After he had been there three days, he said to me,

'I must go tomorrow and you must come with me. I revere my mother, but she is low-spirited, and frankly two days of her company is all I can normally manage. How you have stood it for so long I can't imagine. Perhaps you are a saint. Your father, my poor, poor brother, had of course always aspirations to sainthood, which was perhaps why he loved Provence and was able to abide in his mother's house, but, though you resemble him, I have been watching you, you see, and there are significant differences. After all, you are also your mother's son – I adore her by the way, so sad to think of her exiled in South Africa, you must give her all my love and lots of brotherly hugs and kisses when you see her next, or when you write – do you write? I have never been able to write to my mother of course, but then there is no comparison, is there? What a silly thing to say, there is always comparison between people, I think. We all love X better than Y, and what is that but comparison? So give my adored Polly all my love and tell her not to stay in South Africa, she must be tired of her pilot now, mustn't she – pilots are all very well in wartime when they can be heroes, but tiresome in peace, I think. War and peace are very different, you know, and so different types flourish. I was no good in the war, they gave me medals of course, but I was no good, it was the wrong ambience, that's all. I am a man of peace and affairs.'

'And my father,' I said, 'was he a man of peace or war?'

'Ah, my poor Lucien, I adored him, you know; perhaps we should have some champagne. Let's go and look for some, shall we?'

I hadn't even known there was a cellar below Marthe's kitchen. Only our own wine of the last year's vintage appeared on my grandmother's table. By the look of the cobwebs over the cellar door no one had entered since Armand's last visit home, which – he had told me – had been the previous summer.

'You may wonder,' he said, unlocking the door, 'how any wine survived the visit of our German friends. It is curious that it did, sheer chance. They had a gentlemanly Commander, who was also, uniquely perhaps, a teetotaller.'

'And after the war, or,' I paused, 'during the *épuration* . . .'

'That is odder still, yes, you are right, perhaps the saints interceded for our wine, if not for anything else. I don't know . . . Of course it is not much of a cellar now . . .' he waved the torch he had brought with him, 'as you can see, most of the vaults are empty, your poor father was not interested in fine wine . . . but there should still be some, though I confess that I usually remove a few bottles whenever I visit.'

The cellar must have stretched half the length of the house, and deep into the hillside behind. Most of the bays near the door were empty, though here and there a few bottles, swathed in cobwebs, lay, like driftwood on a beach, eloquent of the rule of chance.

I might have indulged further in such reflections, but my Uncle Armand was hardly the companion likely to respond to them.

'Come, come,' he cried, waving the large torch he had brought with him, 'champagne to the rear.'

He drew out a bottle.

'Perrier-Jouet, '34. '34, ah, Etienne, in '34 I was in love with an actress and we drank this wine's older brother. Perrier-Jouet. '34, was that the last year before the abyss was visible, or could we already see it? It is a lovely pun anyway, though *joué et peri* would of course be more precise. Come, we'll take a few of these . . .'

The second half of the second bottle induced even in Armand a melancholy mood. I had been talking of Polly, of Cambridge and then at last of my father – all in response to his questions, and his statement of the urgent requirement that he should get to know this nephew of his at once – and I said I had been spending hours in my father's study, trying to understand him.

'But though I feel I am getting to know him I still don't know how he died, and no one seems willing to tell me. I don't understand that, especially as my grandmother assures me he was a hero.'

And I repeated what the curé had said: that there were no simple deaths in France then.

'I don't really understand what he meant by that either.'

Armand turned his glass upside down and allowed the last few drops of wine to run down to the tiled floor.

'It was a shambles,' he said, 'France, a shambles, where killing and humiliation were the delight of many. Poor Lucien was a victim, of circumstance and human nature; not his own nature. I've always believed that. Beyond that, I'd rather not talk of it. It's

too painful. I say, let's open the next bottle, and talk of women
. . . you're not a virgin, are you? If you are, that's something we
shall have to remedy, don't you think?'

When we left the next morning, I was surprised that my grandmother made no attempt to delay us, just as she had made no
objection to my announcement that I would like to go off with my
uncle. I had expected her to protest, and was indeed rather hurt that
she didn't. Perhaps she enjoyed having me there less than I was
encouraged to suppose? Now of course I know that was not the
case, but that it was more important for her to have seen me, to have
had me to stay, than to prolong the visit. No doubt she had been
apprehensive all the time I was there that I would suddenly turn
against everything she longed for me to love. But she also experienced the weariness of the old, which is often so easily satisfied by
something less than the presence of those they love, who live at least
as warmly in memory as across the dinner table. My weeks there – I
say this with no personal complacency, you understand – had given
my grandmother sufficient store of memories. This was not something I could possibly have comprehended then; it has taken the
development of my own relations with Sarah to open my eyes to it.

Armand's house in Normandy, just east of the boundary that
separates that province from Brittany, was delightful. It stood less
than half a mile from the sea, but the intervening ground, which
belonged to him, was covered with ragged orchard; all sorts of
wildflowers which I could not name grew round the trunks of the
trees. The house itself was a half-timbered structure with a
verandah running round three sides of it. You approached by
a winding drive which gave on to a little courtyard, out of the
evening sun when we arrived; you were not at first aware of the
wide verandah on which so much of the social life of the house
was lived. It was a pink and white house – pink bricks and white
woodwork which was old and peeling and which any houseproud
Englishman would have renewed several summers previously.
Honeysuckle straggled over the verandah and yellow tea-roses
climbed the pink walls. It looked comfortable and shabby and
quite without pretension. There were deckchairs and wickerwork
furniture on the verandah.

We had left the car in the courtyard without bothering to
unpack anything and had gone round to the front of the house.
A girl was lying in one of the deckchairs; she was asleep and did
not hear our approach, but a white spaniel with lemon markings
came to greet us.

Armand knelt in front of it. The dog – it was an unusually big spaniel – put feathery paws on his shoulders, almost knocking him over backwards with the exuberance of its welcome – and began to lick his face.

'Yes, boy,' he said, 'but we have a visitor, a new member of the family.'

And I felt warm to hear him describe me like that, as if I belonged, and was pleased when the dog turned his boisterous affection on me. Then the girl leapt up, kissed Armand, and extended her hand to me.

'I'm Jeanne-Marie,' she said. 'We're so glad you have come. And this is Henry' – she pronounced it with an open 'e' and put an equal stress on both syllables. 'We call him that because he is an English dog. It was an English friend who gave him to us. He's a love.' She knelt down beside the spaniel and cradled his head in her arms, and he twisted round and licked her face; the long pink tongue was like a slice of mobile ham.

'He's lovely,' I said, and he was, but I meant more than that. I meant it was all lovely, and so was she. She was big and blonde, like a golden heifer. And I knew at once, in the way that you can immediately, that she was good and someone I would love, in a relaxed, sympathetic and trusting way, all my life. It was a long time before I realised Jeanne-Marie's capacity for unhappiness, a capacity that derived from her profound sense of pity, which would lead her into a lifetime of devotion to causes: for animals, for miserable refugee children, for the old, for all the poor and wretched of the earth; a pity which would deny her any conventional sort of happiness, so that throughout her life there have been many ready to say 'poor Jeanne-Marie'. If someone had told me then, as I watched this sturdy goddess cradle her dog's head, that she would be distressed for years over the question of whether she possessed a religious vocation, that it would pain her terribly to decide that she hadn't, and that she would nevertheless pass her life in service to men and animals without any consolation of faith, what would I have felt? The blank incredulity with which we view the lives of others? The sense of wonder that people so different from oneself can exist? And indeed the fact of the existence of others is one of the hurdles one is continually brought down by.

And suddenly there were more girls, three of them.

'Are they all my cousins?'

'No, only two of them, but you'll be overwhelmed by girls,'

Armand said, 'lucky man.' He put his arms round the younger
pair. 'Tot and Toinette.'

It was obvious that Armand adored his daughters and loved to
spoil them. Their mother, whom I called Tante Berthe, though I
called him simply Armand, tried to exercise 'a traditional degree
of discipline. Else they will be savages.' But Armand laughed, and
denied them nothing, asking only that they should be there, happy
and ready to amuse him.

Tot and Toinette were certainly keen to do that. Their conversation was a bubbling stream of jokes, anecdotes and teasing,
much of the last directed at their father, whom they obviously
adored as much as he did them. Tot was twelve, Toinette fourteen, and they were experimenting with make-up – 'It is the
holidays, Maman' – and babbling of film stars, but they were still
clinging on to childhood. Much of their life centred round their
animals. In addition to the Clumber spaniel, Henry, there was a
brace of scruffy terriers, which they swore were 'Aberdeens' but
hardly resembled any Scottie I had ever seen, and there was a big
yellow dog which they called a 'Vendéen hound', but which
looked like a mongrel to me. Cats wandered in and out of the
house, were to be found on the dining table and curled against the
stove in the kitchen, and in the beds. I never succeeded in
identifying all of them, or even in numbering them.

Jeanne-Marie had her own cat, a black Angora with yellow
eyes; she was called Nefertiti, 'because the Egyptians were crazy
about their cats, and so am I about mine. Isn't she heaven? She's
the most intelligent person in the house, her only rival for
intelligence is Henry.'

Nefertiti was given to scratching and biting, and both the
younger girls were frightened of her: 'She doesn't like them
because they used to chase her when they were little. She's
pre-war, Nefertiti' – like the Perrier-Jouet, I thought. But if they
were frightened by her ill temper, Jeanne-Marie valued her all the
more on that account. It was, I suppose, a matter of pride for her
that this savage and independent beauty would drape herself
round her neck, filling the immediate air with a rasping purr.

There were rabbits in hutches in the garden, but often out of
the hutches lolloping round with that air of not knowing where
they are or what they are expected to do which is characteristic of
rabbits. There was a grey parrot in a cage which was placed out on
the verandah every morning as soon as the sun had moved round,
away from its favoured corner; the woodwork there had been

destroyed by its beak, so that it was now only rarely allowed free of
the cage. When it was released it waddled across the floor,
clucking disapproval at any dog that dared to lift its head or at
any cat which ventured within sight. The parrot was Armand's
and 'It is perhaps the only parrot in France which is not called
Polly, and that's not because of your mother, because I had him
before you were born, before they were married, but because I got
him from a Chinaman who had already named him Wu. And Wu
he still is.'

'Daddy will keep calling Wu "him" and "he" but it's really
she,' Jeanne-Marie said. 'It was always he, but then one day Wu
laid an egg, so that proves Wu is really a girl. She's an old lady
now of course, but parrots live for ages.'

'So do donkeys,' Tot said. 'We have one donkey, Etienne,
which is at least forty years old. Jacques, that's our gardener, says
nobody has ever seen a dead donkey.'

'That's nonsense.'

There were three donkeys, and the two younger ones used to be
loaded with panniers when we went for a picnic, either down to
the beach or beyond the house, in the forest. The oldest donkey
had been retired but still insisted on accompanying the party.

These picnics took place almost every day, they were part of the
routine of summer at Les Trois-Puits. Life started early in the
household. Dominique, Tante Berthe's maid of all work, was
busy in the kitchen by six. My bedroom being immediately above
it, at the side of the house, facing east towards the forest, I would
be awakened by her singing as she worked. She was a stout red-
armed Norman girl; I amused myself by thinking that the tanner's
daughter who had caught the eye of Duke William's father had
been of the same robust and sensual sort. It seemed to give a sense
of historical continuity to what was otherwise a very mid-twentieth century gathering. Yet even without such, the continuity
existed. Les Trois-Puits had been in Tante Berthe's family for
several generations, having originally been bought by a Napoleonic General – her great-great-grandfather, I think, though I
may have omitted one generation.

Coffee was served us in big thick white pottery bowls, of local,
or perhaps Breton, manufacture. Milky bubbles frothed at the rim
of the bowls and we would dunk thick cuts of bread, fresh from
the baker, in the coffee. A second slice of bread would be eaten
with white Norman butter and apricot jam. Jeanne-Marie always
slipped a piece of bread and butter to the spaniel Henry, who had,
she explained to me the first morning, a passion for butter and

cheese. There was fruit on the table, but few of us ate fruit at breakfast, though Armand would always take an apple, invariably, to tease his daughters, quoting the old saw about an apple a day; 'Of course,' he would add, 'I know that Toinette has no wish to keep Dr Corbier away. She dotes on him, Etienne, though he has mutton-chop whiskers and is at least seventy.'

'What a fib, Papa,' Toinette cried, 'he's not only seventy, Etienne, but his own breath stinks of rotten apples and when he looks at your throat and commands you to say "Ah", he always contrives to tickle your cheeks with his whiskers. He's an old horror.'

'Don't forget, Toinette,' Jeanne-Marie said, 'that the old horror was a hero during the war. When the Germans were here, Etienne, he kept a family of Jews hidden in the cellar of his house – it's that big one, behind railings and monkey-puzzle trees which you see to the right of the Hôtel de Ville in the square. And he looked after wounded English airmen too, they didn't mind what his breath smelled of. It was one of them gave us Henry, in fact, the sweet. When he came back to say thank you after the war, and we got to know him.'

But the war and its memories cast no shadow on that happy house. It was only mentioned in connection with acts of courage or generosity.

Coming from the pinched aridity of my grandmother's house, and laden with memories of the silent terraces of Roddy's farm where the bottles of Cape gin and Cape brandy served as symbols of the isolation of husband from wife, it was natural, I suppose, that I should fall in love with the whole family, who accepted me as easily and happily as if I had been a new dog, and made no demands on me, but simply showed, by the ease with which I was included in their daily life, that they were pleased to have me there. I would wake up in the morning knowing I would be happy as sunshine all day long.

But there was more to it than that; I had also fallen particularly in love. The girl was Freddie, Jeanne-Marie's college friend, whom, till this moment, I have not mentioned, not knowing how to write about her. And I still don't know.

They say first love is always the same and always individual. But this wasn't first love. I had been in love often enough. And yet it was first love because it was the first love of which I knew I had no need to feel ashamed, and also my first love for a girl which attached itself to a person and not just to a body.

And yet it started with the body, as it always has for me. When I first saw her unfold herself from a deckchair on the terrace, I said to myself, 'This girl is lovely.' That's my abiding impression, though her features, except for big brown eyes which contrasted with her blonde hair, cut short like a boy's, were too clumsy for beauty: her nose was snubby and her mouth too big, and her lower jaw would become too long. And yet she was lovely: she wore that afternoon a white aertex shirt and very brief white shorts, and her legs were long, thin and bronzed. There was a golden sheen to her, touched under her eyes and at the edges with blue.

You cannot conduct a private love affair in a house full of girls, where the whole family is on holiday and people do everything together. I don't suppose in the first week I was there that Freddie and I were alone by ourselves, and I can't imagine how we could have found the opportunity to have any conversation that did not include the others. Yet this wasn't frustrating, though I went to bed thinking of Freddie and woke with her image in my mind. I didn't touch her that week, except once when we were playing tennis on the hard court at the top end of the garden. It was in poor condition, for nothing had been done to it since before the war, and there were several cracks, ruts and bumps. One afternoon, when we were playing doubles – Freddie and me against Armand and Jeanne-Marie – she stumbled while trying to make a return and fell. I helped her up, and for a minute felt the warm weight of her arm, slightly damp with sweat, around my neck, breathed in at close quarters her almondy smell, and found myself looking full into her face, our lips no more than six inches apart. Then she disengaged herself, and sat down, bending her knee to examine the damage, and I knelt beside her, and saw a trickle of blood force its way to the surface and creep, a shy stream, through the grime from the court and break out into a sudden lake on the brown skin below the knee. She dabbed at it with a handkerchief, and swore (very prettily), and licked the corner of the handkerchief, an inch of pointed pink tongue emerging between the lips that I so wanted to kiss. Then she tied the handkerchief round the wound and jumped to her feet ignoring the hand which I hopefully held out.

Sometimes in the evening we used to bicycle down into the little port and sit outside the Café des Marins, drinking *citrons pressés* or beer or perhaps cider, and watching the boats unload their glittering catches while gulls squawked overhead and dived and stole and quarrelled. I think it was there that we were first alone together.

Of course the obvious thing to say was 'I love you. I want you to
be part of me, to share my life for ever and ever amen,' because
that was exactly the thought that filled my mind. But even more of
course I didn't because, first, I didn't dare to, and second,
because that wasn't, with everything it contained even if leaving
unsaid, the sort of thing which, in 1951, it seemed to me you could
say out of the blue to a nice girl who was living in your uncle's
house. No doubt that is absurd, and I could perfectly well have
said it and it would have pleased her. But I didn't. I watched her
thin fingers lie against the frosted glass of her lemon drink, and I
drank my beer, and struggled to find words that would keep her
there, and remove any fear that she would decide it was time we
mounted our bicycles and returned to the house. (But how were
we alone together? I know I hadn't summoned up the courage to
suggest we should ride down to the harbour by ourselves. Perhaps
– surely – Jeanne-Marie had accompanied us, and then gone off
on some message.)

I was ignorant of girls. I had never been to bed with one, and
wasn't, I confess, certain just how one would go about things
when one at last found oneself in that desirable position. I
supposed things would happen naturally. And though I wanted
to take Freddie to bed, I was also terrified of doing so; and was
anyway in that first stage of love, in which emotions just begin to
crystallise, when I would have been satisfied with holding her in
my arms and kissing her. Satisfied is an inadequate word; I would
have been enraptured.

Perhaps we talked of the dogs. I don't remember.

What I do recall is that my nervous idyll was interrupted by the
arrival of Jeanne-Marie – whether she had completed her message
or whether she had sent us on as an advance party – and that I was
as relieved by her arrival as disappointed. Of course it broke into a
beautiful trembling moment, but it also meant that nothing could
go wrong now, and that normality could be resumed. As it was,
and very happily. But that night, I leaned out of my window, and
the air was full of honeysuckle after the day's heat. The dark was
thick and purple. There should have been a moon to complete my
mood, and make it perfect, but thick clouds had blown up, and
now the night was still, heavy and languorous; and in the dark I
saw Freddie, her legs crossed as she sat at the café table, and the
long line of her thigh perfect as the rhythms of a Greek vase.
Naturally I tried to form a poem; naturally it didn't work.

That brief, almost silent, encounter confirmed my love. I felt,
apart from anything else, enormous relief and gratitude. I was

purged. Guilt fell away from me, like the emergence of a butterfly. If anyone had told me Freddie bathed in asses' milk, I would, in love and thankfulness, have made the rounds of donkey-owners to obtain it.

The first time we kissed – leaning against a gate where the garden gave on to the woods – in twilight with doves cooing in the pine trees, I said, as our lips parted and we looked each other in the face and I drew my finger along the line of her eager lips, 'What a lot of time we have wasted.' It was a line from the cinema and I didn't mean it, for I knew we had escaped from time – we were living in an eternal present which enfolded the future and made the past meaningless. Poetry came to my rescue, as it does in youth, ' "I wonder, by my troth, what thou and I did till we loved; were we not weaned till then" ,' and Freddie drew me against her and silenced the poet with a kiss.

'That was English poetry?'

I nodded and kissed her too. The only French poem I could think of was Ronsard's advice to his girl, that she should look at that morning's rose, and I was not, we were not, ready for the mature cynicism of all those poets who have followed Horace and, recognising the brevity of love, told us to 'pluck the day'.

Why should we have been, when we both knew that our love was for all time?

I loved everything about her. I loved her innocent vanity which was coupled with dissatisfaction with her looks. I remember her poring over an illustrated magazine, gazing at the photograph of some famous actress with perfect classical features, and sighing, 'How I wish I looked like that.' I kissed the back of her neck and pressed my hand on her bony shoulder, 'You look better than that.'

'Oh no, never.'

'And my legs are too thin,' she sighed another day, stretching them out in the sun, which they seemed to draw in and then reflect.

'They're beautiful,' I said, and indeed she loved them herself; else why did she wear shorts and acquire that marvellous tan?

I loved pleasing her vanity. One day, in the port, she stopped to admire an embossed leather belt. In the softest, finest leather – kid perhaps – dyed a smokey blue. She hungered for it, and I at once said, 'You must have it.' She protested that it was far too expensive, but I insisted and fastened it round her waist there in the shop. And she kissed me, full on the lips, in front of the shopkeeper, who purred and gloated over us, as happy in our love, it seemed, as if he had been a theatrical producer and we his first and most daring creation.

I loved her in every attitude, and I dwell on them in memory now as if I was pursuing the letters which we did not write to each other. I loved her the way that in those years I loved Keats, whom I have not been able to read for thirty years. Have you ever had the experience of coming, in upland wanderings, to a place that all at once spoke to you with complete familiarity, as if you belonged there, and had come home after weary travel? It has happened to me twice: once in Calabria, in a valley in the high Sila, where in the heat of the day, after crossing a bare ridge of burning lime-stone, I found greenery, and a little spring and a shrine to the Madonna erected by a broken column from the ancient world; distant cowbells tinkled through the blue and golden light and wildflowers grew, purple, pink and white around my feet. And another time in the Scottish Borders, when I had been walking through an October mist, and the sun broke out as I came over a valley and looked down on the ruin of some old castle. The landscape was quite still. There was no sound in the air, and fringes of mist hung around the broken battlements. I can't account for the feeling on either occasion, but there was magic in the air, and peace. That was how I loved Freddie.

But I also loved her with memories of the morning kraal-smoke on the high veld, of the surge of life imparted by a morning gallop across that springy turf. (When we went riding at Armand's, our mounts were two fat roan ponies which could hardly be urged into anything more lively than a trot.) I talked to her of South Africa and promised to take her there.

She used to read in the evening by the light fixed up on the terrace which attracted so many moths. She never seemed to notice them. She read with utter concentration. She read Colette, whom I had never read, but I was pleased to see her doing so because I remembered a review by (I think) Raymond Mortimer in the *Sunday Times* in which he described her as a 'national glory, something to enjoy as well as be proud of, like Chambertin, or the Luxembourg Gardens or the Provençal spring', and it delighted me to see her reading a book which could be compared to a wine or a landscape. It seemed so right.

'What's it about?'

'Oh, love and life. What else?'

'Would I like it?'

'Listen . . .'

And she put her hand on mine, and read to me, her slow delivery not only condescending to any difficulty I might have in following literary French, but also bringing out the melody of the rhythms.

'Beautiful, isn't it?'

'Yes.'

'And like us, darling . . . it says everything, doesn't it?'

It was the first time she had called me darling.

'More than that. Don't read any more. Don't spoil it. Come into the garden . . .'

It was still warm under the apple trees, though the grass was wet with dew. We walked with my arm around her shoulder to the end of the garden and listened to the sea throb below.

Was it the next morning she came into my room and woke me before it was light, and said she wanted to go down to the sea? Perhaps it was not the next morning, and yet the evening and morning are joined together in my memory.

She sat on a rock as the waves lapped below her.

'It was the curlews woke me,' she said, for there was a moorland on which sheep were pastured, beyond the point, and when the breeze was in the south we could hear the melancholy two notes of their cry. The back of her hand lay in a little pool left behind by the receding tide, and when she lifted it she presented it to me to smell and lick.

'I couldn't sleep,' she said, 'I slept badly all night. It was excitement.'

'I fell asleep thinking of you.'

'Did you dream of me?'

'Yes,' I lied.

'I haven't dreamt of you yet, darling. I know I'll do so when I have to go back to Paris . . .'

'It's not yet.'

'No, but it's nearer and nearer. I don't want it to happen.'

'Freddie . . .'

'Yes?'

'I wish . . .' I pressed her hand to my mouth.

'So do I. I've never felt like this about anyone before . . .'

I tasted the salt on her skin.

Nor have I. Nor have I. And I never will. My blood sang the message. My lips formed the words and I leaned over and kissed her below the left ear. Then she turned and was in my arms . . .

'Never,' she said again, 'never, never, never.'

'It's absurd to say there can never be another war.' Armand liked to astonish his daughters with such pronouncements. 'Equally, of course, it's absurd to say that another is likely soon. You're a fortunate generation, my dears. Your sweethearts and husbands are unlikely to be required. But your sons, that's another matter altogether.'

'Armand,' Tante Berthe said, 'eat your pudding. You know I don't like you to talk of such matters to the girls. Or to me.'

Obediently, we dug our spoons into the cake, a gorgeous confection of chocolate, hazelnut and whipped cream, which was Dominique's greatest pride and the especial delight of Tot and Toinette. Armand accepted the reproof with no more than a whisk of an eyebrow in my direction. But it was Tante Berthe who, pausing with the spoon halfway to her mouth, broke her own prohibition.

'It's not as if,' she said, 'we have recovered from the suffering caused us by the last one. Give us time for our wounds to heal. Which some never will.'

'But that's precisely my point,' Armand said, waving his spoon in the air. 'That's precisely my point. We are worn out, utterly exhausted. Nobody in Europe can think of another war for a long time.'

'What about Indo-China?' Freddie asked.

'Oh, colonial wars. I don't count them, they're absolutely of a different order of reality, to employ a phrase which I heard Mauriac use only the other day. No, they are not family wars, you see. Whereas, in this age of ideology, any European war is necessarily and inevitably a civil war too. I grant that may not be the case in the Soviet Union. Nevertheless, they must be experiencing the most appalling weariness after their efforts, which however you may dislike the regime – and I do, despite everything – were simply enormous. I remarked on this to the General last time he honoured me with an invitation to lunch at Colombey, and I'm proud to say he did not disagree. Only he said, "We must never forget the innocence of the Americans, and consequently their ignorance." '

'You are on lunching terms with de Gaulle?' I asked, impressed.

'He's kind enough to seek my opinion, from time to time. And I advise him about his investments . . .'

I was impressed, for I still regarded de Gaulle as a hero, and was accustomed to defend him to those of my Cambridge friends who were interested in politics, and who all found his activities in the *Rassemblement du Peuple Français* repugnant or comic, or sometimes both. Jamie was fond of quoting Churchill's complaint

that the heaviest cross he had had to bear in the war was the Cross
of Lorraine, and I would answer by asking him why Churchill
should have expected the leader of the Free French to put what he
interpreted as the interests of Britain or the United States above
those of France.

'But, you dummy, they were the interests of the Allied
cause.'

'Come off it, Jamie, not even a thoroughgoing Englishman can
still pretend that the interests of the Allies were indivisible. Look
where that pretence landed Eastern Europe.'

'Mind you,' Armand said now, 'I don't go there too often. It's a
dull house. The General is a hero of course, and a great man, but
there's no conversation there.'

'He's devoted to that poor retarded daughter of his,' Tante
Berthe said. 'He is almost human when he is with her. It's a
beautiful sight . . .'

'Do you think, Armand,' I asked, 'that he has any chance of
returning to power?'

'Well, I'm an RPF Deputy. Did you know that? So I must think
he has. But I confess I don't see how, and we are in the odd
position of not being permitted to engage in what all the other
parties – even the Communists, if the others would let them –
regard as normal parliamentary politics, alliances and so on, you
understand. So it will take a crisis.'

'And you said there would be no war. So there can't be another
1940?'

'No, but there is more than one kind of crisis. And 1940
showed this at least, that the system can't cope with a crisis
. . . with a national disaster . . .'

Tante Berthe crossed herself.

'Pray God we are spared that again,' she said. 'With its
perversion of values.'

'Did you know Laval?' I asked.

Armand crumbled his bread.

'Laval? Why do you ask that?'

'Curiosity, nothing more . . .'

'Yes, I knew him. Quite well. Not as well as . . . he was older, of
course. A scoundrel, but such charm. And, in his twisted way, a
patriot. Did you know he once said there were only two men who
could save France in the war; one was Laval and the other was de
Gaulle. He died because he was a realist. But that was the horror
of 1940, that nobody had a monopoly of patriotism. And the
remarkable thing was that the realists got it wrong. Perhaps they

always do. Yalta was realistic, and look how it did for the Poles. But this is gloomy conversation for the summer.'

And there was so much he had left unsaid in it too. It was not the moment, and perhaps he was not the man who could bring himself to speak the words.

For years afterwards I believed that it was that conversation, desultory and trivial though it was, which let the cold wind of reality into the summer. It was a rhetorical way of putting it, which later I tried to deny. Reality, I told myself, is private life. Reality is the touch of skin on skin, it is a flower unfolding, it is weather and the wonderful creamy onion tart that Dominique would give us for lunch; reality was the grains of sand on the beach, the wind in the coarse sea-grasses, Freddie towelling herself by my side, most of all Freddie in my arms and her lips pressed against mine. Reality is sensuous and imaginative; rhetoric is its enemy. Politics, I told myself, represented a denial of reality, the preference of airy abstractions over the primal knowledge of sea, rocks, sand, bones, skin.

Now I don't know. I am a middling-to-old holder of a South African passport, who smokes too much and is inclined to overdo the brandy; and I am properly confused. Words I know can matter as much as a full belly. Sarah believes that words can cause movement, and my own life seems to me a ridiculous attempt to deny that she is right.

And that is mad, for I have been broken by words.

Freddie lay on the beach by my side. A little wind had woken in the east and grains of sand were thrown up against her damp thighs. They sparkled there.

'A diamanté naiad.' I brushed them off, for the pleasure of running the back of my hand over her skin.

'I wish this summer could go on forever,' she said.

'But it will.'

She leaned over and kissed me. We lay there with her hand resting on me and her hair tickling my lips.

'I want to be with you forever,' I said.

We were all but agreed on that. I knew it. Our union was perfect as a rose. We would talk for hours about everything and nothing, and we had as often no need to talk. It was urgent and there was no urgency. We had everything to say, had said everything and need say nothing.

★

I knew all this absolutely. Another morning, unable to sleep, for
sheer unbridled happiness, I slipped out of my bed, pulled on
flannel trousers and a shirt and sweater, and crept downstairs so
as not to wake anyone. The door of the room which Freddie
shared with Jeanne-Marie was open, and I entered on tiptoe to
enjoy the magic of seeing the moonlight rest on her cheek. The
spaniel Henry, on Jeanne-Marie's bed, lifted his great head and
licked my extended hand, and then flopped to the floor and
followed me downstairs and out into the garden.

Tante Berthe had a way of managing to isolate whichever member
of the family she wished to speak to, even in that higgledy-
piggledy holiday house. She took me shopping and then suggested we should go and see a church which would interest me. It
was Romanesque, and she wondered how it would compare with
Norman churches in England. She talked of different styles of
architecture; 'Architecture is one of the things I know about, it
lasts, a feeling for architecture too. I think that's good. So many
things that you care for when you are young don't. But stones and
the way they are arranged have a permanency that you come to
value as you get older.'

It was a little church, set high on a cliff, with the sea foaming
below. The grass in the churchyard was coarse, grey-green with
the sea winds. Gulls swooped squawking down below and as we
approached a flock of jackdaws rose with chattering protest from
the squat tower.

'I like to think,' she said, 'that my ancestors worshipped here,
and they must have done so. My mother's family came from this
village. You have no idea how difficult I found it to persuade
Armand to feel at home here, we're so different of course from the
méridionales.'

She called on me to admire the solidity of the church; it had
been built to withstand Atlantic gales.

'And because of that it has withstood history too. Your
grandmother has written to me that she was so pleased to
see you. You have been much on her mind for years. How
did you find her?'

I hesitated.

'It is not vulgar curiosity that makes me ask. You must believe
me when I say so.'

'I never thought it was. It's only that I don't know how to
answer.'

'Did she talk much of your father?'

'Less than I expected. She made me free of his study. Tante Berthe, how did he die?'

'Ah,' she said, and pulled out a packet of Gitanes, lit a cigarette and pushed the packet across the rock to me. 'I told Armand I was sure nobody had really discussed that with you.'

'My grandmother merely says he was a hero, but if he was a hero, how is it that nobody seems eager to speak about it?'

'Well, of course, it pains your grandmother. She's a difficult woman, as I'm sure I have no need to tell you. She's been hurt too deeply, and in consequence she alternates between desire to hurt others and a terrible fear of doing so. Not that I am in her confidence, she doesn't like me, you understand. I'm a radical in her view, and it's true, of course, that my family has always been on that side. Do you know much French history?'

'Well, the Revolution, a bit; and I did a special subject on the Restoration.'

'Well, you know that the Revolution still divides Frenchmen. There's a clear line, passing through the Dreyfus case. My family and yours have always been on opposite sides of the line. That's all.'

'And Armand?'

'He straddles it, thanks to me, which is why your grandmother dislikes me, in the most civil and punctilious manner, of course. She has never said a word to Armand against me, not since our marriage, though she tried hard to stop it. And now we correspond in the most polite terms once a fortnight. Only she knows that I am reluctant to let the girls visit her. Naturally she holds that against me, but it can't be helped. There's a picnic in the car, would you like to fetch it?'

We spread rillettes of pork on the good bread of those days, and drank cider, which I divined Tante Berthe regarded as an expression of her difference from the Southern family into which she had married, experiencing in doing so a discomfort and difficulty of which I had had, till this moment, no inkling at all. I had been regarding Armand and her as a married couple of unusual and very pleasing felicity, blessed with loving and wholly lovable daughters and surrounding themselves with a warmth and comfort that seemed to come close to the expression of an ideal way of life; and now, all at once, I was aware of strain.

'You brought me here for a purpose, didn't you? Not just to look at the church?'

She shook her head but did not reply.

'Not just to look at the church, and enjoy the sea breezes.'

'Well, that's true,' she said, 'and you've been very good about it.'

She gave me a shy smile in which I could see Jeanne-Marie; it was as if the two of them, mother and daughter, fused into one, and this gave me confidence to repeat my question.

'How did my father die?'

'Hasn't Polly talked about it, hasn't she told you?'

'Would I be asking if . . . and . . .'

'No, of course not, and perhaps she doesn't know.'

'Or care.'

'Oh, I think she would care.' Tante Berthe lit another cigarette and again pushed the packet towards me.

'Yes, I think she would care. She and Lucien loved each other, you know, very much, till, well, till the world came between them. That's the only way I can put it. The crash of the world. Let me ask you a question, it's why I brought you here. I think you have become very fond of little Freddie, haven't you?'

'Why,' I said, 'yes. Yes, I have.'

'There's no need to blush, you idiot. She's a delightful girl and lovely, in a sort of way, an unusual way. She has quality. She's been coming to stay with us for years – she and Jeanne-Marie have been friends for a long time, and besides, her mother was one of my oldest friends. We all love Freddie. And it's been obvious of course that you do. And she loves you a bit too, doesn't she?'

'Really, Tante Berthe.'

'At first,' she blew out smoke which hung blue in the air, 'at first I hoped it was only a summer affair, but I think you both think it's more serious. Am I right?'

I was resentful that she should have had this hope, as if she had thought us incapable of seriousness. I hadn't realised then how impossible it is that people with some store of experience should ever be able to regard the emotions of the young with the respect that the young demand. So I probably sounded indignant when I assured her that we were both utterly serious.

'We haven't talked of marriage, of course. Not as something definite . . . but it's understood all the same.'

'Oh dear,' she said, 'it's as bad as that, is it? What I've been wondering, you see, is whether I am morally required to tell Freddie's father, and I've been hoping I wouldn't have to. As long as it seemed merely a boy-and-girl summer affair, I thought it best to let things run their natural course, but if you are talking this way, my poor Etienne, then he will have to be told. And he won't like it.'

'I don't understand.'

She placed her hand on my arm.

'No, of course, you don't, you poor boy.'

'It's our life,' I said, 'and even if Freddie's father disapproves of me – which he may well not – well, if Freddie loves me, and she does, I'm sure of that, I don't see why. I admit we're young, but I'm prepared to wait.'

'Oh dear,' she said, 'I wish I had never started this. It's far worse than I feared.'

And then, making an absent-minded, indeed unconscious, daisychain from the flowers that grew around us, she embarked, like a reluctant emigrant, on her explanation. What did I know of Freddie's family? Well, almost nothing, so she must start there.

Freddie's father, she said, was difficult. He had always been difficult, but that wasn't really the point. Nor, essentially, was it the point that Freddie was his only daughter, his only surviving child. Well, no, she was wrong, that was the point, the starting-point at least. Had I realised that Freddie was half-Jewish? Of course I didn't mind about that, that wasn't what she meant at all, though she had to admit that my grandmother was certainly a different matter. Which wasn't important, because it could never reach the point of being important.

'I'm sorry, Tante Berthe, but I'm mystified.'

Patience. She was sorry she was attacking it so obliquely, but when she had finished I would realise how difficult it had been, and so perhaps understand. She was chain-smoking as she struggled to find a way into this story, from which she shrank because she knew it would hurt me. And Tante Berthe was, as I had sensed, a sort of earth-goddess whose mission it was to spread fecundity, and who now found herself moving like the angel of death across a smiling landscape. So she lit one Gitane from the butt of another, narrowing her eye against the smoke and the pity which she felt for me.

'Did you notice I spoke of Freddie's mother in the past tense?'

'Yes.'

'And has Freddie ever mentioned her?'

I shook my head.

'She was twelve, perhaps thirteen, when they took her away. And her sisters. To Ravensbrück.'

In those days the Holocaust was not what it has since become, a subject trailed and trampled through the newspapers and across our television screens. It was still a barely imaginable horror. I had seen, like everybody else, photographs of corpses piled high at Belsen, photographs which were beyond words and below them.

So now there was nothing I could say, and I looked beyond Tante Berthe at the wide sea, blue-grey with flecks of foam and the seabirds calling, and at the squat Norman church asserting the indisputable survival of fact and faith.

'Freddie was with us. In hiding.'

'In hiding? I don't understand.'

'They were looking for Armand too, you see, and word was brought to us that they were going to take us . . . to persuade him to surrender . . . so we went into hiding, and, fortunately, Freddie was with us . . .'

'Guy, Freddie's father, has never forgiven, or forgotten. How could he? It's impossible anyone should, and he is a man of deep feeling, a poet *manqué*. No, it's impossible.'

'And does Freddie know?'

'In the manner that the young do.'

The breeze, which did no more than touch the grasses with movement, sent a cloud scudding over the sun. Tante Berthe drew a cardigan around her shoulders.

'And Guy always disliked your father, poor Lucien. So, you see, in the circumstances it is impossible that he should permit Freddie . . . he disliked him from the time they were students. And then politics intervened . . . so you see that it can't be. I am sorry for you, and for Freddie.'

'But I still don't understand. In fact, I'm mystified. What have politics got to do with it? I mean, it's a question of Freddie and me, surely. We love each other. Of course I can see that it's possible he might not approve of me, but unless he's unbalanced, then surely . . .'

'Oh now, Guy is very balanced. That is why he has survived. He has an icy balance.'

'Then . . .'

'I said he disliked your father. That's not true. He hated him. He could never allow Freddie to marry you.'

'But Freddie is not his possession . . .'

'Of course not, but, Etienne, France is, despite everything, still a civilised country. Nice girls like Freddie don't marry against their father's wishes. Especially, they don't choose someone who merely by being who he is will hurt their father. That's all there is to it, and I am afraid I should have told you some time ago, but I did hope it was only a summer affair.'

She began packing our few picnic things into her basket.

'We'd best get home. There's going to be a storm. Now that

you know, I think it would be better if you leave, don't you? Less painful for both of you.'

I nodded.

'But I must speak to Freddie first.'

'Of course you must, my dear. This isn't a melodrama. I'm not throwing you out or expecting you to leave first thing in the morning. We'll all be sorry to see you go, we've loved having you here, and grown to love you for yourself. The whole thing is wretched, an absolute shame. An absolute shame.'

We scudded through the villages, scattering chickens, which fled squawking in response to Tante Berthe's strident horn. The sky was darkening, the predicted storm racing in from the sea and flinging the tops of the poplars around like angry hair.

'Stop a moment, please,' I said.

And when she had done so, 'You must tell me now, now that I know all this, how did my father die?'

'Oh, you poor dear, someone must tell you. He killed himself, nobody knows precisely why. From misery, I think, sheer misery,' and she leaned across and kissed me.

'Where did it happen?'

'In a prison.'

The storm had driven everyone indoors, and the house, which had seemed so charming when life spilled out of it on to the terrace, into the garden and down to the sea, now appeared like an overloaded and leaking ark, in which it was impossible to be alone. And if it was impossible, it was yet absolutely necessary. I lay on my bed only too aware of how full the house was. Music came from a wind-up gramophone immediately below my room; a tinkling piano playing Paris street-songs that bore up to me all the yellow-leaved melancholy of the abrupt arrival of autumn.

Tante Berthe had said there was no need to leave at once, but it was clear to me that departure was inevitable: 'Suddenly comes over one the absolute necessity to move.' Tante Berthe had thrust the apple of knowledge between my teeth.

Someone knocked at the door, and I was tempted to pretend to be asleep, as one may when waking from drunkenness and unable to tolerate company. But the door opened nonetheless, and Armand stood there. He carried a bottle of wine and two glasses, the stems between his fingers and the bowls inverted, rather than the flaming torch with which the angels guarded the gates of Eden, and yet I knew that he came to confirm the expulsion order.

'We should have talked before,' he said.

'We should have talked before you brought me here. Then I would never have come.'

'But we wanted you here. We have all grown so fond of you.'

He poured wine, murky in the half-light that entered the room through the closed and slatted shutters, and handed me a glass.

'Berthe had to speak to you. That's the way she is. I wouldn't have done so. I would have let things take their course.'

'I'm glad she spoke.'

'Well, that's something.'

He sat down on the bed. He sipped his wine and lit a cigarette.

'Freddie wants to see you.'

'Has Tante Berthe been speaking to her too?'

'Oh yes, of course, it was necessary.'

'Then there's nothing to be said, is there? I think I'll leave in the morning.'

'I suppose you feel a victim.'

When he said that, I burst into tears. It was, I'm sure, the first time I'd cried since I was a child, and I was ashamed of myself. I wouldn't be ashamed now, when middle age has made tears seem natural again, and, in retrospect, I even acquit myself of self-pity. I wept, I think, because life refused to take on the pleasing shape of art, because it had torn the canvas of the Impressionist painting of that summer. He let me weep without telling me it would pass or advising me to buck up. I was grateful for that.

'I know it must seem to you,' he said at last, 'that Lucien has destroyed your life. And it can be little consolation that he destroyed his own more thoroughly.'

'Why was he in prison? Why did he kill himself?'

'Well, I could answer that, but the words I would have to employ would be misleading. They always are. I could talk of honour, I could say he killed himself because he had been betrayed and had betrayed himself too. But in the end, you know, all that is meaningless unless you understand his whole life. I don't know if you want to do that. And ultimately you know people kill themselves for a very simple reason: because they have come to the end of the road, and discovered it's a one-way street. They missed the sign "*sens interdit*".'

The rain hurled itself against the shutters. Thunder, distant now like the memory of war in peace, grumbled in another valley. A dog howled.

'I've been all wrong about him, haven't I?'

'Probably not, though importantly yes.'

'I don't understand anything.'

'Your grandmother calls him a hero. She's not wrong, you know.'

I put my glass to my mouth. It was a northern wine, tasting of flowers.

'I don't think I can bear to see Freddie,' I said. 'Can you just say I want to sleep?'

'I'll leave you the wine then.'

And in fact I did go to sleep. I had not thought it would be possible. I was sure – it was perhaps the only thing of which I was sure, except for the certainty that I would adore Freddie till the day I died and that my life was ruined by Fate – that I would lie tossing and questioning, given up to anger and grief; but emotion must have exhausted me, and my sleep was abrupt and dreamless.

The night was still when I woke, but for the murmur of the sea. Moonlight slanted through the shutters in broken patterns, and then, as if I had woken in expectation of the event, the door opened. There was a shimmer of white nightgown and Freddie slipped into bed beside me. Our arms enfolded each other, our mouths met. We kissed long and hard and when we withdrew my lips felt bruised and my tongue explored the sticky residue of lipstick which she had left on them.

'I couldn't bear to think of you and not come,' she whispered.

I ran my fingers over her face like a blind man and touched a single tear that had escaped her eye.

'You've been crying,' I said, and kissed her again. 'It's as bad for you as it is for me, isn't it?'

'I feel as if my heart is breaking,' she said, and the romantic commonplace, evidence of how in the most sincere moments of emotion we fall back on words that one might have thought so shop-soiled as to have lost all meaning, which nevertheless strike the lover who hears them as absolutely fresh and authentic, touched me more than the most original and brilliant lines of poetry have ever done. She leaned over and kissed my eyes, her lips soft and light.

We were both unpractised and without skills, and our means of expressing what we felt were crude and tentative. Our movements were hesitant and, because we were so inexperienced and pro-foundly fearful of any sort of damage we might do the other, our love-making scarcely advanced beyond kissing, hugging, stroking and murmurs of adoration; and yet every moment has been with me in imagination ever since. And I have had no regret as to its inconclusive nature, not even when I have wondered, as of course I have, if things might, somehow or other, have turned out differently if I had forced the issue and possessed her. But, hardly possessing myself, I could not think of it. Freddie had not been given me to possess, and even though she was in a sense offering herself, I do not believe that she was offering what any robust interpretation of her behaviour would insist she was presenting to me, though that same robust interpreter would mock me for my restraint. Yet that restraint was not an act of will. It was natural.

In a little she slept in my arms, and I lay happy as a child whose teddy bear has been restored to him, my happiness sharpened by her confidence and my fear, by my knowledge nevertheless that I had been given what not even Time could take from me.

I woke to find her stroking my cheek. Seeing my eyes open, she rested her finger on my lips.

'S-sh.'

It was half-light, blue-grey and cool.

'It was so nice watching you asleep.'

She leaned down and kissed me.

'Let's go swimming,' she whispered. 'Give me a moment. Meet me downstairs.'

There were touches of strawberry-pink in the eastern sky, but the sun was still below the line of the little hill. The morning air was sweet with the scent of wild thyme, cut grass and awakening flowers. The long-parched ground had swallowed up all the night's rain but the darker green of the trees showed how the storm had refreshed the summer. The pink and yellow roses that clambered over the trellis were opening to the morning, and Freddie slipped on to the verandah wearing a dark-blue dressing-gown and sandals. Her legs were bare. The spaniel Henry galloped past, disappearing into the shrubbery and, as we walked, not touching each other, to the garden gate we could hear him snuffling among the bushes.

I took her hand as we slithered over the rocks, and then we were on the beach; I stripped off my jersey and flannels, and Freddie let her robe fall to the sand, and, without saying anything we swam, racing each other, to a large rock which stood three or four feet out of the water at low tide, about fifty yards from the shore. We climbed on to the rock and looked back. The sun stood, a red ball, on the fringe of the world and Henry was planted on the beach, gazing after us, like one neglected.

'Oh, the poor love,' she said. 'I hadn't realised he had followed us to the beach, he so hates being left alone.'

'Look,' I said, 'there's Jeanne-Marie. Perhaps you woke her when you were changing. You don't think she knows, do you?'

'She was asleep when I left, but it's a regular habit of hers, this. She loves the beach in the early morning. Besides, if she did know, it wouldn't matter. She's good. I wish I was good like her.'

'You don't have to be good, you're perfect.'

'Oh no,' she said, 'you say that because you're in love with me, but really I've a terrible character. That's what I'm afraid of, that I won't be able to be faithful to you. Do you think you . . . no, it's not fair to ask . . .'

'Freddie,' I said, 'we don't have to accept. We don't have to let our lives be ruled by what other people have done in other lives.'

'Oh, darling, you don't understand . . .'

She laid the back of her hand against my lips, knowing how I loved to taste it when it was cold and salty from the sea.

'No, you don't understand. Perhaps after all that is why I love you so much.'

And of course she was quite right. He didn't understand – I see now – understand anything, that young man. He didn't understand how Freddie was preparing herself to play the renunciation scene, even while she was sincere in saying she loved him and, with one part of her being, was unwilling to give him up without a fight.

'If the world was like this rock, just the two of us,' she said, 'but, don't you see, there's Jeanne-Marie on the shore and Henry with her, and they both love us too. They have rights too. Oh, how sweet,' she said, 'isn't that sweet and tactful of her?'

And looking up, he saw that his cousin had turned away. As she did so, her arm moved in a benign and generous wave, to let them know that she respected their desire to be alone together and that she wished them well.

(I put it like that, in the third person, because the scene remains framed in my memory like a film sequence: the two doomed lovers on the rock, and the large fair girl turning away on the beach, walking with a resolute and lonely benevolence away from intimacy, the spaniel at her heels, his nose to the ground. The dog stopped every now and then to investigate a rockpool or twist of seaweed, but the girl, having ascertained where the lovers were, and assured them of her sympathy, neither paused nor looked back. Then the dog would be after her in a busy shambling trot. And the rising sun picked out rainbow colours on the wet beach.)

So I didn't leave that day, because departure was impossible in the state of exhilaration I felt as a result of my certainty that

Freddie loved me, but it was never as good again. Prudence kept her from my bed, prudence and fear; she must have known it could not be as innocent a second time. It is easy now to suppose that she played with me – and for a time I tried to tell myself that – but in reality she was as confused as I was. She had warned me not to trust her resolution. She was far more aware than I of the weapons which a well-organised family could bring to bear. That was natural; my own family wasn't organised at all.

But hers was different. What did it consist of? Surely, I said, remembering what Tante Berthe had told me, there was only her father.

'Oh no, my father and a weight of aunts and uncles and grandparents. Moreover, my father has married a second time, and my stepmother is very severe.'

'She couldn't dislike you.'

'No, not that at all. But she adores my father and is fiercely protective of him. He is rather a great man in his way, you know, and she trembles in case either I or my half-brother and half-sister should do anything that would displease him. Though they are babies, they don't have much chance yet.'

'And I would?'

'It never occurred to me. How could it? I was a child in the war, and it isn't real to us, is it? But to Papa, it's quite different. The war and everything that happened then, in those terrible years, is, well, it's like the clothes he wears.'

He was a writer, she told me, and a politician.

'Like all French writers,' I said.

'Well, perhaps,' she smiled, and in that smile acknowledged a distance between us; it told me that, though I was French, yet I could not be said wholly to belong, even though it was the French side of my inheritance which came between us. And, as she spoke, I realised how much her father mattered to her, how important it was to her that they should be at ease together.

'I am all he has left of Mama – except for memories.'

In my imagination I saw myself confronting her father. I would speak out to him. I would say that the sins of the fathers should not be visited on their children. But, even as I prepared speeches – and I lay abed, while the night scents drifted in from the garden, running through a succession of rhetorical pleas – even as I did so, I knew it was no good. The past had divided us as surely as if a drawbridge had been raised. Resentment swelled within me. I conceived a disgust for everything French.

*

The crossing was satisfyingly rough. Along the rail of the boat men and women spewed out the last of the Continent. Others lay on the deck, in the passageways, and moaned; it might have been a refugee ship, or one of those allegorical representations of a vessel laden with the damned.

With the self-conscious swagger of the good sailor I brushed passed the sufferers and settled myself in the bar. I ordered brandy and ginger ale, defiantly English.

'You look a bit low, young fellow,' said a tweedy man who had settled himself next to me. 'Not suffering, are you?'

'Not in body,' I said.

'Ah, love, I suppose. It's an awful business.' He shook his head, pursed his lips, flickered his eyelids. 'Thank God I'm beyond all that. Still, it's always nice to meet another good sailor. We should stick together. What's yours?'

'Brandy,' I said, confident of my ability to handle his ineffective and old-fashioned approach. 'With ginger.'

'What a very good idea. Just the right drink for a rough crossing. Been in France, have you? What a mess they're in. Mind you, I'm fond of the Frogs, which is more than most Englishmen would admit. But if ever a people could do with a dictator, it's our poor friends across the *Manche*. Steward, two big brandies, please.'

In those days my grandparents, who had sold their town house before the war, retained a flat in Hyde Park Gardens, where I was accustomed to stay while in London. I parted from my new friend at Victoria, resisting his invitation to accompany him to the Savoy Turkish Baths in Jermyn Street. ('Cheaper than a hotel, awfully useful place to know, and they ask no questions. Often stay there when passing through the old Metrop or up on business. What do you say?' 'I'm afraid I'm expected at my grandparents.' 'Too bad. Some other time, perhaps.')

Waiting for Higson, who had been my grandfather's batman in the First War and now cared for the flat, to make his slow way from the basement (it was a double flat) to answer my ring, I looked back across the road towards the park, but the trees were no more than dark shapes looming out of a thick darkness. There was a whiff of autumn in the air. I shivered, shifting my feet. At last, with an almost inconceivable slowness, Higson unbolted the door. His wizened face peered into the dim streetlight. He looked like the reluctant denizen of some unknown underworld, summoned to the surface by a power he could not quite bring himself to resist.

'You should have let me know you were coming. Your bed'll be damp.'

I heard him bolt the door behind me and his slippered feet followed me through the cavernous hall.

'And what would you have done if I had been away?'

'But you're never away, Higson, are you?'

'Might be in hospital. You can switch on the electric fire in His Lordship's library. You won't be staying long, will you?'

'No, Higson, I don't expect so. Is there any brandy?'

'Brandy, is it. No, there's not a drop. You know his Lordship's forbidden it.'

'Or whisky?'

'Not whisky either.'

'Come on, Higson, what is there?'

'Might stretch to a drop of gin. It's my own gin, mind you. But I'll not grudge it to you.'

He shuffled off, returning a few minutes later with a bottle, perhaps a quarter full, and a jug of water.

'There's some letters come for you. Mostly bills, though, so I burned them. That's what you wanted, isn't it? Always burn anything in brown envelopes, that's what your uncle used to tell me. There's one from Miss Polly though. I'd have sent it after you, if I didn't think it would get lost. "Better keep it for the boy," that's what I said.'

He pushed me the letter with the South African stamp.

'Oh dear,' my mother wrote. 'I wish you'd consulted me first, and now I'm afraid this letter will be too late. You really are silly and tiresome, darling.

'You tell me you were off to see your French relations, and it's really not an awfully good idea as I'm afraid you'll have found out by the time you get this. Your grandmother's an old witch, you know, and I daresay completely bats now. Frightfully pi, and like most pi people I've ever known, the most awful liar. She absolutely loathed me of course, whatever she has told you. Forked tongues also ran where I was concerned.

'Oh dear this is difficult. I absolutely loathe writing letters, and wish you were here, though poor Roddy doesn't. He's not making much sense these days, poor lamb. Not that I can really think of him as a lamb because most of the time he's an absolute swine. His ma's doing – I have been a teeny bit unlucky with my mas-in-law.

'But that's not what I wanted to say, only it's awfully hard, dearie, to get to the point. Which is that I have tried to keep you from the French side of your family, and you may not have liked it, but it was for the best. I know you think I'm a featherbrain, and I daresay you're right, but there are some things I can't stand. Aurora was all wrong in what she did, and so was your father, and that's why I left him, because I knew in my bones what was going to happen. France was no good, we both thought that, but his way of making it better was worse.

'I knew all that straight away that time he took me to Germany. He said they were awful, but I could see he was impressed. And it's ever so silly to be impressed by Germans, they always get things wrong, even I know that.

'Please write to me and tell me if you have been to France. I am anxious, really I am, darling.

'Love and kisses, Polly.'

I didn't write. I let France and my French visit fall like a silence between us. What was there to say? That my heart was broken?

Instead I sat in London, moping and pretending to read for my next term, Higson grumbling round me like a mother hen. And Cambridge, when I returned, was flat as the surrounding country. I wrote to Freddie and even posted some of the letters, but got no reply. Perhaps my letters were intercepted. And when a letter came, with a French stamp, from Jeanne-Marie, it was days before I could bring myself to open it.

1951–9

OVER THE NEXT few years it was only from Jeanne-Marie that I heard. She wrote to me every two to three months, though I rarely replied, and then briefly. I had conceived a loathing of France and the French, and there were times when this seemed even to extend to my dear and delightful cousin. Those were bad years for me, and I don't want to write about them. Fortunately they are not part of the story which I am trying to tell, for there is little in the memory of that period of my life which does not make my flesh crawl with shame and disgust. There was indeed too much flesh in it. I had, through my grandfather's influence, found myself a job in a merchant bank – it would be more exact to say that the job was provided for me. I worked hard because industry deadens feeling, and I was successful. None of my colleagues can have felt any warmth for me, and I was satisfied with this.

Everyone I slept with was Freddie, and I abused them. Looking back, I think I was a bit mad in my twenties.

I had one other contact with France. Twice a year I wrote to my grandmother, a formal, cold letter in which I assured her I was well and enquired after her health. I was perversely pleased to perform this dead duty. I told her how much money I was making. It was a sort of mocking triumph.

Jeanne-Marie wrote to me that Freddie was married, then that she was going to have a baby, then that she had lost the child, and sunk into depression. I told myself she wasn't even a memory, though scarcely a night passed that I didn't long for her. Jeanne-Marie informed me that Freddie had been committed to a clinic, that she had run away, taken a car, crashed it and killed herself. 'Whenever we met in these last months, she used to talk of you, Etienne. With a faraway look in her eyes. It was terrible what was done.'

So we were both victims. Very well. I picked up a slut in a coffee-bar and took her to Brighton for the weekend. I doubt if it was what she had hoped for. Anyway, there was a bit of bother, we were asked to leave the hotel, and only my full wallet prevented it from becoming a police matter. When we parted, she told me I should see a doctor. I think that was brave of her, and kind, in the circumstances. Needless to say, I didn't follow her advice; not then. Psychoanalysis came later; without success.

The next death was my grandmother's. I was in New York at the time, and so there was no question of my attending the funeral. Probably I wouldn't have gone anyway. But I was, of course, her principal heir. It was necessary to visit Provence. I travelled south in the first days of December.

The business with lawyers was transacted as briskly as is possible with French country notaries. My own experience had made me sharp in such affairs (as in those which, for want of a better term, may be called 'of the heart'). I was aware that they looked on me with some curiosity, but I answered few of their questions and no direct ones. It was impossible to say what I would do with my inheritance.

My visit to the house was brief. Its air of desolation was more intense than I remembered and anyway the *mistral* was blowing. Marthe had gone – had Jeanne-Marie told me of that? – and a slatternly domestic was acting as caretaker. I confirmed her in her post and told her that I would arrange for the lawyer to continue to pay her wages. Why now? Someone had to live there.

My grandmother had gone out of life very neatly. There was only a tiny void where she had been. Her smell still lingered in her bedroom, and the velvet that covered the *prie-Dieu* was worn to shreds.

I unlocked the Bluebeard's Chamber that had been my father's study. The room was cold and damp, but I sat there behind his desk, and smoked a cigar. It was later that I had his papers collected and sent to me in London.

I stayed in the hotel in the town and ate little and badly. After my meal I took a turn along the street but, soon defeated by the morose wind and rain, returned to the hotel bar and settled myself with a cigar and the inevitable *pastis* of the South, which, without meaning to, I had felt myself compelled to order. There was a group of four men playing cards and drinking *pastis* like myself, while half a dozen young men disported themselves around a billiard table.

One of them broke away and lounged across the room in my direction. He swung out a chair from the table and sat astride it, his forearms resting on its back. He looked at me without removing the cigarette which dangled from the corner of his mouth.

'I've been wondering when you would show up,' he said. 'You don't remember me?'

I didn't like the mockery in his eyes and told him that I had no recollection of him at all. But I did of course; it was Marthe's son Yves. He had been angry before; now my first impression was that he had come to terms with himself. Yet there was something repellent in his air of a lounging beast, the suggestion which emanated from him, that always, given the chance or the opportunity, he would do the dirt on life. So it amused me to force him to tell me who he was, to admit to having made less impression than he was accustomed to leave.

'All the same,' I said, 'I'm sorry, but I don't remember meeting you.'

'So the old bitch is dead,' he said, 'and the other, well, she's had her come-uppance too.'

'The lawyers tell me she's ill. I'm sorry to hear it. She served my grandmother well.'

'That's not the way we talk now,' he said.

'Perhaps not, but it's true all the same.'

'I remember you,' he said, 'you were stuck-up then too.'

'Oh, stuck up,' I said. 'That's your choice of word. I don't suppose I have a higher opinion of myself than you do of yourself.'

'So you do remember me?'

'I remember an angry boy.'

I was tired of the game.

'But you remember my little brother better. My little half-brother. You were soft on him. I reckon you fucked him. Well,' he laughed, 'you won't have the chance to do that again, not unless you arrive where the likes of you deserve to be.'

'Look,' I said, 'I don't know what you are talking about. Why don't you go back and join your friends. They must be missing your conversation.'

'Oh, but I've been waiting to speak to you.'

And then he told me how Jacques had killed Simon, the *garagiste*. He dwelled on the details. And how Jacques was now in prison, and how Marthe had had a stroke when she heard.

'Catatonic,' he repeated the word several times. 'Catatonic, that's what they call it. Makes me laugh.'

Then, changing his tone, he told me about himself, about the difficulties he had experienced, how he was out of work and how his wife had . . . oh, I forget what; it spilled out in the practised tones of the beggar and indeed, by the end, I was glad to pass him a wad of notes simply to be rid of him. It was a gesture of disgust, using money to put him at a distance, but the disgust was not directed only at him, for, looking at that ugly yellow face, listening to him spew out his accumulated resentment at the hand life had dealt him, I saw my own image there. His coil of bitterness was mine too; his vomit and self-pity mine.

He stuffed the notes in his pocket.

'I wonder how you dare to come here. After what your father brought on the place. And Jacques too. Simon has a family, don't forget. Why, there are times when I wonder if my own life may not be in danger because of what they did. No fault of mine.'

'Nothing is,' I said.

As he made his way into the street, he paused under the lamp-post and spat into the gutter.

Have you ever visited a French prison? I would not recommend it. Doubtless they are no worse than prisons elsewhere, in material conditions, and better than some. That's not the point. It is rather that a French prison expresses the Cartesian duality of mind and body, and at the same time a hideous distortion of it. Intellect rules the bodies of certain men in order to annihilate their minds. Moreover the stench of shit permeates the disinfectant.

It had taken a long time to get an order to permit me to see Jacques. By some quirk or anomaly, though too young to be guillotined, he was old enough to be lodged in the adult section of the Saint Paul prison in Lyon. (I don't know why he was in Lyon; but that was where the prison bureaucracy had assigned him.)

'This is where the Gestapo murdered the heroes of the Resistance,' he said. 'Perhaps that's why I'm here. After all, Simon was a true hero of the Resistance himself. There were many women, not only my poor mother, on whom he revenged the insults they had inflicted on our beautiful France. Can I have a cigarette, brother?'

'I didn't know you knew.'

'I always knew.'

'Why didn't you say, years ago?'

'What was there to say? Besides, perhaps it never occurred to me that you didn't.'

He smiled. His smile at least hadn't changed. He was very thin, and the bones stood out on the back of his hands. His hair was cropped close as it had been when we first met ('because of the lice') and his cheekbones were sharp, but they hadn't managed to suppress his capacity for laughter. I looked on him in wonder.

'I wish I'd known you knew. Your mother told me you didn't and made me promise that I wouldn't tell you. Otherwise . . .'

I waved my hand, as if to wipe away the years and assure him that everything would have been different if we could have confessed our fraternity to each other.

'What about the cigarette then?'

I pushed the packet towards him.

'Ah,' he said, drawing the smoke into his lungs, 'a real cigarette. If you want to do something for me, fix with the guard to give me a regular supply. You could afford that, couldn't you? It'd make all the difference.'

'Could you trust him?'

'Sure, I'll show you which.'

'Jacques,' I said, 'I didn't believe you. When you said you would shoot Simon. I thought it was just a boy talking.'

'It was a boy talking, brother. But it was a man who did it. Even though, according to the law . . .' he laughed.

'But why? What good did it do? What about your own life?'

'Oh, my life? Well, that has to take its chance. Besides, I couldn't bear seeing him about, strutting round his pumps, thinking himself a hell of a fellow and sure he had got away with it. That's all really.'

'I saw Yves,' I said.

'He's not your brother, you know.'

'Thank God for that.'

'Did he touch you for a loan?'

I nodded.

'Same old Yves. But there you are. When you look at Yves . . . OK, he's a shit, pure and simple. Well, not pure and not simple, but you know what I mean. And that's it, isn't it? He accepts everything they've thrown at him and does nothing but whine. But I acted, you see. I did what I had to do, and that makes me a free man, even here. But Yves is not only a shit, he's a slave.'

'But Jacques, can it matter to you what other people have done to other people? Matter enough to land you here?'

'Evidently, brother, since it has done just that. I had a choice. I could have let Simon live and in doing so I would have abandoned what I had intended to do since I was a child. Perhaps it would have been right to do so. Perhaps my dream of killing him was only a childish dream, to be put away when I became a man. Instead it is I who have been put away, as a man. But I can stand up. I have done what I set out to do, what seemed right. If Simon had lived, if I had not brought myself to shoot him, all my life I would have been conscious of what I had failed to do. Every day would have been a reproach to me, and I would have asked myself if I had declined to act simply because I was afraid. Now I know, do you understand? Descartes said, "Conquer yourself rather than the world," and that is what I have done. I acted, without hope, which, brother, is ultimately the only way to act and the justification of all actions. And now there is no Simon to reproach me. It is really quite simple.'

I leaned across the table and kissed his cheek, and then left.

Jacques was released some years ago and now runs a bar in another part of France. I sent him the money to establish himself. He is married, and sends me a card at Christmas with a photograph of his two daughters. I am glad they are daughters, though my experience with Sarah had proved to me that not even daughters are safe. Safe from the temptations of idealism, I mean.

PART THREE

1898–1945

CHAPTER ONE

Hôtel des Bergues,
Geneva
2nd November

'DEAR HUGH,

You said to me: "I would rather write it as a novel". I sympathise with that. There are too many dissertations, theses, and dead books.

Well, it is the Day of the Dead. All over Catholic Europe, people are visiting cemeteries to lay flowers on family graves. And on an impulse, which will, I think, appeal to you, I called at a florist's yesterday afternoon and arranged, through Interflora, that a wreath of white chrysanthemums – the flowers of the dead – should be laid at the base of my father's tombstone. Of course, he doesn't rest there himself (if indeed he rests anywhere), for my grandmother was unable to retrieve his body; but she used her influence to have the stone erected in the municipal cemetery; and indeed her name is now on the stone also and she lies there herself.

But this is by the way. I am sending you, as arranged, a packet by registered post. The material for your perusal is very much a mixed bag. There are some of Lucien's own writings, which you have certainly not seen. I have tried to provide a biographical framework, or biographical notes, and I have also offered a reconstruction of certain episodes in fictional (or perhaps to use the cant term of a few years back, factional) form. That seemed to me the only way of presenting the material to you without constant resort to "may have beens", "must haves" and "*peut-êtres*".

I would ask you to remember that we agreed that you should use nothing, and particularly quote nothing, without my approval. This is for background, but I hope you will find it interesting and helpful.

The end is murky, and my version speculative.

When you have read it all, I shall be happy to see you again, if you care to come to Geneva. I recall our previous meeting with pleasure all the greater because I regarded your arrival with a mixture of boredom, suspicion and scepticism.

With all best wishes,
Etienne de Balafré

PS. I have added, by way of introduction, to each passage, an explanatory note, giving its provenance, authenticity, etc.

PPS. I had left this letter open, knowing that there was something nagging on my mind. And I have found it in that *soi-disant* fictitious journal which Malcolm Lowry – a Canadian like yourself, though an adopted one – fathered on his alter ego Sigbjorn Wilderness: *Through the Panama*. It is this:

"I am capable of conceiving of a writer today, even intrinsically a first-rate writer, who *simply cannot understand*, and never has been able to understand, what his fellow writers are driving at, and have been driving at, and who has always been too shy to ask. This writer feels this deficiency in himself to the point of anguish. Essentially a humble fellow, he has tried his hardest all his life to understand (though maybe still not hard enough) so that his room is full of *Partisan Reviews, Kenyon Reviews, Minotaurs, Poetry* mags, *Horizons*, even old *Dials*, of whose contents he is able to make out precisely nothing."

In the margin of my copy I scribbled years ago, "this is me", though I am not of course a writer, let alone "an intrinsically first-rate one". Yet it is how I stand in relation to our times.

And how delightful, if *frissonable*, to find the *Minotaur* – a magazine of which I confess I never heard – in that list. The Monster in the Maze; what an apt description of the quest in which you have to my surprise involved me. And I am still more astounded to discover a lifting of my spirit.

But what colour of sail shall we hoist when we sail back to Athens?

E. de B.

I have numbered these documents for your convenience.'

Document 1

(This is an autobiographical fragment which I discovered in my father's desk in our house in Provence, which, as you know, (don't you?) is called the Château de l'Haye. It may be part of his confessions, or a rough draft; I have never discovered that manuscript in its entirety, though our Parish priest assured me Lucien had worked on it. Various pieces in this collection may have been intended for these confessions, which he was perhaps working on in December '42–January '43, months which he spent at the Château d l'Haye. I have noted these accordingly.)

It was only a few weeks after the outbreak of war, and an autumn day of surpassing loveliness. The huge leaves of the chestnuts in the Luxembourg Gardens were crisp, red and golden, fragile and defiant in the afternoon sunlight; and I felt that the people of Paris were like those leaves. We were caught in a moment of beauty made all the sharper by our apprehension of what was to come.

It was the first day in which I was back in uniform, and I walked with the proud step of the soldier into whom I have been again transformed. And it was also just a week since I had received a letter from Polly saying that she wanted – somehow – the divorce to which she knew I could never consent. And as I looked across the gardens I could see mist gathering, heralding the night.

I was however on my way to the Palais-Royal to drink chocolate with Colette; and to see her sitting in the window as I approached, her Russian Blue cat pressed against her shoulder, was to be reminded of the solidity of France. She had just come back from Dieppe: 'I pass all my wars in Paris,' she said.

I sat with her an hour among the paperweights, the bibelots, the fussy draperies in a room filled with the mingled smells of roses, pot-pourri, the violet scent she wore, and black tobacco. She called me, as she has always done, to admire the paintings and drawings, each chosen for a particular reason, rather than for their intrinsic value, but all in the most exquisite taste. And all the time the cat lay on her lap and purred, or walked over the table-tops picking its way among the knick-knacks with inevitable delicacy.

That was for me the last afternoon of peace, true peace. Maurice, Colette's third husband, Maurice Goudeket, was absent as he generally was when I called by appointment, for he knew I did not care for him and was tactful enough to remove himself.

'The poor cat,' Colette said, 'isn't going to last much longer.

See how thin she has become.' And she ran her hand along its spine, while it lifted its tail erect in ecstasy.

She asked, as she has always done, after my mother.

'You won't let her down, I know, my dear,' she said. 'It's one of the things I like about you, your love for your mother and your respect for her, all the more because I know she disapproves of me and would never read my writings.'

A shadow crossed her face.

'It's absurd,' she said, rolling her Burgundian 'r', 'to talk of being an artist, and, ultimately, I despise all those who do, but it amounts to this all the same: we write what we have to. I have written much about Sido, my mother, so much that I sometimes wonder if I have invented her, and perhaps I have, for my readers, but then, she invented me, in her way. And after all, what matters most in life is that one should have had a happy childhood. It's something no one can ever take away. If you have lived in the earthly paradise of childhood, you can never abandon hope. I pity all those poor things who were wretched children. But you were happy, weren't you, my dear?'

Yes, indeed.

For many years I was a little Duke, a prince for whose delight the world arranged itself. I would run to the sunlight, with the morning mist still clinging about my ankles, while all things woke for my pleasure, and life danced in the dew. Is there any happiness to be compared to the moment of waking up early, perhaps four o'clock, and seeing the first swallows dart past your window, and then slipping downstairs, your little dog at your heels, and bounding through the garden which would be silent but for the blackbirds, and which is at any rate reserved entirely for you?

All this is at the same time memory and actuality; it is gone and yet remains. I have lost the key to paradise and yet it comes back to me in sleep.

I was Maman's favourite. Other people, even then, I suspect, thought her harsh and severe. She has never been tolerant, and her sympathies are narrow. I know that very well, from observation, and Armand, though my younger brother, her youngest child, and the one whom you might therefore suppose to have been indulged, has always been afraid of her. But in her eyes I have been perfect, and it gives me a glow even to write these words. Was it really because, as she told me, she carried me high in her womb and so my birth was difficult?

I have known Colette for almost twenty years, and I have never parted from her without feeling refreshed. I love her, though all we have in common perhaps is a reverence for the French language and a respect for the provinces. But that is real. In one of her books she wrote – I quote from memory, for my copy is in Paris – and I wonder if I shall ever handle it again – that one should understand by the word 'province' not merely a place or region which is distant from the capital, but a sense of social hierarchy, of the need to behave, of pride in an ancient and honoured habitation, which is closed on all sides but yet capable at any moment – and here her exact words return to me – 'of opening on to its lofty barns, its well-filled hayloft, and its masters apt for the uses and dignity of their house'.

Precisely. Though I adore Paris and can wander for hours in its streets tracing lost splendours and eating with my eyes the many variations on life which it presents, I know that, in the long quarrel between Paris and the provinces which has lasted, in my opinion, since the days of the Frondes, though many would date it merely from the Revolution, it is the provinces which have been solidly and magnificently right. Which is why I feel a sense of comfort that the Marshal has established the government of our renascent France in Vichy. The temporary loss of Paris, with its despicable and hysterical enthusiasms, its unfailing capacity to come to the wrong conclusion, is surely a blessing in disguise.

As for Maman, so admirable in her Faith and the security of judgement which the possession of Faith gives her – and after all, this possession is worth so much more than all the knick-knacks and *objets d'art* in which my dear Colette delights – it is thanks to her that my life has been built on that rock of a happy childhood.

Not for nothing do we think of France as feminine; Maman and Colette are the two poles of the France which I adore and serve.

How dated is the language of patriotism. Could anyone, I wonder, write in such terms now? But Lucien, my poor father wasn't alone in writing like this. You have only to think of de Gaulle with his 'certain idea of France'.

I wonder if he had been one of Colette's lovers. Being one year older than the century he would have been just twenty-one when she published *Chéri*, that wonderful and desolate account of an affair between a middle-aged woman and a boy. Not that Chéri, quite without intellectual interests and interested, as I remember, only in his appearance, was at all like my serious father. Nevertheless, I wonder.

There is a singular absence of his own father in the fragmentary jottings Lucien made concerning his early life. Indeed, he never seems to have been there at all. He was a regular soldier of course, and this displeased my grandmother's family, who were the Blackest of Blacks – by which I mean – I write for those ignorant of the language of Third Republic France – zealous clericals, Royalists also, who disapproved of the recognition of the Republic implicit in a military career. The Balafrés however were proud of their tradition of military service – they saw themselves as soldiers of France irrespective of the regime, and one of them indeed, though brought up as an émigré after the Revolution, had been so fired by the splendour of Napoleonic warfare that he had been among the numerous Royalists who had found service in the imperial army an irresistible temptation; he never returned from the Russian campaign. Accordingly, my grandfather, Etienne like myself, may never even have questioned the suitability of a military career. Anyway, like so many of his fellow officers, he saw the Army as the bastion of the real France against the Jews, Protestants, Masons and Socialists. French life has always been complicated; at least since the Revolution. He was of course convinced that Dreyfus was guilty, and, even when his innocence seemed to have been proved, continued to believe the whole thing was a Jewish/Socialist plot to discredit the Army.

Lucien easily falls into sentimentality when he writes of his childhood in 'thyme-scented Provence'. You can see him looking back in pity and regret. Yet when he says, 'the only question seemed to be where to be happiest', I believe him. The sun always shines, the dew sparkles and the *mistral* never blows in these selective memories, which are nevertheless, I insist, sincere.

He went to school first with the Dominicans.

CHAPTER TWO

Document 2

MY MOTHER WAS determined that I should have a truly Christian education, and she regarded the State schools as nurseries of infidelity. From my present position I both understand her feelings and deplore them. It is surely precisely because so many good families have thought as she did that infidelity and Socialism have gained such ground in our schools. You may say that the teachers have been selected by an infidel and Socialistic regime, and this is undeniable; nevertheless, I cannot but think that if so many good families had not chosen to boycott the education provided by the State for children in their formative years, the influence of these teachers would somehow or other have been curtailed. Such, at any rate, is my intention now, when we are left with the legacy of those years in which the fundamental virtues attached to the idea of God, Country and Family were so scandalously neglected; even disparaged.

The Dominican Fathers who taught me were narrow, zealous and honest men. They held before us an ideal of Christian virtue and Christian stewardship which was wholly admirable in its austerity. The curriculum was severe and demanding. We learned by rote and we were discouraged, by the rod and the exercise of a short sarcasm, from any rebellious tendency to question what we were taught. In this way I achieved a mastery of Latin and the French language and a tolerable understanding of mathematics. Philosophy, other than Christian philosophy, was a closed book. And I have never regretted this: it is only when a boy has been grounded in the earthy realism of Aquinas that he may safely be allowed to gambol in the speculative meadows of more extravagant philosophers. It is only when he has accepted and understood these profound truths that he can be exposed without danger to the illuminating, and yet profoundly deceptive, imaginings of such as Plato, Hegel and Nietzsche. There are certain rocks of thought on which alone a man can safely build his house: *nihil est in intellectu, nisi prius fuerit in sensu*; the mind can perceive nothing that has not previously been perceived by the senses; that is the first. And the second is: *quicquid recipitur, secundum modum recipientis recipitur*: whatever is received is received according to the mode of being of the recipient; from which it follows that *cognitum est in cognoscente per modum cognoscentis*: what is known is in the mind of the knower according to his mode of knowing; and it is a recognition of this gritty reality which alone makes a man capable of accommodating uncomfortable truths and discarding illusory consolation. I could not see France as she is, torn and bleeding on account of what she had made of herself, if it were not for my schooling in the lucid realism of St Thomas. But for that I too might have fallen victim to the seductive sophistries of Marxism or the frenzy of Fascism; and, indeed, the first did for a time beguile me till I was recalled to Reason by the sublime influence of the Angelic Doctor. If I am to be remembered for anything, I hope it will be because I have managed so to alter the educational values of France that every child will learn to insist on the reality of things; and will come to understand that change is not a denial, but an affirmation, of that reality, which can ultimately only be explained as part of a greater and complete reality, which is God.

How strangely influence operates. Though I now recognise those years when I studied under the Dominican Fathers as being exactly complementary to the delights of my adored childhood and my certainty of my mother's love, they seemed at the time barren, wretched and vile. Our life was Spartan. In winter the water in the basins in our unheated dormitories froze overnight, and worse than the physical conditions – which in retrospect appear to me to have attractive rigour – was the absence of love. I experienced a new and terrible sensation: of being unwanted and uncherished. I was alone in the midst of many. It seems to me now that those years were passed entirely without conversation.

My poor father. Did he really imagine it was possible, in the twentieth century, in the age of the Panzer divisions, the barbed wire, and the operatic delusions of Nuremburg, to base his life on mediaeval theology? Or, more extraordinary still, that he had in fact succeeded in doing so?

Of course I must admit that my eyes glaze when I attempt to read philosophy, and the *Summa Theologica*, on which I did once embark, made a mad whirlpool of my mind. What about you, Hugh? Can you read such stuff? Can you imagine mastering it? And if you can't begin to, then can you still hope to make something of my, rather more complicated than perhaps you imagined, father?

CHAPTER THREE

Document 3

IT WAS MY Uncle Charles, my mother's elder brother, who persuaded her, when I was sixteen, that I should move to school in Paris; and so I arrived at the famous Lycée Condorcet. She was loth to send me there, in the middle of the war, when there were already rumours – or had they been confirmed? – of shells falling on the boulevards.

'But,' said my Uncle Charles, 'though it is not of course for precisely that reason that I recommend you to send the boy to the Lycée, yet, even if I did not already have a sufficiency of cogent motives, I think I would be swayed by the consideration that, in this moment of agony for France, this young man' – he placed the palm of his hand, from his great height, flat on the top of my head – 'in whom we all place such great hopes, of whom we have such lofty expectations, should acquire, by personal experience – I repeat – by personal experience, an understanding of what France today is suffering; and that cannot, I assure you, my poor sister, be acquired skulking in the Midi under the direction of some perfectly outmoded Dominicans . . .'

My mother was displeased to hear the friars whom she revered, and of whose worth she had indeed a far juster appreciation than my Uncle Charles could ever have, disparaged in this manner; but she had been accustomed all her life to regard my uncle with a mixture of love and reverence – he was five years older than she, possessed of a remarkable, if now forgotten and obsolete, distinction, and besides, even as he spoke so of my tutors, he laughed and stroked the point of his long waxed moustaches with his long bony parchment-skinned fingers which you could see had never been subjected to toil; and, in short, she found all this perfectly irresistible, as she had always done, and so consented to his argument – as she had always done.

You would not have thought they came from the same litter, for Uncle Charles seemed, apart from a certain swagger, to have shed the provinciality which long years of neglect and indifference have made an apparently inescapable element of the Southern character. He was indeed perfectly a Parisian, dazzling as the lights of the capital, trailing behind him the glamour of an ineffably superior and world-weary sophistication which made it possible for people to believe they knew him quite well and yet fail to realise that he possessed a will of iron. And ultimately, of course, it was this will which conquered my mother and caused her to consent to a proposition which she viewed with a principled disgust.

I went to lodge with Uncle Charles in his apartment in the Boulevard Malesherbes.

The introduction of Uncle Charles may have puzzled you, Hugh; indeed I confess that I had never heard of him myself.

Charles de Fasquelle (1872–1935) was born, according to the Larousse *Dictionary of Biography* which I have consulted, in Aix-en-Provence, and is described as 'poet and critic'. Only one volume of verse is recorded however, *Vers le Minotaure* (1895) – the Minotaur again, Hugh! – and 'his promise as a poet was never fulfilled. However, his study of Baudelaire (1899) remains one of the most fruitful explorations of the poet.'

Not much there, I'm afraid, and, however fruitful, his Baudelaire had been out of print since 1925. He was apparently a friend of Robert de Montesquiou, generally considered to have been the principal model for Proust's Charlus; and Charles de Fasquelle himself is also said to have been one of the originals of Robert de Saint-Loup, though there are in truth so many of these that I don't know that the identification is worth much.

However, these identifications may suggest the world in which my father found himself plunged. Charles had himself been two years behind Proust at the Lycée Condorcet, and there are three letters to him in Proust's published correspondence, all couched in the floribund hyperbole employed equally on objects of his adoration and those who had merely lent him a book.

I wrote to my mother to ask her about Uncle Charles: 'The most awful pansy,' she said, 'of the kind who adores Cardinals. Actually, I thought he was rather sweet because he had such lovely manners – when he chose – but your father couldn't stand him, though he always admitted that he was grateful to him for many things. But I can't think why you should be bothering with all this, darling.'

CHAPTER FOUR

Document 4

I SHALL ALWAYS be grateful to my Uncle Charles for having insisted that I should go to the Lycée. It provided me with a depth of education which I could not have won elsewhere. In particular it furnished me with a full understanding of the varieties of French culture. My uncle supplemented this.

'I daresay Balzac is quite out of favour with your teachers who, I am told, regard him as "old hat". But this is nonsense. No one with the profound understanding of obsession which Balzac possessed can ever be out-of-date. Believe me, I speak as a man of the world. Obsession is the governing factor in life. No one without it achieves anything great. Do you believe that Cardinal Richelieu would have made France the first power in Europe, which is to say the world, if he had not been a man in the grip of as powerful an obsession as that which held mastery over the soul of old Grandet himself? Moreover, in Vautrin, you will find the most profound revelation of those subterranean and unconscious impulses which, disregarded, even shunned, in youth, come to dominate life, and which demand respect even when they can be seen to lead to disaster . . .'

And with these words a frown would come over my uncle's face; he looked like a man who sees everything in which he has put his trust crumble before his eyes; and, as he laid his hand, almost beseechingly, on my arm, I realised that he was quite unaware of how he had exposed his true nature to me.

I was so innocent when I came to the Boulevard Malesherbes. I merely thought how charming and remarkable it was that a man of my uncle's age should be able to attract so many friends scarcely older than myself, and I couldn't understand it when one of my school-friends, Edouard Binet, told me, in an embarrassed and indirect manner, that while his mother was delighted that I should visit their house, she had forbidden him to call upon me at the Boulevard Malesherbes.

'But why?' I insisted. 'I am sure you have had nothing but politeness and a warm welcome from my uncle.

'Is it politics?' I asked, for I had only recently come to realise that people of a respectable family, such as the Binets, could differ from my own relations, that, in short, not all nice people thought just the same.

He gave me the most charming smile which robbed his words of all considerations.

'I think it is a sort of politics, but not perhaps those of which you are thinking.'

'Well, Edouard,' I said, 'naturally I shall fall in with your mother's wishes, because it would be wrong for you to disobey her, and, besides you are my best friend, the only person here indeed with whom I feel absolutely at ease, in whom I can confide everything, but I still don't understand. The only point which really seems to divide us is the old Affair, and that after all is twenty years ago, so that it hardly seems to me to matter now that your family believed Dreyfus innocent and your father should have campaigned to that effect, while my Uncle Charles still asserts that he was guilty.'

'Oh,' Edouard said, 'you are so nice, and I wish I could explain everything, but I am afraid it would spoil things if I did.'

'I hope you haven't dropped your friend Binet,' Uncle Charles said to me. 'I thought him charming. His eyes are so candid, and anyone can see that he is as virtuous as he is good-looking. I had thought he would be a pleasing influence on you.'

I assured him that we hadn't quarrelled.

'Then do bring him here please. I grant you, of course, that his family is not distinguished, while as a historian, his father is really absurd. Do you know he wrote an article recently in which it was quite clear that he wasn't aware that Marshal Davout was well-born? But all the same, I am prepared to forgive the father for the sake of his delightful son.'

What was I to say to that?

When I arrived at the Boulevard Malesherbes, I thought Uncle Charles not only immensely distinguished, but universally admired by all right-thinking people. That was what my mother had led me to understand. It was painful to learn that he might be distrusted, and still more painful when some of my schoolfriends made it clear that he was a figure of fun.

'It's not exactly good for your reputation,' one of them said, 'to live in the house of a man who puts rouge on his cheeks, even if he is your uncle.'

And I hadn't realised.

Yet, when news was brought of my father's death, no one could have been kinder or more tender in his sympathy than my uncle, even though I now knew that he and my father had long disliked each other.

'It's only when there is this dislike between people,' he said, 'that it is possible for a true respect, untarnished by affection, to develop.'

My own response to my father's death was a determination to become a soldier as soon as possible. Of course, in the normal course of events, I was due to be called to the colours in a few months, but I now began to look for ways to accelerate my call-up. And, in the midst of that horrible and grotesque war, when every post brought news of death, when everyone was aware of a miasma of death even in the spring air, I fell in love with the idea of uniform. That was a taste I shared with my uncle, who wore himself out in charitable work for the forces, and I shall not myself be so uncharitable as to suggest that his motives were not mixed. It seems to me that, trapped in the network of his affections and desires, he yet retained some noble element in his character which made him far more responsive to suffering, to courage, to the prospect of annihilation which forever stared young men in the face, than were most of those who despised him for what he had allowed himself to become.

Of course everything about him was equivocal; and, in moments when he could escape from the monstrous self which, avid for self-display, thrust his better and more modest nature into the shadows, he recognised this. So, just at the moment when my school-friends' revelation of how he was generally regarded disgusted me, making me ashamed of him, the sympathy he offered me when my father died and then the case of young Marcel Pougier let me see that my mother's estimate of her brother, however ill-founded in misapprehension, nevertheless approximated more closely to being a true judgement of his essence than the ridicule and contempt poured on him by others, who knew him better and less well, could ever be.

I was prepared to dislike Marcel from the moment he jumped up from the sofa in my uncle's library, an eager smile of welcome on his face. He was wearing a private's uniform, and his hair was cut ridiculously short. I had no doubt why he was there, and the dancing mockery in the look he directed at me made it clear he was in no way embarrassed by my arrival.

'The butler told me to wait,' he said. 'Or perhaps he's a valet. I don't know about such things myself. If you've been given the same message, it's rather a joke, isn't it?'

His assumption angered me. I felt myself blushing. He giggled, but kept his eyes on my face.

'The old boy has made a *bêtise*, hasn't he? How do you come to know him? I've not seen you around before. Where did he find you?'

'I'm afraid it's you who has made a mistake,' I said. 'I am Monsieur de Fasquelle's nephew, Lucien de Balafré.'

'Oh, golly,' he said, and the schoolboy expression dispelled my hauteur and made me smile. 'What an ass you must think me. No wonder you're blushing, but it's my cheeks that should be red.'

Yet he was still enjoying the situation.

'It's not possible,' he said. 'Why, if you put it on the stage . . .'

'Well, then, we'd both have to be girls, wouldn't we?'

'Absolutely, and you'd be ever so stiff and proper.'

'As I was, I'm afraid.'

At that moment, while we were both overcome by a fit of giggles – like the girls whose image I had evoked – Uncle Charles entered the room, and stopped, mouth open, the picture of a man surprised by Fate, exactly indeed like an adulterer in the sort of Palais Royal farce we had been envisaging.

Marcel lifted a plate from the table which, I now saw, was set for tea.

'Have a chocolate éclair,' he said. 'There is no embarrassment that can't be eased by a chocolate éclair, you've got to concentrate so hard to keep the cream off your clothes, especially if it's a really luscious one like these, which come from the best patisserie in Paris.'

'Don't let's talk of the trenches,' he said later.

'But I want to know. After all, I expect to be there myself very soon.'

'Well, all I can say is, I don't recommend them.'

We became friends during that short leave of his, and have remained friends ever since. There was a sweetness to his character such as I have rarely encountered, and in those days a gaiety that was infectious. To meet Marcel then was as enlivening as a glass of champagne. His vivacity has been dulled by experience and the struggle for success, but, with old friends at least, the sweetness has survived.

He was a dancer, he told me.

'Well, I used to do female impersonations on the halls and sing naughty little songs. That was where Charles first came across me. He was furious, isn't it strange? "It's disgusting," he said, "a nice boy like you singing such stuff. Don't you see it's degrading?" Well, I didn't – do you? – but I could see he was nice. He doesn't act like he is, but he's really an old softie underneath. Can you imagine, he's given my old Ma what he calls a pension, so that she doesn't have to go out to scrub floors any more. Well, that's hardly typical, let me tell you. Not many of his sort would do such a thing. It's not what you'd call necessary. There's plenty of flowers he could pick up in the market without concerning himself with their old mothers. And that's not the end of it. He goes to see her, chats with her by the hour, makes plans for me after the war – if I survive it, that is.' (He made a quick sign of the cross.) 'He doesn't have to. I think he actually likes doing it. And she thinks the world of him. "He's a real gent," she says, which he is of course. "You've got a good friend there, Marcel," she says.'

'But doesn't she know?'

'Course she does. She's no fool, my Ma. You can't be if you grow up on the streets of Paris, and in a poor quarter like ours you soon learn all the facts of life. No, what she says is, "There's many worse things. Some greedy slut of a girl might have got her painted claws into you. As it is, Monsieur de Fasquelle's a proper gent. You treat him fair and he'll look after you." And she's right. Besides' – he opened his soft brown eyes wide and held my gaze – 'I'm fond of the old boy.'

'Really?'

'Really and truly. You don't understand, do you, what someone like Charles can mean to a boy like me, with my temperament and background. But just take my word for it. Please. I am fond of him.'

And indeed it was Marcel, by then established first as an actor and then as a film director, who closed Uncle Charles's eyes in death. He was holding his hand, too. It's a ridiculous, sentimental picture, isn't it? Only it happens to be true, and it was their real love for each other, enduring despite infidelities on both sides, which taught me the complexity of human nature. I owe them both therefore a debt which I can never repay.

CHAPTER FIVE

MY FATHER SPENT only two months at the front, but they were bad months, for he was wounded in the great German offensive of March 1918.

'He never spoke of that time,' my Uncle Armand told me, 'but you must know it marked him forever. Indeed I would go so far as to say that the strongest elements in his character, and the most persistent traits in his outlook, were the direct consequence of his weeks in the trenches. Like so many people, he was a little deranged by the experience. For some years at least. His first response was pity. It's not too much to say that he was consumed by pity, for the ordinary Frenchman, you understand, who had to endure such atrocities. That was what he said: "There's no denying it, war today, modern war, is simply an atrocity, an offence against God and a surrender to whatever is infernal in our nature. When you have seen a young boy, draped over barbed wire, half of his jaw torn away, and then you realise that the screams you hear come from that ruined boy, well, I assure you, Armand, that everything we imbibed in childhood about the glory of war, the heroism of Roland and Oliver and the glamour of the Napoleonic campaigns, falls away, falls absolutely away, and, quite simply, you find yourself retching." '

And so, determining to have a public life – 'because after all it is my duty, it is the duty of people like myself' – he vowed that he would do his utmost to ensure that no war was ever again fought in Europe.

There were of course countless such young men, in France, England and Germany. They were by no means the majority. It is easy to forget this, because they were the most articulate of their generation. But of course the greatest part of those who had survived the war, many after personal experiences far more frightful than Lucien's, went back to their work, their families, their wives, almost as if nothing had happened. Many of them, even at reunions of old comrades' associations, were light-hearted or nostalgic when they fought their wars over again. They were proud of what they had achieved, and they accepted the horrors as being part of life. In Germany particularly, the horrors of peace often seemed to outweigh the remembered horrors of war, and it is well-known that Hitler and his first Nazi colleagues were ex-soldiers who regarded the war and the Army with a loyalty that was sentimental in its fervour.

Lucien couldn't feel like that, but he did experience the same warmth for his own generation and the same impatience with the old men who had condemned so many to die as cattle. His position was intellectually and emotionally confused, and Armand may not be far wide of the mark when he says that he was indeed deranged.

Yet the derangement was only partial. He attended to his career, for instance. He attended the Sorbonne, studied law with distinction. It was clear that his intellectual abilities had not been impaired, and when he sat the exam for the Foreign Office, he passed out top in his year.

CHAPTER SIX

Document 5

WAS IT BECAUSE I was so unstable that in these years I knew a drive to succeed which I have now lost? I mean, a drive for personal success: to make myself known, to be somebody, precisely because, inwardly, I had become uncertain of everything? And, writing this now, looking back half a lifetime at the self I was then, whom now I find unrecognisable, I wonder how such as Hitler and Stalin are in solitude. Is Hitler as full of certainty in the dark hours of the night as on the podium? Or does he drug himself into nightly insensibility to avoid the questions that might rear out of the dark?

Then I lost my faith in the Faith, and for the moment rested in a false Faith with determined infidelity.

It is easy to blame others, and I could pin the responsibility like a badge of infamy on Gaston Hunnot who constituted himself my mentor and was accepted by me with glad, even gay, abnegation of judgement as such.

He was my senior by five years and walked with a limp occasioned by a piece of shrapnel still lodged in his right calf. It was this which first attracted me to him, but at the same time I was repelled by the bevy of thin-faced girls by whom he was so often surrounded. He had secured for himself a corner in a café which I frequented with some friends, and I was impressed when one of them told me that, though a student like ourselves, Gaston had already found himself a niche in journalism, and even wrote for the *Nouvelle Revue Française*. We first met because the little dog which used to accompany him to the café insistently sniffed my trouser legs.

'It's all right,' he called, 'he doesn't bite, you know.'

It was the scorn in his voice which made me reply with some remark about dogs generally liking me.

'There speaks a man confident of his social position,' he said, and I laughed because it seemed to me absurd.

From that moment we were mysteriously friends. I thought that he was irritated by the unquestioning devotion he received from the girls and half a dozen young men who had constituted themselves his court.

Gaston had been doing his military service when war broke out. He endured the retreat of August 1914, was first wounded at the Marne, returned to the front line and was wounded again at Verdun.

'My father was killed there,' I said.

'And more than half a million others. Have you read this? It's just been published.'

He pushed a book which I had never seen before across the café table; it was Spengler's *Decline of the West*.

'No,' I said.

'You should. It's the book of our times. Listen to this: "Man is a beast of prey. I shall never tire of proclaiming that. All the moralisers and social uplifters who would pretend to be something better are only beasts of prey with their teeth drawn." Do you like that? Do you agree?'

And without waiting for a reply, he opened the book at another point marked, I noticed, by a cinema ticket.

'Or this: "A time is coming – more, it is already here – which will have no room for sensitive souls and frail ideals. The ancient barbarism which for centuries lay fettered and buried beneath the strict forms of a high culture is awakening again, now that culture is consummated and civilisation has begun: the warlike and healthy joy in a man's own strength, which an age of rationalist thought saturated in literature despised; the unbroken instinct of race, which is resolved to live otherwise than under the oppression of dead books and bookish ideals . . ." '

I thought to myself: how can a man be so horribly wrong and yet strike a true note? But I did not speak and waited for Gaston to continue.

'Delightful, isn't it? Yet that nonsense will find willing ears in Germany, it will enter and take possession of generous and idealistic souls there. Yet it's pernicious and frail itself.'

'Frail?' I said. 'It doesn't sound frail, and doesn't your author, whoever he is, condemn frailty?'

'Each man reprobates the weakness which he recognises in himself.'

Gaston closed the book and smiled. I said:

'And what is your weakness?'

'Optimism,' he said.

'What do you mean?'

'Simply that I believe in the future of mankind and am horrified by the temerity of such belief.'

As he spoke, he lifted his head to gaze across the Place

St-Sulpice, and this let me see the strong line of his jaw, like the jaw of an ideal self-conscious dictator. He picked up his glass of Vichy water – Gaston never drank alcohol in those days – and his long upper lip extended itself along the rim like a serpent drinking. I was all at once aware of the force emanating from this spare man in the neat dark suit, and surrendered to it.

For perhaps two years I was intellectually intoxicated by him.

'Spengler is false history,' he said, 'and yet it is the historical view of life which can alone make sense of the world today. That is why what is happening in Russia is merely the logical extension of our own Revolution, which overthrew feudalism but then found itself trapped in bourgeois aspirations and surrendered to them. Pointless to blame the men of '93; they could not be other than they were on account of their historical conditioning. But we, at a distance of more than a hundred years, can now properly recognise them as a link in a necessary chain. It is therefore all the more evident when we look at our France of grocers and country notaries, that our Republic cannot endure, and that we must, and inevitably shall, aspire to the eradication of class conflict through class conflict and so arrive at the Dictatorship of the Proletariat.'

I condense a thousand conversations in a paragraph, and when I asked him how we, who were not proletarians, could possibly belong to the new order of things, he explained that as intellectuals we were the fulcrum of change.

And for two years I believed him. I all but joined the Party. I contributed to the review he established. I did so anonymously, at his suggestion – a suggestion which in fact amounted to a command.

'There will be a time,' he said, 'when it is useful to have your name. At present it is more useful that you should not be publicly associated with us . . .'

He breaks off there, and indeed one of the features of these papers, intended, I am almost sure, as a draft of these by now tantalising confessions, is their inconclusive nature. It is as if Lucien always draws back from any full commitment even to his own past. Of course, if he was writing this in the winter of '42–'43, it's not entirely surprising that he should have hesitated to reveal much about his association with the Communists. Stalingrad had after all been fought – or was still being fought, about the time he started on his confessions – and the Communists had moved from the support for the Vichy regime which they displayed till June '41 towards taking the lead in the Resistance. Nobody could then be sure that anything he wrote was safe, even in his mother's house, and so I wonder less at Lucien's reticence than at his willingness to commit himself to memorising at all.

And of course the question which is always asked of any Communist, or former Communist, rears up, particularly in the light of that last sentence: when he broke with the Party, was the rupture sincere or a tactical ploy?

His close association with Gaston Hunnot seems to have been limited to these two years, but Hunnot, himself a somewhat mysterious figure, one whose achievement always fell short of his promise, was to play a part in my father's tragedy.

Lucien's emotional life during the 1920s, which were also his own twenties, was barren. He mentions briefly that he and Marcel Pougier were lovers, and that surprised me, because elsewhere Lucien shows himself hostile to homosexuality; yet he continued to be friends with Marcel to the end. I leave it to you to make what you can or like of that. Otherwise he was involved with nobody. He lived only through his intellect, and that was in a state of continual ferment. He didn't know what to believe from one year to the next.

It was his instability which exposed him to Charles Maurras. I'm sure, Hugh, that you know more about Maurras than I do. My early ignorance was of course such that on that visit to my grandmother's after the war I quite failed to detect the influence of Maurras in those essays of Lucien's which I referred to. Maurras now seems absurd with his ideas of racial purity, his Latinity, his notion that the four enemies of *la vraie France* were the Socialists, the Freemasons, the Jews and those whom he called *métèques*, people of mixed blood. Or have I got that wrong: weren't the Protestants also one of the enemies? Poor Maurras: he concocted an ideal France that only a very few Frenchmen could recognise. Unfortunately, Lucien was one, though even Lucien at times was able to recognise his mentor's absurdity. When Maurras said in one of his articles: 'One would have preferred to give this advice to the King in his cabinet rather than through the pages of a newspaper,' Lucien scribbled, 'But what makes the poor dear man believe he would have been one of the King's counsellors?'

Nevertheless Maurras was important to him, even though he was never himself a member of *Action Française*. He wrote of Maurras once, in 1935: 'I respect his diagnosis of our condition, which is absolutely just, but like many doctors he can prescribe no remedy that does not fill one with incredulity. For the fact is, that we are landed with the regime of the parties, unless some exterior or interior tragedy occurs. And because I can't help believing that the worst regime may yet be preferable to even the best-intentioned revolution – for revolutions never perform their best intentions – I accept it as it is, and am even prepared to serve it, in the hope of mitigating its worst absurdities and ameliorating its defects.'

Pompous, ridiculous, yet somehow decent: there you have Lucien.

CHAPTER SEVEN

HE WAS ATTACHED to the London Embassy in 1928. For his first year there he was lonely. He had all the prejudice against England which Maurras encouraged in his disciples, and he hadn't yet realised that there were sectors of London society ready to adore any personable young Frenchman of good birth and pleasing appearance who could speak tolerable English. So he attended only official dinners, and in his free time, which was plentiful, read in his own rooms or browsed round art galleries. He read seriously, for he was consciously preparing himself to play some great role, the exact nature of which had not yet been revealed to him, in his country's history. There are a good many letters to his mother from this year. Few are worth reproducing in full. They are mostly banal – commonplaces about the frightful climate (till he suddenly realised the delights and beauty of a London spring), enquiries about her health, reassurances concerning his own. There is some political talk, even though he must have known that she took no real interest in that. These were optimistic years, after Locarno, and one can see Lucien moving into a more centrist position, convinced that French interests could be secured through international co-operation and the League of Nations. More than once, he expresses the hope that he might be transferred to Geneva: 'It is there that the future of civilisation will be forged.'

Then, in his second autumn, he discovered a new and surprising enthusiasm. One of his few English friends, a banker called Nicholas Elbeach – he had a French mother who was a distant cousin of ours, which was how the acquaintance had been formed – invited him to Northamptonshire for a weekend. The local hunt was meeting. They found a mount for Lucien, and in the damp morning, with mist shrouding the beechwoods and the air soft and tremulous, Lucien fell in love with the activity and with an aspect of England which was altogether new to him. He returned again and again. By December he had two hunters of his own, which the Elbeaches amusedly stabled for him. He rode with an audacity which seemed foreign to his nature, and perhaps it was;

perhaps it was his nature's response to this foreign and unexpected delight. He became for the first time in his life – for the only time, I'm afraid – a popular figure. People – the squires, the farmers, the scattering of country gentry and their progeny who zoomed up from London in Bentleys or Vauxhall sports-cars, or piled into early-morning trains – were first amused and then a little flattered and finally delighted by the zest with which this taciturn young Frenchman, whose silence and generally reserved manner contradicted the national stereotype they had accepted, threw himself into their favourite, their (in their view) national sport. 'That young Frog rides like the very Devil,' they chuckled. By the New Year he had four horses and was hunting three days a week – the Embassy was not demanding and the hours he had formerly spent in the Tate or at the Wallace Collection were now devoted to pursuing the fox over the ploughed fields of the Midlands. By March he was ready to ride in the members' race in the point-to-point, though Lady Elbeach warned him that he would probably break his neck.

'However,' she said, 'you ride like a man born to be hanged, so you probably won't. I must say, when Nick brought you down that Friday, I never thought we would be preparing you to race. Actually, when he said you were prepared to be put up, we all thought it a great joke. Just shows how wrong you can be about people.'

It was on one of these March days that he met Polly. Their encounter was lacking in romance, for Lucien rose covered in mud from a ditch to see his horse galloping away, and at that moment Polly, clearing the hedge, sent him sprawling again as he had to dive to escape her horse's hooves.

'You might have killed me,' he said to her that evening. 'In fact I thought my last moment had come.'

'I'm so sorry. There was no chance of stopping. Did you catch your horse?'

'He came to rest about a mile off, and one of your peasants obligingly seized him. Do you call them peasants?'

'I call them chawbacons, but most people say farm-workers,' she replied.

Polly was eighteen, dark as a gypsy and thin as fashion dictated. She was ready for love, having endured one London season where she was bored by the callow boys she met at dances, and then having spent the winter in disgrace in her father's house because of some transgression which any girl of today would regard as absolutely normal behaviour. She was indeed ignorant in the way no modern child could be, but that, I suppose, is the way things were then.

Lucien fitted the ideal on which she had brooded through the wet and windy months of her sequestration. He was ten years older than she; he had a career – girls at that time seemed to revere the Diplomatic in a way that they haven't for thirty years or more. He was silent and distinguished in appearance, and looked as if he was nurturing a secret sorrow. He rode gallantly and was not given to boasting; and he was foreign and it had become smart to have a foreign lover. It was not surprising that she should fall in love with him, and it was in her nature that, having done so, she should set out to get him. She had after all been brought up with a single-minded intention; her duty in life was to marry suitably and well, and part of Lucien's attraction was that, being foreign and Catholic, he strained the concept of suitability to the limit. Polly did not share her sister Aurora's determination to shock, but she had a sufficiently rebellious streak, which expressed itself in an impulse towards the unconventional, and a willingness to act in a manner likely to dismay her parents.

Certainly her father, who was quite convinced that an unnecessary war had been fought entirely because Great Britain had been inveigled into it by the perfidious French, who had then let down their allies, was not likely to welcome the idea of his favourite daughter marrying a Frenchman – not even one who displayed conspicuous courage in the hunting-field. He always indeed regarded Lucien's enthusiasm for hunting as some sort of trick.

And then there was the matter of religion. That question delayed the marriage for at least six months. My grandfather could hardly contemplate the idea of his daughter marrying a Roman Catholic. He was an old-fashioned Low Church Anglican who regarded the Roman Church as all 'stinks and lace'. The delay made Polly desperate. She proposed to Lucien that they should live together; 'That will force his hand,' she declared. To her dismay he was as horrified by the notion as her father was intended to be. He couldn't consider 'compromising' her in this way. She was very angry and threw a shepherdess (Dresden ware) at his head. For a fortnight there was a coolness between them. Each thought the other was being unreasonable. Then Polly went to him, and told him she was sorry. He broke down and wept, assured her he adored her, and that the proof of his great love was his willingness to wait till her father consented. But of course it had to be a Catholic marriage, otherwise he wouldn't feel 'properly married'. And there was nothing he wanted more.

Polly saw she was caught in a trap that could contain her for ages, and she couldn't bear the idea of being so contained. The high-minded obstinacy of her father, and of the lover who refused actually to become that till formally bound, exasperated her. It seemed absurd, out-of-date, and she couldn't bear anything old-fashioned. So, to resolve the matter, she went to her father and told him that he had better consent to the marriage on Lucien's terms because she was already his mistress, was going to have a baby, and he refused to marry her except according to the Catholic rites.

'So,' she said, 'either we do it his way, or your grandchild will be a little illegit. I don't mind because I love Lucien anyway and am quite happy to go on being his mistress.'

My grandfather was furious, naturally enough, but couldn't contemplate the prospect of his daughter's disgrace. He gave way, fulminating against the serpent-like perfidy of the French. The odd thing was, however, that from the day of the wedding he developed an enormous respect for Lucien. Himself a man of imperious will, he was enchanted to discover, as he thought, that he had a son-in-law whose will was even stronger than his own. The respect even survived the revelation that Polly wasn't pregnant at all. Indeed this gave him a wonderful opinion of his son-in-law's cleverness. From that moment for the next ten years he would justify any position he adopted by saying 'and I know Lucien will agree'; conversely the discovery that Lucien on any occasion thought differently from him caused him great disquiet. In the end this was to his advantage. It was Lucien's doubts about Hitler, more and more freely expressed as the decade advanced, which prevented him from following his younger daughter Aurora's lead and conceiving an admiration for the Führer. The Nazis were eager to flatter him, as an English Lord and the father of the Führer's English friend, and he did enjoy being treated as someone important. All the same, the reflection that Lucien thinks 'there's something a bit off about the fellow' prevented him from making a complete fool of himself. Indeed I suppose it saved him from being imprisoned under the notorious Regulation 18(B) of the Defence of the Realm Act in 1940.

Do I seem to make light of this, Hugh? To treat this question of their marriage so much less seriously than they would have regarded it themselves, at the time? It is because it is so difficult to take other people's lives seriously. At one point in my life I tried to write fiction, you know. I failed because I could never imagine reality. Then I turned to biography, and my victim – Smuts, if you must know – seemed even less real. And yet I fully agree with that thing of Ortega's about man's best image for himself being a novelist and that 'man is what has happened to him'. The trouble is that, as I am aware of how fully my own existence can only be explained by what goes on in my head, I am baffled by the unreality of any portrayal of a person which is unable truthfully to tell me what is happening in his. And so I fall back on irony, while real novelists, I suppose, turn to invention; and make their lies seem the better truth, which is what Polly did in respect of that mythical and decisive pregnancy. But if the novel is an image of life, or life a sort of fleshy novel – and the two propositions seem opposite sides of a coin which is valid currency – then the problem must be the existence of other people. Man himself may be a novelist, but he can't make a novel only of himself; and the trouble is that other people are only seen from the outside, however skilfully novelists try to disguise the fact.

Take for example that scene, remarkable, grisly and, as it were, authentic in *Le Temps Retrouvé*, in which the narrator is invited by Jupien to spy on Charlus being whipped by the young butcher or whatever he is; well, there everything about the feelings which Charlus experiences would be, if representing a scene from real life, only supposition. Of course, as criticism, you will say, this is so much nonsense, because it is not real life, but a novel; and you are quite right; yet if real life is a sort of novel, then it remains one told in the first person, and the only sure knowledge we have is of the narrator. Everyone else is only observed, as in a film, in which one action is required to stand for a whole way of life, ocean of feeling, or history of experience. Choose the significant detail, you say; but the choice is arbitrary. We cannot play God in the novel of life.

CHAPTER EIGHT

IN 1930 MY father was transferred to the Berlin Embassy. Now, when I write the words 'Berlin 1930', you, and most Anglo-Saxon readers, will at once summon up a picture of which I can hardly suppose myself capable of disabusing you. You already have all the significant details you need, and you know the city too well. Isherwood has written it all for us, and it is almost impossible to think of Lucien and Polly there without wondering when they will encounter Mr Norris, whether Sally Bowles will be found singing in the *Nachtlokal* they frequent, or whether, stumbling through the economic disruption of the Depression, they will bump into Otto Nowak. If none of these, surely Bernard Landauer (whom we know, do we not? to have been in reality Wilfrid Israel) will invite them to dinner. The fact is that anyone trying to create Berlin 1930 is up against a master; it is like attempting a tragedy in blank verse and avoiding echoes of Shakespeare. This is part of what I mean when I say that our knowledge of what is real is conditioned by the imagination of others.

'I suppose I heard of Hitler, darling, but I don't recall doing so,' Polly once sighed.

Was she pulling my leg, and the legs of those assembled on her South African terrace, or could she have been speaking the truth? She may well have been, for Polly was the most apolitical of women.

Surely, Lucien was much better informed.

Well, of course he was. Nevertheless he wrote a long memorandum – I'm sending you a copy, but won't trouble to reproduce it here, because its banality is so easy to summarise – in which he analysed the threat to Germany's parliamentary democracy solely in terms of the Communists, and concluded that the French Government should do everything in its power to ease matters for Bruening and the Conservatives. He insisted that they must be involved in the work of the League, and even speculated on whether it might be desirable to restore German sovereignty over the Rhineland. He didn't mention the Nazis. They were a mere temporary phenomenon of no historical significance. And Lucien wasn't a fool.

History is written from then to now, but understood back to front.

The Berlin in which Lucien and Polly lived was a dull, correct place. They knew nobody except other diplomats and a few German aristocratic families. Some of these had lost their estates in old Prussia or the Mark of Brandenburg or Poland as a result of the frontier changes which had followed the war; they talked of themselves as exiles. Both Lucien and Polly found this appealing.

For a year or eighteen months their isolation from any lively or interesting company didn't distress them. They were wrapped up in each other. Their conversation was full of the private jokes of happy couples, and they would cut across a dinner table with a raised eyebrow or half-smile. Polly wrote letters to her parents which were rare and scrappy because she was too happy to be able to feel homesick for England. Lucien naturally wrote far more frequently to his mother, but his letters were dull and dutiful things. For both of them family had become for the moment concentrated in their four-roomed apartment.

Two or three times in the winter they were invited by their Prussian friends to shooting-parties. Standing in a butt, his face frozen by the grey wind which cut across the marshy wastelands from the Russian steppes, Lucien sniffed the immensity of Europe, the cruelty of history, the fragility of all he valued. He watched the sullen peasants who acted as beaters, heavy, clownish and indifferent in their leather breeches; he found something 'Slav, barbaric, utterly miserable' in those faces with their high cheekbones and full inexpressive eyes. When in the evening his hosts talked of the lost mission of civilisation which had been Germany's historic role in the east, he understood the sense of deprivation which they experienced. Ancestors, they assured him, had belonged to the Teutonic Order of Knights; he could picture them in black armour setting their faces against that east wind, venturing into a land of dry magic, where no values of Christian man were known. The thought made him shudder. He, who had been accustomed to think of Germany itself as something barbaric, who was conscious of everything that was Roman in Europe to which Germany had stood opposed, now felt that Rome was like a stone hurled into a deep black pond, which sent ripples, diminishing in size, from the spot where it had landed. He had believed that Germany was beyond the ripple; he now saw that he was wrong. The Germans were not only the remotest of ripples themselves, but the guardians of all that that rippling water signified. He listened in the evenings to Brahms on his wind-

up gramophone; there was forest-music there, but beneath its
pagan mystery throbbed the affirmative note of Rome.

Often, in the evenings, after the day's sport had been discussed,
the talk turned to these matters. Lucien was made aware of how
these Germans lived as exiles in their own land, bewailing their
lost estates and, perhaps even more powerfully, the lost mission of
Germanitum. He found himself in sympathy with them; they
echoed the tunes that Maurras piped over the marshy delta of
the Rhone. When one of them said, 'The historic antipathy of
France and Germany has been worse than a blunder, it has been a
crime against the fundamental integrity of Europe,' the words
conveyed to him the idea of a mission that went beyond the
narrow nationalism in which he had been reared. He all at once
saw that France's old alliance with Russia had been a betrayal of
her true self. 'In order to fatten a few thousand greedy bond-
holders, we were ready to squander a thousand years of Europe,'
he wrote in his diary.

Disinterested idealism was still possible then. There was no
fear of a new war. Certainly the world was a mess, for the
economy of the Western world had plunged out of control into
a black and incomprehensible whirlpool. Yet it seemed that men
of goodwill could shake the bag and reassemble the pieces
coherently. Lucien believed this, though below the conscious
level of his mind he still heard the barbaric drumming of Spengler
threatening doom. Yet, despite the pervasive sadness of these
country visits, of which the abiding image remained for him a
flight of duck, necks outstretched, lost in the thin grey of evening,
he experienced a new optimism and sense of purpose. It was
partly because he had found a friend.

This was Rupprecht von Hülenberg. (Does that name ring a
bell, Hugh? It should, you know. I shall call him Rupert because
that is how Polly and Lucien came to speak of him.) He was
hardly more than a boy, in his early twenties, too young of course
for the war, though – in his own words – 'not without its
souvenirs'.

'We had to fly before the Russians. In carts. Then, when we
recovered our estates in '17, it was the peasants. Filthy beasts,
they raped my sister, you know, and we only just escaped with our
lives.'

He told them this in a flat matter-of-fact voice, which horrified
Polly. She didn't know what to make of Rupert. She had been
quite certain at first. He was beautiful, blond, of middle height,
quite sturdy, with a straight nose and curving lips; she fell in love

with him. But his seriousness repelled her. She didn't understand
a boy who would rather, it seemed, talk politics and philosophy
with Lucien than love and gossip with her. She told Lucien she
was sure he was a pansy; 'like so many of these Germans'.

'Not at all,' Lucien said, 'that's ridiculous. He is just a serious
young man. And a very intelligent one.'

For a couple of months she sulked, then discovered, when they
were back in Berlin, that he had taken to calling at a time when he
must know Lucien would be at the office.

'Why do you come here?' she said.

'Because I feel comfortable. You have no idea how uncomfortable I feel most of the time. I live with my mother, you know. She
has never recovered from our experiences during the war, and I
am all she has. It is not very exhilarating.'

'You never seem very exhilarated here. You don't even laugh at
my jokes.'

'Well, no. You see, I am not very good at understanding jokes. I
am even stupid when it is a question of jokes, I am afraid. I only
see that you have made a joke when the moment for laughter has
passed. Nevertheless, Polly, I really do like your jokes. They are
one of the things I like most and which bring me here. There you
have your answer. I come on account of your jokes which I do not
understand.'

She looked at him carefully to see whether he was in fact
laughing at her. But she saw a perfectly blank face, with the deep
blue eyes steady and serious.

'You like jokes which you don't understand?'

'Yes, you see, I like the idea of jokes.'

'You are an ass.'

He touched his mouth with the back of his hand.

'Are you laughing at me?' she asked. 'I always have this idea
that you're laughing at me.'

'Certainly not,' he said. 'Do you like flowers?'

'Everybody does.'

'Not everybody, I think. My poor mother, flowers mean
nothing to her. But next time I will bring you flowers.'

He did so, and soon after that Rupert and Polly became lovers.
It was her first infidelity, and it amazed and disconcerted her; she
had not been aware of anything lacking in her marriage, and now
all at once she found herself in bed with this blond young
German, whom she was not even sure she liked. And Rupert
himself was, I think, also taken aback by the affair. He liked
Lucien, admired him and deferred to his intellect; and yet he

couldn't keep his hands off his wife. He indulged himself in outbursts of self-recrimination, which soon bored Polly. She has always been the least introspective of people, and she couldn't understand her lover's delight in declaring that he was 'utterly contemptible', or his moaning that he had 'lost his honour' and that the 'only thing left to him was to blow his brains out or set off for China'. It seemed all the stranger when the next minute he was urging her back to bed. Yet for all her irritation, she couldn't help adoring him; his photograph was to reappear on her dressing table during the war. I grew familiar with it then; he had rather high cheekbones – perhaps there was Slav blood in him as in so many Prussian aristocrats. (Didn't Bismarck always say he himself was a Wend, not a Prussian; but what exactly is a Wend?)

In the end nothing would serve but that Rupert must confess to Lucien. This disgusted Polly, who believed that the decent thing – if you were engaged in adultery – was to keep the betrayed husband in the dark. But Rupert insisted on 'total honesty'. He took Lucien out to dinner and Lucien talked so determinedly about Spengler and his debt to Hegel (neither of whom Rupert had then read) that Rupert couldn't broach the matter. He therefore suggested they move on to a casino, where, over indifferent champagne, he explained that he was in love with his friend's wife.

'Of course,' he said, 'I must get out. Perhaps I will go to China. There are openings for German officers there.'

'But you are not an officer,' Lucien said. 'You have never been a soldier.'

'No,' Rupert said, 'that's true. But the Army is in my blood. In China I could be an officer. It is a wonderful country, a mysterious one, and there is no future for me in Germany, where my own personal disgrace now mirrors that of my family. But in China I might perhaps fulfil myself.'

'I see no reason for you to go there. You are exaggerating the gravity of things. What has happened has happened to others before us. It is unfortunate, but in another sense, well, Rupert, it binds us together. We both love Polly, and you have proved that you are honourable by confessing to me what you have done.'

Was it Lucien's vanity that caused him to speak in this way?

'But I don't only love her. I have slept with her.'

'I don't regard my wife as my possession,' Lucien said. 'The time for that has passed. Of course I am sad that she does not love me exclusively, but I do not believe she loves me less because she also loves you. And in a curious way my friendship for you is strengthened by your love for Polly. I feel it is somehow symbolic.'

To a German of Rupert's generation, the word 'symbolic' was decisive. At any rate he now called for another bottle of champagne and lifted his glass.

'I shall never forget this, Lucien. This nobility of soul. And I accept the symbol. The three of us, you, Polly and myself, represent the three great powers of Europe, the three cultures of Europe. Let us drink to the idea of Europe as expressed by our love for each other, and to you, Lucien, I protest my undying friendship. Let us drink to – what is your phrase – "to the fundamental integrity of Europe", that's it.'

'The fundamental integrity of Europe.'

Lucien, who normally drank little, threw back his head and quaffed his glass. One thing led to another. The fundamental integrity of Europe was subjected to full baptismal treatment, drenched in the Jordan. Soon people at other tables were drawn into the celebration. As they staggered, arm in arm, into the bald streets of the sunless dawn, Lucien assured Rupert that they were now joined in an immortal brotherhood.

'Like the Teutonic Order of Knights,' Rupert said.

'Or the Knights of St John.'

'Or the Templars.'

They woke Polly up to tell her the good news. She was not pleased.

'When chaps go out to fight over you and come home rollicking drunk having had a jolly whale of a time, a girl begins to feel a bit on the outside looking in. Still, one thing, it ended my little romp with Rup, and do you know, I was so jealous of him that I got to work on Lucien and we started you off. So something good came of the whole nonsense.'

'And did Rupert go to China?'

'No, of course he didn't, it wasn't like the pictures.'

CHAPTER NINE

Document 6:

Memorandum note by Lucien de Balafré

I AM NOT ashamed now to write that I made many good friends in my time in Berlin. Those were years of hope when it seemed that we could build a better Europe without war. Neither I nor any of my friends foresaw that the barbaric savagery of the Nazi movement would introduce an imponderable X into the equation; though it has become an X whose riddle we have to solve, the consequences of which we must elucidate. In those days it was already clear to me that the Treaty of Versailles had been, as Talleyrand said of the murder of the Duc d'Enghien, 'worse than a crime, a mistake'. It had destroyed the stability of central Europe, or rather any chance that the stability might be restored; it had inflicted injustice on many, especially Germans, even while it aspired to eliminate injustice; and, in consequence, it had bred up a generation of fanatics whose one thought was revenge. Such were the consequences of the myopia of Clemenceau and Lloyd George; such was the bitter fruit of rational liberal statesmanship! As the decade of the 1930s appeared to be stumbling into the shadows of night, walking with the carelessness of a doomed man towards the very jaws of Hell where Mars lurked, so I grappled with the terrible dichotomy created when Versailles spawned Hitler, as, in Milton's epic, sin gives birth to death. To be brief, this consisted in the contrast between the justice of Hitler's demands and the injustice of Hitlerism. We were being compelled, step by step, to do the right thing for the wrong reason, the wrong cause and the wrong man.

There was such hope and ardour hidden in Germany then. My friend Rupert von Hülenberg may be taken as an example of all that seemed to warrant optimism there. A young man of rare capacity and generosity of spirit, hardly impaired by the misfortunes to which his family had been subjected or the interruptions which his education had suffered, he was firmly opposed to the extremities of the Right and Left, firm for the enduring traditions of Germany. That said, the purity of his spirit was displayed by his refusal to succumb to false comforts, assurances that tried to conceal the nullity of their message by the stridency with which they were uttered. He was one of those who clung, while all around him fell apart, to the central conviction that truth could be identified and maintained.

Note (*scribbled by my father on the back of this manuscript sheet*): I write this, and it is true, it is all true, but it is also the sort of truth which one utters in public or might publish in a formal auto-biography.

Or obituary notice?

And the time, I fear, may be close when I do indeed feel the necessity to write Rupert's obituary.

If indeed I dare then to write anything, which, certainly, I would find no means of ever publishing.

Consider too: a conversation I had with Drieu in – May '37? – about Rupert as an example of the self-hatred manifested by so many young Germans. 'A poisoned legacy of Romanticism,' Drieu remarked.

Yet, when I write of self-hatred in connection with Rupert, what exactly do I mean? That he had a sense of what must be done, could see no way of achieving it, and shrank from the attempt, hating himself for his fear. And his courage, which I don't doubt, has always nevertheless had its roots in terror.

'When I look in the mirror at night,' he once said to me, 'or in my dreams, I see a stormtrooper.'

He is so nearly everything which he fears and detests.

Five years after their affair, Polly said to me: 'You think the sun shines out of Rupert's backside. You don't see how ordinary he is.'

What she didn't realise is that it was his ordinariness I loved: the fact that he wasn't really clever, that he was so easily per-plexed; that his stocky confidence was assumed, that he swag-gered in order to disguise what he knew of himself.

Who said: 'The relation between France and Germany is sado-masochistic. France is the woman who submits'?

But with Rupert, wasn't I the sadist? Didn't I insist, after he had confessed his adultery with Polly, that he remain our friend, on spaniel terms, not only because I could not then contemplate not seeing him, but, far more significantly, because I knew that he could no longer make love to Polly, even while he longed to do so? I used to watch his eyes following her round the room.

I have had mistresses. After Etienne was born, when Polly began to *tromper* me again and again, I had mistresses: clever girls who wanted to write poetry and some who actually wrote essays. Polly laughed at them, but it reached the point when she could not bear to see me with Rupert, whom I have never so much as touched since that evening when we staggered arm in arm back from the casino where he confessed his adultery to me. That was the only night in my life on which I have been intoxicated.

Marcel Pougier spoke to me in Paris last week about a young officer in the Gestapo with whom he is infatuated. He used the word 'infatuated'; it is his, not mine. He looked at me with the dirty face of a broken angel, and whispered about 'irresistible cruelty, the surrender to everything in oneself one fears' – the whisper came to me on a foul breath, stale with brandy, and his hands shook. He spoke for himself, but the eagerness with which he opened his arms to humiliation – haven't we all experienced just that in the last years?

Yet, with Rupert, it was I who played the part of the Gestapo officer. Or of the inquisitor to whose coming the truly devout heretic looks forward with terrible adoration.

Two nights ago, as I lay with Anne, she looked at my hands, took them in her pale fingers, and said, 'How dirty your nails are.' There was a fleck of blood under one of them too.

And in dreams, even when I lie with Anne, I see Rupert, as I once saw him, stretched out naked on the shingle by the lakeside. It is cold, a March wind is blowing from the east, and the daffodils that fringe the wood shiver. His legs are quite white except where they are touched with a buttery sun. He is waiting for the punishment which I refuse to grant him. When he told me that he had made love to my wife, what did he want? Did I please him by offering forgiveness? Insult him? Or was that the punishment he sought? Who can bear to be forgiven? Even by God?

I write this almost automatically, as if another – The Other perhaps – possesses my pen. It is midnight. Tomorrow I have to make a speech to schoolchildren. It is my duty to tell them what France requires of them. I shall fulfil my duty. Nevertheless I have written these papers.

Which it is madness not to destroy.

Yet I know I shall not destroy them.

CHAPTER TEN

THAT PASSAGE, RETROSPECTIVE as it is, Hugh, is leaping
ahead of my narrative. Yet I have thought to include it here
because I am afraid that you may be revising your previously high
opinion of my father, and concluding that he was indeed – as I
tried to tell you when we met – a dull dog. That was disingenuous
of me, but I had no wish then to find myself obliged to embark on
the quest to which you have directed me. I wanted to be left alone
with my brandy, my mutterings through the back streets of pacific
Geneva. But now that you have forced me to it, I find myself
anxious that you shouldn't begin to be disappointed in my father.

He was disappointed in himself, of course, and Polly was
disappointed in him too. As the thirties began to creak like a
B-movie that has exhausted inspiration, so Lucien came to regard
himself as a superfluous man. He had no sympathy with the mood
of France. He lacked any political direction. And his marriage was
beginning to disintegrate, far earlier than I had supposed. He was
recalled from Berlin in the autumn of 1931, spent two years at the
Quai d'Orsay, and then – evidence, as it seemed, of his superiors'
lack of confidence – was offered a posting in South America. He
rebelled, for he had become a diplomat to play a part, as he saw it,
in European affairs; he had no interest in a conventional career
that would see him at the age of fifty-five Ambassador in Para-
guay. Polly supported him in this; she had, for different reasons,
no more wish than he to exchange Europe for the fringes of the
old Spanish Empire. So he resigned from the service, or, to be
more exact, requested to be placed *en disponibilité*.

For the next two years they seem to have lived chiefly at the
Château de l'Haye. This was not at all to Polly's taste, and she
would take off for England or Paris several times a year. I suppose
she was unfaithful to Lucien on these jaunts. Certainly they were
growing apart from each other.

It was in these years that he came to know Maurras, who was a
frequent visitor; his photograph used to stand on a table in my
grandmother's drawing room, though I didn't recognise it myself
during that visit I made while at Cambridge. Lucien was im-

pressed by Maurras, but he could not constitute himself a whole-hearted disciple; he saw that the great man's thinking was confined in the last decades of the nineteenth century; he understood neither Hitler nor Stalin.

As a result of his time in Germany and his continuing friendship with many Germans, especially of course Rupert, Lucien developed an obsessive interest – Hitler. He found almost everything about him repellent.

I know that that statement will be questioned. It is bound to be. Nevertheless it is true. The evidence is, I admit, widely scattered. For the moment, Hugh, I merely ask you to take my word for it.

But consider this also: my father condemned Maurras for his continued immersion in the last century, but the frame of his own mind was cast there also. He retained the idea of the gentleman. He believed that the statesman owed a duty to his social inferiors; and he recognised that Hitler being, as he put it, *canaille*, could have no grasp of such a concept. Lucien had no objection to authoritarian government, but his rulers were to be Platonic personages.

Letter from Hugh Challefray:

> Dear Mr de Balafré: I am more grateful than I can say for what you have sent me. But I do not want the history of the twentieth century. I want to know what sort of man your father was. And the more detail you send, the more obscure he becomes. Do try harder.

Well, this is blunt and exigent, and I have nothing to say in extenuation. Except this, on a postcard.

> Hugh: It seems to me the more I write, that my poor father is a pale reflection of the twentieth century. If that's not what you want, too bad. It's what you must take if you want to approach understanding. E. de B.

That may quieten him a moment while he struggles to see what sort of sense it makes. But I mean it. It was the history of his time which determined what Lucien became. In saying that, I am not attempting to deny free will. Or am I?

But Hugh's objection worries me more than I pretend. I have little faith in my own judgement. How could I have?

In the autumn of 1934 Lucien established himself in Paris. He hoped this would appease Polly, on whom he depended more than he knew. Like many nervy men of fluctuating will and some imagination he felt a need for an unreflective and confident companion. Polly's blithe indifference to everything outside the immediate sphere of her personal interests irritated him, and comforted and strengthened him at the same time. There was much to be said for a wife to whom a spaniel puppy was more important than Hitler's latest speech. He had accepted that she and his mother were incompatible, and that she could never be happy in Provence; Polly was one of those for whom the South of France already meant the coastal strip.

Colette said to him about this time: 'Your pretty wife is much wiser than you. She knows that the correct way of making an omelette matters much more than a theory of economics.'

He found this comforting even though Polly was – and has always been – a terrible cook. Not that she needed to cook; they had a maid of all work to do that, or they ate in restaurants. But he liked the symbolic truth and the insight of Colette's observation. He repeated it often in conversation, and in one of his essays you will find the sentence: 'Civilisation depends more on the quality of bread than the quality of thought,' which seems another way of saying the same thing.

But there was more to the move to Paris than an attempt to please Polly and revive his marriage. The two years in Provence had been a bad time for Lucien himself. He thought he was happy to live there, but he found his mother oppressive, and in fact was able to tolerate her company only when his own vitality was low. And in those years he had been, as it were, lying fallow. He didn't know in which direction his life should move, and he was disturbed by the conviction of failure. He was after all now in sight of forty, his hair had turned grey, there were lines on his face, and he had achieved nothing.

He was casting around for some means of fulfilling himself. He had no desire to return to the Quai d'Orsay and in any case the Foreign Service seemed to have been a false start. Political life did not attract him; the traditions of his family were still strong enough to make it hard for him to see himself as a deputy in the despised Assembly of the shameful Republic. To put it like that exaggerated his feeling. He would never have spoken in just such reactionary terms. Yet that was how he felt; social prejudices of family and caste are damnably persistent.

One day he met his old mentor Gaston Hunnot. He used to wonder later if he hadn't in fact set out to meet him, though unable to bring himself to admit that this was his purpose. At any rate he went to the café where he used to talk with Gaston, where Gaston had introduced him to Spengler (whom by now Lucien had dismissed as a windy rhetorician), and there he found him sitting at the same table where he had held court fifteen years before, and surrounded by what might have seemed to Lucien the same little congregation of disciples if he hadn't at once realised that their familiarity was of a different order; they weren't the same people, they were the same age. All at once, though he had been dismayed by the thought of how little progress he had made in his own life, he found himself despising Gaston: to have lived so long and still find your audience in students – wasn't that a sign of a failure as complete as his own?

Was Gaston pleased to see him? He couldn't tell. Gaston fell straight away into the old tone of ironical superiority, but now that his old spell was broken, Lucien heard in this the same note of failure which he had diagnosed in his circumstances. He all at once saw Gaston as a wretchedly peripheral person: for all his intellect he remained just where he had been, in the same café chair, with the same cup of coffee in front of him. The man didn't even look any older. When they were both young, Gaston had worn an air of maturity that made him seem older than his years; now time had slipped by him.

'So what are you intending to do, now that you are back in Paris?' Gaston asked. He winked at one of his coterie of admiring girls, as if promising her fun.

'Oh,' Lucien said, 'I'm starting a magazine.' He hadn't known this was his intention. 'Would you care to write for me?'

Gaston blew smoke out of his nostrils.

'I hardly think,' he said, 'that our politics are still sympathetic. I take it there will be politics. You're not talking of a purely' – Lucien caught the inverted commas that enclosed the word – 'purely literary paper.'

'Oh no,' he said, 'I think that would be impossible now.'

'Well,' Gaston spread butter on his bread, 'there you are,' he said. 'I agree with you on that point – naturally – but I am told that you have become a friend – disciple was the word employed – of Maurras. I hardly think we could discover common ground.'

'Disciple was the wrong word. I admire Monsieur Maurras. I find much of what he has to say interesting. Nevertheless I don't believe his politics are applicable. We have to deal in possibilities.'

'Absolutely.'

'Which in my view rules out not only Maurras, but Marx also. And as for our incompatibility, yes, I grant you that. It's precisely why I should wish to have contributions from you in my magazine. I seek to establish a forum for serious discussion. I'm no preacher with a message of salvation. And I remember, Gaston, how incisively you used to be able to write, though I regret to have to say that in the sort of magazines where I discover your recent writings, I find an atmosphere which does not encourage you to produce your most intelligent work.'

'But who are you to judge intelligence? How can you hope to do so when you have no understanding of history?'

'Oh come, there is more than one form of history, Gaston.'

'No, this is something to which I don't have to listen. But I have no wish to be ungenerous. I cannot write for you myself. But there is a young lady here who will, I am sure, be delighted to do so, and whom you will find more agreeable to your sentimental-romantic taste . . .'

And he gestured to a thin girl with a beaky nose.

'Mathilde is a poet who finds even Surrealism what is it you find Surrealism, my dear . . ?'

The girl lit a cigarette.

'As self-indulgent as Marxism.'

'There you are. Isn't that quaint? Mathilde, allow me to introduce Lucien de Balafré. Lucien: Mathilde Dournier.'

'That was how I met him,' Mathilde told me some twenty years later. 'In an atmosphere of mockery.'

Do you recall Mathilde, Hugh? She was that woman who had defended my father at that appalling dinner-party given by Mrs Fernie. I had not spoken to her on that occasion, being far too embarrassed. But sometime in my dead years, being in Paris on business, I encountered her again, and, remembering her gallantry at Mrs Fernie's table, on an impulse introduced myself, and proposed lunch.

She shied away. I persisted. I told her it would mean much to me. Her hand shook as I spoke. At last she consented.

'But not lunch,' she said, 'I am never out and about in the middle of the day.'

'Dinner then.'

'No,' she said again. 'I can't bear the idea of meeting someone for a meal. It's something I haven't done for too many years. But if you'd like to give me a glass of wine, then I'll talk to you.'

She directed me to a workers' café near Les Halles. It was a mean sort of place half-full of men in blue overalls. There were pictures of boxers – one the late Marcel Cerdan – on the smoke-stained walls. One or two of the clients eyed me when I entered. She was sitting in a corner. She wore a thick black jersey and black trousers, and her nails hadn't been painted or cleaned for several days. They were cracked too.

'I can't tell you how I am regretting this,' she said, 'I never go out.'

'What about that reception I met you at?'

'That was different,' she said, but didn't explain why, and called the waiter and asked him to bring two *gros rouges*.

'If I had known you at that dinner-party,' she said, 'it might have been different. But now – anyone will tell you, I'm just a drunk.'

And she knocked back her wine and at once called for another.

'There's no need to be nervous,' I said: a silly remark.

She looked at me and didn't speak. As for me, I didn't know where to begin. The whole thing was absurd. I had no interest in my father. Perhaps I had merely been curious about this woman who disrupted a stuffy party in his defence. And now she turned out to be 'just a drunk'.

'I wasn't in love with him,' she said. 'You must know that. There were people who said he had mistresses, even then, and some thought I was one of them. But it wasn't like that. Our relations were those of editor and protégée. He had a real talent as an editor. You remember that dreadful Philippe Torrance, at the party where we met? Lucien made him, just as I said then. Philippe's writings were crude, bombastic, utterly absurd in their egotism; yet Lucien saw below the surface. Oh yes, he had true genius. I myself owed so much to him, that is why I am seeing you now.'

'I scarcely knew him myself,' I said.

'Perhaps nobody knew him, not really. He only allowed us to see aspects of him.'

And then, ignoring the second glass of wine for which she had called, she leapt to her feet and, knocking against one of the tables, fled from me. A laugh followed her out of the bar.

But a few weeks later, I had a letter from her – and how it found its way to my London address I don't know. Here however it is.

Document 7: Letter from Mathilde Dournier, 11 May, 1959

I read in the newspapers yesterday about a case of torture in Algeria, and, no sooner had I done so than I found myself crouched on all fours in the toilet, vomiting like a dog. Then I lay on my bed, realised that I had no money, that there was only one bottle of wine in the apartment, and that I had exhausted my supply of morphine.

So there it is, I said to myself: in Algeria the flower of the French Army, of the officer corps, are applying electrodes to the genitals of Arab boys, and here in this mean room, for which I owe two months' rent, I am almost entirely without the means of oblivion.

Therefore I am emitting this letter, to the son of my only love and my patron, in the hope – which is a word I have abandoned – that somehow or other he will find it serviceable, if it should ever find him.

Ah me, it is a confession, the record of the death of talent, and, I suppose, some would say, evidence of obsession.

I do not know where to begin and I do not know if I can bring this to a conclusion. As the morphine ebbs away, I grow ever more confused and nervous.

Let me start with the colour 'grey', which is the colour of the city, of my dreams and of the suit which Lucien was wearing. And I am a grey woman now, whose life is measured out in café saucers. But I wasn't then. I used to dress in red. Flaming red blouses and even skirts. He joked about that: 'Clothes are one thing, politics another.' That was the nearest to a joke I ever heard from him. He wasn't a laugher. I liked that. So much of my life had been passed among folk who saw a laugh in everything, and I was tired of such falsity. Humour is the devil's device to encourage us to tolerate the mess he has made of God's world, and the mischief he does there. The Christian view of life without God is tragic. I insisted on that to Lucien, and he did not deny me.

But I am rambling. I intended to set this out for you in orderly fashion. So let me try again. At the beginning.

I was so tired of Gaston Hunnot. For two years I had thought him wonderful, so wonderful I all but let him enter my bed. I stopped short of that because I have never been able to bear being touched. One of the things I adored about Lucien was that he never touched me, he was as fastidious as me.

Gaston tried to corrupt me. He was like so many in France then – why do I say only 'then'? – a corrupter by nature. How deep was his Communism? I could never decide, have never been able to. It pleased him to be a rebel, but such an established one. He knew he was certain always to have a new succession of disciples every year, a little claque of bourgeois innocents who liked the idea of making society rock. Hunnot played the Bohemian, but he lived in a *pension* and never failed to pay the rent. Why should he have failed? He had his salary as well as whatever he gained from his articles, many of which, I must tell you, were in fact written by the disciples, Gaston merely revising them and adding those characteristic turns of phrase which we called – admiringly – *Hunnotismes*. Oh, we were so proud of the Master's *Hunnotismes*.

But I was different. I found nothing amusing in his painless Bohemianism, though I tried to persuade myself that I did. Far from it.

I knew what poverty was. I knew how the aroma of the first soup for two days could trouble the stomach. My poor widowed mother was a shop assistant. She suffered from ulcers, and we had often literally neither food nor money in the house. And then, whereas Gaston's claque were dilettantes, I was a true poet. Poetry in those days burned me up inside. And they laughed: 'Mathilde writes such strange stuff, as if she had read nothing after 1880.'

But Lucien, who had more taste in his little finger than all of them in their gross bourgeois bodies, knew this from the start. He read one of my poems, and said, 'something here', and took a batch away and then called me to the office he had taken – he sent a *pneu* in fact – and said to me, 'It's absurd no one has heard of you . . .'

No one had ever spoken to me like that before. No one had believed in me. His office was like him. You would never have guessed he was a rich man. The furniture was heavy and very obviously from a second-hand dealer, not the best kind of dealer either. And there were steel engravings of official ceremonies on the walls, and a framed photograph of his father in his officer's uniform. I found that touching, none of the *Hunnotistes* would admit that the Army deserved honour. But my own father had been killed at the Marne, and I, who had never known him, knew, from my mother, that he should be honoured.

That first day Lucien said:

'One thing I must tell you, nobody deserves anything which he has not earned. And something else: the love of pleasure and the capacity to nourish resentment are closely allied.'

If only he could have seen that they were united in Philippe Torrance. Torrance was another of Hunnot's disciples. He was indeed one whom Gaston was eager to shed. There was something insidious about him which disturbed Gaston's complacency. And so he passed him on to Lucien; and Lucien welcomed him and made his name.

Somebody once said: 'I don't understand why you publish that Torrance. Surely you know that he is a Communist.'

'Oh,' Lucien replied, 'I'm not ignorant of that. How could I be? He shouts it from the rooftops of Paris. But it's not his cries from the rooftops which interest me, it's the murmurings he brings of his boyhood in Le Havre. Now they are tender and original, it's the way he catches the shadowy yellow light of November afternoons on the quays and overhears the conversations in his father's drapery shop.'

Everything in fact which Torrance came himself to despise . . .

Do you know, Monsieur, writing of your father, I hear his voice with the rolled 'r' and it comforts me, I almost forget that the morphine is finished.

And then I remember how Torrance betrayed him, and I pour myself a glass of red wine, and curse him. I saw him on television the other day, so pleased with himself.

One day I remember your mother came to the office. That was a surprise. Though he always talked of her in tones of respect, we had gathered that they were incompatible. Hunnot of course had made it his business to know that – he used to say that the efficacy of the Party depended on the knowledge of the private lives of its enemies, and would pronounce this with that laugh like a hyena which I so disliked. All the same we believed him, he was always very convincing.

So – but you wonder why I should have been there. The fact was that your saintly father, having learned of my circumstances, said to me:

'But my poor girl, you can't work at your poetry if you are exhausted by a day behind the counter' – for, following the example of my poor mother, I had taken refuge behind a counter, since it was a clothes shop I worked in – me, with my lack of taste and absolute lack of interest in dress – where I was worked off my feet by the proprietrix, a stout, but not ill-natured, Jewess with dyed yellow hair.

'No,' he said, 'you can't do that. I know: you must become an assistant editor.' So I spent my days correcting proofs and writing letters to our contributors soliciting copy, and I must tell you, I greatly preferred it. I was happy, for the first time in my life. I felt I was part of something which mattered.

But it was obvious that your mother didn't belong there. Quite the reverse. I could tell from her silly little hat and the way she tugged a fur stole round her neck that she was incurably frivolous, and that she had come to make trouble for Lucien. He knew it too, though he greeted her with grave courtesy. He even introduced me as his 'invaluable assistant'.

I could see that she had never heard of me, and this proved to me that they were incompatible. That is not conceit on my part. But I knew how he regarded my poetry – oh, it still warms me to remember how he would speak of it – and it was evident that he had never so much as mentioned my name to her. He was devoted to the magazine, he really believed that it was the first thing of importance he had ever done or made, and she flicked dust off his desk, and said,

'Really, ducky, does everything you touch have to be so tatty?'

He wasn't offended, for he had this amazing ability to refuse to take offence, but I am sure he was hurt. He knew, you understand, that he had married the wrong woman.

Let me tell you something which may help you to understand this remarkable man and the times in which he lived.

I have never been much interested in public affairs, believing that a poet's real life goes on in the head. Poems are made with words, as Mallarmé told Degas, not with ideas, but there are also poets who do not write verse. Of such the two poets of modern Paris and our modern times are René Clair and Georges Simenon. That surprises you, that I should admire two such lightweight artists: you have no right to be surprised, for you know nothing about me, and preconceptions are always wrong. Torrance despised them, I must tell you that, partly because it embarrassed him that Simenon should have given his name to one of Maigret's inspectors. But that is not the point, which is rather that the first half of the decade before the war belongs, despite everything, to Clair, and it is still, despite everything – the unemployment, the memories of 1914 – a city lit by the sun, where the evenings are mild, fragrant and full of joyous possibility. But Simenon's Paris is not like that; it is sombre and a place where life is drawn in behind shutters. Well, Paris belonged to Clair till the mood soured after the Stavisky Affair, and then to Simenon; it was no longer a city of make-believe. And your mother, this light and frivolous Polly whom I saw only that once, plucking her fur stole so delicately around a pale and slender neck, belonged to the films of René Clair, which, though shot – naturally – in black and white – nevertheless still possess for me a rosy glow; but your poor and admirable father, taking the burden of an unforgiving future upon himself, recognising that obsession is the inescapable condition of the serious man today, why, he is of the Simenon period, which, I say, is where, despite my reverence for Clair, I belong myself.

Do you understand these divagations? Or do they seem to you the demented warbling of an old drunk and morphine addict?

Ah, but your father would not have despised my condition. He would have understood: 'Reality,' he observed once, 'is painful for those of us who face the future with our eyes open. But my dear Mathilde, we must always be ready to engage the Minotaur, even in the labyrinth built for him.'

You will forgive this long letter, which is written out of love and respect, by one who reveres your father's memory and would wish you to do so also.

CHAPTER ELEVEN

Document 8:

Memorandum by Lucien de Balafré, December 31, 1936

THIS YEAR HAS been the most momentous, and the most useful, of my life. I have established my magazine *L'Echo de l'Avenir* as one of the most influential and most highly regarded in France. Tributes to its authority and integrity have poured in from all sides, and the attacks which have been made on it have come from disreputable quarters and have therefore only enhanced its prestige. For the first time in my life I am regarded as being of account. I must guard against vanity, I whose previous tendency has been towards self-deprecation.

And I have found a father, who is also a hero, and one who has supplanted my adolescent tendency to look to Monsieur Maurras for advice and comfort.

I still tremble when I think of the audacity of my approach. At one of our weekly luncheon parties at which we discuss ideas for future articles in the magazine, the talk turned, naturally enough, in this year of the Popular Front, in which Hitler has also reconquered the Rhineland, towards the notion of a whole number of the magazine devoted simply and terribly to the idea of imminent crisis.

'Which one of us,' young Louis Deverger said, 'is not disturbed by the sense that the Four Horsemen of the Apocalypse are once again riding round the encampment of civilisation. It's like a Western, we have made a corral of our wagons, and we await destruction. I tell you, thinking like this the other morning – no, thinking is the wrong word, sniffing their presence in the thin air of a cold morning – I cut myself shaving, a deep two-inch cut.'

And one after another, everyone at the table recounted a similar apprehension; even Mathilde, who has no interest in politics, confessed that she dreamed of bodies twisted round barbed wire.

'Is it true,' I asked, 'that we live in fear?'

There was a silence, and the feeling of shame hung over all of us. The mood became foggy as the November afternoon. Louis crumbled his bread-roll. Even Philippe Torrance had nothing to say.

'But in that case,' I said, 'our crisis is moral, not material.'

'There is only one man,' young Louis said, 'who can write on this subject with the authority which France longs to hear; and that is the Marshal.'

And so I resolved to approach him.

He received me in the study of his apartment at number 8, Place de Latour-Maubourg; a Spartan room, with no fire, though the afternoon was cold, with sullen clouds hanging over the leafless trees. I felt obliged to stand to attention while I was introduced; no one else has ever had that effect on me. He listened very carefully while I explained why I had come; all the while he made notes in writing with a pencil on a thick yellow pad. Once he asked me to speak more slowly, but that was all he said while he heard me out. Once he licked the point of his pencil like a tradesman – I have seen the same gesture from a carpenter to whom I was giving instructions.

Then he asked me to sit down. His secretary, who had stood silently by, indicated a straight-backed leather chair losing some of its stuffing at the corners. The Marshal ordered the secretary to leave the room. He fixed me with his gaze. In that dim light I could not be certain of the colour of his eyes, and previously I had only seen him on parade; but their lucidity had a remarkable effect on me. I felt that he knew me utterly. I knew I was in the presence of a true father.

Then, as if he divined my thoughts, he said to me: 'Your father was Etienne de Balafré, Major in the X Infantry, killed at Verdun, October 16. Is that correct?'

'It is, Marshal.'

Of course I realise that this display of knowledge only means that he was well-briefed, that he had his staff do their homework. Only a fool would fail to understand that, and we all know that when Napoleon during an inspection would recognise a man as having fought with him at Marengo or Austerlitz, he was only able to do so because he had taken care to be supplied with a list of such veterans and an assurance of their exact position in the ranks. But the veteran did not realise this, and took the Emperor's recognition as a sign of his humanity and intellect. And at this moment I felt the same about the Marshal, who said:

'I confess I cannot escape the conviction that I stand *in loco parentis* to the orphans of Verdun. And now you wish me to write an article for your magazine, of which I have seen the two copies which you have been kind enough to send. I approve of them, though many of the contributions are too clever for a simple soldier like myself. But I approve the magazine's tenor.'

He fell silent, and I respected his evident wish for silence. Then he stretched out his hand and tinkled a little brass bell.

'We would like some coffee,' he told the maid, and then fixed his eyes on the door closing behind her as if following the sway of her hips along the corridor. He did not speak until she had returned with the coffee and laid it on the desk before him. He stroked the corner of his moustache; the brown blotches of age marked the back of his hand.

'I don't write articles any more,' he said. 'I haven't time at the moment. But I will talk to you, and you can write it yourself and attach my name to it. Of course I shall want to approve it before it is published. As to the style, remember mine is clear and distinctive. There must be a central theme which sustains the text from start to finish. Few paragraphs, and remember that the sentences must be properly formed; subject, verb, object. Remember too please that I deplore adjectives. They make writing furry. I don't object to a tone of irony. I often allow myself irony, though I forbid it to my subalterns. In my view, irony works from top to bottom. It is after all an expression of superiority.'

Then he smiled. It was the first smile he had given me, like the sun emerging to light up the winter afternoon.

'But we haven't discussed the subject.'

'This issue of the magazine,' I said, 'will be devoted to the general crisis which threatens civilisation.'

'You refer to the danger of war?'

'And worse, Marshal.'

'Yes, you are correct in that. There can be worse things than war, though war, as every soldier knows, is terrible. Some of my friends tell me that Herr Hitler does not want war, because he fought as a private soldier and then a Corporal and so knows its utmost horrors. But I tell them, no, for two reasons. In the first place, the private soldier does not know the horror of responsibility. He has not ordered men, good men like your father, to necessary death. And in the second place, the Corporal always believes that the General Staff are idiots, he believes that he could correct their blunders or avoid repeating them. He does not realise that blunders are an inescapable feature of war, because choice in military affairs lies generally between the bad and the worse. The defence of Verdun was appalling; failure to defend it would have been intolerable.'

Outside in the square the light was fading to a dusky yellow and the plane trees stood out bare as figures in no-man's-land recorded by the war artists. The Marshal made no move to light the lamp which stood on the desk, and in the gathering gloom the features of his face became indistinct, Gothic, mediaeval.

'Nevertheless,' he said, 'there are indeed worse things than war. Peace can be more terrible. When I say that I do not speak as one who welcomes war, merely as one who observes that in war man loses his Self, which in peace too easily rules him. The subject of France and the French nation and our problem which you must elaborate in the article, the nature of our crisis, is not material but spiritual. If France is at a low ebb, it is because we have put enjoyment of the fruits of our victory in 1918 before our duty to the country. This year, you know, I refused to take my place – the place which is mine by a right which I have earned – in the official grandstand for the parade on the Quatorze, because, as I have said publicly, the front rows will be filled with all those politicians who have for the past twenty years been denouncing the Army and the spirit of the Army, and advocating renunciation and surrender. It is time to speak out. I am not, I must tell you, altogether opposed to Blum and his Popular Front. Blum is at least demanding discipline of his supporters. I do not agree with his politics, but he is a man, he has a fist. Most of our politicians are no better than old women, and, though I honour and love women, there is no place for old women – of either sex – in the government of a nation.'

What is truly extraordinary about the Marshal is his serenity. It is the serenity of a man who has suffered much, and learned the lessons of life.

'There are no rewards and many duties,' he said.

The Marshal is the true moral chief of the nation. He has been close to our misery. And he confronts the worst of experience with that level gaze. Are his eyes blue or grey? I don't know. But they are candid. He incarnates the strong, calm and humane virtues of eternal France. If it were not absurd, I would say I am in love with him. No, 'in love' is wrong, ridiculous, a debased term. What I mean is an emotion much closer to the love of God. I am ready to put myself and my conscience entirely in his trust.

Will the day come when I have to act on that commitment?

CHAPTER TWELVE

Document 9: Copy of letter from Lucien de
Balafré to Count Rupprecht von Hülenberg

October 4, 1938

MY DEAR RUPERT: It was as ever a pleasure to hear from
you, and on this occasion a relief also. I understand that you
feel the need to be cautious; we live in times when each of us
may be convicted out of his own mouth, so rapidly, in-
comprehensibly, and unpredictably, does the wheel of
Fortune, to which History itself is bound, make its revolutions.

It is a relief that there is no war. To have fought over an
artificial country like Czechoslovakia would have been an
absurdity, especially if we had gone to war in order to force
Germans to remain under the government of Slavs in a
State created by the ideologues of Versailles on the prin-
ciple of national self-determination.

Nevertheless for several weeks fear of war sweetened my
appreciation of my daily life, while the thought that in such
a war you and I will necessarily find ourselves on opposite
sides was bitter.

And it will come. These idiots of politicians talk of having
achieved peace in our time, even peace with honour, but
you and I know this cannot be true. We have talked often of
the nature of the forces which move the world, and we can
recognise when appetites are insatiable. Believe me, my
dear, that all which has been achieved at Munich is a pause.
It is one which, I fear, France will not know how to use. I
have had conversations with the Marshal on this subject. He
believes that we have let ourselves be lulled by material
pleasures and desires. Though he has no more respect for
the masters of your country than I have myself – or certain
of my dearest friends whose names I shall not mention – he
recognises nevertheless, as I do myself, and as any thinking
man must – that the Führer has given Germany a sense of
spiritual purpose, by which I mean that men in your
country are now prepared to put national interests above

their personal wishes. As the Marshal says, 'The world is governed by ideas,' and in Germany there is a ruling idea and in France none.

The source of that idea I will not mention. The Marshal attacks the lack of seriousness in French life which, he says, 'causes all our divisions'. He is perhaps simple in that judgement because I recognise that true seriousness such as you possess yourself may well lead to even more bitter divisions. He believes that when the politicians have brought France to the brink of the abyss, then they will turn to him.

Pray God they do so before then.

But these grave matters are things to be discussed in that warm dialogue which we have been fortunate enough always to enjoy. So let me turn to a happier and more social note. Polly and I propose to take a winter-sport holiday in Switzerland at New Year. We would both like you to join us.

And send you love,

Lucien

(*Note scribbled below*)

Dearest Rup, Haven't read all L has said because I can see it is dreary politics, and I leave that to my sister. But do come please. Too long since we have seen you. Love and kisses, Polly.

In those days winter sports were still the preserve of the few, and at Zermatt where Lucien and Polly had been several times they were sure to meet those whom they knew and only people of their own class. There was nothing remarkable that Rupert should join them there, though he himself told Lucien that he could have wished that the invitation had been less explicit.

'What do you mean, my dear?'

They were sitting in the hotel foyer drinking brandy. Polly had retired to bed, announcing that she would be stiff the next day and she couldn't bear it if she was short of sleep also.

'This mountain air makes me yawn my head off. Heaven knows why these idiot doctors call it bracing.'

Rupert held up his glass to the light. He had aged in the two years since their last meeting. His youthful freshness had withered, his blond hair was receding from the temples, which gave him an unexpected craggy look, and lines had gathered under his eyes and at the corners of his mouth. 'He looks as old as I do,' Lucien thought, and was pained by the realisation.

'It's a relief,' Rupert said, 'to be free, out of Germany. Isn't it a terrible thing to say of your Fatherland?'

'It is not how I could imagine feeling about France.'

He looked round the big *belle époque* hotel. A thin dragonfaced waiter flicked crumbs off a table with a corner of his napkin. Even the potted palms looked ready for sleep.

'No,' Rupert said, 'but France is different, a mother or a mistress. Perhaps both, thus fulfilling what the good Dr Freud of Vienna would suggest is every man's ideal: to make a mistress of his mother. But Germany at the moment is a rather heavy father, a tyrant, not the kind you can respect. It's as if your father turned out to be a nasty small boy who pulls the wings off flies. What I meant when I said that I wished your invitation had been less explicit is that I am quite sure I am watched, sure my correspondence is opened.'

'As bad as that?'

'As bad as that.'

'But why?'

Rupert sighed. He lit another American cigarette. He had been smoking one after another since they sat down. A little tic flickered at the corner of his mouth.

'People employ these categories of Left and Right, which are meaningless. The true opposition is between decency and indecency. I'm on the decent side, and my closest colleagues are Generals whom the rest of Europe ignorantly stigmatises as warmongers. Do you know, Lucien, if that ass Chamberlain had not flown to Munich, my friends were ready to arrest Hitler?'

'And now?'

'And now of course he is a hero. The German people worship him, and believe it is on account of his genius that we have avoided war. Do not be deceived by the press. Few in Germany desire war. That is true even of those of us who, like myself, have personal reasons for believing we might benefit from war in the east.'

Lucien thought, as he often did, of those winter plains stretching to nowhere and of the wild geese flying across the evening sky.

He said: 'Have you considered emigration?'

'Naturally, and rejected it. I am a German. I must remain in Germany. When there is a war I shall fight, but I shall fight on two fronts, against Hitler and for Germany.'

He laid his hand on Lucien's arm.

'There is no one except those who think like me to whom I could say that but you.'

The waiter opened the great double doors to clear the air. A breeze stirred the fans. Looking through the doorway and into the night, Lucien saw only a deep and intense blackness. Then a sleigh passed with a jingle of harness.

'The question is no longer,' he said, 'where to be happy, but how to remain oneself.'

'The question,' Rupert said, 'is whether decency is possible.' He drank his brandy.

'That waiter wants to go to bed. I think we should let him.'

'One thing I haven't mentioned. Polly's sister Aurora is joining us here. Does that distress you?'

'Little Adolf's friend? No, on the contrary, it intrigues me.'

The first attraction of a ski resort is that the world stops there; Zermatt itself is a cul-de-sac. The day after Aurora arrived there was a heavy fall of snow. The railway line was blocked, the telephone wires brought down. Only the radio, to which they did not choose to listen, would have connected them with the outer world. They ignored it however, preferring for a few days in that winter of '38–'39 to pretend that they had no lives beyond the valley. In the evenings after an early dinner they went to the town cinema. The programme changed every third night. They showed mostly American films. Some were dubbed rather badly, others played in American English, for there were of course many English speakers among the holidaymakers. They would see the same film in both versions, and return to the hotel humming Irving Berlin tunes. Fred Astaire was popular and Rupert would do a soft-shoe shuffle along the snowy pavements. Then he would stop, point to the sky, link his arms with Polly and croon a ballad to the moon. Back in the hotel they would drink coffee and kirsch, and eat *Sachertorte*. The night they saw *Top Hat* was the last time Lucien and Polly made love.

They were all highly keyed. Even Polly, for whom the whole of life was normality, experienced a sense that these few days were, in some way which she couldn't understand, special; they were like the little hush that can come over a forest before the wind rises. For the rest of his life Lucien remembered them as the last time he felt safe.

He knew of course that the safety was illusory. Nothing they felt now could obliterate what was going to happen. They were behaving indeed like the man who on the point of disgrace or bankruptcy or arrest on some vile criminal charge, nevertheless goes out and gets drunk, picks up a woman, or just laughs with friends, as if by such simple and normal actions he can arrest the future; yet who knows of course that he is not even postponing it; that it is all pretence.

Polly and Rupert sat on the terrace of a bar and let the morning sun warm their faces and watched Lucien and Aurora on the slopes.

'It's a shame you can't ski now,' she said.

'Dicky knee . . .'

'Not my thing ever. Skating, now, I used to love to skate. D'you know I could have been a champion, they wanted me to train for the Olympics, but Mummy said "No, school first." So here I am, no skating champion and absolutely uneducated. Lucien's good, though. He goes at it the way he used to ride a horse, when I fell in love with him.'

'So's Aurora. She's very good.'

They watched her swoop down the slopes, blonde hair flying behind her, for in those days of course no one bothered with protective headgear.

'No wonder the Führer dotes on her. Is "dote" the right word?'

'Last year's word, Rup, no one would use it now.'

'Ah well, like me.'

'Not like you.'

'Like the Führer's taste then. He thinks of himself as the modern man, but really you know he's something out of Grimm's Fairy Tales. That's what's so frightening.'

'Maybe Aurora is too.'

'The enchanted princess.'

'Sort of thing.'

She looked up the valley. The pine-needles shone golden in the sun, like a false future.

'Are you still in love with me, Rup?'

'Oh,' he said, looking at her soft mouth and the blue eyes that glistened in the mountain air, 'I wish I was, Polly. But no, I can't lie to you.'

'That proves you're not, if you can't lie.'

'I'm sorry. But the way things are now, the way they are going to be . . .'

'You haven't turned pansy, have you? Maybe you have. Most Germans are pansies, aren't they, especially the tough ones?'

He placed his hands on hers.

'You're laughing at me, aren't you? The English sense of humour.'

'That's right, I'm laughing at you. The English sense of humour, God help us. I didn't really mean it, Rup.'

'Well, I am not offended in any case. But no, I have not turned homosexual. It doesn't attract me. No, Polly, it is simply that there is no place for love in my life now. I don't dare. I have only so much courage and that must be directed elsewhere. Do you know what is really wicked about the Nazis? It is that they deny the reality of private life, of individual life. Everything for the Fatherland – monstrous. Even those who are against them must be totalitarian. So, no, Polly, I'm not in love with you now. I love you of course, always, but at a distance.'

'Ah well, too bad, old thing. Now was your chance.'

'What do you mean?'

'I'm leaving Lucien, you see.'

'Oh,' he said, and took out his cigar-case, cut the end off a cigar with a pen-knife, and lit it. He puffed out smoke, thick, blue-grey, aromatic.

'It's because,' she said, and sighed, 'because . . . we've come to the end. I suppose he's like you, I hadn't thought of that, he has no time for me now. I used to love his seriousness and now I can't stand it, simple as that. Shall we have some champagne?'

'Have you told him?'

'Not yet . . .'

'I think he suspects,' he said, and summoned the waiter. 'I'm sure he knows, in fact.'

Rupert was right. Lucien had seen it coming. He was surprised only to discover that it hurt him. He had found himself so often exasperated by Polly in recent years that he had often looked forward to the moment when she would tell him it was all over. When she interrupted a serious dialogue with some piece of whimsy, or when she showed herself bored, 'fed-up to the back teeth', with matters that he knew to be of the first importance, he had even wished for it. He had found himself rehearsing the conversation in which they would annul their marriage, and in these rehearsals he always managed to be judicious, kind and superior. He had so frequently told himself that he had made a mistake in marrying her, that they weren't fundamentally suited, that it was irritating to find now, when he was on the point of regaining his freedom, that the line which thumped in his brain was Colette's: 'Your pretty wife is much wiser than you. She knows that the correct way of making an omelette is much more important than a theory of economics.' 'But it's not a matter of a theory of economics,' he wanted to cry, 'it's a question of whether civilisation survives, of whether France survives, of whether, in short, there will be any omelettes.' But it would be absurd to put it

to her like that. It was better to let things go. If only, however, she
would admit that he was in the right. But he knew she could never
do that, and after all wasn't that innocent certainty that she could
not be wrong, that therefore she was always justified, one of the
things which he had loved in her? All the same, he wrote in his
journal: 'If I ever love again it will be a woman with whom it is
possible to hold a conversation. It has been my misfortune to
adore a woman who is not my type. But how could she have ever
thought me hers? Well, we shall both be better off apart. The boy
too will be better for the time being out of France, for I cannot
share the certainty that the Maginot Line will protect us. After all,
my own personal Maginot Line has been breached.'

'Has Polly spoken to you?' he asked Rupert.

Rupert didn't pretend not to understand, merely nodded his
head.

'If things in the world had been different . . .' he said.

'I don't know. Perhaps it has been wrong from the start. We are
not, when you come to think of it, each other's type.'

'So what will you do?' Aurora asked.

'Go home to Mummy and Daddy, I suppose. Collect little
Etienne on the way, of course.'

'How does Lucien feel about that?'

'Do you know, darling, I've only just realised that I don't know
what Lucien has ever felt about anything. I've been an absolutely
blind bat.'

'They'll be pleased anyway.'

'No they won't. Daddy thinks Lucien's the tops. It's stopped
him from making a fool of himself.'

'I do wish Daddy would see the point about the Führer. He's a
terrific friend of England, you know.'

'What you don't understand,' Aurora lifted her glass of champagne, 'is that the Reichsmarschall is an utter kitten.'

Then, for the first time in three days, they heard the telephone
ring at the hotel desk.

'We're back in the world,' Rupert said.

Lucien escorted us – Polly and Mrs Thompson, my governess –
to the Gare du Nord. We rode there in silence. There were grey
skies and the people in the street all kept their eyes to the ground.
The station was not very busy and we had a long wait standing on
the platform till the train was ready to depart. He must have had a
last message for me, something significant, but I don't remember.

His moustache tickled my cheek as he kissed me. I think he told me to look after my mother. I remember I told him that she was going to get me a spaniel puppy. 'That will be nice,' he said, 'treat it kindly.' Then they talked so that I couldn't hear. A whistle blew. Mrs Thompson hustled me into the train. They embraced, as people might who expected to see each other in a few weeks. He stood on the platform till the train was out of sight. Mrs Thompson pulled me back in. 'You don't want your head taken off, do you?'

It rained in the Channel, but the crossing was calm, though Mrs Thompson was sick despite the pills she had taken.

Lucien walked back to his empty apartment. He felt flat. He wondered what Rupert was doing in Berlin.

CHAPTER THIRTEEN

LUCIEN LAY ON his back just beyond the parapet and watched larks swoop and soar above him. He turned on his side and the country rolled towards the German lines; there were poppies and other blue and pink flowers, which he could not name, among the grasses. He knew that if he stood up and looked back he would see peasants ploughing the stubble fields behind their heavy chestnut horses which the Army had not commandeered. A reconnaissance plane flew over, its engine throbbing. He stood up and waved to the pilot. Then there was silence. He lay down again and waited. His mouth felt sour and dry from the single glass of wine he had drunk at lunch. In the mess two or three of his brother officers would have finished off the bottle and would now be downing nips of cognac or armagnac as they played their interminable games of cards. What else was there for them to do?

He pulled a volume of verse from his pocket and began to read, mouthing the lines to himself:

> Mon coeur, lasse de tout, même de l'espérance,
> N'ira plus de mes voeux importuner le sort;
> Prêtez-moi seulement, vallon de mon enfance,
> Un asile d'un jour pour attendre la mort . . .

Of course, he thought, it is always tempting to suppose that other times were simpler than our own, to dismiss such murmurings as self-indulgent affectation, even while they continue to appeal powerfully to our own modern sensibility.

The afternoon sky was pale, trees touched with gold. The smell of wet grass and heavy earth seemed good. He shifted on the groundsheet again, and pressed his nose to the clay.

Voici l'étroit sentier de l'obscure vallée . . .

The path was always narrow, the valley dark; naturally enough, for we each trod a lonely and frightening measure. When he watched the private soldiers, many of them only boys, he could not escape the feeling that they should rather be lying in hedgerows cradling their girls. But, across Europe, Poland was dying. 'Poland is the test,' the English poet Belloc, who talked so much of his French ancestry, had once said to him at a London dinner table. He remembered the cigars and brandy, and Belloc, a thickset man, dressed in black, with a curiously high thin voice, leaning over him, fuming, jabbing him in the ribs with two stubby fingers as he said again: 'Poland is the test.' Well, Poland itself was being tested now, cruelly tested, but that was not what the man had meant. Poland is the test for Europe, by which Belloc signified in an old-fashioned manner which appealed to Lucien, Christendom. He himself had never doubted the fact of Christendom; it was denied in those lines opposite.

Yet, for all that, it was a civil war too. All European wars were civil wars. Had he not learned in those Prussian marshes how the Teutonic Knights had carried Christendom to the East on the point of a lance?

The Sergeant who had welcomed him back to the regiment had said, 'Well, sir, it's got to be finished this time.'

He seemed to believe that, and he was a good man, admirable in his decent discipline, and one whom the boys respected. What were his thoughts as he composed himself to sleep? His breath had been heavy with wine when he told Lucien things had to be brought to a conclusion.

Just before leaving Paris, when he was already in uniform, he had bumped into Gaston Hunnot. Gaston looked him up and down. Lucien saw a sneer form.

'So you think I am playing at war, Gaston?'

'The whole of France is playing at war, and each of us wishes for a different conclusion.'

'What do you mean by that?'

'I mean that primarily each of us sees this war as a means of resolving personal difficulties. That is France today, a mere collection of personalities.'

As he spoke, he tapped the lamp-post with his cane. Lucien remembered that Gaston's newspaper had been closed down, as a result, it was thought, of an article which Aragon had written welcoming the Nazi-Soviet pact as offering the hope of European peace.

'And how will you occupy the war, Gaston?'

'I am writing a journal.'

'And isn't that somewhat egotistic?'

'No egotism is without value, so long as it is sincere. Then it can also be of enduring interest.'

Lucien was astonished to realise that Gaston welcomed the

outbreak of hostilities simply because it heightened his own awareness of his own feelings. Young boys would be killed so that Hunnot could observe his indifference to their deaths as a mark of his own superiority. He watched him limp away, more heavily than he used to: to divert any suggestion that he too should have been recalled to the colours?

But of course Hunnot was too old. Lucien was indeed too old himself. It had required persistence and the use of such influence as he had to bring him to this point where he lay, on a fine autumn afternoon, in front of the French lines watching the larks in the sky and a magpie swoop from a nearby copse.

Yet this ground too had been stained with blood – Hunnot's also, he must not forget that – and would be again.

Waiting. He had spent all his life waiting.

> *O Seigneur! J'ai véçu puissant et solitaire.*
> *Laissez-moi m'endormir du sommeil de la terre . . !*

It distressed him that he could find no language in which to speak to the private soldiers. He wanted them to know that he shared their fear of the future, their longing to be back home with their families – he whose family had torn itself from him – that he sympathised with their knowledge that reality consisted of the tram-ride to work in the morning, the game of cards in the café, the Sunday afternoons strolling hand-in-hand with their girls along the riverbank. And all he could do was comment on their drill and turn-out. He felt so much for them, and they saw him as almost an alien, someone who kept them up to the mark, who insisted that they paid attention to matters that were quite meaningless to them.

Not that it was much better as far as his fellow-officers were concerned.

After all, to talk of a death-wish, still more to fear that such possessed the nation, was merely fashionable nonsense.

Was a single magpie unlucky? He couldn't even remember that.

Weeks of waiting, of performing necessary tasks which were all part of preparation for the day when the waiting would end, when the grey uniforms would swarm towards them, to batter themselves against the impregnable fortress of their lines of defence.

'Of course they won't attack,' Major Delibes was accustomed to say, twirling his glass of Calvados. 'It would be madness. And we are not going to because our strategy is to remain on the defensive. So we have evolved the perfect strategy to make war obsolete: we refuse to move and they dare not. Take it from me, chaps, this joke-war will continue until . . .'

'Until what?' little Arquier, who admired Delibes, could be counted on to ask.

'Until we have to go home to Normandy to replenish our stock of Calvados,' someone said.

This was a new Lieutenant who had just joined them and whose name Lucien did not yet know. His intervention was thought presumptuous. Delibes smiled at him.

'It's easy to see, young fellow, that you don't know much about these things. I don't imagine you even understand what we are doing here.'

'No, tell me,' the Lieutenant said.

'We are performing a comedy. Hitler has no reason to wish to fight France, and, believe me, he has too much sense to think of doing so. That is why there is no action on the western front, unlike 1914. No, no, laddie, all his ambitions are in the east. Which is just as well, let me tell you, because if he knew how those scoundrels of Jewish-Socialist politicians had neglected the Army, he would be here tomorrow.'

'But I thought,' the Lieutenant said, 'that you had given it as your opinion that we would throw the Germans back, if they chose to attack.' He spoke in a modest, enquiring tone.

'Precisely.'

'Despite the way the politicians have neglected the Army?'

'Despite that, young man, I am a soldier of France, and I understand the spirit of France. It is indomitable. We shall triumph, if we have to.'

'If? Do you mean that you really think it will not come to a battle?'

'Why should it? Who wants this war? Not France, not Hitler. Only Jewish politicians, and those who have sentimental ideas about Poland, ideas which in this context of our present difficulties amount, in my opinion, to treason.'

Delibes seized the bottle of Calvados by the neck, almost as if it might have been a Jewish politician whom he wished to strangle, and tilted it towards his glass.

'No, no, young man,' he said, 'you have no need to be afraid. Things will arrange themselves, never fear.'

Hearing this officer, Lucien understood that the war would be lost. He had already seen the negligent manner in which Delibes supervised his men's training.

Later that night he sought out the young Lieutenant and tried to assure him that not all French officers were like Major Delibes.

'Of course I understand that, sir. Nevertheless I am afraid there are a good many who think like him.'

'Naturally,' Lucien said, 'nobody of sense wants war. That doesn't mean however that . . .'

He stopped, his fluency deserting him. He was unable to pretend to the young man that he was confident of victory.

'You're almost young enough to be my son,' he said. 'Let's just say it will be a long war in the course of which we shall doubtless suffer reverses before victory.'

'What I'm afraid of,' the Lieutenant said, 'is that we should have acted sooner. It seems to me that we are in danger of being left alone at the mercy of the enemy.'

They stepped outside. It had started to freeze. There was silence under a white moon. A windless night in which they could have been two men in a desert landscape.

'It will be a cold winter and a long one,' Lucien said. 'All we can do is whatever duty demands of us.'

It seemed strange to him to speak of duty after hearing Delibes. Fortunately the young Lieutenant appeared to find it natural enough.

'I find myself praying,' he said. 'I never thought I would do that. I was quite convinced that I had put aside any belief in God. It distressed my poor mother. And now . . .'

'This sky, this situation . . . there are moments in life which must convince us that God exists.'

'Do you think they feel like that on the other side?'

'Many of them do, Lieutenant,' Lucien said, thinking of Rupert.

Lucien knew that he was an object of interest and suspicion to his fellow-officers. Most were solid professional soldiers who had spent the last ten or fifteen or twenty years in provincial barracks. Only the Colonel was a veteran of the last war. None of the others had seen active service even in the colonies. They were puzzled by the determination Lucien had had to employ to return to the Army. Those who were reservists, recalled from their civilian occupations, were mostly resentful that he had chosen a course to which they had themselves reluctantly submitted. Then he lacked the easy camaraderie which could make life there tolerable. They thought him a snob and a prig. When he received a letter from the Madrid Embassy, where the Marshal was Ambassador, franked with the Marshal's own stamp, some were impressed, but more wondered if he was not in some sense a spy who would pass on reports about them to higher authority. Even if he wasn't a spy, he was clearly a pet of the War Office. A few however, Delibes among them, now began to try to ingratiate themselves with him, as someone who might advance their career. He disliked them for this.

All in all it made for a difficult atmosphere. The weather too turned bitterly cold. The troops were bored and indifferent to their duties. Morale was low. Lucien shared in the general mood of despondency.

The Marshal's letter did nothing to raise his spirits. Though reticent in speech, he was indiscreet in correspondence. He told Lucien that while he believed he was doing a useful job in Spain himself – it was necessary to convince Franco that France's struggle was 'a continuation of the Nationalist cause in the Civil War' – he was gloomy about the state of affairs in Paris. There was 'poor organisation' at the Ministry of War: 'Indeed, my friend, I must call it by the right name, which is anarchy. It does not surprise me. At my age few things do. The truth is that there is a notable lack of resolution in this Government, which prefers words to actions. Life in France has been too easy-going. The spirit of sacrifice is missing. To stimulate energy, which is sadly absent, there is nothing like suffering. And I fear we shall soon discover this.'

The old man's letters might have dismayed Lucien more, but for two things. The first was that he found himself in agreement with the Marshal's criticisms, and indeed fed them by relaying to him his own appreciation of the mood in the Army. (To this extent those of his brother officers who thought him a spy were quite correct.) Second, the Marshal hinted that he expected that he would be recalled from Madrid, 'sometime in the spring' to take part in war planning, 'though I shall refuse to have anything to do with cabinets of politicians whose influence has been so disastrous'. When that happened he would wish to make use of Lucien. 'Your lucidity, patriotism and intelligence are just what I need.' He added that while he understood Lucien's wish to take 'a direct, personal, manly and honourable' (no shortage of the despised adjectives there) part in the war, he must nevertheless 'nerve' himself to understand that the hour would arrive when he could serve France better, according to his special gifts, in another capacity. 'There are many brave officers, few wise counsellors.'

Lucien had become friendly with the young Lieutenant who had argued with Delibes. His name was Alain Querouaille, and he was Breton, with the reddish hair and pale skin often found there.

For Lucien his enthusiasm was invigorating. He was intelligent too, high-spirited; he confessed that he would have chosen to be an actor, but his mother, to whom he was devoted, was horrified by the suggestion.

'All the same,' he said, 'I intend to write plays, indeed I have had one performed, but only at a local festival, you understand.'

Despite his high spirits, Alain was pessimistic when they talked of the forthcoming battle.

'It's all very well for a fat imbecile like Delibes to talk about spirit, but the only spirit I connect with him is the Calvados he swigs. And look at the men. They are all under-trained and they don't trust their officers. Half of them don't even think we should be fighting – not when the Soviet Union is Germany's ally.'

'Not as many as half,' Lucien said. 'Only a few.'

'I would say half. We have the wrong Army for the wrong war, I'm sure of that.'

'We have perhaps no choice but to wait on the defensive. That is the penalty of democracy.'

'And half the officers wouldn't be unhappy to see a German victory.'

'Again surely not as many as half.'

Their arguments were circular, as men's usually are in such circumstances when one day repeats another.

Alain said: 'We are preparing to fight the last war, and I don't think the Germans are.'

Lucien argued against him, but he suspected the boy might be right. He was always ready to believe anyone younger than himself. Besides, there was something of Rupert in his new friend, though Alain's features were more fine-drawn and nervous.

'Don't you sense,' Alain said, 'a simmering undercurrent of self-hate in our Army. There are a good many officers who will be lucky not to receive a bullet in the back if they lead an advance. Perhaps that accounts for our Maginot-Line mentality.'

Lucien would have liked to disbelieve him.

He admired the boy's tact. Alain often talked about his own family, never asked about his. His grandfather had been a sea-captain, drowned somewhere in the Pacific. His mother had conceived a hatred of the sea.

'It's a tradition in my mother's family, but one we could not follow. Anyway, we have perhaps the wrong temperament, I don't know.'

There were two brothers and a sister. His elder brother was a notary in Rennes, the second a schoolteacher, while his sister

Anne had joined the administrative branch of the Ministry of Education.

'We are a very respectable family,' he said.

He passed Lucien a photograph.

'I took that last Christmas.'

He sighed.

'I wonder if we shall ever have another Christmas all together. Don't you think my mother has a remarkable face?'

Lucien nodded. He almost said, 'It's for mothers like yours that we are fighting,' but it would have been absurd and sentimental. It was a fifteenth-century face, from a stained-glass window. Loving and passive. All he could do was nod.

'Hervé is a bit of a fanatic.'

Alain indicated the thin-faced boy with a lock of dark hair falling over his left eye. He was fondling the ears of the spaniel which sat between his legs looking up at his face with an expression of adoration.

'Yes, he's a Breton nationalist. He's even taught himself Breton. We're all a bit worried about Hervé.'

But it was the girl who held Lucien's gaze. He couldn't tell why. She was not especially beautiful, though that might be the result of the quality of the photograph. But there was a promise of serenity there. What had he said to Rupert: 'It's my misfortune to have fallen in love with a woman who is not my type'?

'What colour are her eyes?'

'What colour are my sister's eyes? What an extraordinary question. They're blue or I think they are.'

'She has . . . an uncommon look to her.'

'She's an uncommon girl.'

He took back the photograph and replaced it in his wallet.

'You must think me an awful fool,' Alain said, 'pressing photographs of my family on you, just like a little private soldier. But we are very close.'

'Of course I don't think you a fool. I'm honoured. But you are quite right. People are doing just this all along the line. In the end, it's hard to distinguish between love of family and love of country.'

'I suppose one's family is a microcosm of the country.'

'Well, certainly,' said Lucien, the man who had lost his family, 'it's for the family that most men will fight.'

These months were a kind of limbo for him. He went through the motions of being a serving officer with such diligence as he could muster. He was far too proud not to do his work efficiently, but he knew that he had made a mistake in insisting on returning to the Army. He couldn't believe either that he might make a useful contribution to the war effort there, or indeed in the war effort itself. His diaries are full of doubts. Even the Colonel, whom he had admired at first, proved to be 'obstinate and old-fashioned to the point of imbecility. It is like serving in the Royal Army of 1788.'

In February he went to Paris on leave. The atmosphere of the city astonished him. At first he told himself it was because he had forgotten the sound of conversation, which was unfair to young Alain. But it wasn't that. It was rather that Parisians seemed to him to have become already indifferent to the war. It was a joke-war in which nothing was happening, and soon a peace would be agreed.

'After all,' a woman said to him, 'it was only about Poland, wasn't it, and now that Poland has been gobbled up by the Germans and the Bolsheviks, there seems little reason to continue to pretend that we have anything to fight about.'

She waved a cigarette-holder in his face, and he remembered from that gesture that she had been a friend always ready to encourage Polly in some frivolity.

When he met Marcel Pougier, he found him only able to speak of a young actor he had seen in a play.

'What I'm terrified of is that he will be called up. It wouldn't suit him at all.'

Lucien wondered how he had escaped call-up already.

He walked by the Seine. The hard frost held the sky motionless, blue-grey and shiny like a suit of armour. Birds huddled black on the black branches. Even the chestnut-sellers, round their braziers, stamped their feet to keep warm. The smell of the roasting chestnuts hung in the air. A hearse pulled by four black horses passed, its driver muffled to the ears. Sheets of ice had formed round the parapets of the bridges, supporting seabirds the colour of fog. Every now and then came an echoing creak as a barge broke through the ice. As night approached, the horns of the barges sounded melancholy as funeral music and the wretched tramps who slept under the bridges made their round of the dustbins collecting scraps of food and discarded newspapers with which to cover themselves.

But in the brasseries and cafés things were different. In the first weeks of the war, when he was last in Paris, many had been closed. Now their proprietors had accommodated themselves to the blackout. In the evening, tarts, assembling at street corners, swung gasmasks in their hands. There was a note of gaiety there once you were past the misted glass doors. Inside the babble of conversation rose: 'like incense' he said to himself. 'We talk, therefore we are.' In the Brasserie Lipp he watched men gobble sausages and fried potatoes as if their meal represented their last tomorrow. And yet, there, voice after voice asserted that of course the Germans would never come. 'But if they do,' he heard a stout red-cheeked man with stiff moustaches shout, 'it won't be a moment too soon to rid us of these damned Jews.' Was he oblivious of a party of very obvious Jews eating at the next table but one, or were his remarks directed particularly at them?

Lucien felt a hand laid on his sleeve. He turned to see a small man with a black beard whom he did not immediately recognise. Then he realised it was Léon-Paul Cebran, an essayist who had been an occasional contributor to *L'Echo de l'Avenir*.

'Lucien,' he said, 'so the future echoes more loudly.'

'I'm not sure that I understand what you mean.'

Léon-Paul smiled. Surely the beard was new, that was why he had failed to recognise him.

'What do I mean? Why, that we see before us our two possible futures. Either France is confirmed as a Jewish State or it is not. Look at that collection of Hebrews. Are they not evidence of the moral muck through which we are wading? Do you see the fat man there? He has made millions selling rotten beef to the Army. Yes, I assure you. And the man with him, the lean one who looks like a satyr, well, he is a Communist schoolteacher who has debauched the youth of France. They are brothers, my dear.'

The smell of aniseed rose from the glass Léon-Paul was waving under his nose.

'Are you looking for someone?' Léon-Paul asked him.

Lucien did not know how to reply. He wasn't sure why he was there or what he was in search of. He shook his head, letting his eyes rove. Death, he said to himself, would undo many of these; but not the worst, not the worst.

'I'm told you are in regular touch with the Marshal,' Léon-Paul said. 'Now there's a real man. A pity he is so old. He's not one of these politicians ruled by their mistresses and by an ignoble desire to curry favour with the mob. No fear: they say he even tells his mistress where to get off.'

Lucien wished the little man would go away and leave him in peace. He had not realised how tired he was. He wanted to go home to sleep, but the thought of the journey – on foot, for he was doubtful whether he would find a taxi – dismayed him. Léon-Paul pulled him towards his table and he sat down. A waiter appeared. He asked for a glass of lemon tea.

'There will have to be a real clear-out, a purge,' Léon-Paul said. 'France is disfigured and made disgusting by intellectual ordure. It's got to be cleaned up.'

That week in Paris was like a kaleidoscope. Everything familiar seemed to be shaken out of place. His ears were assailed by a babble of rhetoric, which seemed to him less and less real. Every day he found himself walking for hours without intention and ignorant of any destination. He arrived in districts which were unknown to him and where even the accents were unrecognisable. Then he would sit, his feet sore from walking, at café tables, watching the other customers by the half-hour. It came to him that he was seeking signs of hope, but then he thought that anyone watching him would think he was looking for a pick-up. But if he had been, his gaze would have been sharper, not the dull brooding thing he knew it to be. Then he said to himself: 'I am preparing my soul for suffering.' He even scribbled that sentence in a note-book where it rested alongside scraps of conversation he had heard, and stray reflections.

On his last night he met Marcel Pougier for dinner. They had fixed the date at their first accidental meeting, and when the evening came, Lucien was tempted to break the engagement. After all, if he talked of the private soldiers whose bewilderment bewildered and disturbed him, Marcel would wonder whether any of them were pretty.

But Marcel was in a sombre mood himself. For the first time Lucien realised that his friend was middle-aged. There were bags under the dark lemur eyes, and the skin of his face was shrivelled. There had always been something simian in his appearance, but now the prettiness and gaiety had been eclipsed; he looked like one of those little old monkeys one sometimes sees huddling in the corner of their cage in the zoo. When he removed the beret which he had been wearing on their encounter in the street Lucien saw that the front part of his head was entirely bald. Curiously this emphasised his resemblance to the monkey.

He talked first and for a long time of Charles de Fasquelle.

'Do you know – would you believe, my dear? – that there's hardly a day I don't miss the old thing. Oh, he was so difficult and demanding with his jealousy. You know, once, I woke up very early, about dawn, and went to the window in the way one does, and looked out on the street. It was summer and a lovely morning, and there, standing under a chestnut tree, just next to a *pissoir*, was Charles, gazing up at my window, keeping an eye on me, watching, I daresay, to see if anyone slipped out in the morning. It was absurd – he couldn't have known, could he, whether that someone came from my apartment or somebody else's. I wondered if he had been there all night, and I hoped not because the old dear was already sixty. He used to pay the concierge to report on my visitors. Oh, his jealousy never stopped. Even on his deathbed all he could talk of was a young actor he had once seen me with. 'Your concierge tells me he called on you three times in a week last month,' he complained, for by that time he had accepted that I knew he was spying on me. I don't know. It gave him some satisfaction. Isn't life sad, my dear . . . I owe him so much, and yet sometimes I wonder if my life mightn't have been better if I had never met him . . . nobody would know of me, and I would just be a nice old queen . . . or perhaps not, I might have married and had children if I had never met him . . . people do change – our natures are not immutable but each step that we take in our progress through life leads us in a certain direction, and meeting Charles was such a big step for me.'

It was a Provençal restaurant. They ate red mullet, which, Lucien reflected as he always did when he ate that favourite fish in Paris, never tastes as good as when you eat it fresh from the sea, on the coast, on the terrace of a restaurant where you can breath salt air.

'How is your mother?' he asked.

Marcel smiled, as he always did when his mother was mentioned.

'She's very fat,' he said, 'and complains of her liver. I'm not surprised. I tell her, "If you will spend the day sitting in your kitchen sipping white wine, what can you expect." But I'm worried about the silly old dear. She absolutely refuses to leave Paris. I have a nice house, you know, a few miles from Cannes, but will she go there? "I'm a Parisian," she says, "and I stay put . . ." '

'Like Colette,' Lucien said. 'She tells me, "I pass all my wars in Paris." '

'So much for her provincial wisdom,' Marcel said, 'but I tell Maman they are going to bomb Paris, and all she says is, "that will be interesting". "Besides," she says, "if we are going to be occupied, I don't know that I don't prefer Germans to Italians." "But we are not at war with Italy," I say, and she nods her head and says, "We will be." Then I remind her that Italians have always been perfectly sweet to me, and she just says, "Anyway, I've worked all my life for this apartment" – which you must know, Lucien, is a lie because Charles gave it to her – "and I'm not going to abandon it now," and I'm just terrified as to what will happen to her when the Boches do arrive.'

'You think they will?'

'My dear, we both know they will.'

The mullet was succeeded by the lamb and then by an anchovy tart. Seeing Marcel dig his fork into this, Lucien recalled how, as a young man, Marcel had detested anchovies.

'You used to like everything sweet.'

'And now I have come to appreciate bitterness.'

They drank Tavel rosé, because it reminded Lucien of summers such as he did not hope for again.

'Do you know,' Marcel said, 'I have never been more in demand. Your tastes are of course more austere, but my particular brand of bitter-sweet comedy is exactly what the public want just now. I suppose it's a form of escapism. I'm a minor artist, but, within my limits, a good one. It's a light truth that I tell, but at least my form of sentimentality is not a lie, like so much art that is both more pretentious and more noisy. Yet I don't deceive myself, it's an art for the end of a particular civilisation.'

He scrunched out his cigarette.

'Like that,' he said, 'a fag-end.'

Then, with the arrival of the coffee, he began looking at his watch.

'Have you an appointment?' Lucien asked, offended that Marcel might have one. It seemed an indication that he had expected to be bored, that he had viewed the prospect of the dinner – which he had proposed himself – with an enthusiasm that had diminished as it approached; rather as Lucien himself had done. But now that they were there together, at a restaurant table as they had so often been, Lucien didn't wish their conversation to come to an end, didn't wish to be forced out into the streets, and back into responsible life again. It was so pleasant and undemanding sitting there with Marcel indulging in mild melancholy. There was nothing important in their conversation, and that pleased him.

'No,' Marcel said, 'not exactly.' He lit another cigarette.

'I asked David to join us here,' he said.

'David?'

'I told you about David.'

Of course, David was the new lover whom he was trying to keep out of the Army.

'He's late. It worries me when he's late.'

Lucien smiled. 'Is he unfaithful?' He tried to make it sound like a joke.

Marcel waved his cigarette.

'Of course he isn't,' he drew on it, puffed out the smoke. 'Of course he is. I'm terrified that he is. I'm getting like Charles, you know. It's humiliating. I smoke such a lot and he doesn't like it. Or I'm afraid he doesn't, which is absurd because he smokes himself, you know. It's humiliating to be helplessly in love with someone who can't love you. But then, I'd rather be like that than not in love at all.'

'Of course I don't understand you, but I don't see why he shouldn't love you. After all, since you have made the comparison, you loved Charles didn't you?'

'Not as he wished to be loved.'

'But is anyone – are we ever – loved in that way? Isn't the whole business of loving cursed by discordancy of emotion. You never love anyone so much as at the moment when you fear your love is lost forever.'

'When I was confident,' Marcel said, 'I always sat facing the door of a restaurant. Now I sit with my back to it, hoping to be taken by surprise.'

'Tell me about him,' Lucien said, to comfort his friend.

'I saw him first on the stage, in an absurd comedy. He had a way of touching his lips with his fingers – to show surprise. There was something so vulnerable about it, and then he had to throw himself on a couch, weeping, and it was the way he lay there with his feet trailing on the ground . . . he's very young, an American mother and a French father. The mother's Jewish, which is why he is called David, but . . .'

Marcel ran on and Lucien thought how absurd it was indeed that he should be sitting at a table covered with white linen, empty bottles, glasses, coffee-cups and a brimming ash-tray, listening to this, while, a few hours' train journey to the north, his men lounged bored and apprehensive in their lines, longing for their girlfriends, or for their mothers to wake them in the morning with a bowl of coffee. Then he thought of his own mother, asleep in Provence, having prayed for him before he went to bed, and of Polly, perhaps in a nightclub in London, and it seemed to him that life was made up of a network of affections, like a spider's web, spread over experience and over the physical world; and as fragile as that web.

Marcel stopped. Lucien looked up and saw that a young man had laid his hand on his friend's shoulder.

'I'm so sorry I'm late. There was a bit of trouble at the theatre. It was rather horrible. One of the understudies tried to hang herself. Fortunately she didn't succeed. You must be Monsieur de Balafré. I'm so pleased to meet you. I loved your magazine. I do hope the war isn't going to interrupt publication indefinitely.'

He sat down. Marcel fussed over him, persuaded him to drink a glass of armagnac 'for the shock', enquired about the girl, announced that he knew her mother, 'the poor thing', smoked cigarette after cigarette, while the conversation bubbled.

The telephone rang just as Lucien had finished writing an account of the evening in his diary and was preparing for bed. His last words had been: 'Despite my preconception, David is indeed charming. But I tremble for Marcel. He has given his heart to him, and the price of such gifts is always high. Yet I envy him too. The ability to lose myself in another would at least be a distraction from the torments and uncertainties that beset me. I suppose I should do so in devotion to the interests of the men who are my responsibility. But I cannot, I feel only pity for them, and yet they exasperate me. It is their dull readiness to take life as it comes which is the cause of my exasperation. Someone like Marcel is at least always attempting to make life the right shape.'

The caller was Philippe Torrance. He sounded nervous and aggrieved. He told Lucien that he had been trying to find him all day. He implied that his failure to do so was to Lucien's discredit. Lucien smiled at that: Torrance was the sort of egotist who expects the world to arrange itself to his convenience. Now he insisted that he must see Lucien. That was difficult. Lucien was due to return to the front the following morning. To the front? Well, nevertheless Torrance must see him. Besides – with a harsh laugh – just at present there was no front, not in reality, was there? Didn't Lucien understand that it was urgent? He would not have been trying to reach him all day if it wasn't. Very well, he would come round now, even though it would be almost impossible to find a taxi. No, Lucien said, that wouldn't do. Torrance protested. They argued for some time. Eventually they agreed to meet in the buffet of the Gare de l'Est at half-past nine the following morning. Lucien replaced the receiver; the room seemed to be filled with dislike and resentment. He reminded himself that Torrance was a writer of real talent – 'limited but intense, and very fine', as he had said – who required to be cherished. He was difficult, because of his disposition. Nevertheless, Lucien continued to feel protective towards him as his own discovery.

The morning was cold, grey and windless. His knee, which he had banged against a stone during one of the first exercises of the war, ached. Unless it improved he could not be considered fit for active service. On the other hand he had not mentioned it to the Medical Officer.

The station was thronged. So many girls, wives and mothers were seeing off young soldiers returning to the lines after a brief leave that he had the sensation that the air was full of sobbing. The cavernous station was like an antechamber of the infernal regions, as men surrendered themselves, their individuality and their free will, to a malevolent force over which they were powerless, against which they had no protection. As each man placed a heavy shiny boot on the high step of the train, he lifted himself into a realm where he was at the disposal of the Fates. Behind him, the women held out their arms as if he had been torn from them. And then there were handkerchiefs dabbing at the eyes; arms were placed round shoulders; girls clung to mothers, mothers to daughters and sweethearts, all thrown into limbo, their eyes still fixed on the carriages which the railway company had consecrated to the service of death. Even three tarts standing near Lucien were sobbing. He heard one of them say, 'He kept telling me he wished I hadn't left off wearing my mascara, and I said I couldn't because of my gasmask. But I wish now I had put it on for his sake.' One girl was leaning against a pillar. Her pale face, which was thin and bony, was lifted up so that she was gazing over the top of the train at the girders which supported the roof. There were piles of newspapers tied up with string around her feet, as if they were faggots and she a sacrifice to the gods of war. But the train needed no favourable wind to carry the men to their Trojan War which this time – Lucien felt his temple throb – was definitely going to take place.

He turned away and made for the buffet, crowded and steamy and noisy without hilarity. There was no sign of Torrance, though Lucien's delay by the troop train had already made him a few minutes late. He was not surprised. Torrance's insecurity would never allow him to be first at an appointment. It was impossible to reach the counter which, however quickly the barmaids worked, was always jammed with people who thought service overdue. He took up his place instead at the door of the buffet watching for Torrance.

He had consulted his watch twice before he saw him approach. Torrance carried a cane and wore a light-coloured tweed overcoat and a soft hat.

'I've had a terrible journey,' he said, his tone establishing that this was not an excuse for his lateness, but rather an expression of a just grievance at the way things were arranged.

'This place is awful,' he said, 'it's impossible to talk here.'

They crossed the square into a café which was less crowded. As usual Lucien ordered the drinks – a *café filtre* for each of them and also a *fine à l'eau* for Torrance – knowing that he would have to pay. The elderly waiter shuffled off.

Lucien said, 'I've just half an hour before I must board my train.'

Philippe Torrance looked round the café. It seemed to Lucien that he was anxious lest they should be overheard. He dropped his voice, speaking in a husky manner, unlike his usual tone, which was that of a schoolmaster dominating a class of boys for whom he had no respect.

'I've been to your office twice,' he said. 'It's all locked up.'

'Well, yes, I'm afraid it is. I can't produce my magazine while I'm in the Army, you know. There are more important matters.'

'I thought you believed in the magazine and in your writers.'

'You know I do, and perhaps I shouldn't have said "more important" but rather "more urgent". Anyway, it's partly a question of time.'

'Yes, I understand that. You should have appointed a deputy, however.'

'Perhaps I might have, but it's been a very personal thing, the magazine.'

'Yes,' Torrance said. He spooned sugar into his cup. 'That's what has been wrong with it. It has been too personal, too much the expression of your own tastes.'

'I'm sorry you should think that, but I'm bound to point out that your own writings have been to my taste, which is why I have published them.'

He paused: there was nothing to be gained from reminding Torrance that he had had little success in finding an editor sympathetic to his work till Lucien accepted two or three stories. It would only irritate him further.

'Yes, yes,' Torrance said. 'I won't pursue the matter, though it's not just my opinion, you must know. But the point is, you have an article of mine, which you were going to publish, and since the magazine is in abeyance I want it back, and the office, as I say, is locked.'

So it was simply for this that he had brought him here, for the return of a manuscript to which he himself hadn't given a thought for months. Lucien remembered it. He had never intended to publish that article, but Torrance was, he knew, likely to be offended by an outright rejection. So he had temporised. The fact was that Torrance had real gifts as a writer of fiction, an individual point of view, an unexpected capacity to evoke the bitter poetry of *petit bourgeois* life, but he also fancied himself as a political commentator, and in that capacity seemed to Lucien absurd. His opinions were volatile, but always vigorously held and stridently expressed. This particular article had insisted that war would find Germany out. Hitlerism would appear hollow, Hitler's preparations a sham. If he didn't actually say that the German tanks were made out of cardboard, he didn't stop far short of that assertion. He insisted that Germany was in no condition to make war; there were shortages of oil, steel, grain and other essential foodstuffs. His conclusion was exultant: 'Herr Hitler's verbal belligerence cannot any longer conceal the inescapable truth that Nazi Germany is insubstantial; it is a rhetorical performance. Consequently, France, strong, honest and determined, will etc., etc.' It had been, though forcibly expressed, too feeble for words. Lucien had done Torrance a service by pushing it under a pile of manuscripts in a bottom drawer and forgetting all about it.

He said now: 'Do you want to publish it elsewhere? I don't think the mood is ripe.'

Torrance snapped at his cigarette-lighter, which refused to work.

'No,' he said. 'I've decided I don't want to publish it at all. But I want the manuscript back.'

'If you don't want to publish it – and I think you are wise – then it's safe where it is. There's no urgency, is there?'

Torrance said: 'It's you who doesn't understand. I want the manuscript back precisely because it is not safe where it is. When the Germans arrive they will raid your office, as they will raid the offices of all newspapers and magazines of any influence, and they will find the article, and where will I be then? Who has the keys to your office?'

'Mathilde.'

'There. I have always told you that girl was a liar. She denied any knowledge. Will you write a line instructing her to give me the key? Why do you hesitate? Don't you realise the danger I'm in?'

'So are we all,' Lucien said, but he scribbled the note. He picked up his cup. The coffee was cold but he drank it all the same.

CHAPTER FOURTEEN

'NO,' SAID THE farmer's wife. 'I've no milk, or anything. It's all gone, you know. You're not the first. Not by any means.'

She wiped her hands on her apron. 'Just like a peasant woman in a film,' Lucien thought. 'I must remember to tell Marcel.'

'Do you mind if we rest anyway?' he said.

'And if I did mind, you'd still do it.'

She turned away from him and disappeared behind some farm buildings. He could hear her grumble like distant birdsong. He found it reassuring. She would sit things out: the eternal France? Perhaps. It was absurd how, when you were very tired, phrases kept forming in your head. There were birds too, for it was a beautiful evening of early summer, and the light was long. The last pink hawthorn blossom took on a darker sheen as the sun slipped behind a line of poplars. They sat with their backs against the wall, resting and trying to forget that they were hungry.

Had he even been in a battle? That was the question which perplexed Lucien. There had been battle all round them, but he hadn't so much as seen a German tank. Nor a French one, come to that. Only the aeroplanes. Was it a battle when an aeroplane swooped low and strafed you? The question was meaningless. There were dead bodies, anyway, all along the sides of the roads down which they had retreated. His feet ached, and he had an itch between his toes.

Worst of all was the shame. They would never forget the shame. It would return in dreams. He knew that. To have run and not to have seen the enemy, not even to have seen a single grey uniform since they pulled back from the line without firing a shot. Useless to say that it wasn't their fault, that the line had given way on either flank and so they had had no choice. There was still the shame, which no one would forgive them. And he had lost control of his men. He didn't even know where most of them had gone. All he knew was they had gone faster. He wished the woman had been able to offer them some milk. It was precisely milk that he craved, though he knew it wouldn't assuage his thirst.

He never drank milk normally. Always preferred his coffee black. But it was milk he wanted now.

There was a scent of honeysuckle. It came from a trellis at the side of the house, which meant that the breeze was in the east. He rubbed the itch with the heel of his left boot.

'Can you get the wireless to work?' he called.

His operator shook his head.

'The battery's completely dead. Finished.'

The old woman plodded back.

'Aren't you going to move?' she asked.

'Are you sure you have no milk? Nor anything to eat?'

'Nothing at all. You're not the first, I tell you. All running as if my man hadn't died for France last time. He didn't run. Anyway, if I had anything I'd keep it for the Germans.'

'Dirty bitch,' muttered one of the men, but the woman, who was probably a little deaf, didn't seem to hear him.

'Yes, I'd keep it for them,' she said. 'God knows what they'll do to us if we can't provide them with food.'

She crossed herself.

'Don't bother about them,' the Corporal said. 'They'll have plenty of food. They're not neglected like us.'

Three hours later they came to a village where they found a group of their comrades resting in the square. They had got some bread and were passing round little bottles of red wine. One of them spat when he saw Lucien.

'Officers.'

Lucien paid no attention. He hunted about till he found a Sergeant, a man he recognised and respected, a regular, and a Southerner like himself.

'Is there anything left to eat?' he said. 'These chaps with me are starving. They're all in.'

'I kept something,' the Sergeant said, 'in case we were joined by stragglers. It wasn't easy, I can tell you.'

Lucien called his companions over, and the Sergeant handed out hard bread, biscuits and a bottle of wine.

'I paid for these things,' he said. 'Can you give me a chit, sir?'

'I don't know that it will do much good,' Lucien said, 'but here you are anyway.'

'You're probably right, sir. It's hard to believe that money means much just now, or will again. Still, you never know.' He put the piece of paper in his breast pocket and buttoned it. 'It's surprising how things get back to normal.'

He fished out a packet of cigarettes.

'Like one, sir?'

'I shouldn't be smoking your cigarettes.'

'That's all right. There's lots of them. No shortage there. The local tobacconist's run away, leaving his stock. I commandeered them. After all, he's a government servant, in a manner of speaking. And it calms the boys.'

Lucien drew on the cigarette though he had given up smoking two years before. He would never do so again. He decided that straight away.

'Are there any officers with you?'

'Well, no, sir.'

'Then I'm the only one. I'd hoped . . .'

'I wouldn't make too much of that, sir. Not if I was you. Officers are not exactly popular just now. Major Delibes was with us . . .'

'What happened to him?'

'We came on a staff-car as we entered the village. There were three in it, all dead. Shot from the air, you see. The car had slid off the road, but the fields round here are flat and it was easy to get it moving again. "I'll go and find out what's happening," says the Major, and jumps in. He calls the two Lieutenants and they whisper together, and then all three drive off. We haven't seen them again. That was six hours ago.'

'I see. Something may have happened to them. Any sort of delay.'

The Sergeant tugged at his chin.

'Plenty of delays on the road south, sir, I expect. Half of France is on it after all. As for the Major, I daresay he might have got a bullet in the back as he drove away if most of the boys hadn't already ditched their rifles. I'd play down your rank, sir, we're all in the same boat. Would you like a piece of cheese? I saved some in case you turned up. And a piece of chocolate. Here, let me top up your mug.'

Lucien took a swig of the harsh wine. Delibes' conduct was deplorable, it shamed his rank, and the taint spread to himself. Which was itself absurd. Like everything else.

'You said two Lieutenants. Was either Lieutenant Querouaille?'

The Sergeant shook his head.

'Come, sir, what sort of question is that? Lieutenant Querouaille, you know yourself, sir, none better, I'm sure, he was a good boy.'

'You say "was".'

'I'm afraid so, sir. He caught it on the road back. From one of the aeroplanes it was too. He was trying to get everyone to take cover, some of the men being a bit slow, and it caught him . . .'

'You're quite sure he was killed . . .'

'I've seen dead men, sir. I was at Verdun as a mere boy myself. Instant it was, like switching off an electric light.'

He dreamed that night, but not of Querouaille, though he had gone to sleep thinking of him, and after saying a prayer for the repose of his soul. It was not till weeks later that he made a note of this dream, so it may not be as he dreamed it. Still, this was his memory:

I was walking in a wood with Rupert and we were talking of Polly. I can't remember what we said, but the mood was warm, affectionate and forgiving. (What did we have to forgive? I don't know, but I am fully conscious of the glow I experienced at the knowledge that we had come together in an act of forgiveness.) The bells of a distant church began to toll the angelus. We looked out from the edge of the wood towards the churchtower, and the fields were pale gold in the declining sun. As the last note of the bell struck, the sun dipped behind the tower and a chill breeze crept over the wood. We hesitated, as if unable to decide whether to cross the fields or return by the woodland path which would lead us home by a shorter route. I took Rupert's arm and we turned back into the wood. All at once the light was murky. Rupert caught his arm on a thorn, tearing his shirt (which was one of mine from the Rue de la Paix). The blood gushed out, as if from a knife wound, and I tore the sleeve of the shirt to make a tourniquet. His bare flesh felt cold. Then he placed the forefinger of his right hand on the blood and touched me on the forehead. 'Now we are joined,' he said. We came into a clearing, formed by a ring of oak trees. An altar made by laying one slab of pinkish stone on top of two dark grey columns stood in the middle of the grove. It was attended by a priest, an old man in a saffron robe. His back was to us. We paused. The calm music of the angelus bell still echoed. The light faded as we stood there, and the silence was absolute. Then in the distance rang the challenge of a hunting-horn, followed by the tramp of feet and the breaking of branches. We were surrounded, jostled and seized by men in uniforms with much gleaming leather; they wore wolf-masks on their heads. Someone gave an order in a tongue I could not understand, and we were released; but in that moment I know that I surrendered Rupert to them, and I woke.

'You were screaming, sir.'

The Sergeant's hand was on Lucien's shoulder. He held a bottle to his lips.

'Take a swig of this, sir. It's brandy. Bad dream, eh? I reckon there's a lot of bad dreams in France tonight. And for nights to come. You might say, a bit fanciful like, life's turned into a bad dream.'

'Yes,' Lucien said, 'it was a nightmare.'

They rose before dawn and made ready to march again. Lucien made no attempt to give orders, and, as far as he could see, any organisation was spontaneous. Everything had broken down and the men were acting by instinct. There had been no planes. All but a couple of the houses overlooking the market-place had their shutters closed and bolted, but an old man wearing a nightshirt, leather slippers and a black beret appeared at one of the doorways. He held a mug in his hand and watched them a long time without speaking. Then he spat, twice, in the gutter, and turned back into his house. Lucien's foot was itching again, and his bad knee was rebelling against yesterday's long march.

The Sergeant brought him a mug of coffee, some hot water, soap and a razor.

'You'll want to shave, sir.'

He made it sound like an order.

'Is there any news? Someone must have a wireless in the village. Can you go and ask that old man?'

'Oh yes, there's news enough, sir. We're falling back all along the line. The Boches are south of the Meuse. On the other hand, it was announced yesterday that old Pétain's back. I don't know as what, but he's in the government.'

'At last.'

'Well, that's as may be, sir, he's well over eighty, isn't he?'

'Nevertheless, I assure you, he's the only man who can save France.'

The Marshal's return made Lucien ashamed of his acquiescence of the night before. He drank his coffee and shaved, then called the Sergeant over.

'We are still part of the French Army,' he said. 'It's not right that we should allow the men to come and go as they please. We have to restore order and discipline. After all, our men haven't themselves really been in battle, and as for the Army as a whole, yes, we have suffered a reverse, but we can recover. It was worse at the Marne.'

The Sergeant did not reply at once. He stood in front of Lucien, not quite at attention. His wide face gave Lucien no idea of what he was thinking.

'Will you call the men on parade,' Lucien said. 'I want to inspect them and speak to them. Make it clear that there will be no recriminations concerning lost rifles and so on. All that is in the past. And get someone to fetch me a map.'

Still the Sergeant looked at him without moving. A trickle of sweat ran down from his temple.

'If we don't do this,' Lucien said, 'we're finished. You're a regular soldier. You know we have no choice. It's a matter of pride. You've been decorated, haven't you?'

'Yes, sir.'

'Then show yourself worthy of your medals. Last night you did admirably, as a sort of nursemaid. I'm grateful. Now it's time to be a soldier again. Otherwise, you and I, Sergeant, we're no better than Major Delibes.'

The Sergeant's hand shot up in a salute. Two or three men, sitting nearby, looked up in surprise, and got to their feet. The Sergeant about-turned, stamping his feet. Lucien himself turned away and lit a cigarette.

'Here's the map you wanted, sir,' said a soldier.

Lucien had time to shave, drink his coffee and consult the map before the Sergeant got the men in order. There were about twenty of them. Perhaps a few had slipped away before it was light. Two of those with him the previous day were now missing. As he was about to speak, the Sergeant touched him on the elbow.

'Don't pitch it too high, will you, sir. They've had all that stuff they can take.'

Lucien nodded:

'Soldiers,' he said, speaking in a voice distant from the parade ground. 'We've had a rough time, no question of that. And you haven't been well served by your officers either. I'm ashamed of them and I apologise for them.' He paused. What was he saying? Suppose they found Delibes waiting for them at battalion head-quarters, wherever they were, supposing they reached them? What would be the consequences of his criticism then? Conduct prejudicial to good discipline? Though the sun was not yet hot, he brushed his sleeve over his brow.

'That will be a matter to be gone into later,' he said. 'We have more important things to deal with. We have to rejoin the main body of the battalion. I fought in the last war. I've been in retreats then too. But we recovered. We'll do so again. We're Frenchmen after all, and it's been our ill luck to have had to retreat without even engaging the enemy. But we'll do so. We'll get back at them. As for now, we have half an hour to clear up here. Then we'll march. Where's the wireless operator? I need you now. Sergeant, dismiss the rest, and have them stand up again at 08.30 hours.'

It had been a lame speech. The men would obey, but only because it was easier for a little longer to surrender their will, because they would be more fearful cut off from the pack. That was all. He had failed to convince them, he knew that; he was no leader, no sounder of the trumpet-call. And of course he couldn't believe his own words. All around him, in the abandoned equip-ment, the rifles thrown away, the dull look of the eyes, the regression of smart private soldiers to suspicious and secretive peasants, he read evidence of a lost war.

Nevertheless his wireless operator was able to establish where they might join up with whatever remained of the battalion, and the men fell into column of march, the Sergeant coaxing them along. Mutiny and desertion had been avoided. That was something.

Five hours later they reached a village where the battalion was regrouping. The journey had been slow. They were hampered by the flock of refugees, in cars and motor-wagons, on bicycles, on foot and in farm-carts. Half a dozen of the troop fell out, stragglers who would throw off at least part of their uniform to mingle with the fleeing civilians. It was impossible to prevent it. He saw one man climb on to a wagon and sit down by a peasant girl who was carrying a black cockerel in her arms. He shouted at the soldier, who looked him straight in the eye, challenging him to act; and he dared not.

He reported to the Colonel, relieved to find him at least still there. But he scarcely recognised him. The Colonel was famed for his elegance, disturbed only by bouts of malaria (for he had served in Indo-China) and not at all by his taste for opium. He had treated Lucien with respect, aware of his connections beyond the Army. Now Lucien found an old man suffering from lack of sleep, whose hands shook and whose voice had lost its customary precision. He even wondered if he might have had some sort of stroke.

'We're on the run.'

That was how Colonel Vidal greeted him.

'Aren't we regrouping here?'

'What is there to regroup? It's a débâcle. No other word. Do you realise I have lost half my officers, and only one of them dead and one wounded? What sort of Army is that? And now I'm going to lose you.'

'But I've just arrived.'

'And must leave. Where's that motorcyclist? He has a summons for you. You're getting out. You're climbing to the top, and will sit there like a monkey on a stick.'

'I don't understand.'

But, instead of explaining, the Colonel put his head in his hands and began to sob.

CHAPTER FIFTEEN

THE FAT GENERAL and the lean senior functionary from the Ministry of Defence complained about the absence of a dining car.

'It's outrageous when they knew that so much of the train was reserved for senior personnel.'

'And why have we stopped here? We haven't moved for a quarter of an hour.'

'My adjutant confirmed that there would be a dining car.'

'We have been so overwhelmed – no other word for it – at the Ministry' – the initial capital sounded in his talk – 'that it has been quite impossible to lunch for several days. Only a bowl of soup and a sandwich at my desk. Can you believe that? And now, when I was looking forward to, well, nothing excellent, you understand, for I am a reasonable man, but at least a chop and some fresh vegetables, what do we find? Not even bread and cheese.'

'It's sabotage, a deliberate attempt to impede the war effort. Brainwork is impossible without . . . and why don't we move?'

'It's twenty minutes now . . .'

'We'll find the hotels in Tours closed, certainly the kitchens . . .'

'I happen to know that the Reds are everywhere on the railways . . .'

'My brother-in-law, who is a judge, tells me . . .'

Lucien closed his eyes. He had had no sleep for three days. The orders to him had been changed and countermanded more than once. But, though he ached to sleep, when he closed his eyes Colonel Vidal's yellow face, twisted in disbelief, rose before him – he heard him mutter again, 'You're flying to the top of the greasy pole, my boy' – saw him twitch at the lapels of his jacket as if he could pull himself and his troops back into military order, and saw them fall away, leaving the jacket, which he hadn't perhaps removed since the first day of the battle, looking only a little more creased.

'My son was killed in the first hour of the battle,' he heard Vidal say, 'and they brought me news only yesterday, and my soldiers keep running, I've no time to mourn. Tell them what it's like, Monsieur de Balafré, tell them what they have done to us.'

But what in fact was it like, and what had been done to them? Lucien realised that either he did not know or had lost the power to command the words which might tell them. And the itch in his right foot was worse.

A girl was driving red-and-white cows through a watery meadow beyond the train's smeared and yellowing window. She lifted her hand as if to wave to them, and then stopped in mid-gesture; had it come to her that the train was carrying them to participate in what was left of the government of what was almost no longer France? Her hand dropped to her side, and the sun shone on her yellow headscarf. One of the cows broke away from the others and trundled in a clumsy confused gallop – like a French soldier, thought Lucien – towards the stream that ran under a row of elms. It stood knee-deep in the water, surprised as if it had never intended to arrive there. The girl laid down the pail she was carrying and, abandoning the other cows, which continued to stroll across the meadow in the direction of the train, turned back to chivvy her out of the water. But the cow just looked at her, uninterested. Its whole attitude said that it had had enough. Meanwhile the other cows lowered their heads and began to graze again. Without warning the train moved. The girl and the cows slipped out of sight. Lucien shut his eyes again. This time he slept.

When he woke it was dark and there were no lights in the compartment. It was still warm, and a little orchestra of snores played around him. His eyes adjusted themselves and he realised that it was not quite dark, he could discern outlines. But he could see nothing beyond the train. The man on his left, who had said nothing since they drew out of Paris but whose disapproval of the General and the civil servant had been transmitted to Lucien, said:

'Don't ask me where we are. I've no idea.'

He passed Lucien a bottle.

'It's rum, I warn you.'

'Rum? I don't think I've ever drunk rum.'

But he took a mouthful.

'Not bad, not bad at all,' he said. 'Thank you.'

'Have some more. We're all going to have to get used to things which we haven't known before.'

'Like that girl and the cow,' Lucien said. 'I wonder if she managed to persuade it out of the water.'

'What girl and what cow?'

'Oh, you didn't notice? When we were stopped . . . ' And he explained. 'It looked so obstinate standing there,' he said, 'I felt sorry for the girl.'

'Have you been in battle?'

'If it was a battle, yes.'

'At any rate, if it wasn't a battle, it was a disaster. It's up to us all now to see what can be saved.'

He closed his eyes, the train trundled through the night, at last it halted. Lucien rubbed his sleeve against the window. He couldn't see whether they were in a station or in open country. He rolled down the window. Rooftops outlined themselves against the sky, blacker than its dull matt. There were no lights visible anywhere. He sank back on the cushions.

After what seemed an eternity, the door of the compartment opened. A railway official stood there. He announced that they had arrived.

'The train terminates here, gentlemen.'

'There should be a car,' Lucien said.

'How would I know?'

But there was a car, a big open staff-car waiting in the station yard. The chauffeur explained that he had been unwilling to leave it to search for them. 'It was the choice of two evils,' he kept saying. They climbed into the car. Without asking anyone, the general lit a cigar. They drove off into the night. Lucien experienced the powerlessness of a dream narrative.

'The castle's called Nitray,' a young Lieutenant said. 'The Marshal has retired hours ago, naturally. We expected you earlier. He has left instructions that he will see you at eight-twenty in the morning.'

Lucien looked at his watch. It was five past four. The Lieutenant escorted him to a little room at the top of several flights of back stairs. One bed was already occupied. Lucien asked to be called at seven-thirty. He took off his boots, tunic, trousers and shirt, and fell on the bed. Then he stirred again and removed his socks also.

He woke to find the sun on his face and the other bed empty. His watch said five minutes past eight. He jumped to his feet, and had to steady himself, resting his hand on a table, as he experienced a wave of dizziness and nausea. There was some cold water in a jug and he shaved, wincing as the razor tore the beard from his face. It was eighteen minutes past when he left the room, and he had no idea where he was to report to the Marshal.

'You're two minutes late,' Pétain said. 'I expect my staff to keep military hours, with a soldier's precision, Captain.'

The Marshal was pink and gleaming as a strawberry ice. Sunlight danced from his buttons. The great white moustache fluffed out as he spoke. Lucien read benevolence and candour in his steady gaze.

'Come, sit you down,' Pétain said, 'and tell me about the battle.'

'There is nothing, Marshal, I can tell you in general terms, which you don't already know, and as for my particular experience, it is perhaps too particular to have much value.'

'Just so. All battles are the same in detail. Only this one is lost.'

He paused. Lucien realised that he was expected to recount his impressions of the battle, nevertheless. He began to do so. After he had been speaking for some five minutes, he saw that the Marshal's attention had wandered. He was gazing out of the window in a manner which suggested that he saw nothing. Parkland stretched away till the view was closed by dark green laurel bushes behind which rose beech trees.

'I encountered a former protégé of mine yesterday,' Pétain said. His voice seemed to come from a great distance, as if from the past. 'You won't have heard of him, but he's a General now. I told him I didn't congratulate him. "What good is rank in the midst of a defeat?" I said. He reminded me that I had myself received my first stars during the retreat in 1914. "The Marne followed a few days later," he said. The Marne, yes, but history doesn't repeat itself. It unfolds new shapes. It has its rhythms. I told him it wasn't the same thing.'

Then, with just the same gesture he had employed on that first occasion they met in his Paris office, he tinkled a little bell, relapsed into silence till an orderly arrived to receive his request for coffee, and again sat, as if carved in stone or at least posing for a sculptor, till the coffee was brought. Lucien couldn't take his eyes off him; he was fascinated by the old man's impassivity.

'I need you,' the Marshal said, 'on my staff for the time being. I've arranged it all. That was a good article you wrote for me, you caught my style exactly. It was lapidary, classical. It represented me. Good. I want you to prepare a paper for the Prime Minister. It has to convince him. He's not much of a man, little Reynaud, just a politician, but for the moment he's the man we have to convince. It's not only that we need an armistice, we have also to resist the British who are proposing that the French government abandon the French people and the soil of France and carry on the war beyond the seas. Bah, there is no France beyond the seas. You'll find the right words, I'm confident of that. Churchill – I knew him in the last war, a man of no judgement – says England will fight on. I have my doubts. One other thing, we must accept suffering, you understand that? Can you say it well?'

Lucien thought.

'Perhaps we could say that our Renaissance will be the fruit of our suffering.'

'Yes, that is true.'

'For the government to leave France would be the line of least resistance . . .'

'That's true. Remember, France is its soil, and the most true Frenchmen our peasants who are attached to their land by bonds of history. But remember suffering. We must suffer in order to revive. First winter, then spring.'

He stopped. Lucien felt the candid eyes searching his face. He felt the Marshal's power and wisdom. Pétain stretched out his hand. For a moment it seemed to Lucien that he was going to receive the old man's blessing, and there would be nothing presumptuous or blasphemous in the Marshal adopting the role of the priest.

'Good,' Pétain said. 'We understand one another. Drink your coffee. Good. Ah, I see they've brought madeleines. I like these little cakes.'

He took one and bit into it.

'Don't forget. The importance of suffering,' he said.

That was June 13. The next day the whole party of Pétain's entourage left in motorcars for Bordeaux. They dined that evening, twelve of them at a big table, in the Hôtel Splendide, their quarters for the next fortnight. During the dinner a very tall Brigadier-General approached the table and shook Pétain by the hand. The Marshal proffered his hand in silence and barely looked up from his plate.

That was the only time Lucien saw de Gaulle, and it was only his unusual appearance – 'like a disconsolate stork' – and Pétain's evident indifference, which made the occasion remarkable; but six days later, when the armistice had been proposed, when Pétain was Prime Minister and de Gaulle had already made his first, subsequently famous, broadcast from London, he talked of him with his brother Armand.

Armand had arrived in the city with de Gaulle, in whose regiment he had been serving. Lucien did not know that he was there, and was surprised to be summoned to the telephone and then hear his brother's voice. They hadn't met for almost a year. Armand explained that he wanted to see him – 'urgently' – but he didn't wish to come to the Hôtel Splendide.

'The fact was,' he said later, 'that I wasn't at all sure of my status. I was really afraid of being arrested. It was known by then that de Gaulle was in London, and I thought it quite probable that I might be charged with having deserted my regiment, since it had only been with de Gaulle's authority that I had come to Bordeaux. Of course everything was in a state of such confusion, and so many people who should in theory have remained with their regiments were to be found in the city, and indeed elsewhere all over France, that this may have been unlikely. I couldn't tell, but I had nevertheless been very happy to slip out of my uniform and hoped that I would be taken by anyone who didn't know me for a Bordelais businessman or civil servant. You can't imagine the confusion there was.'

So he persuaded Lucien to meet him in a café in a little sidestreet off the quays.

'We were entering a time of little cafés in sidestreets, you know.'

The brothers looked on each other as opposites; each saw the other as a sort of alien being who nevertheless compelled him to gaze into a mirror in astonishment. There were the simple questions: how could they have sprung from the same womb? From the same seed? Nurtured – to speak the language of 1940 – by, in and from the same soil? Lucien could not understand Armand's talent for making money; it was the sort of thing he couldn't himself conceive of. Money for him was simply what you drew from the bank and deposited there. The fertility of credit was a mystery to him, a veiled abstraction. But his own abstractions were equally veiled from Armand, who had an un-Latin distaste for general ideas. There was a Northern strain in the family – a grandmother from Lorraine – and perhaps that emerged in Armand, though it was Armand who had been educated entirely in the Midi.

Yet, behind or below, or circling round, these differences, there was much, despite the gap in age, that was shared, so that now, when Armand saw Lucien push through the beaded curtain, and stand for a moment blind in the dark of the little café, he knew a tenderness which he could never have felt for anyone so different unless they had been fundamentally one. I often feel there is no relationship stranger than that of brothers; as an only child I am mystified by the tenderness which can join incompatibles, and which is manifested in the phrase one often hears: 'Of course my brother is entirely different from me, but he's a remarkable chap. I'm really proud of him, though we never see each other.'

'And most of the time,' Armand said to me, 'we had no idea what to talk about.'

This time of course it was different. There was too much to talk about, and it was the consciousness of this superfluity of experience and emotion to be exchanged which for a few minutes kept both silent. They fingered the glasses of armagnac which Armand had obtained and looked at each other as if they could wordlessly divine what had been endured in the weeks of war.

Then Lucien said, 'Do you know, I found myself drinking rum in a train the other day. A fellow whose name I don't know gave it to me. Extraordinary stuff, never drunk it before. Rather liked it actually.'

Armand was amazed by the abrupt jerky delivery; he wondered if his brother was drunk. That wasn't possible, but it was surprising even to hear him talk about drink. He drank wine, of course, like anyone else, but he would no more talk about it than about water. Less, actually, for one of his favourite tags was to quote the Greek saying, 'water is best', lifting a glass of the stuff to prove it. He wasn't drunk, however, only very tired. He told Armand he hadn't enjoyed a night's real sleep since April.

'You have to remember,' Armand said to me, 'that in the early summer of 1940 all decisions were made by men who were exhausted, had gone without sleep. I made my own decisions, such as that which I now communicated to him, in the same state. Would I have determined to get to London to join de Gaulle if I hadn't been so short of sleep?'

'Pétain was the exception, surely,' I said to him. 'He slept enough, didn't he?'

'Oh, the Marshal, yes, but his waking life was a sort of dream, though I didn't understand that at the time.'

Lucien said: 'Don't you know he's deranged?'

He scarcely knew anything of de Gaulle, but he believed that. It was what was put about in the Marshal's circle; deranged, consumed by vanity, his mind enflamed by chimeras.

'Besides,' Lucien said, 'you are evading your duty. Your duty is to remain here and repair the damage of our débâcle. That at least is clear enough to me. And the chance exists. We are offered the opportunity to take part in a national revolution, which, unlike previous revolutions, is not founded on spite, hatred, the desire for revenge, and all the irrationality of destructive natures, but rests on a tranquil confidence and a profound love of France.'

I condense what he said. There was a bright light in his eye which Armand had never seen.

'Perhaps you ought to have me arrested then,' Armand said.

'For your own sake perhaps I should, but for my sake I must do you the honour of leaving you free to follow the course you have mapped. Let me try to dissuade you. England too will make peace by the end of the summer, and where will your renegade general be then? Do you know the Marshal's opinion? "In six weeks," he says, "Hitler will wring England's neck like a chicken." '

'I had hoped to persuade you to come with me,' Armand said, 'but I see it is hopeless.'

'As hopeless as your mad adventure. Believe me, my dear brother, there is noble work to be done here. The Marshal has promised me a share in it, and I had hoped to make room for you . . .'

Armand ordered more armagnac. They talked of the Château de l'Haye, and of the Provençal summer, and then of their mother. Lucien stretched over and pressed his hand.

'I must go. I am required in attendance. Good luck. I shall pray for you. At least we are both acting in accordance with the dictates of honour as we interpret it.'

Before he left he asked his brother to seek out Polly, to assure her of his continuing love and respect, etc., etc.

'She won't lack for anything with her father there . . .'

'And,' he said, 'give this to the boy.'

He took a crucifix from his tunic pocket and handed it to his brother. It is round my neck still.

Had he brought it on purpose, knowing of Armand's intention?

CHAPTER SIXTEEN

ON JULY 3 the British Navy attacked the French fleet in harbour in Mers-el-Kebir, the French Admiral having concealed from the new government that he had been given the option of sailing to a port in the French West Indies. The news of the attack was received with horror all over France. Philippe Torrance, for instance, who had arrived in Vichy by a train the previous night, and who had at once sought Lucien and requested him to exert his influence to secure him 'some employment, distinguished employment, you understand', fulminated at 'the treachery of the English'. 'They have always been our enemies,' he told Lucien. 'We should at once retaliate against them.'

'No,' Lucien said, 'the Marshal is wiser than that, though I believe both Laval and Darlan agree with you.'

'There, you see. Can you get me an introduction to Laval?'

'To Laval? I scarcely know him, and anyway, Philippe, I wouldn't advise it even if I did.'

It is ironic to think that this refusal perhaps saved Torrance's life, and so enabled him to speak against my father at that dinner-party given by Virginia Fernie ten years later.

What Lucien didn't however confess to Torrance was that he himself was fascinated by Laval.

Five days later he was in the little gallery of the Petit Casino while the last Assembly of the Third Republic debated its own suicide. He heard the Radical ex-Premier Edouard Herriot declare: 'Our nation has rallied in its distress to the side of Marshal Pétain, in the veneration his name inspires in us all. Let us take care not to trouble the accord that has established itself under his authority. We must now render more austere a Republic that we have made too easy.'

He saw Laval, grey, white and jerky, his lapels dusted with cigarette-ash, rise to present, in his coarse and seductive voice, a plan for 'a new regime, audacious, authoritarian, social, national . . . Capitalism,' he said, 'would disappear and be replaced by a new order'; and later, when a Deputy proposed some revision, he heard Laval snap, 'Don't fool yourselves, gentlemen; we are living in a dictatorship now.' And at ten minutes past seven, at an hour when in a normal summer all those taking the cure at Vichy would have been dressing for dinner, he saw the Assembly pass a motion which accorded all powers to the government of the Republic under the authority and the signature of Marshal Pétain, for the purpose of promulgating, by one or several decrees, a new Constitution of the French State. This Constitution should guarantee the rights of labour, of the family, and of the Fatherland. Only eighty deputies were found to vote against the motion; five hundred and sixty-nine approved it.

The corpse of the Third Republic was ready for burial.

Later that evening Lucien saw the Marshal sign three decrees: all beginning 'We, Philippe Pétain, Marshal of France . . .' The signatures were firm, the Marshal calm, the mood of all assembled had a strange exhilaration.

'It is like Louis XIV,' Lucien noted in his journal.

'And that's how you overthrow the Republic,' Laval said, taking the fountain-pen from the Marshal and screwing on its top. He put the pen in his own breast pocket, took out a cigarette and lit it. Pétain kept his eyes for a moment on the sheet of blotting-paper, then turned it over as if reading the reflection of his signature.

'Well,' he said, 'I was only fifteen when it was inaugurated. If my mother could see me now. I'm hungry.'

He retired to wash his hands, then they all descended – the Marshal and his immediate aides in the lift, the others by the grand sweeping staircase, to the Chantecler restaurant. A screen had been erected at the rear of the room and the Marshal's table was laid there.

'Where is Monsieur Laval?' someone said.

'Monsieur Laval has no time to eat.'

'Not chicken,' the Marshal said. 'A boring dish. I should like a beefsteak.'

Lucien was impressed by the old man's appetite.

'Who would have thought he could still chew a steak?'

They ate for the most part in silence. When they spoke, the war was not mentioned. All felt that they had participated in something momentous which made ordinary conversation ridiculous. Yet, unless the Marshal led the way, they were conscious that it would be indecorous to discuss what was to be done. That, after all, was his business. The French people had made the future the Marshal's province.

Lucien lay long awake after he had retired to bed. He heard a woman crying in the park: 'Pierre, Pierre.' She must be seeking her son. The thought pained him. All over France families had been divided in the confusion of the flight from the German Armies. There were several thousand people camped in the park, and one, at least, hunted through the night for a child who had strayed. 'Pierre, Pierre . . .' In the morning he must telephone his own mother to let her know where he was and what was happening. He wouldn't of course mention Armand, he would say he knew nothing of him. For one thing it wasn't safe. People were already saying that the Germans were intercepting telephone calls. He didn't know if it could be done, at such a distance; but even if they weren't, it would be unwise to advertise his own connection with a brother whom he must describe as a traitor. 'Pierre, Pierre,' the woman's voice was fainter now. He fell into a fitful sleep as the new dawn broke over the mountains and touched the walls of Vichy with rosy summer fingers.

Lucien had had no private conversation with the Marshal since their meeting at Nitray. His memorandum had not convinced Reynaud, and he wondered if Pétain might not have decided, on account of this failure, that he had overestimated his abilities. The thought depressed him. On the other hand he could not bring himself to join the host of supplicants who sought personal interviews with the Marshal. These were to be seen at every corner, and in every lobby, of the hotel. Of course he had no need to associate himself with them; he was still welcome, apparently, at the Marshal's table behind the screen in the dining room and, if Pétain said nothing directly to him, that was not so very different from his treatment of others.

All the same it was a relief when Bernard Ménétrel, Pétain's doctor, stopped him as he was going out for a walk one morning, and suggested that he might perhaps be permitted to accompany him.

'Only I don't like to be absent for too long,' he said. 'I never know when the Marshal is going to need me, and I don't care that someone else should perhaps seize the opportunity to substitute for me. However, the truth is that I do need some fresh air, and besides, I have something to say to you.'

It was with that speech that Lucien realised that a court had been established at Vichy. As he wrote in his journal later, 'To understand Vichy, read Saint-Simon.'

Ménétrel was not only Pétain's doctor. Some said he was his bastard son. Lucien had never talked with him alone before, but he had noticed that he was the only member of what he thought of as the dining-club at whose jokes Pétain condescended to smile. They were coarse, crude, vulgar jokes, the jokes of a man who was still in some ways the callow medical student from a dull province and a *petit bourgeois* background, and Lucien thought that only affection could persuade the Marshal that they were to be tolerated.

'The Marshal however wants to speak to you. This afternoon. He is, I know, sorry he has not had the opportunity to do so before, but you can't believe the strain he is under, the demands that are made of him. I'm always anxious about his health. He has arthritis, you know, which I treat by a hot-air method invented by my father, and as a tonic I inject him with oxygen. It's a great responsibility to know that the health of France is in my hands, and you can't wonder if I am protective.'

Holding Lucien's elbow he steered him round the square in front of the hotel. Every now and then he glanced up at the balcony of the Marshal's suite. Perhaps he had arranged a system of signals whereby he could be warned if his presence was required.

'Laval is bad for him, you know. The Marshal's blood pressure always rises after he has had an interview with that dirty type. And then he feels both giddy and faint. There's no end to my problems. Furthermore, the Marshal's still a lusty man, you understand, it's a great mistake to think he is past the sexual act . . . but if he should happen to overdo it . . . and wine, I put water in his wine, but if I am not alert, he seizes the bottle himself. Not that he drinks, you understand, only what is temperance in a man of sixty can amount to excess when you are eighty-four. Yes, what is it?'

This remark was addressed to an elderly lady whose approach Lucien had not observed. Now she was plucking Ménétrel's sleeve, and Lucien felt his own arm released while the doctor tried to shake himself free of her.

'What is it? Oh, it's you again, Madame. Can't you see that I am busy? I've no time for your little troubles now. You will hear from me in due course. When the time is ripe, I say, when it is ripe.'

He seized Lucien again and hurried him forward, leaving the poor woman lamenting behind them.

'Such importunity,' he said. 'I can't even put my head out of my hotel to take a little exercise and fresh air, both of which are necessary to my health, but I am seized by the arm and bothered.'

'What does she want then?'

'That one? Oh, merely that I should trouble the Marshal. She has a son-in-law, a Jew if you please, and she seeks security for him. At present he lives in the occupied zone, where he is a schoolmaster, yes, indeed, yet another Jewish schoolmaster corrupting the youth of France, and she is requesting a transfer for him; and she claims to have influence with the Marshal, because, if you please, she says she had an affair with him before the last war, when he was a Colonel. I said to her, "What makes you think the Marshal will remember you, you're not unique, you know."'

He laughed and gripped Lucien's arm harder.

'She actually confesses to an affair?' Lucien said. 'A respectable woman like her?'

'Not in so many words, it's true. But it's obvious. And all for a Jewish son-in-law, who is a schoolteacher. If I had my way he would go down a coalmine. But that will be your responsibility.'

'What do you mean?'

'Oh,' Ménétrel clapped his hand over his mouth, with an exaggerated gesture like a music-hall mime's, 'I've spoken out of turn. But you will soon find out all about it. The Marshal will see you at half-past four.' He glanced up at the balcony again. 'Excuse me, I'm needed. At half-past four then.'

Lucien waited till he had entered the hotel, then turned back looking for the woman. He wasn't sure that he would recognise her. There were so many old women in black, and he had noticed nothing more about her. For a moment, he stood lost, and then he realised that he was being observed. That must be her. He was about to approach her when it occurred to him that it might be injudicious to be seen talking to her; he wouldn't put it past Ménétrel to be keeping an eye on him from a window. He was surprised by this thought, for such imaginings were unfamiliar to him. However, he acted on it, and strolled out of the square, not looking behind him. He walked along the boulevard, pausing at a flower stall. He glanced up. The woman – if it was the same woman – was following him. He turned the next corner which led into a long, narrow street, deserted in the heat of the afternoon. There was a café about halfway along. He looked back to see the street empty but for the old woman, who was moving towards him in a determined fashion. Of course she might be followed herself, but, if he entered the café and sat down, and was accosted by her there, it would be easy to explain matters. Certainly he couldn't be thought to have accosted her.

As he ordered a *café crème*, he was astonished by the way his mind was working.

He sat at a table. She came in and, ignoring the waiter, made straight for him.

'Excuse me, Monsieur,' she said, 'do you mind if I sit here a moment? It's because I saw you talking with Dr Ménétrel that I wish to speak to you.'

'But of course,' Lucien said, rising, 'if I can be of any assistance.'

'It's a sad state of affairs when a respectable lady like myself finds herself accosting strange men. But I saw you talking to Dr Ménétrel. Do you think he can be trusted?'

'The Marshal trusts him, I believe.'

'Ah,' she said, 'but then the doctor has something to gain from the Marshal.'

She hesitated, embarrassed, as if she had already said too much. Lucien recognised in her something with which he was to grow all too familiar in the next months: a recognition which perhaps accounted for the full account he wrote of this otherwise – one would have thought – unimportant incident. It was the look of a person who understands that the confidence which experience had persuaded him or her to repose in the way things were ordered was no longer justified. People could in short no longer believe anything life had taught them. Actions could no longer be spontaneous. Everything had to be considered in advance. You could no longer speak your mind because you had to be sure of your auditor's. And that was impossible; even those in whom you had hitherto reposed infinite trust had become unaccountable. Everyone was an unknown quantity. Here, for instance, was a lady whose dress and general demeanour (the neat black suit – for it was neat, he saw that now, and had been elegant and expensive; the carefully coiffured hair, which actually needed attention, but still spoke of hours at the hairdresser; the soft unused hands) proclaimed her as someone who had never questioned that the world was well-arranged, now, at an age when her life's pattern should have been assured, brought bang up against the fact that she understood nothing.

But if certainty had vanished you had nevertheless to take more risks. You could no longer dare speak intimately even to friends, but you might find yourself compelled to approach a stranger.

'What is your problem?' he said.

Ménétrel at least had not deceived him; it was as he said. Her son-in-law, married to her only daughter, her only child in fact, was a schoolmaster in Paris, and – again she hesitated, then brought it out with a little flush – a Jew.

She looked up to see how Lucien received the news.

'I don't like Jews myself,' she said, 'and I must tell you that I was against the marriage. Nevertheless they went ahead, and I'm bound to say it's been a success. Simon is a good husband, and I have grown fond of him myself. He's dutiful, and, though he is much cleverer than I am, he has the good manners not to show it.'

Lucien told her that, though he was flattered by her confidence in him, he didn't see what he could do.

'And that's not all of it,' she said, as if he hadn't spoken. 'It's not only that they live in Paris and that Simon being a Jew is in danger there, but he is also an intellectual, he's written things against the Nazis. I've told him it's unwise, but why should a clever man like him listen to me?'

'Is he a Communist?' Lucien asked.

'A Communist? Of course not. I told you he is my son-in-law.'

What was there to say? Lucien knew that he had no power to effect the transfer of such a man, of anyone indeed; moreover it really was a case of 'such a man', who sounded precisely the type that the Marshal blamed for the demoralisation of French youth. Lucien suspected that this demoralisation was exaggerated, but didn't deny that it existed. The woman toyed with a string of pearls. For a moment he entertained the absurd idea that she was going to offer him a bribe. He wished she would. It would make it easy to get up and walk off. But of course she did nothing of the kind. Instead a tear, almost as big as a pearl, escaped her eye.

'Have you grandchildren?' he said.

'Two girls.'

'And are they in Paris still?'

'I don't know,' she said.

'But if you don't know, isn't it possible that the whole family has managed to leave?'

'That's not the point,' she said. 'The war's over, isn't it? He must earn a living. They can't expect me to keep them. I'm a widow. My investments are already threatened. As for Simon, he has no money of his own, merely his salary, and it's not safe in Paris.'

She spoke on, telling him her family history. It was a chronicle to which he hardly listened. The details didn't matter. His pity had been stirred. It was a small thing, but he would speak to Ménétrel, try to see if something could be done.

Later that afternoon, the Marshal told him he was appointing him to the position of Under-secretary in the Ministry of Education. He spoke of the force for good that Lucien would be; and Lucien found that his first thought was how he could serve the mother-in-law of the Jewish schoolmaster, Simon Halévy.

CHAPTER SEVENTEEN

FOR ALMOST EIGHTEEN months Lucien contented himself with the administration of French schools. I rather think that, despite moments of loneliness, these held the happiest months of his adult life. He stopped keeping a journal, itself perhaps a sign that he was content. He believed that he was doing good and necessary work, every morning he went to his office with a song in his heart. He was by nature a teacher himself; one of the pleasures of running his magazine had been the opportunity to collect round him a group of young people whom he might influence and guide. And now the youth of France was entrusted to him. What more could he wish for?

Of course there were problems. The Marshal had decreed that secondary education should no longer be free: 'We don't wish to create an intellectual proletariat.' Well, Lucien conceded that that was certainly undesirable. Since there had to be a proletariat as the world was constituted, it was wrong that they should be educated in such a way as could only foment dissatisfaction. On the other hand, he found it distasteful to think that intelligent children of any background should be denied the chance of full development. Was that proper? Was it Christian? There is a long memorandum – some 10,000 words – in the Ministry's archives, in which he argues this question.

And then there was the problem of personnel. This revealed the weakness of my father's character. He was quite ready to declare that there were certain types who, simply by reason of belonging to particular groups, were rendered unsuitable for employment as schoolteachers. But it was a different matter when it came to the individuals belonging to these groups; that is, when they presented themselves as individuals. The case of Simon Halévy is sufficient example.

But for his meeting with Halévy's mother-in-law, Madame Villepreux, he would never of course have considered intervening in the affairs of a Jewish teacher. Though he would never have claimed, in that phrase which has become a mockery, that some of his best friends were Jews, and indeed this would be untrue in his case as it is in that of most of those who make such an assertion, he wasn't in any deep sense anti-Semitic. He was inclined to deplore excessive Jewish influence if it seemed likely to dilute French culture, but being an intelligent man he also knew that it had often rather enriched it. (There is, Hugh, an unfinished essay on 'The Jewish Contribution to French Literature', which I shall send you.) All the same, he accepted the Marshal's views, even if with reservation. That was fine. But he had nevertheless taken some trouble to find Halévy, and had then invited him to Vichy.

The young man who appeared in his office was, to his disappointment, distinctively Jewish. He clearly belonged, as Lucien's superior would have put it, 'to the large-nosed fraternity'. That was a pity. He was also hostile.

'I can't think what you want of me,' he said, lighting a pipe and sitting down.

Lucien explained that he wanted to help him.

'I understand that there have been difficulties in Paris.'

'That's an understatement.'

'And you realise, I'm sure, that some of these difficulties will emerge again wherever you are.'

'I realise that your Ministry is likely to prohibit the employment of Jews, even when they are good Frenchmen as I am.'

He blew smoke across the desk, into Lucien's face.

'We live, unfortunately, in a time of categories,' Lucien said. 'The problem is how can I help you?'

'Why, if I may ask, should you wish to do so? I can't say that I would look for help in your direction.'

'I was approached personally. That is, I was asked to see if I could do something for you. By your wife's mother, in fact.'

'Old Mother Villepreux? Well, that's kind of her. I wouldn't have looked for that either.'

'She spoke of you in warm terms.'

His own tone was cold.

'She admires your intelligence and she is aware of course that her daughter loves you and depends on you, isn't that enough?'

'Enough? I don't choose to be beholden to her. Or to you if it comes to that.'

'Believe me, I understand that,' Lucien said. 'However, you must see that you will have to be beholden to me, as you put it, or your family will suffer.'

'My family will suffer in any case. Whatever happens. And why? Because I am a Jew. Monsieur de Balafré, I used to be a subscriber to your magazine, and then I thought you an intelligent man, and a man of honour, but when I find you sitting here, in this office, as a functionary of a regime built on a foundation of lies, lies which are to my mind all the more reprehensible because they have a spurious sound of nobility, then I must consider you either a fool or a hypocrite. There: I have spoken.'

He sat back, folded his arms, his pipe replaced at a jaunty angle in his mouth, as if, in that time of half-truths and outright mendacity, he was satisfied to represent the honest man of good sense. He had put himself in the ascendancy, and Lucien was disgusted by his assumption.

'It is never,' he thought, 'as easy as that.'

'What do you want then?' he said.

Halévy took his pipe from his mouth and, holding the bowl, jabbed the mouthpiece in Lucien's direction.

'Perhaps the first satisfaction would be to compel you to admit that your establishment in that chair is offensive – an offence to your own history and intellectual honesty, among other things.'

'You're being ridiculous, you know.'

He lit a cigarette himself, got to his feet and crossed the room behind Halévy to the window. The late-afternoon sun still shone on the boulevard, which was not busy. A few girls, typists probably, going home from their offices, strolled past; their laughter rose to him. Most of them were wearing coats, for it was now autumn, and the breeze brought a chill air from the mountains towards evening. He imagined they were discussing the problem of where they might find winter clothes, even winter fashions, in this resort town; his own secretary had asked him that morning whether it was possible to go north, to the occupied zone, to Paris actually, to restock her wardrobe. 'Why not?' she had said. 'The war's over, isn't it?'

'You're being ridiculous,' he repeated, without turning round. The man who accused him of hypocrisy was a hypocrite himself; how else had he impressed the mother-in-law he so evidently despised with his 'good manners'? Lucien was conscious of the man's immobility behind him, an immobility that was moral also. Why didn't he reply? Dislike filled the room like the stench of rotting food. And yet, wasn't it precisely Lucien's consciousness of this dislike which made him determined to help Halévy? We are all hypocrites in our fashion. He turned the thought over like a coin he suspected of being counterfeit. But no, it was valid currency. Rhythms of hypocrisy ran through the social order; he had learned that from listening to Gaston Hunnot. The *Hunnotismes* which his disciples so relished, which they admired for their cynical 'realism', displayed the flower of hypocrisy in full bloom. But wasn't hypocrisy part of any public statement, his own included? When the Marshal had said in a recent broadcast that 'the National Revolution means the will to rebirth . . . the determination of all the elements of the Past and Present which are healthy to make a strong State, to remake the national soul and to restore to it the lucid confidence of the great and privileged generations of our history, which were often generations on the morrow of civil or foreign wars' – weren't those words, some of which Lucien had himself supplied in an early draft of the speech, evidence of hypocrisy on a grand scale? They contained truth but they concealed a lie. He had known that even when he supplied the phrase about lucid confidence. Because confidence was as impossible as lucidity. Moreover, though the Marshal was perfectly right in asserting the need for a National Revolution, the effect of the self-conscious nobility of his utterances on those who heard them depended on their willingness to forget that the Army had not wanted to fight. He had seen Major Delibes in a restaurant the night before last and heard him speak in a language which echoed the Marshal's; and Delibes had run away, deserting his men, while Alain Querouaille had been killed.

But it was necessary to ignore Halévy's gibes. He wanted to send him away, but the consciousness of his dislike and the memory of the worn parchment of Madame Villepreux's face prevented him from doing so.

'What do you want then?' he said again. 'And this time please try to give me an answer which will be of some help to us both.'

'I'm a teacher,' Halévy said.

'And that's impossible.'

'And a writer.'

'Which is dangerous.'

'So,' Halévy said, 'I am unemployable in France, and have wasted my time in coming here.'

Lucien said, 'And yet I promised Madame Villepreux.'

This was not true, for he had not been in a position to make such a promise and was anyway too wary to do so.

He said, 'I think you must leave the country.'

It was his first act of treachery, and he was not sure even that he knew what he was betraying. He took such measures as were necessary – the provision of suitable papers – to make it possible for Halévy to do so. It seemed an act of humanity to him. He was acquitting himself of a debt which he had voluntarily incurred. He was salving his conscience by proving to himself that the individual counted for something. There were all sorts of soothing explanations he could offer. But it was still an act of betrayal. In helping Halévy, he was confessing that the National Revolution was a lie, that he had bound himself to a monstrous farce.

He hid this knowledge from himself for a long time. When, that winter, he visited his mother at the Château de l'Haye – and must incidentally have held his little bastard son in his arms – he was still free from distress because of what he had done; able to present it to himself as an act of exceptional benevolence, exceptional precisely because it had no wider significance.

His mother sparkled with pride to see him. He was the servant of a State with which she could at last identify, to which she could give her blessing. She invited his uncle the Bishop to visit, and they joined in a purring communion. Lucien expanded in the sunshine of her approval. When he talked of the Marshal and what he was doing for France his mother crossed herself and the Bishop said he regarded him as a Redeemer, for whose continued health he prayed every day.

'I can see,' he said, 'the mark of his benevolence in your demeanour. You are a different man, dear boy. It must feel as if you have come home, working in close association with the Marshal. It is like coming to a knowledge of salvation.'

One subject was forbidden. This was his brother Armand. When, on his first evening home, he tried to tell his mother of his last meeting with Armand in Bordeaux, she said, 'Don't speak of him. He has brought disgrace on our name.' That was of course a common reaction among good families.

'In his way, mother,' Lucien said, 'Armand is a patriot too.'

'A patriot,' she said, 'associating with riff-raff.'

When he had first mentioned the possibility of emigration to Halévy, the schoolteacher had objected to 'those Monarchist corner-boys around de Gaulle, that absurd little General'.

Lucien had always loved winter in Provence even more than the hot weather. It delighted him when the *mistral* blew icy gusts as he struggled up a jagged hillside to see snow-capped mountains. He loved to hear the rattle of the naked olive trees, and to smell roasting chestnuts in the cafés of the little town. It was a pleasure to turn up the collar of his coat as he sat outside in the late afternoon, and to experience the moment on the terrace when he had at last to admit that it was impossible to sit there and read any longer. What he valued most was the assurance of brevity the winter brought.

Only one thing depressed him that first winter of the war. This was the stream of people approaching him to beg that he should intervene on their behalf with the authorities, to procure a licence for this, a post for a son, a special concession of some sort. He did not yet admit that their importunity defined the regime to which he had given his heart and mind, but he was embarrassed to be seen as the fount of favour. The most persistent of these clients was the *garagiste* Simon, who not only besought favours for himself and his family – in a wheedling tone that was especially irksome – but was also quick to relay information to him about the misdemeanours of his neighbours – how Jean was already working the Black Market, Pierre contravening licensing regulations – and so on. Eventually Lucien was forced to say:

'I'm not the police, you know. These are matters for them.'

'Ah,' Simon said, 'but they will listen to a big shot like you, whereas a poor man like myself is quite without influence . . .'

IN MARCH '41 Lucien paid his first visit to occupied Paris. He was prepared, of course, to find the streets full of German uniforms and empty of civilian motorcars, and for the shabbiness of the children's clothes, but nothing had prepared him for the emotion he felt on unlocking the door of his own apartment in the Rue Claude Bernard and finding a pile of the last number of his magazine in the hall, with dust lying thick and unruffled on it. He went through to the cold bedroom and looked at the bed he had shared with Polly, and wondered who she was sleeping with now. He had accustomed himself to the knowledge that she would be unfaithful and that his marriage was over, but he had not imagined that the sight of his marriage bed would distress him. He lay down on the bed and looked up at the dark ceiling, and then at a photograph of Polly which stood in a silver frame on the table beside him. There was nothing else in the room to remind him of her, and yet her presence pervaded it.

He thought, and spoke his thought aloud: 'Will I ever be ready to love another?'

He had come to Paris on government business, and yet the next morning found it impossible to leave his apartment. For a long time he could not even rise from the bed, where he had lain sleepless, listening to the night, the cats, and the awakening city. He tried to telephone the office of the Ministry where he was expected, but, despite orders, the telephone had not been re-connected. There was nothing to keep him in the apartment, and yet he could not leave it. Across the hall, in the dining room, Gaston Hunnot had once lectured him about the power of the Will, until Polly, pushing aside the brimming ash-tray which was a measure of her boredom, had said, in English and with a rose-garden English sigh, 'This particular Will is to be fucked. Good-night, Monsieur Hunnot,' and drifted through to the bedroom, beckoning him with a glance so utterly compulsive that he had had Hunnot out of the house within five minutes.

'Whatever made you speak out like that?'

She had put naked arms round his neck, and thrust her tongue into his mouth, and for a long time they had stood, still, entwined, like a statue of love; and there had been no need of words to . . .

Remembering it, standing there, in the cold dusty room, he felt an upsurge of desire; the memory of lust sharper than anticipation can ever be.

'What have I done? Whatever has made me act as I have?' There came a knock at the door. They had sent someone from the Ministry to find him, and his state must be obvious and shameful.

It was, to his confusion, a girl who was standing there. She was slim, pale, and wearing a dark suit cut like a uniform. That was all he took in at first.

She explained that they had been worried when he did not appear, and she had been sent to find him. There was a driver downstairs.

'I'm not ready,' he said, 'Come in, though I can't even offer you coffee.'

She entered without speaking. He was grateful for that. He sensed, though he couldn't say why, that she was a girl who would be able to deny herself unnecessary words.

'I've been confused,' he said. 'It's my first visit to Paris, you understand, since the Occupation, and I came to this apartment where I used to live with my wife, and I shouldn't have done so.'

She sat on the arm of a chair. He saw that she had dark chestnut hair, cut short, a clear skin, and big eyes to which he couldn't put a colour: they were dark, yet with a shade of blue.

He was surprised to find himself noticing this. He wanted to break down and weep, and be comforted by her. Instead, he held out his hand and watched it tremble.

'You must think me absurd,' he said. 'I didn't think coming here would affect me as it has.'

He went through to the bathroom and shaved in cold water, cutting himself twice. The sky was as grey as a German uniform, and the nearby dome of the Val-de-Grâce disappeared into mist. A clock struck, twelve times. 'I've missed an important meeting,' he thought.

'We put the meeting back,' the girl said, 'till the afternoon. We said you had been delayed, or weren't well, I don't know which excuse they used. But a satisfactory one, I'm sure.'

'So we have time,' he said.

'Time?'

'Is it possible to have lunch somewhere? I have realised I'm hungry.'

'Of course.'

'Well, then . . .'

'You'll need a coat,' she said. 'It's bitter outside. No wind, but gripping cold.'

'But you haven't got one.'

'I'm not susceptible to cold. I don't feel it. My mother says I have the Atlantic in my veins and icebergs in my bones.'

They ate in a little Alsatian restaurant behind the Panthéon to which she directed the driver without consulting Lucien, who was both amused and impressed by her certainty.

'You'll want a cup of coffee while we order,' she said. 'For some reason that I don't understand, the coffee here is still genuine. That's why I chose this place.'

Lucien was grateful for the good coffee. He told her that her advice had been so good he would leave her to order the lunch. She nodded her head and told the waiter they would both have onion tart, followed by smoked sausages, and to drink, a bottle of Gewürztraminer.

They were sitting at a little table in the back of the restaurant, which was beginning to fill up. Lucien found himself trembling again; his coffee-cup rattled against the saucer. He was afraid someone he knew would enter. As if she divined the reason for his agitation, the girl told the waiter to bring a little screen and cut them off from the general view. He obeyed in a manner which suggested that she was known there and respected.

'I'm so sorry,' Lucien said, and wondered again if he was going to break down completely. He dug his nails into the palms of his hands.

'I'm not usually like this,' he managed to say. She lit a cigarette and pushed the packet across the table in his direction. When he looked at it doubtfully, she took the cigarette from her mouth and offered it to him. Their fingers brushed as he took it from her, and then she lit another for herself. They smoked in silence. She inhaled, and held the smoke for a long time in her lungs. She didn't look more than eighteen.

The tart arrived. It was creamy and sharp-tasting and went well with the smoky wine, but he was not able to eat more than a few forkfuls, till he had finished his first glass and was drinking the second. He never normally drank more than one at lunchtime, and was accustomed to put water in that. Was this girl going to change all his habits? It must be a dozen years since he had eaten in an Alsatian restaurant.

She said, 'I wangled this job with you. I had a reason.'

He didn't understand what she meant, and could only look at

her. Her mouth was soft and curving. She had eaten her tart, and there was a little crumb adhering to her upper lip. She flicked out her tongue and removed it, and then, with a gesture as if to ask a permission that she knew would be granted her, lit another cigarette. They were ordinary Caporal.

'My name's Anne Querouaille,' she said, 'and my brother Alain was in your regiment. He wrote to us about the conversations he used to have with you, which I suppose he shouldn't have done, but my mother and brother and I are all grateful to you. Alain was so sure that he had found a friend, his last friend as it turned out, and so I wanted to know you. I hope you don't mind.'

And now, at the mention of Alain's name, he was at last crying indeed. It seemed as if all the tears he had restrained since childhood welled up and broke forth. He felt the awful delight of surrender. The girl, Anne, laid her hand on his, and said nothing. Then, as he dabbed his cheeks with the napkin, she said:

'When we knew Alain was dead, which wasn't for some time, not till the letter you wrote to my mother – we hoped of course he had been taken prisoner till then – well, at first, I couldn't weep for him, not a single tear, and, do you know, I resented you because you had had the chance to talk to him before he died, and that had been denied me, and then even more because you brought us the news we feared to receive.'

'Forgive me,' he said, 'I have never broken down like that before.'

'There is nothing to forgive.'

She stayed by his side throughout the meeting, at his urgent request. It strengthened him to know that she was there, and he was able to conduct himself in a satisfactory manner. Various problems relating to the difficulties experienced in the Ministry in exercising their continuing responsibilities for the appointment of teachers in the occupied zone were discussed; suggestions were advanced which, when suitably examined, might form a basis for developing a means of resolving the difficulties which nobody of course had anticipated. Altogether, it was generally agreed, the meeting was 'useful'. Lucien contrived, by the exercise of his will, to disguise his inability to follow much that was said; nobody appeared to find his behaviour odd or out of the ordinary. That was a considerable achievement on his part. It left him exhausted.

He said to Anne, as the others gathered up their papers, 'Do you know anywhere else, nearby preferably, where we can get real coffee?'

'Yes,' she said, 'I'll take you there.'

'And can you stay with me this evening?' he said when they were settled in the corner of a little bar.

He had already dismissed his driver.

'I can't,' he said, 'promise you anything amusing. Far from it. It's difficult, in fact. I must go and see my brother's wife.'

'Would I be in the way?'

'No, you would help me.'

'Then of course I'll come.'

CHAPTER NINETEEN

Document 10: Letter from Madame Berthe
de Balafré to Etienne de Balafré

MY DEAR ETIENNE: Of course I was surprised to receive your
letter, and yet, even though it is so many years since we have seen
one another, it was as if I had always expected it. I have never
ceased to think of you with affection, and to pray that you have
been able to forgive me for the part I have played in your life. And
I suspect that, despite everything you so kindly say now, I have, if
not destroyed it, yet twisted it in an appalling manner. As with all
the really damaging acts one performs, I did it with the best
motives. But I take your letter as evidence, in a sense, of
absolution. I am grateful, and to be able to feel gratitude in
old age is so rare that your letter indeed brought tears to my eyes.

Yet the discovery that you wish to delve deeper in the past
alarms me. I wish for your sake you would let it go. At the same
time I realise that I have no right to say 'for your sake', con-
sidering how mischievous my previous intervention was.

I am therefore assailed by doubt, amounting to anguish, and I
only wish my poor dear Armand was here to give me, as he always
did, fortitude.

But, in all the circumstances, I am bound to accede to your
request, though I do so reluctantly, for a host of reasons.

Yet – a final confession – in some mysterious way I find myself
welcoming the opportunity you force on me. It is like opening the
last door of a haunted house in a nightmare. It sounds pretentious
to call life a nightmare, but it is certainly true that one contains the
other.

It was horrifying, you know, how accustomed one became to
the Occupation in its first year. That ass de Beauvoir said in one of
her interminable books of memoirs, which are, as I have always
said, orgies of egotism, that 'the same violent prejudice and
stupidity that had darkened my childhood, now extended over
the entire country, an official and repressive blanket'. But it
wasn't like that at all. Even those of us who disapproved of the
armistice, whose husbands and lovers had joined de Gaulle in
England, as my dear Armand had, felt a certain relief, a deep

sense of comfort, when we thought of the Marshal. That was in the first year, when we trusted that somehow or other he could protect us. There was no Resistance then, you know, and there were days, many days, when I thought Armand had been mistaken. One reason I looked forward to seeing Lucien was because of my confidence that he was acting as a moral guardian for me and the children. I gave out of course that I had no idea where Armand was, and said I believed he had been lost in battle. Later I wondered if I had been cowardly, but it seemed sensible then.

So I was eager to see Lucien, and it was unfortunate that Guy called that evening. (Yes, my dear, the same Guy whose name you have so often cursed, the father of your poor Freddie.) I didn't want him to meet Lucien because they had never liked each other, and also because, though Guy had not joined de Gaulle, whom he regarded as impossibly right-wing, he nevertheless deplored Vichy; and I knew he would pick a fight. He was always argumentative. I knew also that if I told him Lucien was coming he would certainly stay. Anyway, hard though I tried, I couldn't get rid of him, and I was even wondering if I should endeavour to do so by pretending that I was expecting a lover (which he would not have believed) when the doorbell rang, and it was Lucien.

I was surprised to see a girl with him, and then I thought, after all, why not, Polly has left him forever. But I thought it in poor taste of him to have brought his mistress to my apartment. It was surprising because Lucien's manners were usually perfect. The girl couldn't keep her eyes off him. That was the next thing I saw. And several times, when he hesitated and seemed lost for words, he would turn to her looking for help. I thought, you know, they had been living together for weeks, but they hadn't.

Lucien was clearly tired, and he wasn't pleased to see Guy, because – I suppose, or I learned later – he had really wanted to talk to me about Armand and wasn't willing to trust Guy. That was quite right of course. In those days who could you trust? But Lucien obviously trusted the girl. Anne, that was her name. Do you know, my dear, for a moment I couldn't remember it. But I forget so much now.

I couldn't forget the way Guy looked at Lucien. When one person really hates another and the second isn't aware of anything more than a certain incompatibility, the atmosphere can be very strange. It was like that afternoon which I know you will never forget, in the churchyard when we were waiting for the storm to break.

Guy at once berated Lucien about the anti-Jewish decrees. You will remember that Freddie's mother was Jewish, but you may not know that she taught philosophy at the university, and she had of course been dismissed from her post as a result of the decrees. Lucien was perturbed; it was as if he had never considered that the decrees which his own Ministry had drafted could have any personal application. He couldn't imagine they could affect people he knew. This is so often the case with anti-Semitism, people make exceptions of their personal acquaintance, so that Jews only exist in the abstract. But Danielle wasn't abstract. She was a lively, beautiful, intelligent woman, and a good one, and Lucien knew this. So that when Guy exploded, 'You are destroying lives for a theory, and a disgusting one at that,' he had no answer.

'The whole of Vichy is only a theory,' Guy said. 'These idiots have their certain idea of France, but the France which they would wish to impose on us has never existed.'

'You can't believe that,' Lucien said. 'You know very well that our ideals are admirable, and if perhaps they do represent an ideal society which has never been, why, that is true of Christianity also, and, if I may say so, Guy, for I think you now incline in that direction, of the Marxist Paradise too. A man's aim should reach further than his grasp. If not, we achieve nothing.'

'Ideals!' Guy said. 'You talk of ideals, but who really runs your France? Laval! I confess I find it hard to associate Laval with any ideals whatsoever.'

'Laval,' Lucien said, 'is not entirely to my taste, I grant you that. There is a coarseness, an abrasiveness to him which I find displeasing. Nevertheless, Monsieur Laval is a patriot. I have no doubt of that. The trouble with people like you, Guy, is that you are guilty of precisely the same fault as you attribute to us. You are living in an imaginary world. Even if we set aside the vices of the Republic – and it is hard to do so – you cannot pretend that the events of last summer did not take place. We have lost a war. That is the starting-point. What do you do when you have lost a war? Believe me, it is a real problem, and not everyone can retire into private life and pretend it hasn't happened or doesn't matter. The truth is, you have to come to some sort of terms with your conquerors. That is the starting-point. Once you admit that, once you have the virtue to confront the facts, then you will find yourself compelled to act as we have acted, often, I confess, in ways that we would not choose . . .'

You may wonder, Etienne, that I remember so clearly. Of course, I don't pretend that these were exactly Lucien's words, but I hope to give you the sense, and the passion. He trembled as he spoke, he felt it so. And one word is, I promise you, exact. The word 'virtue'. That phrase – 'the virtue to confront the facts' – those were his precise words. I admired his use of the word 'virtue', which I understood in the full Latin sense.

'You cannot construct a politics, or a theory of action, on the basis of what you would like to have happened,' he said.

All the time the girl Anne watched him. She had curious dark eyes which kept changing colour according to the expression on her face. Once she laid her hand on his forearm, with a gesture of the utmost tenderness. It was obvious to me not only that she was in love with him, but that she recognised that this fine and tortured spirit sought comfort.

How, I have often wondered, remembering that evening and the way she looked at him, could she have been brought to betray him?

For she did that, you know.

That was the only time I saw Lucien during the war, therefore my last meeting with him. We went to Normandy the following spring, and remained there. Of course he wrote to me, but that's not the same thing. I don't have any of his letters. It was not a time to keep letters.

I tremble to think into what depths your investigation will lead you. But I would impress this on you: there was nothing dishonourable in Lucien's adherence to Vichy, no matter to what terrible actions he may have been led.

You ask about my health. It is poor, which must be expected. The twins and my other grandchildren are a great comfort. It is not often that I hear from my dear Jeanne-Marie. She is in the Sudan now. She writes of the bones sticking out of the flanks of cattle and of children with the swollen bellies of starvation. But you will have seen all that on the television. If you should find yourself in Paris, please come and see me.

Your loving aunt,

Berthe de Balafré.

CHAPTER TWENTY

LUCIEN WAS UNABLE to arrange immediately for Anne's transfer from Paris to Vichy, or perhaps they hesitated before an act which must be regarded as one of definite commitment. But she was there early in the spring of 1941, and they were certainly living together soon after her arrival. Despite the insistence of the regime on high standards of personal morality and all the stuff about the sanctity of family life, such irregular liaisons were common enough. Pétain after all, octogenarian though he was, still had his mistress, and was indeed known to claim that women continued to try to force their attentions on him; one of his biographers tells us that he made love for the last time in 1942, at the age of eighty-six.

My grandmother never spoke of Anne, though she certainly stayed at the Château de l'Haye. I can see that she might have wished to pretend that the girl did not exist, but surely the fact of betrayal might have opened her lips. It is very strange; I wonder if young Hugh will be able to guess a reason? American biographers are good at divining what nobody knows. But I keep forgetting that Hugh is Canadian.

I have a problem in dealing with this part of Lucien's life. He wrote nothing about it, for he did not resume keeping his intermittent journal till the end of that year. I find myself unable to imagine its details without the help of any documentary material. It is a task for an Israelite – making bricks without straw. Exodus doesn't tell us however whether they were successful in doing this or not; and were such bricks as they made of tolerable quality?

The blank period was obviously passed in the unremitting duties of administration, and in what I would like to think of as domestic bliss with Anne. Because they were together, no letters survive, and, though I have talked to a couple of his old associates in Vichy, their evidence was of no value. 'They seemed happy enough. She was good for him, you know. Oh yes, there is no doubt she loved him. When we dined together, she would order for him, and she couldn't keep her eyes off him. As for him,

I remember the tender manner in which he held her coat for her when we rose to leave a restaurant.'

That sort of stuff; not very illuminating. But it is useful perhaps if it serves to remind us that life in Vichy was distinguished by its normality. One is so apt to think of war and defeat as wholly disruptive that it is useful to remember how powerful is the human instinct to create order. You can see it in prisoners who put a glass of flowers on a table in their cell. We aspire to domesticity, for we are domestic animals. Lucien and Anne were clearly not exceptional.

There are however two moments in the summer of 1941 to which it is worth drawing attention.

All spring there had been a debate in the Ministry of Education. The subject was what would be a suitable monument to the Marshal and the National Revolution. It's normal of course to reserve monuments till the person to be honoured is dead, but that argument was quickly disposed of. The Marshal should be honoured in his life by an act which would bear witness to the nobility of his task and the nature of the glorious revolution (it has become glorious early in the memoranda) which he had inaugurated.

Some suggested that statues of the Marshal be erected before the town hall of every municipality. One supporter of this project wrote: 'They should bear the simple legend: Blessed Saviour of France.' This proposal won general applause, and was rejected only when, after consultation with the Ministry of Beaux Arts, it was realised that they could not possibly find a sufficient number of sculptors of requisite quality. A suggestion that the statues should be cast-iron replicas of a masterwork was rejected on the grounds that it smacked of industrialism. Besides, some said, both stone and ironwork lack the note of humanity which the Marshal gives to everything he touches; this was undeniable.

'Napoleon is commemorated by the Arc de Triomphe,' one minute ran. 'The hero of Verdun and the Saviour of 1940 requires a comparable monument.'

General applause again. Unfortunately, however, new objections were advanced. It might have been thought that these would be put forward on the grounds that a triumphal arch was scarcely the most fitting monument for a leader who, whatever his virtues, had assumed power as a consequence of a national disaster, a resounding defeat – and indeed this view was advanced, though anonymously and timidly. That however was an argument easily

overturned: the call to Pétain, and his response, after all represented a moral triumph in the hour of adversity. Therefore, a
triumphal arch was perfectly appropriate. The trouble was quite
different. The proper place for such an arch was Paris. To raise it
in Vichy was to subscribe to the treasonable theory that France
had been divided; it was to admit that the Marshal was head of a
State that was less than France. Impossible and repulsive thought!
But, alas, it was inconceivable that the Germans would permit the
erection of a new Arc de Triomphe in Paris. The proposal was
rejected.

The committee's debate was now becoming wider. Proposals
flew hither and thither. One cynic even suggested building a
mausoleum, but he made the suggestion *sotto voce*. The argument
lasted for several sessions. At last Lucien, who had up to now
contented himself with offering restrained and, as it were apolo-
getic, objections to each new proposal, addressed the committee.

'Gentlemen,' he said, 'we seem to have reached an *impasse*. It
is, I think, because we have been proceeding in the wrong
direction. We have been thinking of man-made objects. But
the Marshal is both our gift from God and a force of Nature
in himself. I think we should base our thoughts on that understanding. Now, on the one hand, as Under-secretary of the
Ministry of Education, I know very well where the true and
enduring monument to his work and influence is to be found;
it rests in the hearts and minds of our schoolchildren. They are
the future of France and they are being formed according to his
wisdom and understanding. It is possible, therefore, to argue that
we need no other memorial to the National Revolution. Nevertheless, I recognise the desire of this committee to have such a
memorial, to have something tangible and enduring which will
say to future generations: thus we revered Pétain, thus we ask you
to remember him. But we cannot agree on such a memorial
because, as I say, we are thinking in the wrong manner. Let us
therefore pause to consider the Marshal and what he represents,
to consider this gift from God and force of Nature. Is it not then
apparent that it is in Nature itself that we must seek the right
memorial? The Marshal shelters us from sun, rain and adversity.
His strength gives us strength, and a suitable memorial will bear
witness to the nature of his strength. He is simple and serene and
enduring. Does it not seem that he is like a great tree, and that
only a tree – let me be more specific – a great oak tree – will be the
proper monument to his Being and his Work for France.'

This speech was greeted with general acclaim, and so it was

that, on a May morning, a cavalcade of official cars lurched out of Vichy, into the mountains, to the forest of Troncais, for the ceremony of dedication. They had brought a tame Bishop along, of course, to do the deed. All the court was present, but Lucien, as the author of the plan, was granted the privilege of travelling with the Marshal. It was unfortunate that Pétain was in a bad temper. He was suffering from indigestion, and complained for most of the journey. It must have been disappointing for Lucien, but then, I suppose indigestion is a force of nature just as the Marshal was; though I doubt if he consoled himself with that thought.

However, they arrived at last, and Pétain pulled himself together. He was always admirable on parade. Seeing him stand, erect, on the little podium provided (after much debate), his moustaches puffing in the breeze, his face pink and glowing, was to understand the rightness of the ceremony. He didn't even fidget when the Bishop spoke for much longer than he had been told to, though later in the car he said to Lucien,

'Went on a bloody bit, didn't he. All the same, these preaching fellows. What they need, I've always told my chaplains, is a half-hour square-bashing every morning.'

For the Marshal, though loquacious on the subject of Christian values, had in fact little time for the Church's ministers. If it was really the Army of Christ, he seemed to feel, they should be a damn sight more soldierly.

You may wonder at my tone. I treat this affair as an absurdity, because when you come to think of it, there could hardly be anything more absurd than lugging an octogenarian suffering from indigestion into the middle of a distant forest in order that he might be present at a ceremony in which he was compared to an oak tree and at which he would stand solemnly and watch this tree being dedicated to his memory.

Still, he was pleased enough.

'Went off very well, I thought,' he said to Lucien. 'Good idea of yours, makes me feel my self-denial is appreciated.'

Then he fell asleep and didn't wake until they stopped for lunch.

Lucien published an article: 'Reflections on the Pétain Oak'. Its peroration ran: 'Finally, we ask, what does this signify for France, for our country which the Marshal loves, serves and incarnates? When our children ask us to explain the meaning of the Pétain Oak, what shall we finally say? In one sentence, this: The National Revolution is also a Natural Revolution. Its roots are buried deep in the soil of France, like the oak tree's, and it rises from the good earth of France sturdy and magnificent. Our children are young saplings under the protection of that mighty oak.'

Poor Lucien, I don't think it can have occurred to him that the spreading branches of a great tree deny light to whatever grows under it.

For a time that spring and early summer Vichy was quiet. The war seemed far away. There was no resistance, even in the occupied zone. The censorship authorities reported that of the more than five hundred thousand mentions of the Marshal they had recorded in the two and a quarter million letters intercepted in April, 95 per cent were wholly favourable. There were rumours that he maintained contact with de Gaulle. 'He's an old fox, playing a deep game,' people said. But in May Lucien was told that the British had offered information about a journey de Gaulle was planning to the Near East, so that French planes could intercept him, and thus rid both Churchill and Pétain of an embarrassment.

'The Marshal would never consent to his murder,' Lucien said. 'On the other hand,' he told Anne that evening, 'his arrest would be another matter. Do you know that the Marshal now refers to him as a viper he nursed in his bosom?'

Anne said: 'Your brother is with de Gaulle. You ought to find a means to warn him. It's not right that Frenchmen should conspire against each other in this way.'

'When have we not done so?' Lucien asked.

They were happy together that summer. They went to the races, ate in restaurants, walked in the mountains. Lucien commemorated their activities in a long poem, indifferent in quality, but sure in feeling.

On the 8th of June they heard that British forces had attacked French troops in Syria. 'It's war again,' people said, the Marshal himself among them. But that war was far distant. Then on the 22nd of June Hitler invaded the Soviet Union. For the first days Lucien was jubilant. If there was a crusade against atheistic Bolshevism, then there could at last be no doubt that Vichy was on the side of virtue and the angels. I have a witness who remembers him saying that: a curious story, for he had concealed such doubts till then, from all, I suppose, except perhaps Anne.

Hugh, these notes grow ever more fragmentary, and, I fear, unhelpful. The fact is – you will have to accept it – that the period of Lucien's life between the fall of France and the invasion of the Soviet Union is largely time lost. Only a few shafts of light penetrate the darkness. I have given you what I can; you don't want me to invent what I neither know nor can truly imagine.

We are trapped here, it seems to me, in the lie of biography. Biography pretends to tell the truth about people's lives, but it can deal only with what is revealed, and this is not the most truthful element. Autobiographical revelation is always itself an artistic construction, and therefore unreliable: it offers an approved version, it is like Soviet history, from which everything inconvenient is expunged. When biography relies, as it often does, on letters, we, the readers, receive the least characteristic of utterances.

What I would really like to know is what Lucien and Anne said when they were alone, on the terrace of their apartment, dining at the corner table of a little restaurant, lying in bed after lovemaking. I don't know this, and I'm not capable of making it up, and I don't think it would help you if I did.

Here I sit, in my dull hotel room, with its stained mahogany, and a table flecked with cigar-ash, the brandy bottle at my right hand, and a smeared glass showing that I have been drinking for a long time, listening for voices. But all I hear belong to the present. There is the absurd Baroness, there is the clerk who every morning tells me that the *Journal de Genève* may be a dull paper, but is to be believed, 'and that's something, sir, in the world of today'; and I feel oppressed by the thought that I have failed you, Hugh, in this task which I so reluctantly undertook, as I have failed myself in every part of my life.

Thinking of Anne, I thought and dreamed last night of my own wife, and she seemed equally remote and insubstantial.

My hotel room begins to seem like a prison cell, like the one in which my father hanged himself.

Forgive this melodrama. You will be relieved to know that I have something authentic, in my father's hand, to send you in my next batch. But I want to read it again myself first.

CHAPTER TWENTY-ONE

Document 11: Manuscript of
Lucien de Balafré, dated December 31, 1941

AM I AN egotist? Certainly. I dislike myself but am fascinated by
the story of my own life, and by my own thoughts. Yet these are
frequently banal, or would seem so to me if presented by others.
This is perhaps why I dote on Stendhal, though finding his
opinions ridiculous and disagreeable. It's his honesty that ap-
peals, even when he does not realise he is deceiving himself. Or do
I mean 'especially when . . .'

In several of his books I have made marginal notes reading:
'This is me.'

'All my life,' he says somewhere, 'I have had a horror of coarse
individuals.'

Yet, like me, he couldn't remain in his own room with his
books.

This has been a momentous year in which the agony of the
world has intensified. And I have found happiness. Is that absurd?
Or wicked?

There is a frost outside, a mild frost. The trees sparkle and the
air is like champagne. I have just drunk my coffee, and the little
black cat which Anne brought home last month is stretched out in
the sunshine on my desk. Anne herself is still asleep. I looked
through a few minutes ago, and she was curled up like a child. I
touched her cheek with my fingers, and she uttered a little moan,
as if of pleasure, or rather as if asking for the postponement of
pleasure. My heart turned over.

I had lunch in Paris in the autumn with Monsieur Laval. He
wishes to return to the government, but on his own terms, and he
believes I might be useful to him. 'You have, I know, the
Marshal's ear,' he said.

For a moment I thought he was going to reach forward and
tweak mine, as if he was Napoleon.

Laval is disgruntled. He believes everything is in danger of
going wrong. This is because he is excluded from government.

'It is absurd,' he told me, 'not to desire a German victory, however much one dislikes Germans. That is the best hope for France. Otherwise we shall have a Communist government or else become mere appendages of the Anglo-Saxons. Believe me, if Germany loses the war, Europe is finished. The new world will be divided between the Anglo-Saxons and the Russians. We'll only be a battleground. Do you know, when I was in Moscow in '35, I saw nobody smile. There was only one exception: Stalin himself.'

He smoked incessantly, sipped brandy and gulped mineral water.

'Of course de Gaulle is necessary, in case that happens,' he said. 'He would then do what he could to save something of France. But the Reds would be too strong for him. Believe me, I know, I've been in my time a man of the Left myself. No, my friend, there are only two men who can save France. One is de Gaulle, the other Laval. You realise this in your own family, for your brother is with de Gaulle, isn't he? As for you, you should stick to Laval.'

He was loquacious, indiscreet, charming and repulsive.

'Pétain thinks he is in charge, but he's too old. He no more steers the ship than the figurehead does. As for Darlan, the beautiful Admiral, he's an imbecile, believe me.'

Laval bites his nails, and when he smiles you can see his bad teeth. Yet he's right. He is our best hope.

When you talk with a man of power you are easily seduced into thinking: 'This is real life.' But it's only a parody. Kneeling in prayer in a cold church just after dawn, holding your mistress in your arms, watching the first morning sun touch the branches of winter trees with pink and gold: all these, appealing at first to the senses, or perceived by the senses, belong to the whole man.

Moreover, they are good.

Speaking with Laval, I experienced the thrill of pain and its infliction.

Anne met me at the railway station. She was wearing a fur coat and a little fur hat.

'You look like a kitten,' I said; but her cheek was icy.

She kissed me and I came alive.

One popular lie: that we wish to be understood.

In fact, we flee understanding. My marriage to Polly dissolved because we understood each other too well. Anne does not understand me at all, and has the good manners not to wish to do so. That is the first reason why I live comfortably with her.

I do not believe God understands us either. Freedom from understanding is a condition of the freedom he has accorded us.

I saw others in Paris: Colette, who spends hours every day

watching the coming and going in the Palais-Royal; she talked to me of the sufferings of the poor. 'I know,' she said, 'that the poor have always suffered, old women especially; but this is more bitter. They have no hope and they haven't enough to eat.'

I called on Drieu at the offices of the *NRF*, which he is now editing. He folded me in his arms. Since he failed to remove the cigarette which is held perpetually, like an Olympic flame, in the right corner of his mouth, I was apprehensive. But his delight in seeing me was itself delightful.

'At last,' he cried, 'a true civilised friend. You've no idea how awful it is here in Paris. Sometimes I even find myself believing that Otto – you know the German Ambassador Otto Abetz, don't you – is the only civilised man except for myself in the city. But they tell me you are in love, my friend, charming, charming. If it wasn't for women, I would cut my throat, I get so depressed sometimes.'

Nobody could seem less depressed than Drieu. He swept me off to the Brasserie Lipp, to eat frankfurters and potato salad. He talked merrily, all the time, and smoked between forkfuls.

'I am a Fascist now, you know,' he said, and laughed. 'Yes, I have the courage to call myself that, which is burning my boats if you like. But I am a Fascist, Lucien, because I have seen, I have measured, the progress of European decadence. We need a clean start, a break. Snap: that's the past gone. Do you know, Mauriac was here the other night and they shouted at him, "Get out, Mauriac, friend of Jews, you've no place in Paris," and he called back, "You don't frighten me, lice." You couldn't imagine an exchange like that in Pericles' Athens, could you?'

(But I could.)

'It's what I mean by decadence.'

We drank Alsatian wine.

'I regard it as a symbol of Franco-German solidarity,' he said. 'A French wine with a German name. Perfect.' (But the Germans have annexed Alsace: has he forgotten?)

He talked and talked, smoked and drank, pressed my arm as if we were the dearest friends he said we were, though we are only good friends, even friendly acquaintances, spoke to me as if he needed me, and urged me to write for his magazine.

'You've no idea the tripe I get, ideologically sound perhaps, but of no literary quality. Sometimes I think even the Germans could do better.'

He called for another bottle.

'Let's put the snake back on the tree,' he said.

'Shall I tell you a secret?' he said.

He leaned across the table. There was a little twitch in his right cheek. He took the cigarette from his mouth and stabbed it at me.

'There are times when I'm afraid the Germans are going to lose the war. They're such fools, you see. To invade Russia. That's really crass. It's breaking the first law of war: don't invade Russia. Their only hope is the sheer inefficiency of Communism, and that's really staggering. Stalin murdered the whole officer corps, you know.'

He stubbed out his cigarette, lit another.

'I don't mind confessing to you, Lucien, because you're discreet, and a gentleman. My position is frightfully boring: the magazine, the whole business of collaboration, of being a responsible person, it's irritated me from the start. Yet I was so eager to get my hands on it. Strange. And I'm stuck. I've got to play the part to the end. To the curtain. And it's absurd. To work, to labour, for an idea of Europe, when the Germans, who are alone in the position to remould Europe, really have no idea what they want, when my fellow-collaborationists, which is a good joke in itself, are divided, and divided fools; and to do all this in the middle of a population that wants Europe to be English, American or Russian, it's wearying. I'm so tired and we're not halfway through the comedy. The invasion of Russia is the opening of the third act, at most. And weariness breeds fear. I often feel like killing myself . . . Are you afraid, Lucien? Do you think we have been dealt the wrong cards . . ?'

What could I say? That in such times as ours fear stalks the corridors of night like a corrupt policeman?

To all appearances the war goes well. Hitler has advanced deep into Russia.

'Remember,' Drieu said, 'Napoleon took Moscow.'

He already believes, clearly, that Germany will lose the war.

I said, 'Collaboration is not a faith, it's an exercise, in which we shouldn't put our trust. Let's not think of Europe, which is a myth and delusion. Remember we are French. The interests of France, the interests of the historic sovereign State which is France, and the interests of Frenchmen, are all that need concern us. We have to play a waiting game, to tolerate' – did I lower my voice, to a whisper, as I spoke of the interests of France in the heart of the French capital? I, as a Minister of the French State? – 'to tolerate the Germans as our conquerors. But we need do no more. Friendship is unnecessary. It's a mistake, my dear, to bind yourself to the occupying power. Perhaps I see that more clearly, being based in Vichy. But that's the Marshal's opinion also. We must consult only the interests of France.'

'Oh yes,' he said, 'but when you play roulette, zero belongs to the bank. We have no choice but to put our stake on the red or the black, odds or evens. That's the nature of the game, and therefore of our choice, and you can't shift your stake while the wheel spins. Besides, I'm afraid that the Marshal inhabits a world remote from reality. It's the privilege of the old, denied to you and me. So I think we should have some more brandy. Cognac can do more than commonsense to reconcile us to destiny.'

He talked of killing himself, of the temptation of the gun, razor and medicine bottle, but my memory of the evening is of his laugh ringing out, mocking and free. Was it however the notion of freedom that he really mocked?

I was so busy, this time in Paris. I had no time to reflect. My time was taken up by a stream of visitors, too many of whom seemed to be seeking some form of reassurance from me. I strove to supply what I could not feel myself. Or perhaps feed to myself.

When back here in Vichy I thought of my talk with Drieu, of that confession of faith which I had made, it seemed to me that, without realising it, it was also a confession of infidelity. After all, for years, thanks to my long and enduring conversation with Rupert – and of course thanks to my reading – I have believed in Europe. What did I used to call it: the European Idea? And I have been driven to abandon that hope. Christendom is dead. The black uniforms of the SS are a vile parody of the Teutonic Knights of whom I dreamed. We are inhabitants of a besieged city, driven back into the citadel. No one in a citadel ever believes in the Future. *L'Echo de l'Avenir* is drowned by the clash of the present.

Perhaps it is only a personal disillusion? Among those I met in Paris was Anne's young brother Hervé. I felt a tremor of excitement at the thought of meeting him; the idea of the brothers and sisters of someone one loves is always entrancing, though the reality so often disappoints.

He is very thin. I found him biting his nails. But his quick smile was Alain's, and that touched my heart. And pained me also. I passed on Anne's message of love, asked how his mother was, and said that I so much hoped eventually to meet her.

'I hope,' I said, 'that she is not distressed by my relationship with Anne. Anne of course assures me she isn't, but I fear she must be. Believe me, I regret its irregularity myself.'

'It's a time when we can't avoid irregularity,' he said.

Certainly Hervé is irregular enough himself. Like many young men his passion outstrips his judgement. He spoke rashly to me.

His passion, as both Alain and Anne had warned me, is for Brittany.

'I have no feeling for France,' he said. 'You must realise that for me France is the historic enemy.'

His smile was so charming that I forgave the absurdity. Politics is still a sort of game for him, even though he recognises that, like a bullfight, it may result in death.

'At first I believed the Germans,' he said. 'They promised us self-government, you know. But it is all a sham. Like your government in Vichy. So, I have altered my views. Isn't it time you altered yours? Don't you see that we have been deceived?'

No one, since May 1940, has spoken to me so frankly, and I risk my life, and his, in writing it down.

Yet the compulsion to write these things is irresistible. It is like a drug. And, in my heart, I believe I am safe. I even wonder whether that sentence about the risk isn't an example of contemptible rhetoric.

Young Hervé is evidence of our failure. What have we offered to ardent youth? Youth such as is ready to speak without calculation. When I told Anne how he had spoken, she said:

'He is so brave and foolish. He talks like that to you, and he will talk in the same way to everyone. At a time like this.'

Marcel came to see me, and dissolved in tears as soon as we were alone. His lover David had left him, accusing him of being, in his heart, a collaborator.

'I denied it furiously. I told him he was only deserting me because I could no longer get him a part. As if it is my fault he has a Jewish mother. But he has fled. Of course, his American passport helped him.'

Marcel snivelled.

'But that's not the worst of it. The worst of it is that he is quite right. I am a collaborator, not because I believe in collaboration, but simply because I am afraid. And worse still, as a symbol of my collaboration, as you might say, I have fallen in love with a German boy who is an officer in the Gestapo. What should I do, Lucien?'

They come to me asking such questions. Marcel deluged me with descriptions such as he would in the past have been ashamed to proffer. I can't repeat them. They render him abject and disgusting. He is a sort of slave to images of cruelty which excite him unbearably. I suppose the easy thing to say is that he is mad, that he is not the Marcel who has been my friend for a quarter of a century. But this is not true. He is the same man. We are all, always, the same man. What he reveals now is only the longing he has hitherto concealed.

And when I look at him, and when I see that kind, intelligent monkey-face rivered with tears, and yet somehow gloating over his shame, what do I see but a mirror, in which I am reflected, and behind me, the shade of France? Isn't our acceptance of the Occupation an acceptance of rape? Isn't the humiliation and pain what we – I – have for so long and so intensely desired?

I left Marcel, and walked out on the boulevards, and along the Seine. Everything was grey as morality. There were no colours and no black and whites. I went into a bar, the sort of place to which working-men resort on their way home, and ordered a glass of rum. As I drank it a Negro boy approached me and began to talk. His conversation was rambling and incoherent. I don't remember what he said. But I was glad to have him burble beside me, offering at least the imitation of human society. There was nothing personal in his conversation, and nothing political. He wore a thin shabby suit and complained of the cold. I bought him a glass of rum and another for myself. I think that was all he wanted, just to be bought a drink. I don't think he would have taken it further. I don't think he intended to make any proposition. Anyhow, it didn't matter, for a group of other young men, evidently friends, entered the bar, and he joined them. I was left with my stubby glass held in both hands, which were clutching it hard, as if it represented something of great value.

I walked out of the café into the dusk. There were only a few people in the street, all moving with their heads lowered as if wishing to suggest that they recognised they had no right to be there. There was no live smell in the air, only a damp muddy odour rising from the river, and the silence was oppressive. Then I came on a little group of half a dozen who were gazing at a notice fixed to a fence. One of them was directing a torch at it, and I was able to read what was written.

Jean Lafond, house-painter, of Paris, having been condemned to death by a German Military Tribunal for an act of violence against the German Armed Forces, was executed this morning.

Later, someone told me that such notices, which are printed in red ink, have been more common recently. Nobody in the little group said anything. They stood with their heads bowed – but that was necessary to read the words – and then turned away. But they had remained there longer than was necessary to read the words as if by doing so they were paying some kind of tribute. As for me, I stood still for a long time after the man with the torch had moved on.

Of course, it can't be denied that such deaths are unavoidable. Our peace is a sort of civil war. An act of violence? What does that mean in a world in which every gesture signifies violence, in which every decision condemns someone to death?

I was on my way to a reception at the German Embassy. For a moment I thought of abandoning my intention. Nausea disturbed me. A policeman came and stood beside me, shining his torch on the notice so that I found myself reading the words again – as if it was necessary to do so. I felt the policeman's gaze shift to my face. He was summing me up, or rather trying to assess my feelings. It would have been important to give nothing away, if I had had anything to give. But it occurred to me that I was as ignorant of his reaction to the notice as he of mine, and that policemen are after all citizens with their own sentiments and opinions. I should have asked him what he thought of such things, but I didn't. Instead, with premeditation, I enquired if he knew how I could best find my way to the German Embassy. Was I near a Metro station? He said, abruptly, that he had no idea, and I guessed that the notice offended him. Then, as if remembering that he was a functionary subject to discipline, and suspecting that I might be someone of some influence – or else why would I wish to go to the Embassy? – he pulled a map from his pocket, made great play of consulting it, and then gave me the directions which, I was certain, he could perfectly well have provided without this comedy. But I understood why he played it out, and liked him for doing so.

Chandeliers, lobsters and champagne, and a covey of hack writers, little functionaries and black market businessmen seeking legitimate contracts, all sweating in the brilliant light. Drieu was there, and Robert Brasillach, which pleased me. I congratulated Robert, at a moment when Drieu had gone to the sideboard to replenish his glass, on the last number of his magazine.

He said, 'It grows more difficult and more necessary to maintain the faith.'

We were joined by Gerhard Heller, who works in the German Propaganda Department. He is a Rhinelander and a Protestant. Drieu introduced him to Scotch whisky, of which he contrives to retain a small supply, and assures me that Heller is devoted to the interests of France.

'He's a civilised man,' he said to me the other night.

We talked for some time about common ground between our responsibilities. He told me that he strove to avoid censorship.

‚'I always tell French publishers that that's their business, not mine. As long as they are careful what they publish, and refrain from putting anything out which is overtly anti-German, they can keep and exercise a surprising degree of freedom. After all,' he stretched out a hand, seized a glass from a tray being carried by a passing manservant, downed it, and replaced it on the tray, 'after all, very few of my colleagues can really read French, and even fewer have any interest in literature.'

What surprised me was that he spoke as if we were allies.

Robert, who had been distracted by someone who wished to speak to him, turned round.

'Nevertheless,' he said, 'it can't be denied that nine tenths of what people would write – if they weren't afraid – requires to be censored. Furthermore, there's a certain magazine, *Confluences*, published in Lyon, Lucien, and therefore under control of your own Ministry, which should be shut down. It reeks of the Third Republic, and half its writers are Jews or pederasts. I'm told they are even planning to publish the ravings of the American Jewess Gertrude Stein, to say nothing of a scurrilous review of my own poetry. I don't give a fig for that, but the former is serious. Have a word with whoever is responsible, won't you. There's a good fellow. Ah, here's Otto. You know the Ambassador, of course, don't you, Lucien? If only people realised what a good friend you are to France, Otto, we could sign a treaty of perpetual friendship tomorrow.'

'Why wait till tomorrow, Robert?' the ambassador smiled. 'Why wait?'

There was an ease and intimacy to the conversation which were delightful; or should have been. There is absolutely no reason to doubt the benevolence of men like Abetz and Heller. They are true friends of France, and both recognise our cultural primacy. Indeed, their appreciation of French culture is so extreme as to be almost shameful. That is why they are so anxious to please. They are in awe of our cultural heritage, and, being in awe, they are even ready to underrate what Germany itself has contributed.

'You are the Greeks in the new Roman Empire,' Heller said. He spoke without irony.

'No,' Abetz said, 'that is not accurate. It is true that culturally France stands to Germany as Greece did to Rome, but in the New Order of Europe that will develop from this war, we must be equal partners.'

For a moment, as he spoke, in that drawing room, under the shimmering chandeliers, I could believe him. His sincerity was apparent, and the social ease, with the suggestion that differences were valuable, even fruitful, gave a hint of how things might be in a Europe where war has become an impossible thought, in which a recognition of common heritage and common interests could create a real sense of community. This was, I told myself, the civilisation which we were struggling to create; this was the promise of which even Monsieur Laval had had an incongruous glimpse. The doubts I had expressed to Drieu appeared defeatist. I could imagine a Europe in which Hervé's Brittany had its own proud distinct identity, in which France and Germany, and of course Italy and other countries, retained their own historical validity, but in which also a true spirit of community and co-operation prevailed. Rupert and I used to talk of Charlemagne as the inspiration of that Europe, the reviver of Empire in a Christian form; we thought of ourselves as the new Carolingians . . . it was possible.

Jean Lafond, house-painter, of Paris, having been condemned to death by a German Military Tribunal for an act of violence against the German Armed Forces, was executed this morning.

I looked past the Ambassador's shoulder at the framed photograph of the Führer which brooded over us, and I remembered what they had cried at Mauriac in the café.

Drieu caught my eye. He raised his glass of champagne.

'*L'Echo de l'Avenir*,' he said.

'A remarkable magazine,' Heller said. 'I could almost wish, Monsieur de Balafré, that you would lose your Ministerial post, if it would enable you to resume publication.'

'With that title?' I said. 'It seems unlikely. Isn't it perhaps a little sombre?'

I spoke of course without premeditation, as I might have spoken before the war persuaded us to think first, then bite back intended words. A few minutes ago I gave Anne an account of the reception. When I had finished, she kissed me. Was I wrong to read pity in that kiss? Certainly, she had nothing to say. We both know we have not reached the worst. I am going to be compelled to do things, support actions, which disgust me because they are unworthy. There is talk for instance that French labour will be conscripted to work in Germany. It will be dressed up in some way: a returned prisoner of war for each conscripted labourer, perhaps. It will be impossible to prevent this, even to ameliorate it. We took the first step in that direction a long time ago.

Are there sadder words than these: 'There is no turning back'?

Yes, there are others: 'There is no alternative to our present policy.'

There is a café on the pavement below our terrace. My attention was caught by a peal of laughter. It came from a girl in a yellow dress. She was leaning back in her chair, her black hair loose and gleaming in the snowy sunshine. The movement of laughter had pulled her skirt up to reveal a long shapely thigh. Her boyfriend leaned towards her and tugged the skirt down. When he had done so he did not remove his hand, but let it rest there pressing gently on her leg. She swung forward, bringing her elbows down on the café table and dropping her chin into the cup formed by her hands. They gazed into each other's eyes. She moved her legs together to hold his hand where it was. Then she touched his lower lip with her forefinger. He wore the blue uniform of the Service d'Ordre Légionnaire. He was telling her how he and his colleagues had ransacked the apartment of a Jewish woman. 'You should have heard how she caterwauled,' he said. There was a frost this morning and his happy voice cut the air. The girl pressed her legs together, holding his hand fast. At that moment Anne came back into the room with our little cat in her arms.

'You don't think Hervé is going to do anything silly, do you?' she said.

'I'm not sure I know what is silly any longer.'

'I mean,' she said, putting the cat down on the table and stroking the length of her back, 'join the Resistance.'

It is the first time we have given disaffection that name by which it chooses to be known.

Then she said: 'Are we going to lose the war?'

'Do you mean lose it again?'

IT IS A romantic fallacy to suppose that anyone's story is an individual thing. We share with our contemporaries emotions as well as ideas, hopes and fears as well as political convictions. In trying to decipher Lucien and tell his story, I find the picture blurred. He becomes one of the crowd of History's victims. To call him that will seem to some special pleading, as if I am saying that he was not responsible for his actions. Of course he was – and wasn't.

We are all placed in History, landed there, involuntarily and unconsulted. Some generations have the apparent good fortune to be able to feel free of History. No great questions disturb the tenor of their life. Yet even such people are formed by their historical experience. The questions posed may seem trivial to another more strenuous age. They are still not of their own making. Every new age asks new questions of candidates who have had no opportunity to prepare for the examination.

No one in France was prepared for the examination of 1940. How could they have been? How could Jean Lafond, house-painter, of Paris, have imagined that a day would arrive when he would be given the opportunity of performing 'an act of violence against the German Armed Forces'? And could he have guessed before he committed that act that he would take the chance?

Moreover, it is not only History that acts on us. Sartre's drama which tells us that Hell is other people is too glib. The fact is that life here is other people too. If Lucien had not been posted, by the whim of a superior, to Berlin, if he had not crouched in the butts watching for the geese to fly across the Pomeranian marches, if he had not sniffed the grey wind in the east, would his journey from Bordeaux in 1940 have taken him to London, not Vichy? And would he, in any case, have acted differently if Rupert had not said to him in Zermatt that the true war was between decency and indecency, adding that if that ass Chamberlain had not flown to Munich, his friends in the Army would have arrested Hitler?

There are so many ways of interpreting every decision, even while one realises that the very word 'decision' is itself misleading, suggesting as it does a degree of consciousness which is very often not there at all. I am tormented by the thought of inextricable triangles: Rupert, Lucien, Polly; Germany, France, Britain; love, hate, fear; Christian, pagan, Jews; good, evil, indifference; reality, unreality, surreality – each of these groupings resembles the Trinity, three in one and one in three. Even the least probable of them. My poor father wrote once: 'The reason the Jew is hated is that he has broken into the Christian world, and returned it to paganism and the worship of the dead goddess, Moneta. In retaliation, especially in Germany, many born Christians have abandoned their faith and themselves reverted to the vile enthusiasm of paganism. Hitler hates the Jews because this hatred justifies his own killing of Christ in himself.'

So where, in this maelstrom, can responsibility lie? We are responsible for actions performed in response to circumstances for which we are not responsible.

Everything I have written about Lucien, Hugh, is likely to mislead you precisely because I have written about a single man. Only a fool however can pretend to singularity, though only a fool denies it. This is the bottom line: our actions are compelled by circumstances and yet we choose to commit them. Lucien could not have avoided following Pétain and committing himself to Vichy, and yet can be seen to have neglected the chance he was offered to avoid doing so. But Lucien cannot be understood if we try only to understand Lucien.

This is one lie of biography. It separates the individual from his circumstances, and grants him an individuality he did not possess. But there is a second lie, characteristic of political biography, and this eliminates the subject of the biography, so that the book becomes merely a record of his words and acts. Such biography cannot accommodate that moment when Lucien looked down from his terrace and saw the girl's legs close on the boy's hand. It cannot do so because moments like this which are deeply moving are nevertheless insignificant. And if I went on to describe how the boy was promoted when the Service d'Ordre Légionnaire was converted into the *Milice*, the secret police of Vichy, the next year, of how he was guilty of 'atrocities' against the Resistance, and then shot during the *épuration*, such information could not fail to affect one's interpretation of that simple and double manifestation of desire which made Lucien aware that it was spring, as he looked down from his terrace, and made him wonder if he himself would feel another spring.

Let me sketch out three other wars to bring Lucien into focus.

If I was an artist, Hugh, I would have contrived to entwine these stories with Lucien's and, if I was writing a novel – and we toyed with making his story a novel – I would devise a cunning plot which brought them together in less arbitrary and more consequential fashion. But that is not how things happen. One life touches another only from time to time – even the girl in the café released the boy's hand, though they were frozen into eternal immobility in Lucien's mind. I have invented one story for him, and let us say she tried to pretend later she had never known a boy who committed atrocities against those he was programmed to consider traitors, atrocities, however, which in another interpretation were expressions of self-hatred rather than hatred directed outward.

The artist labours to bring these things together, to impose a pattern which he pretends he has extracted; but life forces them apart.

So, take Rupert. We left him in Zermatt where in fact he stood on the platform of the little station watching the train bear Lucien, Polly and happiness away. He travelled from Zermatt to Geneva, and stayed there, in this same Hôtel des Bergues, throughout the spring of 1939. He mixed, carelessly, with refugees from Hitler's tyranny, who found him unsympathetic and were afraid that he might be a spy. He considered further and permanent emigration, as he had once thought of going to China. Yet, in May, he returned to Germany, certain that war would break out in the autumn. 'I could not oppose Hitler unless I also fought for Germany,' he wrote. 'I can divorce Germany from Hitler but it is impossible to divorce myself from Germany. The doctrine "my country right or wrong" is too facile. It is not that consideration which moves me. With memories however of the suffering which defeat in war makes inevitable, I cannot work for the defeat of my country in order to be able to preserve my view of myself as a moral being.'

It's absurd, isn't it, to consider someone who chose – that lying word again – to return to fight for Hitler's Germany, which was only his own Germany in as much as he and Hitler partook of the same Germany – to consider such a man 'a moral being'. Yet he had no doubt: he would have been ashamed to have taken any other course. So he returned, committing himself to loyal opposition, disloyal support.

In June 1941 he found himself fighting on the eastern front. That felt right; he was enacting, or re-enacting, the historic mission of his family. He was decorated in the great advance,

then wounded, and sent back, with his Iron Cross, to convalesce
at his mother's house in Saxony. The war was still going well,
which meant that Germany was going badly. Defeat was necessary to dislodge Hitler, but not such defeat as would destroy
Germany. He spent the winter of '41–'42 reading Hegel, Goethe
(*Faust* – what else?), Thucydides and Homer. In the evening he
and his mother played Wagner on the gramophone.

'How can Hitler take comfort from this,' he asked, 'seeing that
the message of *The Ring* is that even the gods cannot do wrong,
commit violence, with impunity?'

In the short hours of daylight, he shot duck. They had devised
a sling for him which let him use a gun despite his shattered left
arm. He was assailed by dreams of bright heroism, wrote long
letters to Lucien which he did not dare to send. In the spring he
travelled to Berlin, and consulted with his well-born friends.
They agreed that the time was not yet ripe to make a move. He
received a posting, as a species of military attaché, to Paris. It
was agreed with his friends he should sound out elements in the
Vichy government, men who might be ready to act as inter-
mediaries with the British and Americans, so that peace might
be negotiated, when they had 'dealt with' Hitler. There were
delays. He arrived in Paris on the first day of the Battle of
Stalingrad.

He had written to Lucien announcing his arrival, and was
disappointed to find no message awaiting him. But for a few days
the pleasure of being back in Paris, even the mean grey Paris of
wartime, was enough to raise his spirits. Yet he soon started
feeling oppressed; relations were askew. He had always been
accustomed to think of France as condescending; he couldn't
adjust to the mixture of subservience and resentment he encountered. In the east there was no difficulty in being a member of the
master race, his family had always been conquerors there. It was
different in France: he felt inferior to those who refused to accept
his superiority, superior only to those who toadied to him. The
French people with whom he wanted to speak were those who
would have nothing to do with him. It seemed in a curious fashion
that this included Lucien, even though he was a member of the
government that was allied to his: which of course he detested.

One afternoon he found himself in the street which had housed
the office of Lucien's magazine. To his surprise the plate announcing its presence was still there, though requiring to be polished.
He mounted the stairs, conscious, as he already to his irritation
found himself whenever he ventured off approved paths, of a

certain tremor: the result of an awareness that he offered a tempting target.

He pushed open the door at the head of the stairs. It led into a passage blocked off by another door, the upper half of which was made of misty glass. He could see two shapes through the glass, and heard voices. The door was not quite shut. They were arguing.

'And if I denounce you . . .'

'You will compromise Lucien. Is that what you wish?'

It was a woman's voice, and it trembled. Rupert hesitated.

'I suppose it is,' the woman continued. 'You will do anything to destroy him. You cannot tolerate the fact of his moral superiority.'

'The moral superiority of a collaborator,' the man said. 'Yes, indeed, you have not lost your capacity to speak the unthinkable, Mathilde. You were always a fool.'

'And you a venomous toad, Philippe.'

Rupert pushed the door open. They fell silent on seeing a German officer. The man snatched up a briefcase from the table. He was tall and thin with a little black moustache; he could hardly have looked less like a toad. A rat, perhaps, Rupert thought.

Rupert was embarrassed by the silence. For a moment, hoping to find Lucien there, he had forgotten his uniform. And it was an absurd hope. He didn't know what to say. The silence alarmed the man, who pushed past him and galloped down the stairs. Rupert listened to the descending feet. The girl watched him. She was waiting for the sound of a shot or at least an arrest.

'May I sit down?' he said.

'Who are you?'

There was silence on the stairs now. It seemed to creep into the room which was lit in the dying afternoon by a single weak bulb hanging on a ragged cord from the ceiling. He moved a brimming ash-tray from the table, flicked his handkerchief to blow away the dust and rested his elbow there.

'I'm sorry,' he said. 'I seem to have alarmed your friend.'

'No friend.'

'I didn't intend to. I called here quite by chance. I am myself an old friend of Lucien de Balafré, I recognised the name of his magazine on the brass plate, and called – absurdly, I understand that, but then I find, don't you, that so many of our actions are absurd – on the mere chance that someone here might know where he was.'

'He's in Vichy. I would have thought you would know that.'

'Oh, of course, that was always likely. I merely hoped. You must understand that I am here in no official capacity.'

He wanted to put her at ease. Perhaps she was the kind of girl who was never that. Now she looked stricken. She was tall, beaky, perhaps a little drunk; her breath carried a whiff of wine to him. It was a very small room, and musty, as if the air had been held in it a long time. It might even be pre-war air. There were cobwebs, big ones, across the window; he could see into another room which was quite dark.

It was not surprising that Mathilde Dournier was perturbed by the arrival of a German officer. Somehow his claim to be a friend of Lucien's made him more sinister. She had always been ready to distrust friendliness. But it was a bad moment.

Mathilde's war had been quiescent. That accorded with her temperament, with her suspicion of commitment. She had tried to live as if it wasn't happening. Politics were for men. Politics were violent. That was why they ended in war. She suspected that all men were invigorated and excited by war. Even perhaps Lucien, who was the best man she knew. As for her, she loathed it so much that she would have preferred to wipe it off her consciousness. In the end that wasn't possible. She found that she couldn't write poetry. She was working in a shop again, but that wasn't the reason. It wasn't because of fatigue and malnutrition that her Muse had fled. She put that phrase in italics, to excuse herself, even while the consciousness that it had come into her mind sharpened her self-contempt. She was sure that Lucien was wrong in what he was doing, but never doubted his good intentions. Indeed his mistaken loyalties only strengthened hers to him.

She could deny herself much, but not pity. In the end pity compelled her to action. She had formed the habit of coming to the office one day a week, choosing for some obscure motive of caution to vary the day, her ostensible purpose in coming being to keep the magazine ticking over, even though it was in abeyance. A few forlorn hopeful manuscripts still arrived; she dealt with them, mustering sympathy, dispensing judgement. That was her duty. Attendance at the office was also her pleasure, it was the only service she could perform for Lucien. It represented, in her mind, the same sort of hope she felt every month when she caught sight of the thin slice of new moon: an assurance that not everything was out of order. Someday Lucien would be back, someday real life would be resumed. She told herself the thought was madness. What was happening around was only too horribly real. But she attended the office in order to deny that reality, to impose a superior reality upon it.

Rupert said: 'I was under the impression that Lucien's magazine had ceased publication.'

'It's been suspended.'

'Not by us, I would hope.'

'No, by Lucien himself. By the war. This beastly war.'

'But you still come here to . . ?'

'Oh,' she said, 'manuscripts still arrive, you see. People who used to read it, or used to contribute, don't always know that . . . anyway, they hope. That's why I come, to deal with these things.'

'To put an end to their hope.'

'Perhaps.'

But that wasn't the only reason, now. They had in the back room a duplicating machine. Mathilde had always disliked it – she was unhandy and couldn't operate the machine without getting her fingers inky – and had almost forgotten its existence. Then a young man, a poet who had had a few verses published in the magazine, asked her if she would run off a sequence of little poems he had written. 'Yes,' she said, 'if I like them.' That was the start. There was nothing political, nothing subversive about it. But the young man had friends, and it was difficult to draw a line between what was political and what wasn't. Soon, or rather gradually, she was committed. Mathilde's duplicating machine became a tool of the Resistance. There was no enthusiasm on her part: she disliked most of those she served, and, though it made her angry, and grieved her, to see the poverty and wretchedness of old women and children in the streets, that seemed to her the consequence of war as much as the Occupation. Besides, her loyalty remained with Lucien, and she resented being used by those on the other side. For all that, she continued the work. Without interest in politics, hating and scorning the war, she still didn't believe that the Occupation would last. It occurred to her that what she was doing might serve Lucien. If the time came, she would swear he had encouraged her. In this way she appeased her disturbed loyalty.

They had never been raided. She couldn't understand why, for she took few precautions, not knowing how she should set about doing so. It was perhaps the very blatancy of her lack of method which protected her; and the fact that the magazine had been closed at the beginning of the war, and that Lucien was a Vichy Minister, and so above suspicion. As the stridency of those Parisian Fascists who regarded Vichy as insufficiently committed to the cause of a German victory grew in volume till it penetrated even her defences, she began to believe in the virtue of what she was doing. And, believing that, she experienced fear for the first time. So it was natural that the arrival of a German officer perturbed her. She must be under investigation. She must have been denounced.

He told her his name. She recognised it, which surprised her. Lucien had indeed mentioned him. She had even been jealous, she remembered, because he seemed to admire him so.

'You were with him in Zermatt,' she said, 'when his wife left him.'

'Yes,' he said, 'it was a tragedy for him.'

'But they weren't suited, I think.'

'Who's to say? They loved each other, I know that. I can say that with truth and certainty because I loved both myself.'

'She wasn't worthy of him, she couldn't share his interests.'

'Don't you think he was perhaps happier that way?'

It was absurd that they were talking together as if they were friends, and a moment ago her heart had stopped when Philippe Torrance had threatened to denounce her and the German officer had entered.

'Who was that man who was here when I arrived?' he asked.

'Just a contributor, just a would-be contributor. I don't know . . .'

'It was such a good magazine, you have no idea what it meant to me to be able to receive it in Berlin. Lucien discovered his true *métier* with it, and now . . . the war. It destroys everything.'

'He was an editor of genius. He is. He . . .'

'You wrote for it yourself . . ?'

'Yes.' She looked away. 'Only a few poems, nothing much.'

'A few poems: Will you tell me your name?'

'Mathilde Dournier . . .' she said, and held her breath.

'But I remember them. They were charming. You can't think what a pleasure it is to me. To meet you, I mean. It's like a moment of real life in this ghastly charade we are playing.'

To her surprise, she found herself liking him. Charade – the word expressed what she would have liked to be able still to believe; there was a scornful innocence to it. She glanced at his left arm and the shattered hand.

'Is that part of the charade?' she asked.

He smiled.

'The Russian front?'

'Yes. Don't let's talk about the war. Let's talk of Lucien or of poetry.'

In a little, he said: 'I wonder, I don't know how you feel about such things, but would you like to have dinner with me?'

'Dinner?'

'Yes. Don't feel obliged. I will understand if you feel it would compromise you, if you'd rather not . . .'

'Compromise me? I suppose it would. But why not?' She poured two glasses of wine from a bottle sitting on the window-ledge where it had been pushed behind the curtain. 'We're not just French and German. We're two people, individuals. I refuse to be bound by a stereotype.'

'Two individuals. A poet and her reader.'

He raised his glass to her.

'We'll go to the Flore,' she said. 'There won't be any other Germans there.'

He understood what she meant.

'You're a brave girl,' he said, responding to her pride, and proud too of the trust she offered. 'But won't that embarrass you? Compromise you further?'

'And if it does?' she said.

Third war: Philippe Torrance.

I haven't, I'm aware, been just to Torrance. He is a man to whom it is hard to do justice. I disliked him so the only time I met him, at Virginia Fernie's table. I have disliked what I have read of his work. Even the early stories which delighted Lucien now seem dated, tainted with affectation and insincerity. In the fifties he wrote a long novel of the Resistance which won prizes; I found it disgusting. His reputation faded in the changed mood of the Fifth Republic; he died a few years ago. Even to the end, or near the end, he retained a constantly renewing bank of admirers, mostly young girls. He made a fool of himself during the Events of May '68, proclaiming that he was a Maoist. Obviously he was everything too late, a man who just missed every bandwagon. Yet there must have been something there which I am too prejudiced to detect.

He almost missed the bandwagon of the Resistance. Lucien's refusal to introduce him to Laval infuriated him. His writing became angrier, more extreme. As Lucien observed however, polemics ill became him; his talent evaporated in rage.

Throughout '41, even after the invasion of Russia, he was a fervent man of the Right. He fulminated against Jews, celebrated the importence of England. Yet a certain Norman caution prevailed; he never burned the boat that had brought him to any shore. Two things happened in the New Year which caused him to shift his opinions. He began to suspect that the Soviet Union would hold out and turn the war; and Drieu La Rochelle refused a short novel which he had hoped to publish in the *NRF*. Torrance discarded his beret, bought a roll-neck pullover, began to frequent the Flore and the Deux Magots. He cultivated Gaston Hunnot, an old friend with whom he had never, cautiously, quite severed relations. He began to spout a lukewarm Marxism, toy with the ideas that would later be called existential. So many people were shifting ground in these months that his own recantation was hardly noticed, his former opinions easily forgotten. There were not after all many people who would have liked to be judged by last year's opinions.

Nevertheless, when he threatened to denounce Mathilde, it was the German authorities he had in mind. It would of course have been an anonymous denunciation, and it was only fear and prudence which persuaded him to deny himself the pleasure.

All the same he was delighted when he heard she had been seen in the Flore with a German officer.

'I always said she was playing a double game,' he said.

He had himself gone into hiding for a week, straight from the offices of *L'Echo de l'Avenir*. That week stretched out in his conversation and memory.

By the end of the evening Mathilde was a little drunk.

'You don't need to worry,' she told several people in the cafe; 'Rupert hates the Nazis, he hates the war, we've been talking poetry, not politics.'

IN NOVEMBER '42, the war took a new turn for France. On the night of the 7th and 8th the British and Americans launched Operation Torch against French Algeria and Morocco. At four o'clock in the morning the American Chargé d'Affaires in Vichy, S. Pinckney Tuck, delivered a letter from President Roosevelt to the Marshal. The President emphasised how France had been humiliated by Germany, which was now threatening to occupy French colonies also. Roosevelt seemed unaware that Algeria was not a colony, but a *département*, of France. However, he assured Pétain that the American forces had been instructed to co-operate with local officials responsible to Vichy.

Lucien heard the news on arrival at his office at eight o'clock. He was told that Tuck would call on the Marshal at nine. It was at once apparent to him that a moment of choice had arrived. He sat at his desk and smoked a succession of cigarettes, unable to give his attention to the papers that lay before him.

'I realised,' he wrote in one of those papers which I found in the Château de l'Haye, 'that everything which we had refused to consider hitherto had now become inescapable.'

Document 12: Manuscript of Lucien de Balafré,
undated, possibly part of his confession

We were the Republic, and the territory of the Republic had been violated by the Americans and our erstwhile allies, the British. They committed this act of aggression under pretext of friendship, but it was nonetheless aggression directed against a sovereign State, against France. That was an argument I would have found no trouble in sustaining.

But France was not a free agent. Half the country was occupied. Monsieur Laval had been forced as Prime Minister back on the Marshal. The Head of State could no longer choose his own Ministers. These were also incontrovertible facts.

Moreover, the act of aggression was not primarily directed against France, however it insulted our dignity.

On the other hand, it must bring even greater suffering to France. It invited the Germans to move into the unoccupied zone. It threatened to destroy even more completely the authority of the Marshal.

These were my first reactions. We had of course expected such news; nevertheless we were struck dumb by it. No one had made preparation for a development which was inevitable. Once again it was clear to me that politics is a matter of reaction to the unwilled and unwelcome. It was true that Admiral Darlan happened to be in Algiers where his son was suffering from infantile paralysis. 'There are no advantages in that,' Laval was reported to have stated. 'The beautiful Admiral is the last man to play a hand intelligently.'

There was a cabinet meeting that morning at eleven o'clock. Half an hour before it was due to begin, I received a message from Dr Ménétrel. The Marshal wished me to attend, as a confidential aide. I was surprised by this because I had had no conversation with the Marshal for at least six months, and believed either that I had offended him or that he had simply forgotten me. It was difficult for him these days to remember things.

The room was bathed in autumn sunshine. The Marshal had greeted me with a firm handshake, but had said nothing to enlighten me as to why I had been summoned. His step was confident, he seemed cheerful. He even hummed a little tune.

'At least it's not *Auprès de ma blonde*,' one of the secretaries whispered. 'That's always a prelude to disaster.'

'Monsieur Laval is late,' the Marshal said. 'But then I believe he was up half the night, and driving here from his house at Châteldon. They let me sleep till seven o'clock, you know, which was considerate of them.'

Did he say this on purpose, to indicate to us that he was acquitting himself of responsibility? Or was he ironical: to arouse our pity?

Then Laval bustled in. He hadn't shaved. He didn't apologise to the Marshal for being late, but at once sat in his appointed seat, stubbed out a cigarette, and lit another. He spoke without removing it from the corner of his mouth, taking charge of the meeting.

'I see some unfamiliar faces. Some of them I know from elsewhere. Well, you're welcome. It's right that, in the gravity of the present situation, some of you Under-secretaries should be intimately involved and share responsibility for our decisions.'

He smiled, enjoying the disturbance which he expected his

words to cause. But I was calm, for I have always accepted that my adherence to the government, my expressed faith in our moral validity, assures me of the responsibility of commitment.

Laval proceeded to give us a full account of the situation. As ever I was impressed, no longer reluctantly, by his lucidity and candour. He didn't pretend it was anything but perilous.

'It's the most dangerous situation we have found ourselves in since 1940,' he said. 'Our decision this morning will again determine the fate of France.'

He looked straight across the table at the Marshal, who pulled out a red spotted handkerchief and blew his nose loudly. He emitted a series of trumpetings. Laval watched him till he had finished.

'We have suffered an act of aggression,' Laval said. 'There is no question of that, and there has been no provocation. The United States, a power with whom we enjoy diplomatic relations, has invaded French territory.'

He paused again.

'Has anyone any comment?'

There was silence. The Marshal was still dabbing at his nose with his handkerchief. He gave a little snuffle which might almost have been a laugh. Sunlight lay on the table between them, and Laval's cigarette-smoke coiled towards the ceiling.

'Good. We have reached a point of choice.'

'The Americans,' someone said, 'have guaranteed our sovereign integrity.'

'Ah, quite,' Laval said. 'And we have reports of an attempted Gaullist coup in Morocco, while General Giraud in Algeria has broadcast an appeal for all French forces to desert to the so-called Allies. Our sovereign integrity is in splendid shape. Nevertheless, that observation makes a valid point, which, you won't be surprised to hear, I have anticipated. I have already told the German Ambassador that we are requesting his government to issue a declaration guaranteeing the integrity of both metropolitan France and of our empire. Such a declaration, I have assured them, would prevent the emergence of a dissident movement in North Africa.'

There were murmurs of assent round the table.

'Meanwhile,' Laval continued, 'it is necessary that we consider offers of help which we have already received from the Axis powers, and to do this, in conjunction with the request already made by Admiral Darlan in Algiers, that the Germans provide us with air support against Allied shipping in the vicinity of the port.

Now I confess to you that there is good reason for hesitation with regard to this request. It runs the risk of calling down the thunderbolt upon us. Nevertheless, it is important to understand the implications of whatever decision we make. Is that not so, Marshal?'

'Important?' the Marshal coughed. 'Yes, it's important.'

'If we decline to accept the German offer, we shall lose Algeria. If we accept it, we shall lose more. For it will be followed by a demand that we declare war on the United States and Britain, and, it seems to me, unless this is accompanied by the guarantee of our territorial integrity which I have sought, then . . . Gentlemen, what then? We must be reserved in our response.'

A little later the meeting broke up, much unresolved. Ménétrel plucked me by the sleeve.

'Don't go. Come to the Marshal's office.'

I accompanied him upstairs.

'This has shaken the Marshal,' he said. 'He doesn't know where he stands. He doesn't trust Laval, but he dare not do anything about it. It's all a scene of indescribable confusion.'

'Things will get worse,' Pétain said, pressing my hands. 'They've escaped my control. Even Darlan is acting independently. There's no respect left, no obedience, no chain of command. It's all breaking up, I would be better dead. On the other hand, France needs me more now than ever. Isn't that so?'

I was dismayed by his appearance and manner. In my diary that night, I confided: 'Physically, the Marshal is still robust. He has, they say, good hours. But morally, it is as if he has suffered a stroke. Anne said to me this evening: "It's like coming out of a matinée performance into the streets and finding that it is already dark." I know just what she meant. It is imperative that I get away for a few days to my home in order to think, but that is impossible. Ménétrel made it quite clear to me that the Marshal is relying on me, though he couldn't say what for. The fact is that the confusion in the Marshal's mind mirrors the confusion of France. He is our King Lear, that's all.'

Over the next few days events moved with cinematic speed and the confusion of a mystery story. Laval flew to Berchtesgaden to see Hitler. We were not told what he hoped to achieve. Darlan was instructed to resist, disobeyed the order, and the Marshal rubbed his hands as if satisfied. The Admiral then proclaimed a cease-fire. Meanwhile, came the most appalling news.

On the night of 11 November, the anniversary of the Armistice in 1918, while Laval was still engaged in discussion with the Germans, Hitler issued an order to German forces to cross the demarcation line into unoccupied France at seven o'clock the following morning. We were told it was for our protection. 'Germany,' Hitler said, in the message he sent to the Marshal, 'has decided to defend the frontiers of your country side by side with French soldiers, and at the same time the frontiers of culture and European civilisation.'

Ménétrel woke me at five o'clock.

'The Marshal has need again of your literary skills,' he said, in that tone which has always left me uncertain whether the doctor is a buffoon or an ironist. I found Pétain sipping coffee. He was wearing a dressing-gown and nightcap. It is the only time I have seen him in such disarray.

'It's all breaking up,' he said. 'I thought I had already lived the darkest days of my life. Monsieur . . . Monsieur . . . Monsieur de Balafré' – he seemed to summon my name from recesses of despair – 'I must broadcast. Will you prepare a draft?

'We protest. We accept. We are compelled to accept. All is gloom.'

So I had to set to work to persuade the French people to face reality again.

Is there no end to reality? I asked myself.

Two days later I was witness to a conversation between Laval and the illustrious General Weygand. Throughout Weygand has been a robust pessimist. It sometimes seems he takes pleasure in exposing the worst.

News had been brought by René Bousquet, Secretary-general of Police, that he had received an order from Himmler to place Weygand under surveillance.

'I assured the Germans, of course,' Bousquet said, 'that you were the Marshal's guest and that I would answer for you myself.'

'No need,' Weygand replied, 'the order places me in a position of honour.'

'Of course,' Laval said, 'it is quite unnecessary. You may disregard the order, Monsieur Bousquet.'

Bousquet withdrew, and Weygand, mindless of the fact that Ménétrel and I were both present, turned on Laval.

'You see how it is,' he said. 'Your policy of collaboration is dividing the country from the Marshal. Authority is fleeing.'

'What do you expect me to do?' Laval said. 'I'm certain that if the Anglo-Saxons win this war, France will be surrendered to their Russian ally, and that will mean Bolshevism.'

'Your policy,' Weygand said, 'in effect makes us the accomplices of Bolshevism. Every French worker sent to Germany becomes a Communist, and so do all his family and friends. Your policy, Monsieur Laval, is opposed by 95 per cent of the French people.'

Laval smiled. It was a curiously impish smile. He waved his cigarette at Weygand.

'The figure is probably 98 per cent,' he said. 'Don't think I don't see the situation even more clearly than you do yourself. I'm determined to save France in spite of itself, to make the French people happy no matter what they think. You, General, are guilty of the sins of pessimism and defeatism.'

When Weygand left, Laval beamed at us.

'In spite of the immediate facts, I'm an optimist. The fundamental question hasn't changed. It remains: who is going to win the war? My money is still on Germany. But even if it wasn't, I have to take account of the immediate question, and that is: what happens to France and the French people while the other question is being decided? Remember this, gentlemen, we are all playing a double game. Some of us however know that, and have another card up our sleeves.'

In this state of secrets, there are no secrets left.

That afternoon, General Weygand was arrested by the SS as he drove from Vichy to Gueret, and taken to Germany.

'He was always a lucky bastard,' the Marshal said.

I left the Hôtel du Parc that afternoon in acute depression. Yet there was still little hint of winter in the streets. The cafés resounded with laughter and well-dressed ladies walked their toy-dogs on the boulevards. Except that the town was full, it might have been any gentle autumn afternoon, and people were obviously thinking of what they would have for supper rather than of the state of the war. Our concerns in the administration seemed to me neurotic, and a troop of schoolboys passing me pulled off their caps and chorused 'Good afternoon, sir.' They had recognised me and I realised I must have addressed their school on one of my many visits. I stopped them and asked if they had a lot of homework, and they assured me they were heavily burdened. 'Good,' I said. 'Good.'

Anne was putting a casserole in the oven. She asked me if I would be in for supper. I told her I hoped to be, but it depended. I might be called back to headquarters at any time.

'That's why I thought a casserole,' she said. 'It's rabbit again, I'm afraid.'

I sat down and stroked the cat. I knew Anne was eager to hear what had happened, but for a moment I wanted to pretend to be living an ordinary life.

She said, 'It's finished, isn't it?'

'No,' I said, 'but it's another turn of the screw.'

And the screw kept on turning. You would have thought it tight fast, but still events turned it.

We had first the news of Darlan's defection.

'He hopes,' the Marshal said, 'that the Americans will set him up in my place. Darlan. Nobody would kill anyone, or die himself, for Darlan. I named him as my successor only to keep him out of mischief. Well, and he has got into mischief nevertheless.'

But his voice trembled. The truth was that in these desperate November days the Marshal changed his mind every five minutes. He had lost the constancy which had been his strength, and, having lost that, was only a poor bewildered old man.

Yet he clung to his duty and to his vision of himself as the saviour of France.

'Laval despises me. He rejects me. Nevertheless he knows he can't do without me. As I said to him and the German Ambassador, "My presence is necessary to you. If I detach myself, there'll be anarchy."'

On the 16th, Laval confronted him with the German demand that France should declare war. Pétain scratched his head.

'You wouldn't make that sort of demand if you were a soldier,' he said. 'It's always you civilians who want to rush into war. You're behaving like a politician, like Reynaud. Besides, I'm exhausted. I've had enough. I'd like to retire.'

'I'm weary too, Marshal,' Laval said. 'You seem to forget I have spent several hours recently listening to Hitler. That's fatiguing, I assure you. But we can't retire. France still needs you, if only as a symbol.'

'What did he mean,' Pétain said to me, ' "if only as a symbol"? That's not the way France needs me. On the other hand, since I can't have my own way, perhaps I should abdicate, and remain only as Head of State without immediate responsibility. That way . . . of course Laval and I understand each other, we're both peasants, you know. And, ultimately, we are both working for the same end.'

Throughout the crisis I was amazed by the Marshal's resilience. It is as if he sinks back into the soil from time to time only to gather his strength again.

'Do you know what Abetz said of me?' A shy smile crossed his face. 'He said I was as troublesome as I was indispensable. That's just how I like it. "We can't do anything with him," he said. "We can't do anything without him." You see I can still resist. I am France, and I am a disagreeable reality that whoever wins this war will have to confront somehow. Meanwhile, I don't mind giving Laval his head for a little.'

On the 19th they commanded him to broadcast again. 'Write the speech,' he said to me. 'It doesn't matter what you say because at the moment we've got to say what they tell us to. It's a speech that won't be supplemented by an official order. So it means nothing.'

'In the dream world of nightmare in which we live, in which terrifying voices howl by night, the Marshal still moves with more serenity than any of us.'

So I wrote in my diary of 20 November.

On the 26th the Germans moved to seize the French fleet at Toulon. According to orders already given, the Admiral in command had the ships scuttled. The news was given to the Marshal when he woke an hour later.

'It had to be done,' he said.

Several of us pressed him to reconsider his intention to remain in France. We urged that this evidence of German ill-faith annulled all contracts and made it impossible for him to stay.

' "Contracts, impossible", I don't like these words.' He pulled at his tunic. I noticed that his nails are still beautifully manicured. 'My poor children,' he said. 'How can I run away? I gave my word to the French people that I would stay with them. I'm not going to abandon them now when things are again as bad as they were in 1940, or even worse. I know you are concerned about my reputation. I'm a proud man and care for it myself. However, there it is. My glory may be tarnished, but I won't abandon the poor people. I'll share their sufferings as Christ was made flesh to share mankind's. In any case I'll follow the path of duty, though it's by no means the easiest one. For me, the easiest path would be to leave.'

He really believes that, though Anne assures me it's not true.

'It's easier for him to stay, don't you see? At least here he knows which part he must play. It would be a new role in a new comedy in North Africa, and that's too much for him at his age. No, I don't blame him.'

Sometimes I think that Anne, who has never spoken a word to the Marshal, has come to understand him better than I.

Then, on 29 November, Hitler announced that he was going to disband the French Army. This, I said to myself, is the final revenge for 1918. The Marshal fingered his moustache.

'Maybe it's for the best,' he said. 'It certainly removes one problem. We no longer have soldiers to command. I shall therefore accede, under protest, and assure Hitler of our continuing loyalty. What else can I do?'

He required one further service of me. This was to prepare a draft of the broadcast which he intended to give at Christmas.

'You'll remind them that I have kept my promise,' he said. 'That's the main thing. And not too many adjectives, remember. Tell them we must be dignified in sorrow. That expresses the right mood.'

So I wrote: 'At this hour when it seems that the earth is falling away below our feet, raise your eyes to the sky: you will find in the celestial majesty of the heavens reassurance of the eternity of light, and you will know how to place your hopes where they belong.'

In the broadcast version, the words 'enough stars so as not to doubt the eternity of light' were substituted, and some said that this was intended as a reference to the American flag. I do not know whether this was true or whether the Marshal merely preferred the homely stars to my more ornate 'in the celestial majesty of the heavens'. Perhaps my phrase was ill-chosen; after all, in 1940 Laval had told the Marshal that he now possessed more power than the Sun-King himself.

I say I do not know, for that draft was the last service I have been able to perform on behalf of the Marshal. On 31 December I resigned my portfolio and retired to the Château de l'Haye. The Marshal had been rendered impotent, and I could not believe that I could honourably perform any useful service to what remained of the French State. Perhaps this was a cowardly decision.

November 1942 was a month of decisive disaster. When it began, France still had a large area of metropolitan territory free of Axis troops, an empire, an Army and Air Force, and a fleet. By the end of the month we had none of these things. Everything had changed. The Marshal had surrendered what remained of his authority to Monsieur Laval, who, poor man, was henceforth doomed to twist and turn, like a rat in a shrinking trap.

As for me, as for me . . . it is now spring, and the question remains open. The Resistance is stirring even in Provence. I sit, read and write. Only the landscape comforts me. The landscape and Anne's love.

Let me put it on record that, but for her, I might have shot myself.

No, that's romantic rhetoric, such as I have always despised.

CHAPTER TWENTY-FOUR

I HAVE ENGLISH friends who love Provence and have never looked at the country. They know it only in summer, when it basks in the sun like a cat, and the fruit ripens. For them Provence is benign, a land of fresh mornings and long hot afternoons, of flowers, fruit and fecundity. They haven't observed how harsh and jagged are its rocks, how thin the soil, how the trees are bent by the icy wind that for five months in the year blows from the high Alps. They take the summer as a right, when it is only a reward or recompense.

That January the wind blew without stopping, day after day, rattling the olive trees; it fell towards evening and then the land was held in a hard penetrating frost. The peasants wore pinched looks, and the German armoured cars clattered through the villages. The cocks crew, the dogs howled, but the people were silent. There was a shortage of fuel; in the château Anne huddled, grateful for Parisian furs which Lucien had found her. They had formerly belonged to Polly, who hated Provence and had feared the boredom of its winters.

My grandmother had asked no questions about what had happened in Vichy, why Lucien was no longer a Minister. Instead she recounted how disaffection was rife in the villages, how anti-clericalism and Socialism flourished. 'They say they are fighting the Germans, but *canaille* like that are always out only for themselves. They are not preparing to fight against something they think is wrong. That's just what they say, but don't you believe it. Fine words don't ripen the harvest. What they want is our property, nothing less. And they attack the Church first.'

Her mutterings had the repetitive quality of madness.

'I never thought I'd be grateful to see Germans, but what would we do without them?'

'Do you know why the young men run off to the *Maquis?*' she asked. 'It's because they're thieves who don't want to work.'

At her request the curé approached Lucien.

'You must understand that I speak out of respect,' he said. 'I'm not a man of the world, but nevertheless I understand how things

are. All the same, Monsieur de Balafré, this irregular liaison . . .
well, naturally, I comprehend . . . but . . . you haven't been to
confession because you can't come and you are likewise excluded
from Communion. Well, I don't have to tell you that your
immortal soul . . . at a time moreover when any of us may be
summoned at any moment to meet our Maker . . . and there's
another thing besides, the example . . . this decision to install
your mistress in what is after all your mother's house, well, it's
offensive to her. Have you thought of that?

'It was astonishing,' he said later, 'with what tolerance he
received my reproof. But that tolerance caused me anxiety, it
was so close to indifference. And moral indifference of that sort is
but the twinkling of an eye from the mortal sin of accidie. I was
perturbed.'

Lucien said: 'Monsieur le Curé, you have done your duty. But
you know of course that I have not been without sin in the past,
even here, in this house. There is poor Marthe after all, and you
know very well that young Jacques is my son, perhaps now – who
can tell? – the only son I have, even though born, as you must say,
in sin, on the wrong side of the blanket. Believe me, however, I
respect you, and I value my soul. But then there's the question of
sanity. Without Mademoiselle Querouaille, I must tell you, I
would have gone mad this last year. I'm sure of that. A madness of
what you call indifference. I trust in the good God and that he will
forgive me.'

Early in February a German unit was instructed to take up its
quarters in the château. Lucien protested to the local Commander, was assured that it was necessary.

'There is notable disaffection in your neighbourhood, very
many young men taking to the mountains to avoid the duty of
labour service in Germany on behalf of the Reich, as ordained in
the regulations of the French Republic.'

The Commander, a fat little man with a Himmler pince-nez,
sat trapped between his chair and his desk. The front of his tunic
was squeezed out like a woman's breasts. His skin shone pink
from scrubbing.

'They're for your protection too, Monsieur de Balafré. We have
information that you, as a former Minister of the French Republic
and a good friend of Germany, have been nominated as what they
call "a legitimate target" by the dissident groups.'

But Lucien could not escape the suspicion that the German
unit was also detailed to spy on him.

'Of course they are,' Anne said. 'You have after all resigned your post. You are known to be a French patriot, and they must be beginning to wonder if your interpretation of patriotism has changed. You will be careful, my dear, won't you? I couldn't bear to lose you too.'

'And do you think it has changed?'

'That depends. Surely no one can be certain of what patriotism means at the moment.'

'One thing I'm sure of,' Lucien said, 'is that true patriotism can't mean the sort of activities which result in reprisals against ordinary decent people. Have you seen this?'

He pushed a copy of a local newspaper towards her. It carried a report of executions carried out by the Germans at a village only twenty miles away. Ten men had been shot because a German lieutenant had been killed in an ambush ten days previously, and his murderer had not been surrendered.

'How many wrongs create a right?' he asked. Then bent to try to kiss her tears away. But she sobbed in his arms, shaking and trembling, her tears salt on his lips, cracked by the wind, and on his tongue.

The German unit conducted itself properly. Its commanding officer was a very young man, a dedicated Nazi, but nevertheless punctilious in his observances of the proprieties.

'He believes it is proper that the master race should set a moral example,' Anne said.

'Don't be ironical, it doesn't suit you. We should consider ourselves lucky.'

Lucien's nerves were frayed. He had never spoken sharply to Anne before; she had often been amazed by his unnatural calm and forebearance.

'I'm sorry,' she said, and kissed him. 'But it's a sort of refuge.'

'It's a temptation.'

He used such influence as he still had to try to persuade the villagers and townspeople to observe regulations and abide within the law.

'And does that mean we must let our sons be carted off to Germany?' he was asked.

'I'm afraid it does. Because if you defy these regulations things will be worse. It will be impossible to offer you any protection.'

He tried, yet again, to speak to his mother about Armand, and to urge her to realise that Armand was, in his own way, a patriot.

'Whom do you respect,' he said, 'those members of families like your own who remained émigrés throughout the Empire, or those who returned like my father's family and served Napoleon?'

'It isn't the same thing,' she said; but he knew it was; people had different, yet equally certain, ideas of France.

Rupert arrived there in September. He had a week's leave. He was surprised to find the German unit in residence. No one had warned him. Surely it wasn't necessary.

'Necessary?' said Lucien with a lift of the eyebrow.

But he felt younger to see Rupert. They embraced each other.

'I have almost full use of my arm now,' Rupert said. 'The doctors thought it impossible. Perhaps we should always distrust experts.'

'What do the experts say about the progress of the war? I'm out of things now, you understand.'

'You're lucky.'

Rupert glanced at the German officer who had entered the room, and barely acknowledged the exaggerated heel-clicking salute he was accorded.

The curé said: 'Yes, I met Rupprecht von Hülenberg. I liked him, he was obviously a good man, intellectual, not very intelligent. Your poor father expanded in his presence. He gave him back confidence and hope. He made him believe in possibilities. I don't know how. I met him at dinner. There was little talk of the war, perhaps because the other German officer was there, very stiff, very correct, very punctilious. Clearly neither Lucien nor von Hülenberg was at ease with him. Marthe served us her famous anchovy tart, I remember. He was very gentle, von Hülenberg. I was astonished that a German could be so gentle.'

Lucien and Rupert walked in the hills, the same hills where only seven years later I went shooting with young Jacques. Did Rupert recognise in those Provençal hills the significance for Lucien which the eastern marshes held for him? Did he recognise in them the strength of Latinity?

They would have talked philosophy, of the amateurish sort in which they had always indulged. Did he ask about Maurras, Lucien's old hero, adhering to fixed ideas which had never been applicable and which were all the less applicable in those years when it was plausible to argue that they were in fact being enacted?

Certainly, it was in these conversations held as they lay on thyme-scented hilltops, under the deep blue sky that promised enduring sunshine, that Rupert opened his heart to his friend. There were things stirring in Germany. He had friends – they were a loosely-knit group of true patriots – who were determined on change. The war?

'The war,' Rupert said, in a phrase that stuck in Lucien's mind, 'has been the wrong shape from the start.'

Germany, as he saw it, had no quarrel in the west. It had long ceased to be the natural enemy of France. He and Lucien had agreed on that over and over again, and nothing that had happened since altered that conviction.

'Overseas colonies? We have never needed them. Our mission is, as it has always been, in the east. It should now be a mission of civilisation, not of war, for the days when you could impose civilisation by war are long past. But we have been dragged into this war, which we are losing. We must extricate ourselves, and to do so we must eliminate Hitler and his gang of bungling cut-throats. To do so effectively, we must be prepared; and if the right results are to follow we must be prepared beyond Germany also. It's the right psychological moment that is necessary. Are you a friend of Laval, Lucien?'

'Laval has no friends.'

'He will need them, and I think we need Laval.'

He mentioned names, since famous: von Stauffenberg, Adam zu Solz von Trott, Bielenberg; Lucien had met some of them. He felt proud of Rupert's confidence. Their conversation inspired him with the hope that something would be saved from the wreckage.

So when, in the winter of '43, two or three months after that visit from Rupert, he received a summons to visit Laval at Châteldon, he acceded eagerly. He left the following report.

CHAPTER TWENTY-FIVE

Document 13: Certainly from the Confessions

MONSIEUR LAVAL ONCE said to me: 'Don't you know Châteldon? There's no other place like it in the world. It's a village in a valley, with hills all round and vineyards on the hills. We make a fine wine there. No Burgundy, certainly, you understand, but a fine wine all the same. I like it, it's what I've been accustomed to drinking all my life, and that sort of knowledge and familiarity means a lot to me. It's an old village, Châteldon, with mediaeval houses, the true France. In the valley there's a knoll with an old castle on it. That's my home. You must visit me there, Monsieur de Balafré, if you really wish to understand me. I have always believed that you can only understand a man when you know his calf-country and have seen him there. It's the east winds of Picardy that have formed the Marshal, you know.'

Since I have never been intimate with Monsieur Laval, I had had no opportunity to see him in Châteldon and to prove the truth of his words. Nevertheless I believed them. In the same way, for all her sophistication and glitter, my poor Polly has never escaped the hunting fields of the soft English Midlands. It's the experience of riding a hunter across a ploughed field and then taking a blackthorn hedge that has made her what she is; it gave her the resolution to follow her own line all her life. And yet though she has seen things clearly, she has never seen much, because there is no definition in the countryside. And Anne? And Brittany? It's my misfortune that I don't know her country.

Monsieur Laval sent a car and escort for me. We travelled by night, and I reached Châteldon on a wet windy morning, when there was mist hanging from the chestnut trees on the hillsides. The castle is a solid edifice at a little distance from the village. It looks down on the valley, and there are fir trees between it and the opposite hill. There were men and women working in the fields as we approached. Two or three looked up and waved at the car, perhaps thinking it contained the Prime Minister.

To my surprise he greeted me at the door of the castle. I was equally surprised to find him wearing breeches and gaiters. I had never previously seen him in anything but formal dress, and it occurred to me that, in his country garb, his protestations of devotion to the soil seemed altogether credible. He told me he had been visiting the dairy.

'I'm a scientific farmer,' he said. 'It's in my blood, and I get more contentment from gazing on a good milking-cow than aesthetes like yourself do from gazing at an Ingres.'

He laughed, affecting an intimacy for which I was unprepared, and was nevertheless charmed by.

'I wasn't born in the castle, you know,' he said. 'On the contrary, down there in the village. We'll take a walk in the afternoon and I'll show you my birthplace. My father kept the inn, but he had a few acres of vines and six horses because he was also the local postmaster. I was taken away from school when I was twelve to drive the mailcart, but I managed to return and so got myself an education; and here we are. But I love the soil, it's the source of everything. I could never leave. I could never be happy anywhere else. Before the war, even during the most intense crisis, I would return here on Saturdays, just to get myself feeling right. It's good of you to come.'

He spoke as if his invitation had not been a command.

'I was puzzled,' I said, 'and curious.'

'Naturally.'

He let me into the library, which is a large handsome room with big windows giving a fine extensive view of the valley. One wall was lined with copies of law reports, another with collected volumes of French classics which looked as if they had been bought by the yard. A maid brought in a pot of coffee and some of those little almond cakes characteristic of the Auvergne.

'I'm devoted to these,' Monsieur Laval said. 'The coffee is genuine, I assure you. Some of my German friends are good enough to make a supply available to me.'

His eyes twinkled as he said 'my German friends'.

He poured two cups of coffee, and winced as he sipped his own.

'I'm addicted to coffee but my wife has just insisted that I stop putting sugar in it. She's worried about my health. It's ironical, isn't it, to worry about one's health with things as they are. But of course, your *patron*, the Marshal, thinks about little else these days. About his health, not mine, you understand. He would be delighted if I was to drop dead.'

He settled himself in a carved chair, made of stained oak in the heavy and deplorable style of the Second Empire, and gestured to me to sit down too.

'Let's not stand on ceremony,' he said. 'I was born a peasant, a superior peasant, and I still think like a peasant. It makes me uncomfortable to let formality interpose itself in personal relations. Even my celebrated deviousness – oh yes, I am quite well aware of my reputation – is only the taciturnity and deviousness of a peasant confronted by his landlord. You're surprised that I have asked you here?'

'Yes indeed.'

'We had a conversation in Paris in the autumn of '40. Believe me, I have not forgotten it. You impressed me. And I have watched you since. In November '42 especially. And concluded: Lucien de Balafré is a man I can trust, a man worthy of confidence. That's rare these days.'

He smiled. His whole face changes when he smiles. It is as if he is making a present of himself to you.

'I mentioned my German friends just now, and I saw you detected the irony in my tone. But you have German friends yourself, without irony? That's right, isn't it, nothing ironical in your friendship . . ?'

'I don't understand you.'

'Oh yes, you do, but you are playing safe. I like that. I admire it. The man who lets his hand be seen is a fool. I can't respect such a man. But I respect you. And I am not trying to deceive or trap you. Read this.'

He passed me a sheet of paper which had been lying, face down, on a little table at his right hand.

'Go on, read it,' he said, and stretched beyond that table to pick up one of the little almond cakes. He bit into it, keeping his eyes, as I was powerfully aware, on me.

It was a report of the visit paid to me by Rupert. It outlined our pre-war friendship. There was a paragraph, couched in general but lucid terms, which indicated that Rupert was regarded as a security risk by the German authorities, on the grounds of his connections with 'subversive elements among the old nobility and the conservative classes'. The author of the report advised that I should be kept under surveillance. He pointed out that my brother was with de Gaulle, and that my mistress's brother was believed to have joined the *Maquis*. He recommended that if any further ground for suspicion should be given – 'and since the subject's telephone calls are intercepted, and his mail routinely censored, it will be easy to establish such grounds' – I should immediately be placed under arrest.

I read it twice before looking up, then waited for Laval to speak.

'That's from our own people,' he said, 'not from the Germans, though I suppose they have the same information on your German friend. Perhaps not, of course, for one can't exaggerate the secretiveness of the different departments in a State such as theirs. Still, you see, you have become an object of suspicion.'

'I suppose we all have our dossiers,' I said.

He lit a cigarette from the stub of the one he had been smoking. 'Of course we do,' he said, 'I'm glad you see it like that. And of course visiting me here will do you some good, in some quarters at least. Conversely, it may endanger me. That's my risk, however. But I haven't really brought you here to talk about that. I merely thought it useful that you should know what's being said about you.'

His smile convinced me that it would be absurd to protest at being threatened; it was the most gentle threat.

'No,' he said, 'I just thought you should see this. But I brought you here – I beg your pardon, invited you here, for you could have refused, you must admit that – because I have been, as I say, impressed by your intelligence, lucidity and, at the same time, your courage and common sense whenever we have met. I don't hold it against you that you were one of those who told the Marshal to have nothing to do with that common intriguer, Laval. Why should I?'

That was a fantasy of course, for I was never in a position to offer such advice to the Marshal.

'I've invited you here because I want your advice.'

He smiled and poured me more coffee. It was really very good coffee, with a flavour of before the war.

'This isn't a French war,' he said. 'It hasn't been a French war since 1940, and I'm determined it won't be again. Unfortunately, the Resistance doesn't understand that. I would wish them to do so. But it's a war in which France can still be destroyed. I wish to avoid that. That's my policy. To protect France, simply that.'

'I've never doubted your patriotism,' I said.

'Only there are moments when patriotism is inadequate? I agree. You wrote an article once which impressed me, about Europe, about the need for a friendship between France and Germany. I approved it absolutely. Europe has been ravaged by our unnecessary quarrels. They threaten, even now, to destroy France.'

'That quarrel?'

'The remnants of that quarrel.'

'But Monsieur le Président, even if I still believe that it is necessary for France and Germany to come together in friendship, I can't conceive of friendship between France and Hitler.'

'Nor, of course, can your friend Herr von Hülenberg. Nor can his friends who are all what our children will learn to call "good Europeans". I think we understand each other. Perhaps you have some means, some subterranean means, of communicating with Herr von Hülenberg? Do please give him, if that is the case, my good wishes.'

He jumped to his feet and, crossing the room, picked up a walking-stick from a stand by the door.

'Let us take a walk.'

The mist had lifted and the air was soft and gentle. The trees were not yet quite bare, but there was a scent of dead leaves. Smoke rose, dark grey and straight, from cottage chimneys. We made our way to some farm buildings. Two or three geese and some ducks were feeding in stubble fields. We paused by a pigsty and Monsieur Laval scratched the back of a big blue-and-white sow.

'She's going to be a mother again,' he said. 'Wonderful.' He moved the tip of his stick so that he could scratch behind the ear.

'You love that, my beauty, don't you?' he said. 'It's imperative of course that the German Armies are not overwhelmed by the Bolshevists. I don't want my Auvergnat peasants to suffer as the Kulaks have suffered. And they would. So we need a strong Germany, if a different one.'

Even by the pigsty, with only his sow listening, I thought, he will use only words which can carry more than one meaning.

'As for France,' he said, 'we need reconciliation, if this terrible European war is not to be translated into a civil war. Come,' he said, 'we'll walk into the village. I'll show you the inn where I was born. That will help you to understand me, yes, and perhaps even to trust me.'

'Do you know,' he said, as we walked down the cobbled street, 'this is the only place in France where I can walk freely, without a bodyguard; it's the only place where people give me good-day. They trust me, you see. They know it's my intention to look after them.'

The inn was a mean-looking house, with a bench and wooden table outside where four old men sat playing cards. One of them removed his pipe from his mouth to pass some remark about the weather to Monsieur Laval. He replied in the local patois, and they all laughed. The innkeeper greeted him as Pierre.

'He's some sort of cousin aren't you, Raoul? My father was his mother's half-brother, isn't that right? Give us a glass of red.'

We sat for some minutes in silence. An old woman was frying sausages on an open range, and, without being asked, brought us some on a plate. They were coarse, highly-seasoned pork sausages.

'How good it is,' Laval said, 'to eat what one ate as a child.'

'Do you think it's possible,' he said, 'for you to act for me?'

'In what capacity?' I asked.

'As an unofficial Ambassador,' he said.

I accepted, and I am nervous on account of what I have undertaken to attempt. Yet I could not have refused.

Laval retains the same aim he has had throughout the war. He wishes to keep the peace in France and to save the country from Bolshevism also. To accomplish this, two things are necessary. First, an understanding must be achieved with those elements of the Resistance which are aware of the Communist menace. This means, as he admits, dividing the Resistance and making overtures to de Gaulle. He will offer to sign a pact with de Gaulle, if de Gaulle will agree to ease matters for him now by restraining his followers from making the sort of attacks on the Germans and the French State which invite reprisals.

Second, there must be a coup d'état in Germany. I am to contrive to assure Rupert that Laval is in favour of their enterprise and will do everything in his power to facilitate its success.

'It's a gamble,' he said, 'because I still think Hitler is strong enough to repel any Anglo-American invasion; but whatever the outcome in that quarter, it is necessary that we have a German government strong enough at least to compel Stalin to accept a negotiated peace in the east, and yet at the same time respectable enough to make it possible for the Anglo-Americans to give them a free hand against the Bolsheviks.

'As for de Gaulle,' he said, draining his glass, 'you must let him know that the Americans have already made overtures to me to establish a provisional government in the event of their successful invasion, which will exclude him. The Americans distrust de Gaulle far more than they distrust Laval. It's one of the few cards left in my hand.'

When I returned home Anne was at once aware of my excitement and apprehension. I told her what had happened.

'It's impossible,' she said. 'Laval has asked you to square the circle, he has sent you in search of fool's gold, he has asked you to reconcile the irreconcilable.'

It was time, she said, to go into hiding, to join the Resistance, to flee the country.

'There is Spain,' she said.

'Don't you understand?' she said, 'I don't want you dead.'

HUGH, I HAVE not been entirely frank. Why should I be? We all have secrets to protect, and sometimes when we are offered those that belong to others, we shrink from accepting the gift.

Two years ago, my Uncle Armand died. I hadn't seen him for more than ten years, and indeed I doubt if we had met more than half a dozen times since I left Les Trois Puits with tears in my eyes and resentment in my heart. Yet, because both Armand and I had a sense of family which expressed itself in the tacit knowledge that we were, whatever happened, obliged to each other, we never quite broke contact; and when he died, he left me certain papers.

As it happened, I was not well at the time. I was indeed in a clinic, receiving treatment for what they call alcoholism – I put it like that because I cannot accept the notion that addiction to the bottle is some sort of illness or disease. It seems to me, naively, yet – I would claim – with justice, to be essentially a matter of choice. Nevertheless, despite my scepticism, I was that year sufficiently close to despair, and yet still tenacious of life, to be willing to seek treatment. It was largely a matter of detoxification; and, having escaped death, I resumed my normal pattern of life fortified. But for several months I was also timid and defensive. I consigned these papers Armand had bequeathed me to my bank. They lay there like a decayed tooth which one cannot forget but which does not imperatively require treatment. I suppose I always knew that some day they would have to be read. But I let them lie there, because I was afraid.

It was only when you compelled me to this task that I wrote to my bank asking them to forward them to me. Banks, in my experience, are rarely efficient, not even when you owe them money. Anyway, it took more than one request before they did my bidding.

Here then is Armand's letter. I think you will find it almost concludes the story, and it seems to me that it makes it very unlikely that you will be able to take your project further, if only because I can't see how you can impose any shape on the material you have.

Certainly, it's a long way from your early intellectual curiosity.

I am afraid you must be disappointed. Perhaps that is why I haven't heard from you for two months. Perhaps, even now, you have advanced to some more fruitful enterprise.

But I feel, now, rather like Ulysses. I'm damned if anything will keep me from Ithaca.

CHAPTER TWENTY-SEVEN

Document 14: Letter from
Armand de Balafré dated 20 July, 1984

MY DEAR ETIENNE:

I shall be dead when you receive this letter. This morning sentence was pronounced: inoperable cancer. Well, I am seventy-seven; no point in grumbling.

Have you observed the date of this letter? Precisely forty years ago, Claus von Stauffenberg placed that briefcase of his against the table-leg of the hut in East Prussia, and departed rejoicing that he had killed the Führer. Within a few days Lucien's friend Rupert von Hülenberg was hanged on piano-wire alongside his friends. Hitler gloated over the film made of the executions which marked almost the last snarl of the beast. They marked in a different way the extinction of your father's hopes also.

How ironical it seems at this distance, when the Franco-German friendship in which both believed, and to a version of which, it may be said, both sacrificed their lives, now seems so firmly established that it has become one of those facts of life, as natural as that people should drive to a restaurant in the country for their Sunday lunch. But yet there is more irony. What has confirmed that friendship has been the Russian domination of Eastern Europe which they hoped in 1944 to prevent.

Half a lifetime ago, Etienne, we told you that your father had killed himself. We had discussed this, Berthe and I, and it seemed necessary to tell you. It may not have been, as you may have guessed, true; except in the metaphysical sense that Lucien, in choosing to be a man of a certain sort of action, chose death. He was, in that last year, absolute for death.

Early in January 1944, I was back working in de Gaulle's headquarters in Carlton Gardens, London. It was a season when rumours of the Allied landing in France proliferated, though, as you must be aware, the British and Americans declined to take us into their confidence. In particular, the American distrust of the General had reached such a point that we could not escape the knowledge that President Roosevelt was determined on only one thing as far as France was concerned: that however the liberated country should be governed, it should not be governed by de Gaulle. All this is well-known history.

Agents from within France sent us several reports of American overtures to Laval. There was still a clique in the State Department sympathetic to Vichy, and we knew that, for many influential parts of the American war machine, the favoured French solution was a purified Vichy, which would contrive to exclude both Communists and Gaullists from the Administration. That was not our only problem. We also knew of Communist plans to take over full control of the Resistance in order that the German expulsion should be followed by a coup or revolution which would establish in Paris a government closer to Moscow than to London or Washington. We of course had no desire to be close to any foreign capital, for in the circumstances of the time, such closeness could only mean inferiority and subservience. Therefore, we Gaullists of the first hour sought a means whereby France could be re-established, free, independent and entire.

All this is common knowledge, but it is a necessary preliminary to the story I must now tell you.

One morning that month I arrived late in the office on account of a vile London fog. Such fog no longer exists, but it caught you by the throat, made your eyes red, and chilled the bones. I was told by my secretary that Colonel Pelissier, my immediate superior, wished to see me.

Pelissier was a man for whom I had little respect. He had been serving in Syria in 1940 and had not joined *La France Libre* till late in '42. He was however a man of considerable acumen.

'There's been an interesting development,' he said. 'It affects you personally.'

He stood with his back to me and gazed into the fog. There was silence in the street below, and, without visibility, we might have existed in limbo. I knew he didn't like me, and was on my guard.

'One of the problems concerning you, Captain, has always been the fact of your brother's adherence to Vichy.'

'He was a Junior Minister from the beginning of the regime till the winter of 1942,' I said. 'It was a time when many who are now with us were against us. Since his resignation he has taken no part in public life.'

'Are you in communication with him?'

I saw the trap. 'Not directly,' I said, 'but, as you know, through our various sources of information, it's easy to know most things about people of any prominence.'

'He went to see Laval at Châteldon last month.'

'No,' I said, 'in November.'

'Well,' Pelissier said, 'The General is curious about that meeting.'

That evening, when I was pondering this conversation, I received a telephone call at home. It was a young man who refused to give his name. He insisted that it was necessary that we meet. He mentioned the names of people whom I knew to be in the Resistance, which would serve, he said, as a form of reference. And then he said, 'It concerns your brother, too.'

We arranged to meet in the Café Royal. He assured me that he would 'make the contact'.

I wondered if I should report this approach to Pelissier, and concluded that could wait. In doing this, I neglected the old military advice that one should always protect the flanks and rear.

The Café Royal was still in those days like a Parisian café. I'm told this hasn't been true for a long time. I chose it precisely because it was public, for I was convinced that I was being followed, and was ready to guess that my mysterious caller might also be an object of interest to both our security service and the British one. It seemed a good idea therefore to avoid anything clandestine.

I ordered a glass of beer and sat down at one of the marble-top tables with a good view of the door. There were many soldiers in the bar, some of them intellectuals whom I knew at least to say good evening to. After half an hour I was beginning to think that my telephone caller was not going to turn up, and was amusing myself by trying to catch and hold the eye of a very attractive blonde girl whose companion seemed to be approaching a stage of tiresome inebriation. I was just calculating that when he had had one more drink she would welcome my approach, when a young man in a belted raincoat and a slouch hat – looking absurdly like a figure from an American gangster movie – paused at the doorstep, scanned the room and came directly to my table. He wore a cigarette in the right corner of his mouth. He made no apology for being late, but sat down and clapped his hands to summon a waiter.

'That's not how it's done here,' I said, but, to my irritation, one at once came to take his order for two glasses of beer.

'You have the advantage of me,' I said, 'for I don't know your name.'

I expected him to be evasive, probably for no reason beyond the love of mystery which afflicted so many then, but he at once replied:

'Hervé Querouaille.'

'I see.'

I knew of course of his sister's liaison with your father. He smiled, throwing off his absurd look of an American gangster and letting me see only a charming boy who had dressed up for play.

'You could have come to the office,' I said. 'Since you're in London, you can have nothing to fear.'

'I've been a member of the Resistance for the last nine months,' he said, 'and in that time I've come to see that I don't like everything about it. That's why I'm here really. But that's also why I have thought it a good idea to meet you away from your headquarters. Do you love your brother?'

'Why not?' I said.

'I am devoted to my sister.'

He began to talk. Words tumbled out with inconceivable rapidity, which would have defeated any stenographer, and with a turbulence which blurred my understanding and quite dulls my memory. No matter. The gist of his rhetoric was simple.

He began by insisting that he was a Breton; a Breton first, and a Frenchman second. (I let that pass without comment; it seemed to me merely the romanticism of youth; and now I reflect that all political activity is a form of romanticism. But his was diseased, perhaps.) However, this wasn't the point, he said; everyone had deceived the Bretons, always. He accepted that for a moment. The question was, how to save the peace which was surely coming.

'You haven't brought me here to listen to some half-baked political philosophy?'

Did I say that, or merely think it? I drank my beer, which was already warm. Possibly I said it, for I remember that he flushed. My brother had asked him to come. I looked up. He nodded his head. I couldn't doubt his honesty, his sincerity. Lucien, he said, remembered our last conversation in Bordeaux: how we were each seeking to serve France, in different ways.

'He says to tell you that the parallel lines are converging. He says you will know what he means.'

That was proof at least that he had spoken to Lucien, for I remembered his fancy that frequently courses which seem opposed have nevertheless the same goal and may be represented by converging parallel lines. (It is curious, Etienne, that this theory was later advanced by that other opaque metaphysician, the Italian Aldo Moro.)

'He has authority to indicate how this can be achieved. And he said to tell you that Rupert has plans to control the east wind. Does that make sense?'

'Did he mention the wolf-pit?' I said.

'How did you know?'

The drunk man at the further table was now twisting the girl's arm. She gave a little yelp of pain and tried to take it away. I got up and tapped him on the shoulder.

'The lady doesn't enjoy that, you know.'

Absurd to remember that. It was so direct in comparison with our conversation. He tried to hit me. I cuffed him across the cheek with the back of my hand, and he subsided, blubbering. The incident caused little stir, but, instead of thanking me, the girl began to comfort him.

'Why don't you go away?' she said. 'You foreigners. Bloody foreigners.'

We went into the blackout. Knowing my way, I took the boy's arm to guide him.

'You will have to come to Carlton Gardens,' I said.

I keep, Etienne, being side-tracked by detail: the feel of the damp mackintosh, and the bony elbow I held between my thumb and forefinger. And all the time the boy's voice throwing waves over me like the tireless sea; it was impossible to believe either that he could keep a secret, or that anyone could recognise one in the stream of rhetoric. He still didn't want to come to Carlton Gardens, but I insisted.

They were suspicious there, naturally. Exiles inhabit a house full of dark twisting corridors, where the air is heavy with resentment, fear, envy and doubt. Whatever someone proposes must be read every way: through a magnifying-glass, before a mirror, tested for invisible ink. It was eventually the General himself who summoned me:

'So, they tell me you want to go to France to see your brother, Laval's friend.'

'He has sent a message by way of a young man in the Resistance.'

'There is not one Resistance. There are many differing acts of resistance. And there are different people to be resisted. Some day we shall have to be friends with the Germans. This is true enough even though Monsieur Laval now enunciates the same sentiment.'

'And who knows? Even the Germans themselves may change direction, sir.'

'I understood that was one point which you were going to ascertain.'

'Our mission has been approved,' I said to Hervé. 'You will have to say your affectionate farewells to that girl you have been seeing.'

There were delays. There always were. Hervé was able to postpone his goodbyes to his little blonde. As for me, I spent evenings, homesick, in the Café Royal. The thought of France was enough to make me tremble; the conviction that I would not be able to see either Berthe or the children dismayed me.

The way young Hervé talked of his sister made me feel happier for Lucien. He made her seem a girl of the utmost sympathy. No doubt, in the private life of the family, she was as he said. We can never tell how we shall behave in extremity, and in her case it was to be a question of loyalties. There is nothing I have found more perplexing and morally confusing than loyalties. They destroyed your life, didn't they, when Berthe told you how your poor Freddie – yes, Etienne, I still attach that possessive adjective to her when I think of her, and always with a little stab of pain – how your poor Freddie, I say, was broken on the wheel of loyalties.

There were a number of us, mostly Gaullists of the first hour, who made a habit of meeting in the Café. I shan't trouble you with their names, for only one is relevant. But a few nights before I was at last, it seemed, about to go, we were discussing just this question: to what should a man be loyal unto death?

Four of us would have called ourselves Catholics, but none suggested the Church, or even God.

'The Protestant vice of private judgement has infected us.'

'France?'

We had all abandoned home, risked much for France, but there was only a raising of glasses and sipping of drinks at the suggestion.

'Naturally we would die for our idea of France, but one has to confess that one would have only a precarious hold on the cliffside of meaning.'

'And what do you mean by that?'

'I mean that each of us has his own France, and that it is impossible to recognise an identity. Would you die for a Communist France? Or for Laval's?'

'Wives and families?'

'Haven't we all abandoned them to the mercy of the Germans?'

One whom you will recognise, though you have never met, Etienne, Freddie's father Guy, raised his head, which in moments of emotion never failed to make me think of a self-consciously weary buffalo – if you can grant the conceit of a self-conscious buffalo – and said:

'I would die for revenge.'

'For an idea?'

'For the fact of satisfaction.'

'You mean you would die content, having achieved revenge? Or that you would be content to die failing to exact it?'

'I mean it is what I want, and I shall put my life at risk to obtain it.'

It was at that moment that I looked across the room and saw your mother. She was with a young officer of the Royal Air Force. Naturally I abandoned metaphysics, leapt up and embraced her. Her young man, from sheer embarrassment, as I thought, made himself useful, bustling around to obtain drinks. Polly reproached me, 'You never come to see me, Armand darling.'

As ever, it delighted me to see her. I have never known a woman who aroused in me such a strong desire to protect her. It was absurd, for none needed protection less. She wore the armour of immaturity preserved in champagne that never lost its sparkle. It had been proved to her time and again that life wasn't a game or a society dance; she acted as if she thought such proofs ridiculous. Whenever I saw her I felt a soberly responsible eighteen, and was possessed by a powerful desire to enter into her world of fixed and naive assumptions.

'I'm going to marry Roddy,' she said, pointing at the young officer, 'as soon as things can be fixed up.

'I'll never stop being fond of Lucien,' she said, 'but I couldn't live with him again. He asks too much of everyone and everything. He stopped being fun a long time ago.'

I would like to think she shed a tear as she said that, but actually she laughed.

'I often think I should have married you, darling, instead.' And do you know, if we had, we would have been happy. Lucien wasn't made for happiness.

At that moment Hervé entered the Café. I made excuses to Polly. As we left I reflected that once I would have found a keen pleasure in introducing the brother of Lucien's mistress to his wife. Now it seemed things were sufficiently complicated already.

Two nights later we were parachuted into France from a Lancaster bomber. Our reception was well prepared. The local *Maquis* took charge of us, with that rough suspicion which they reserved for visitors from London. However, Hervé's credentials were satisfactory: one of the reception committee was his mistress of the previous autumn. The eagerness of her greeting made me jealous.

This cell of the Resistance was run by the local landowner, which was unusual. He escorted me to the château.

'Isn't this a bit risky?' I said.

'It's just as risky to hide you in the forest. Besides, though I used to be a playboy, I'm neither a fool nor an amateur at this business. There's a perfectly respectable identity awaiting you. And papers, of course. You're from the Ministry of Agriculture.'

'Is that credible?'

'Perfectly. They keep sending me circulars about natural fertilisers. I've requested an expert. You.'

I was never for the next ten days quite sure where we were. That was a measure of the distrust which the Resistance on the ground felt for us in London. We travelled by night, though it seemed to me that that made our journeys more dangerous, for anyone moving after dark was likely to attract the attention of the Germans. However, I didn't raise the point; I did our colleagues the courtesy of supposing that they should know what was safest. They were avid for news of the direction of the war, reluctant to offer anything in exchange.

'You mustn't be offended,' Hervé said, 'it's best for everyone that we know only what is necessary about our friends.'

I did not argue, though I thought that their reticence scarcely augured well for us Gaullists. But then Hervé was hardly one of us.

There were delays. I remember three days holed up in a mountain farmhouse. The peasant who owned it disliked having us there, grudged everything we ate, and would have preferred us to remain in the loft above his barn, if he hadn't also been reluctant to let us out of his sight. We had three companions there, young men, whom I would have taken for criminals if they hadn't assured me of their patriotism. One of them had secured himself a bottle of armagnac; as the level sank, he whispered to me that his colleagues had only joined the Resistance in order to escape the labour draft for Germany. Probably this was true. I wondered what his motive was. This dismal trio dampened even young Hervé's ebullience.

On the third evening, as we sat over a cabbage soup, in which a muttonbone had been perhaps perfunctorily dipped, and a little flask of flabby white wine, we were alerted by the roar of a motorbike down the valley.

'It's the boss.'

One of the young men slipped out; the others stood by the door. The old man continued to spoon soup into his mouth without looking up, and Hervé and I sat, listening.

Hervé said: 'When you hear motorbikes you usually think of the Boches.'

The motorbike engine coughed and was silent. We heard footsteps. The door opened, and a thin man with a black beard entered. The thin nose and the beard made him look like an illustration from the Bible. He greeted Hervé with a nod, shook my hand: 'Simon Halévy,' he said.

The three young men who had been looking after us exchanged glances: they had been careful to preserve anonymity.

As if aware of their disapproval, he said:

'Of course, it's necessary for you to know who I am. We have serious matters to discuss, serious negotiations to be undertaken, and it's both ridiculous and insulting to pretend that this can be satisfactorily done if we play games with our identities. You have no reason to trust me if I won't trust you with my name. Besides, there are strands which bind us. You know my cousin and her husband, Guy Fouquet.'

I nodded.

'And,' he said, 'I know your brother myself, who is – what shall I say? – the object of our mission. So, you see, it is quite a family party.'

The family party, as Halévy ironically termed it, congregated two days later, again in a farmhouse, high in the south Auvergne. We were all nervous lest Lucien should be followed, and so the arrangement was that he should arrive there the day before us. The approaches to the farm had been watched two days previously, which was an elaborate precaution, for in fact Lucien had made a rendezvous with the Resistance, some fifty miles away, and had been brought, blindfolded and ignorant of his destination, to our meeting-place. His willingness to entrust himself to those whom he had reason to fear seemed to me irrefutable proof of his sincerity and desperation.

I was shocked by his appearance. He had aged a dozen years since I had left him in Bordeaux, and the formal double-breasted dark grey suit, which he wore even in our mountain retreat, hung loose on him; it might have been made for a bigger man, though Lucien had always been thin. He rose from a sofa as we entered, and rubbed sleep from his eyes.

We embraced of course. He embraced young Hervé too.

'I'm so glad you have come back,' he said. 'Welcome to France.'

Then he was shaken by a coughing fit, which might have been brought on by the depths of his emotion.

We talked for a few minutes about family, about Mother. I told him I had seen Polly, and that you, Etienne, were doing satisfactorily at school in England. He told Hervé Anne sent him love. We were all nervous, anxious to please each other, and fearful of taking a wrong step. I was abashed, as I had been since turbulent childhood, by Lucien's manifest goodness; it's a word I find difficult to use, but no other will serve. Someone ought to write an essay on the decline of our belief in goodness, in virtue; somebody probably has, but I read little nowadays.

I had to stop here, Etienne, and take a pill. Thinking of your father brought on agitation and pain.

Hervé relaxed in Lucien's presence. That impressed me, for the boy's nerves had been stretched taut as piano-wire.

(I didn't mean to write that comparison, and am aghast when I contemplate it. Still, *stet*.)

Only between Simon Halévy and Lucien was there evident tension. I realised that Halévy disliked my brother, and I thought the worse of him for it.

'So, what's your proposition, now we are all assembled?' he said.

Lucien lit a cigarette. His hand shook as he held the match to it. It must have been a strain making that journey, and he would have been too proud to show fear. And I sensed that he felt Halévy's hostility to be oppressive, and was ashamed, for some reason which escaped me, of his own reciprocal dislike. I say, for some reason which escaped me, because I found no difficulty in accounting for my own dislike of Halévy: he was a shit.

'You're Laval's envoy, aren't you?' he said.

'In a manner of speaking.'

'What does that mean?'

'It means that I have reached some of the same conclusions as Monsieur Laval, but that I have also independent reasons for seeking this meeting. And I have knowledge which he lacks.'

'Does that mean you are deceiving Laval too?'

'I hope I'm deceiving nobody.'

That is precisely what he said. It's important to be clear about that, and to remember that I never knew Lucien tell a lie. For that reason, I have no doubt that the accusations later brought against him are false. And I have frequently said as much to Guy Fouquet. But, again, I confess that this certainty is retrospective. 1944 was not a year when one could put one's trust in any past knowledge of anyone, not even a brother.

Then Lucien began to speak. His exposition was lucid as ever, but there was a passion in his voice that was new to me. He stabbed the air with his cigarette as he spoke. And he held everyone's attention.

There would be fighting in France that year, he assured us. But it was not necessary that there should be fighting between Frenchmen. Whatever the attitude of some of his colleagues in Vichy and 'of the Fascist scum who have been kept out of the centre of power there, with the greatest difficulty, I assure you', he had never doubted the patriotism of those who had joined de Gaulle. 'How could I? Doubt your patriotism, Armand, or the patriotism of the many friends who followed the same line as you? I doubted your judgement. That was all.' Accordingly, he had a right to ask for a similar indulgence of judgement to be directed to those who had taken a different path, who, confronted with the responsibility of action in the circumstances of 1940, had tried to save what they could of France, for France and for the French people.

'This is fine talk,' Halévy said.

Lucien looked him in the eyes.

'It's by way of introduction,' he said. 'I have a proposal, sanctioned by Monsieur Laval, whose envoy, as you say, I am. It is this: let us call a truce between Vichy and the Resistance. Let us postpone recriminations. Meanwhile, if the Resistance will abandon action, which, whenever it takes place, invites German reprisals on unfortunate and innocent people, Monsieur Laval will do all in his power, short of himself inviting similar reprisals, to obstruct the occupying forces. Then, when this year is over, we shall see how things stand. If France is free and independent again, Monsieur Laval will at once demit office, and he is ready to stand trial for any offences which he may be thought to have committed against our country, and he asked me to state that he is confident of being able to justify everything he has done before a properly constituted court of law.'

'You're asking us to save Laval. It's absurd.'

'I'm asking you to help us spare the French people suffering. Is that absurd? And I'm asking you to consider my proposal before you judge it.'

He paused, and smiled.

'It's not a lot to ask you know.'

'What of the blood that has been spilt already, that cries out for vengeance?'

It was growing dark. Someone closed the shutters and lit an oil-lamp. Shadows flickered against the wall, making me think of early Christians sheltering in the Catacombs or of those myster-ious late paintings of Rembrandt in which unexplained menace invades tranquil domestic life. Someone else put a bottle of wine on the table and I was grateful for its harsh red assurance of continuity. Yet it was cold as the room we sat in.

'Now,' Lucien said, waving the offer of wine aside, 'let me go beyond my brief from Monsieur Laval, though what I have to say to my mind reinforces the sense of his offer. I have certain German friends. I'm not ashamed to say that.' His chin went up, making his shadow dance on the wall. 'Indeed, I should be ashamed if I had no German friends. These friends are patriots, as we are; like us too, they are not Nazis. Indeed, being German, they have even more reason to hate the Nazis than we have, for Hitler has involved them in the degradation of their people, and they know they are stained by his guilt. They have long nurtured plans against him, and these plans are coming to fruition. Some-time in the next six months – I am sorry I cannot be more exact – they will act. Hitler and his immediate confederates will be removed, a new government established, which will immediately offer peace terms to Britain and America.'

'What about Russia?'

Lucien did not falter.

'I can't answer for the terms which will be offered the Soviet Union, but those proposed in the west will include the immediate evacuation of France by German forces. In six months, if all goes well, the Germans will leave France. I would ask you to consider my earlier proposal for a truce in the light of that . . . possibility.'

He got up.

'You'll want to discuss this among yourselves.'

'We'll need to think about it first, take soundings, try to get in touch with others,' Halévy said. 'And we'll require you to stay here.'

'I can hardly leave without your assistance, since I don't know where I am.'

I remember thinking: its audacity is matched only by its vagueness. Yet there is a naivety which might just make it work.

'They don't like it, do they?' Lucien came and sat beside me. 'I've failed in this, as in everything.'

'Have some wine,' I said. 'I don't think you've failed. I've never thought of you as a failure.'

That was true then. In an odd way it is still true now.

'I don't want wine, thank you,' he said. 'Curiously, I'd like some rum. I don't suppose there is any. It's nice of you to say that, it makes me think of our last meeting in Bordeaux. The tables are turned now, aren't they? Then you were backing the outsider, and I was on the favourite. Well, that horse hasn't stayed.'

I drank my wine, waiting. I waited a long time for him to speak.

'I could envy that boy, Hervé,' he said. 'He retains a zest for life. I wish you had had the chance to know Anne, his sister. She has saved me, made it possible for me to carry on. I owe her so much. Remember that, will you, Armand, please?'

'I won't need to,' I said. 'It'll be over, and we'll return to . . .'

'To what? Normality? Do you know, at home, it's all the worst types who are in the Resistance. The decent family men have too much to lose. Types like Simon who keeps the garage, I don't suppose you remember him, you've never liked our home, have you?'

'You'll do what you can for Etienne, won't you?'

(I nodded. I've failed there, haven't I? Another broken promise.)

'And for young Jacques, Marthe's boy . . .'

(Was it twenty years in prison?)

'Do you remember our last conversation, in Bordeaux? I called yours a mad adventure, and invited you to take your share in our National Revolution. Which has divided the nation as never before, and is no revolution. Laval knows we have failed, that's why he talks for choice only of his village and the land. The land . . . the land . . . we have been so . . . antiquated. I told you it was not based on spite or the desire for revenge. Such self-deception. Do you know, my dear, in the end I have found myself following Laval, not the Marshal, because Laval doesn't hide from the truth.'

'Why don't you say something, Armand?'

I pressed his shoulder, but what could I say? Words of comfort are always impertinent.

'I dream, you know, every night now, and they are cruel dreams. Always cruel. My poor Rupert is the victim, and I am compelled to watch. I suppose, Armand, I have loved Rupert more than you because I have loved ideas more than life. Even the family has been only an abstract noun for me . . . teach Etienne to be able to give himself, won't you? It would be nice if there was some rum. I'm so tired and it helps me . . .'

But, as if despairing, he picked up my glass of wine and drained it.

'I'm sorry. That was yours, wasn't it? Well, at least I have drunk from my brother's cup.'

I don't pretend, Etienne, those were all his precise words. How could they be when I am casting back almost forty years in my memory? But that was the sense. I was overwhelmed by my consciousness of his moral exhaustion. Only a stubborn pride held him from despair.

Nothing was decided at that meeting. How could it be? The matter brought us by Lucien was too momentous to be determined at that level. We would all have to consult. It was something, I thought, that it wasn't rejected out of hand. Even Halévy admitted Lucien's sincerity, and was impressed by it. This did nothing to mitigate his dislike of my brother. That was rooted in his awareness of his own moral inferiority.

To my dismay Lucien's spirits were not raised by this degree of success, which he had certainly not expected. He had come to the meeting without hope. He was tempted by the profound attraction of failure. He would have liked to be able to resign from further commitment. But he couldn't. Pride again held him to his post. I thought of that sentry at Pompeii who held his ground while the lava engulfed him, and of the noble declaration of the Guard at Waterloo: 'The Guard dies, but it does not surrender.'

Surrender, sometimes rational as in 1940, is the great temptation for the man of low vitality.

We parted at dawn. It was cold. A veil of fog concealed the trees that stood only fifty metres from the little hut. Lucien had shaved. He wore a fur-lined overcoat, but still flinched from the cold. We embraced. His lips were dry on my cheek and his own cheek icy. He got into the car with Halévy, young Hervé and two other men, who were to change cars in the nearby town and then escort Lucien, finally by train, to an agreed point. They drove away. I watched the car swallowed up by the fog.

I never saw him again. I had other assignments to fulfil, which would take me to Normandy and give me the opportunity of a brief and dangerous reunion with Berthe and the children. I was gone by another route within ten minutes of the departure of the others.

Their car was stopped by the *Milice* twenty miles from our meeting-place. I had known it was folly to travel like that. When I remarked on this, Halévy said, 'It's my style.'

They were all arrested. I don't know what happened to the two men whose names I never knew, but I believe they blabbed. Young Hervé was tortured by the *Milice*, and then, perhaps because he would not talk, murdered in his cell. Some say he died during torture, others of its effects, but I believe it was as I say. Simon Halévy was also tortured, then surrendered to the Gestapo, who sought him for a bomb attack on a German convoy. They tortured him more. He disappeared in Germany, perhaps in one of the camps, perhaps in a cellar.

There is evidence that Laval tried to protect Lucien, even to have him freed, though, when apprised of the circumstances of his arrest, he straightaway disowned him. I can't blame him for that. Yet . . . it's too difficult.

Your father was taken to Lyons. He was subjected to torture in the prison there, and interrogated by the notorious Barbie himself. Lucien was always afraid that he lacked physical courage – I believe that was why he hunted so audaciously in the year before he married your mother. Fear of fear, and fear of your reaction to pain, is the most desolating fear of all.

He talked. Of course he did. Most of us do. We all do if the torture is gauged correctly. They would have got his friend Rupert months later without his evidence, for they were watching him already; but Lucien talked. There's no doubt that he betrayed him, in circumstances, I insist, in which the word betrayal loses all meaning.

If he was not compelled, five months later, to watch Rupert's own experience of torture or to see him twist on that piano-wire on which they hanged him, he had already seen both too often in his imagination.

They didn't kill Lucien. I think Laval may have saved his life. I don't know, however. What I am certain of is this: it would have been better if they had killed him, and that is what he would have desired.

He returned home, broken, without fingernails, to the Château de l'Haye on the 14th of May, 1944.

CHAPTER TWENTY-EIGHT

Document 15:

From the last journal of Lucien de Balafré

MAY 16, 1944. It is difficult to hold a pen. Acute pain still in my finger-ends. I believe Laval saved my life. Why?

May 18, 1944. Anne left today. She kissed me on the cheek. Only once, but a lingering kiss. I fancy I can still feel the touch of her lips. She explained to me that, now that she knew for certain that Hervé was dead, she must go to her mother. 'I'm all she has left,' she said. Thank God my remnant of pride restrained me from crying, as I wished so much to cry, 'And what about me? You're all I have left.' It would anyway have been a lie, for I have lost her. Whenever she sees me she hears her brother's screams.

May 19, 1944. Yesterday I wrote of my remnant of pride. How can I have even that? After what I have done, after my act of betrayal. When the curé came today, for Maman, not me, I felt an intense desire to speak to him about Judas. Again I restrained myself. (I write as if my life is a series of acts of self-restraint. It's not like that at all. It's not like anything.) The temptation to wallow in self-abasement is extreme.

May 22, 1944. Why not give in? Why not admit that I have always known that I would yield to physical pain?

May 23, 1944. Maman can't talk to me. She can't bear to look at my finger-ends either. She understands nothing of the world that has sprung into being like a monster around her. Do I? Of course not. I'm only a man who used to write essays telling people how they should behave.

May 25, 1944. I woke in the night having dreamed of Rupert again. I was screaming and covered in sweat. In the dream I was made, yet again, to watch as Rupert was stretched out, naked, over a wheel, wrists and ankles pinioned. I got up, came downstairs, found a bottle of brandy. This morning I have the taste of rotten flesh in my mouth. More brandy is perhaps best.

May 27, 1944. The Almighty set his canon 'gainst self-slaughter'. Oh yes, but the Almighty has surely abdicated. He is as impotent as the Marshal, who has – they say – given up any pretence of still taking an interest in what happens around him. Poor old man. Poor deluded substitute for a hero, or a god.

May 30, 1944. Today, as I was walking, I was accosted by Simon, the *garagiste*. I thought he had gone into hiding. He adopted that cringing manner which has always irritated me. 'I've a bit of advice for you, monsieur,' he said. 'I wouldn't offer it if I didn't have your good and your family's to heart. You ought to get out while you can, else things will get rough for you. There,' he said, wiping his hands on his trouser legs, 'it's as much as my own life is worth to have passed on that message.' I thanked him, and said I was grateful for his advice, but I was staying there. It was my home, and I had done nothing of which I was ashamed. If people wanted to put me on trial after the war, then I was ready to speak in my defence and justify myself. I think I kept my voice steady. 'You're a bloody fool then,' he said. I'm mystified as to why he approached me.

June 4, 1944. Three days with the brandy bottle, two of indifference and one of horrid imaginings. But today I found on my study table a letter from Mathilde Dournier, which had been placed there during my alcoholic absence. I can't quote it. My emotion is too extreme. I wept from joy as I read it, muttering to myself, 'At least one person, one single person . . .' And now I'm near to tears again thinking of her words.

June 6, 1944. The Allies have landed in Normandy, successfully it seems. I have just listened to Laval's speech on the wireless. 'We are not in the war,' he said. 'You must not take part in the fighting . . . You will refuse to aggravate the foreign war on our soil with the horror of civil war . . .' And so on. My sentiments exactly. But all around is civil war. Twenty miles away the *Maquis* murdered a Mayor the day before yesterday: for collaboration. Collaboration in his case meant carrying out the orders of the legitimate government of France. Laval's lucidity, like mine, belongs to the asylum, now that its inmates have been let loose in the streets.

June 8, 1944. All I can do is sit it out.

June 12, 1944. More news of Russian advances on the eastern front. Will some of my enemies now admit that we were right? That the danger from Russian Communism is at least as great as the threat from the Nazis ever was, greater indeed because more fundamental? As for morality, what's there to choose between them? For Jews, read Kulaks. The difference is that the Communists would not only subvert French society, but would also destroy everything that we recognise as historic France. What is the position of the Church in the Soviet Union? Yet the myopia of Great Britain and the United States is such that they continue to aid the Russians.

June 20, 1944. It was a mistake to enter public life, for which I have no talent. I should have been content to remain at my desk.

June 22, 1944. A letter from Drieu La Rochelle today. He tells me he now believes in nothing, not even action. He would be absolute for suicide, did he not suspect it as a species of action itself. Drieu and I differ in that he was always a romantic who saw himself in a heroic role, whereas I have only tried to be useful and to do my duty. Well, no matter the difference, we have arrived at the same destination: where the only problem is how best to die.

June 30, 1944. The Allies advance. Two policemen were shot in a neighbouring village yesterday. Ceremonially. Though we have still the protection of German troops, it occurs to me that my presence may endanger Maman. That's impossible. I can't continue to shelter here. I'm going to Paris. Why Paris? Because it began there.

July 6, 1944. Appalling journey, a crowded train that stopped every few miles, and which was continually searched by German soldiers. Their nerve is shattered. One of them struck an old woman over the face with the butt of his rifle. It looked as though he did so from sheer malevolence. But I think it was an expression of his terror and sense of powerlessness. They know the war is lost. We stood by and did nothing. A little businessman whose fingers smelled of cheese talked all the time, in an undertone directed mostly to himself, but interrupted at intervals by questions which he shot at us: his subject was his imminent bankruptcy: 'I've tried to keep things going for my family, only my family, and now I've been blacklisted, boycotted, and I'm in fear of my life.' That was the tenor of his talk, and I was astonished by the temerity of his frankness. But I don't think he knew what he was saying most of the time. He waved his cheese-smelling fingers and sniffed at them.

July 10, 1944. I went to my old apartment. The concierge, who was always so polite, has changed her tune. It was to be expected. She will have to go on living here. My apartment was full of memories of Polly, and also of Anne. There was dust everywhere. I traced their names in the dust on the dressing-room table, and, as I did so, fancied I saw them both sitting gazing into the glass and each other's eyes. I sat down and tried to read. Impossible. We are all waiting, some in barely-suppressed elation, terrified that, even at the last moment, something may go wrong, others, like me, in what would be terror and apprehension, if we were capable of that. I went out, walked the streets for hours. Paris has never looked more beautiful to me: roses and honeysuckle in the Bois de Boulogne. People sitting at café tables as if we were at peace: yet A is only waiting for the arrival of the Allies to denounce B. I sat down at a café and ordered a glass of rum. When I saw Gaston Hunnot limping along the other side of the square, still followed by a troop of girls, I drank it quickly and slipped away. There are other enemies I would happily meet, but I see no reason to subject myself to Gaston's bitter and mocking triumph. Yet I was pleased to see he had come through. For the first instant I saw him, it was like 1919, and I felt happy. Then I went in search of Mathilde. No one knows where she is, even whether she is still alive. Anything could have happened to her in the month since she wrote to me. Then, on a bookstall, I saw a copy of her poems. I bought it and read them: what a relief to find no mention of war. Of course her melancholy has deeper roots; it's Platonic. Her world has always been an ugly shadow of the beauty she has glimpsed. So instead I went to the cinema. I had seen that Marcel's new film was showing at a theatre on the Boulevard Clichy. It's his version of the David and Jonathan story, and it is cunningly made, in such a way as may, I suppose, put him right with the Resistance. That's the intention, no doubt: the Philistines are the Germans, and his Goliath bore a startling resemblance to the Reichsmarschall Göring. But, as always with Marcel, it is the personal note that predominates: the sidelong glances of never-to-be satisfied desire which King Saul shoots at the boy David. What is clever, and in its way touching, is the manner in which Marcel indicates that, even if Saul were to achieve precisely what he desires, what he has set his heart on, he would remain unsatisfied: if only because, in doing so, he would have tainted the object of his love. Isn't this also just what I have experienced with France, and isn't it also what de Gaulle will come to learn? Marcel has lost all his illusions, and so gained a psychological understanding that makes me tremble.

July 14, 1944. Walking in the early morning on the Avenue de Breteuil, I encountered Drieu.

'So,' he said, 'you haven't killed yourself yet either.'

I accompanied him back to his flat. Though it was not yet ten o'clock he insisted that we drank brandy.

'I split my last bottle of Scotch whisky with Heller three months ago,' he said. 'I suppose there will be whisky in Paris again soon, when the Allies arrive. But it won't be for me. I've had it, I realise that.'

He straightened a Matisse on the wall. He was as full of energy as ever, unable to sit still and talk. Instead he walked about the large drawing room, with its magnificent view of the river and the skyline beyond, stabbing his cigarette at me, and drinking three glasses to my one.

'Really, there's nothing for it but to stay half-drunk,' he said, 'only half, I insist. More than that and one is just a drunken terrified beast like those imbecile Fascists of *Je Suis Partout*, the ones who surround Robert, you know. On the other hand, sober consciousness has become intolerable. Don't you find that?'

His mood fluctuated as we talked. One moment he was near despair, analysing the different methods by which he might choose to kill himself. 'After all, that's the only serious question that remains, isn't it, my dear? When and how? To choose one's own death. It's a privilege. Besides, we are both classicists, aren't we?' But, in the next breath, he was discussing how he might manage to survive. 'After all, one has friends, hasn't one, even now?' He pins his hope on Malraux, who has always been close to him; he proclaims that they have always understood each other, 'perfectly'. Besides, Malraux is under obligations to him; so is his mistress, Josette Clotis. 'We've always had a lot in common, you know. Do you remember what she said about Clara, André's first wife, who was Jewish of course? She said, "Their noses aren't in harmony." Do you mean you hadn't heard that one? So amusing. Moreover, it was thanks to me that Josette was able to leave Paris, in some style, I tell you – in a mink coat and a sleeping-car – and join André on the Riviera. Things like that aren't forgotten.'

But he doesn't really believe any of this. He talks to amuse himself and because he has never learned how to be silent. It's his loquacity that has done for him. He's said and written things that simply can't be forgotten or forgiven.

When I told him that I intended to await arrest and stand trial, he laughed:

'My poor Lucien, you haven't a hope. They'll shoot you in a cellar.'

He drank off his brandy and filled both glasses. He stood with his back to me, looking out at the river.

'The *quatorze*,' he said. 'I always thought the Revolution overrated, and besides, I detest manifestations of popular enthusiasm. They might put me on trial, they'd enjoy that, but not you, not with your calm good sense and your air of virtue. Impossible. They'll shoot you like a dog, my dear.'

And he gestured with the bottle again.

July 21, 1944. The worst has happened, and it leaves me calm because it is only the fulfilment of everything I have feared; and when fulfilment comes, and hope is killed, a dead calm prevails, all agitation of spirit annihilated.

Yesterday Rupert's friends tried to kill Hitler. Apparently they believed at first that they had succeeded, but this was not true. It's the end. There's nothing more to write. These vile dreams in which I have seen Rupert tortured and heard his screams ring down dank and chilly corridors must now be reality.

I remember that half-smile he would give when I bested him in argument.

And I thought of how, if I had not appealed to his sense of honour when he was in love with Polly, he might have escaped all this.

But that's not true, Rupert was doomed from the start. That's why I loved him, for his gallant and defeated beauty.

At this moment perhaps, in a cellar, under Berlin.

When I left Drieu the other day, he raised his brandy glass, and, swaying a little, said, '*Moriturus, te saluto.*'

I can't say even that to Rupert. For two hours I have wandered about my apartment, not even weeping.

But I dare not sleep tonight. I dare not contemplate the shape in which Rupert will present himself to me.

Drieu telephoned to invite me to dinner. I shall go of course.

July 22, 1944. It was a wake. Heller was there. Drieu's maid Clothilde served dinner, dressed in a black frock and white apron.

We ate off silver, and drank a good Burgundy. Lucien Combelle, who used to be Gide's secretary, was there. He was amusing now – about how, when he first worked for Gide, the great man – 'and you never met such a conscientiously great man' – was surrounded by Stalinists whose every word he believed. And now?

'Now we believe nothing,' Drieu said.

Heller rose to his feet, a trifle unsteadily, for Drieu had produced the cognac, and made a speech. He praised Drieu for his 'sincere and whole-hearted collaboration which nevertheless never lost a sense of what was due to France and the self-respect of the French people'. It was clear to him, he said, that the responsibility for the breakdown of relations between France and Germany rested with those who were not content with an honourable collaboration, but wished to go much further, who were in fact Fascists more Fascist than the German occupying authorities, who 'as you know, so I may safely state as much here, have never been wholehearted Fascists themselves'. He concluded by saying that it had been an honour to work with Drieu, and that, whatever happened after the war, 'which Germany has lost', and whatever fate befell Drieu, he would strive to do honour to his friend's achievements and intentions.

It was clear that he expects Drieu to be dead by then. 'Well,' Drieu said, 'that's a testimonial to carry to the Shades . . .'

Someone was singing in the street below. It's a sound I haven't heard in Paris since 1939.

Combelle said: 'If they had killed Hitler the day before yesterday, we might all yet have been saved.'

'Let's do something different,' Drieu said. 'Let's go to the Ritz bar.'

It was full of German officers and their whores. There was a curly-haired girl of seventeen or eighteen whose blouse was torn. She carried a bottle in her hand and went from group to group asking if anyone had seen her Klaus. She insisted that he had promised to see her safe: 'Not safe home, you understand, but just safe.' She couldn't however tell anyone which Klaus she meant, or even what his regiment was. A fat Lieutenant pulled her on to his knee and promised that he would do the duty of an absent Klaus. 'No,' she insisted. 'It's only Klaus I can rely on. He has a friend in the Gestapo who will see me safe.'

'Come here, my dear,' Drieu said, 'and let me give you a word of advice. You're a lovely girl, but you should go home to your mother. She's the only person who may be able to protect you.'

'No,' she said, shaking her head and looking at him as if

momentarily sobered, 'when I first went with a German she told me to get out – even though I was bringing her butter and eggs and silk stockings – and called me a disgrace and said she never wanted to see me again . . . I laughed at her. Oh, why has it all gone wrong? Where's Klaus, I'm frightened without him.'

'In that case,' Drieu said, 'my second piece of advice is to stay right here, in this bar. In two weeks it will be full of American officers. Find one of them to protect you.

'What else could one say?' he asked. 'Girls like that . . . do they deserve what will happen to them? You can say we do, but girls like that? I've a good mind to take her home with me, but it would only complicate matters for her even more. Her best hope is, as I say, to find an American quickly. It's like a railway station – have you thought of that, Lucien, that the whole war has been like a railway journey? Now the porter's crying, "All change for America."'

I walked home. It was a soft summer night of calm beauty. The streets were quiet and deserted. It might have been any night of real life.

I climbed the stairs, and found Anne sitting on the doorstep of my apartment. She lifted a face smudged with tears.

'I thought of Rupert,' she said, 'and I couldn't keep away. I couldn't continue to deny my heart. I'm with you, my dear.'

She waited, I held out my arms. 'To the end,' she said, '*contra mundum* . . .'

CHAPTER TWENTY-NINE

Document 16:

Narrative of Armand de Balafré (continued)

I DON'T LIKE to think of those weeks which Lucien spent at the Château de l'Haye, after his mistress left. His loneliness must have been extreme. Certainly he could not have unburdened himself to Maman. Though she never liked me, Etienne, that doesn't mean that I am blind to her virtues. They were considerable, of course they were, but her lack of sympathy, by which I mean her inability ever to put herself imaginatively in the position of anyone else, made it impossible for her, all her life, to offer comfort even to those she loved. And there's no doubt that she loved Lucien. Only they couldn't confide in each other. It's a tragedy, not to be able to speak to the person you love. There's nothing more desolating.

That's what I hoped, and believed, Lucien had found in Anne. I think it's what he did find. All the more reason therefore for him to be desolated when she left. Yet he couldn't blame her, for he held himself responsible for Hervé's death.

I know nothing – I must tell you, Etienne – of how he lived those weeks in Provence and then in Paris. It's only surmise. One friend, who encountered him by chance in Paris, remarked to me years later that it was 'disconcerting: like meeting someone who enquired if you, perhaps, were Charon'. But that's only one personal impression. Impressions, surmises, that's all I can offer.

At some time, before the Liberation, Anne returned to him. I don't know why. Perhaps she always intended to betray him, but I don't believe it.

They remained in hiding during the week of the liberation of Paris. At some point they had furnished themselves with false papers. Her deposition states that they intended to make for Spain. Rather too late. At any time in the previous fortnight they might have managed to get there. So many did, including Abel Bonnard, formerly Lucien's colleague at the Ministry of Education, then the Minister himself, who made his getaway complete with boyfriend. But there were lots of them. Lucien delayed till it was more difficult, and then left Paris by train. The hard-line collaborators had made for Germany, but Lucien was in the unfortunate position of being equally unpopular with both sides. Not even being tortured by the Gestapo could help him with the Resistance.

They reached Orléans on the 1st of September. The train was boarded there by a Resistance unit. I have reason to believe that they had been given advance information. They must have been, for they enquired for Lucien by name. Only Anne could have told them he was on that train, and so she betrayed him. He was disguised, lightly, but at once admitted who he was. It says in the report that he remarked, 'I don't want to cause other people unnecessary trouble.' He was taken to Resistance headquarters. The senior officer there was Guy Fouquet.

I have told this badly. It is partly because the pain makes it so difficult to concentrate.

Pain of the heart at raking over these still burning coals, as well as the sharp nipping of the crab, Etienne.

When I left Lucien after our conference in January, I made my way, as I told you, to Normandy. I saw Berthe and the children. I saw also Danielle, Guy's wife, your poor Freddie's mother. She was in hiding there, in terrible danger as a Jewess and the wife of a member of the CNR. My presence was reported to the authorities. I was quickly snatched away by our boys, but in the search for me, Guy's wife was discovered. You know what happened to her.

From that moment, for the next year, indeed till his second marriage in the summer of '45, Guy was like a man deranged. He was filled with hatred. He had never liked Lucien, now he saw him as the accomplice of murderers.

There was no trial. There was not even one of those speedy executions after a mockery of a trial which were characteristic of that phase of the *épuration*. Lucien was discovered hanged in his cell. They called it suicide.

Guy was absent the night it happened. I verified that. I could not hold him directly responsible. Indeed he expressed his anger to me: he had wanted Lucien to stand trial.

'I disliked your brother,' he said to me. 'I disapproved of him fundamentally, of his political position, and of his actions during the war. But I had a certain respect for him. That's why I thought it so essential he should be put on trial. If we only tried the scoundrels, I argued, the full guilt of Vichy would never be revealed, or at least accepted. I was furious when I returned and discovered he had been left with the means of hanging himself.'

That was what Guy told me. You will wonder that we were able to remain on friendly terms. Perhaps you will blame me for this, and indeed of course in terms of your own life you have all the more reason to blame me. Berthe has never ceased to insist that you were wounded, severely damaged, by the abortion of your love affair with Freddie – I call it abortion, because it was just like that: the extinction of life, a sort of murder. And of course you might never have met Freddie if . . .

If, if, if: life is difficult enough without taking count of un-fulfilled conditionals. (I'm bad at this sort of reflection, I've never been philosophical in my life before . . .)

But: there was so much between us, and I blamed myself for the death of his wife, and then we were, Guy and I, on the same side. We'd risked our lives in the same cause, while Lucien had been opposed to us. And, finally, it wasn't Guy's fault.

I checked up on that. Of course I did. He certainly wasn't there, and he equally certainly instituted an inquiry into the circum-stances of Lucien's death. I don't believe there was any cover-up. I believed then he had reason for suicide: Rupert von Hülenberg's murder, his own complete failure, the grey waste of the future.

So, for years, I accepted it.

We got on with living. Lucien was, I'm ashamed to say it, our private shame; when people mentioned him in print, they asso-ciated his name with Laval's. Only a few rare indulgent spirits conceded that each was in his way a patriot.

Patriotism is like Christianity, you know: what evil has been committed in the name of France, Germany, or Christ!

Then, ten years ago, Guy died. He left me a letter. In it he confessed that he had never believed in Lucien's suicide. 'I talked to him,' he said, 'at great length the night before I left for Paris. I don't know why. I had never found him sympathetic. Yet, waking in the night, missing my poor Danielle, in search of whose body my hand nightly found itself patting a cold unoccupied sheet, I rose and woke him in his cell.'

They had talked, he said, till dawn, ranging over their whole lives, their philosophies, their consciousness that failure corrupts any human success. For the first time Guy had felt in accord with him. As they parted, Lucien said he was glad they had been intercepted. He could not have borne to live on in Spain and had only consented to flight in a moment of weakness, to please Anne. But he knew he had to stand trial, not in the hope of justifying himself, personally, but to defend the memory of 1940. Those were his exact words: 'to defend the memory of 1940'. They impressed themselves on Guy's memory.

So, when Guy returned from Paris to find Lucien dead, he could not believe it was suicide. Yet all the evidence pointed that way. His investigation yielded no new cause of suspicion. There was no way of finding out what happened. He was compelled to accept that interpretation of his death, which then became official.

'There was no obvious suspect,' he wrote. 'There was no one there who had any personal motive that I could discover. So there it was. Another suicide – and there were so many in '44–'45. Nevertheless, Armand, I have never believed it, and my incredulity has grown stronger with the years. You see, I remember that last conversation so well.'

I destroyed that letter, Etienne. I thought it could only add yet another link in the long chain of misery, betrayal, revenge. I thought never to tell you about it. Yet, in the end, I can't die without informing you, even though Berthe has tried to dissuade me.

Let us, at least, expunge the lie.

Don't come to see me. I'm a miserable scarecrow, and can't bear any company but that of Berthe and the girls. And my spaniel. We've always had spaniels, remember? But you have my blessing – for whatever the blessing of a freethinker and financier may be worth.

Not much, eh?

A. de B.

PART FOUR

1986–7

SO, I HAVE reached my fog-bound and murky Ithaca, and find my own Penelope still beset by importunate suitors.

I sent all this to Hugh, and, having on a whim had copies made, to Polly and Sarah also. I thought that when I had rid myself of it all I might experience a sense of liberation. No such luck; I am more restless than ever.

I went from the post office to the café where I have been accustomed to meet my Ukrainian chess-player. He wasn't there. The proprietor said he believed he was ill, but didn't know where he lived, or had been called away, but didn't know where he had gone. I ordered brandy and lit a cigar, for all anyone might guess a prosperous bourgeois, which I am, at peace with the world, which I am not.

Instead waiting. Without knowing what I am waiting for.

The other night there was a disturbance in the hotel. I was woken by the sound of a woman screaming. The place seemed like a madhouse – I thought of *Jane Eyre*. Well, I said, it's nothing to do with me, and turned over. In the morning the manager apologised. It was the Baroness, he said; she had finally gone off her head, absolutely right off, he had never seen anything like it. She had had to be straitjacketed and removed. He was very sorry.

'Yes, it's sad,' I said.

'I do hope you weren't too disturbed,' he said. 'The Americans in the adjoining suite say they got no sleep at all.'

Do you know, I feel envious? There would be an enormous release if one could go absolutely and spectacularly nuts. There are happy madmen, after all, and once she has stopped screaming, and been given a few calming drugs, the Baroness may be perfectly content inhabiting her fantasy of Old Europe.

Her husband, or ex-husband, the press lord, arrived here to pick up the pieces. We met in the little bar of the hotel.

'It's difficult to believe,' he said, 'how charming she was once. And now . . .' he shook his head. 'As I get older, Monsieur de Balafré, I find it harder to accept the pain of life. Did my poor wife speak to you about the photo-girls in my magazines? I'm sure she did, for I know from her letters – oh she was a voluminous and impassioned letter-writer – how she admired you and confided in you. But do you know what it is that touches me in those girls: it's their utter silliness, their expectations, and their ignorance. When I look at those beautiful rounded legs, at that lovely skin, at their untouched smiles, I am intoxicated by the realisation that they are absolutely new, that they have just this moment sprung into being – for of course a girl who suddenly finds herself desirable is an altogether new creature, she has no connection with the child from which she has emerged, any more than the butterfly recalls the caterpillar; and at the same time I know what they don't: that it won't last. I'm sure you understand that . . .'

He sipped his gin and tonic, and crumbled a cheese biscuit between his well-tended fingers. He shone with health and hygiene, and smiled, and adjusted the glass he wore in his left eye.

'I am aware of autumn in spring,' he said, 'of the charm of evanescence and corruption. I couldn't be a newspaper publisher otherwise.'

He smiled at me.

'So much of life is a matter of coming to terms with the way things are, isn't it? It's tempting to refuse to do so, of course. My poor Reineke found the effort beyond her. Instead of welcoming evanescence, accepting corruption, she tried to deny and defy them. Poor woman, I'm sorry for her. We've a choice between disillusion and madness, and she chose the latter. I suppose it's gallant in its way. Tell me, Monsieur de Balfré, why do you live in Switzerland?'

'Because my home is in South Africa and Switzerland is as unlike South Africa as anywhere can be.'

I spoke without thinking. I saw where his success lay: he had the ability, on account perhaps of his easy and confiding cynicism, to make one reveal oneself to him: to say more than one intended, and what, at heart, one meant.

'We must have some more gin,' he said. 'I've long wanted to meet you. And not only because of Reineke. We have more in common than my poor deranged wife.'

I was about to protest that we didn't in any real sense have the poor woman in common; but his smile stopped me; it was both mocking and trusting.

'Do you know,' he said, 'I have extensive interests, not only in Germany and indeed throughout Western Europe, but in your own country too, and, which is more to the point, I am trying to develop them in Eastern Europe also. It's a vast empire, though naturally only a paper one of course. But then paper empires do so much less harm, don't they? People inveigh against the power of us press lords, accuse us of all sorts of corruption, but none of it matters, you know. The opium we peddle is the gentlest drug. Oh, we're a bit sleazy, but no worse than any music-hall comic. Shall we take a walk?'

There was a grey, cold sky, heralding snow. We stepped out by the lake, swinging walking-sticks. The Baron marched, big and blond, in a teddy-bear coat.

'I do like to walk in a comfortable city,' he said.

As for me, I was entranced by his assurance. He had come to Geneva on an unpleasant mission. He was aware of pain and suffering – his conversation had convinced me of that – but it didn't disturb his complacence. I envied him his affirmative nature.

'You don't read my magazines, I suppose,' he said. He hummed a snatch of Rossini. 'No, you wouldn't. Proust and Stendhal, they will be more in your line. You're an intellectual. I'm one myself, though you mightn't think it. I adore Chekhov, you know. But most people don't; pictures and pap and a bit of gossip, that's what they like, and that's what I give them. It's better than politics, you know.'

'It's a form of politics though, isn't it?'

'Absolutely, my dear chap, everything's politics in the end. But my form of conservatism doesn't stir people up, that's the great thing. It's getting cold. What about a spot of Scotch in that bar there?'

When we were settled at a little zinc-topped table, with glasses of whisky and puffing at our cigars, he adjusted his monocle.

'I've long wanted to meet you,' he said. 'I've a story to tell, and a warning to give. Let me take my time about it, there's a good chap. I say, waiter, bring us the bottle, will you?

'It's my life story,' the Baron said, 'I hope you don't mind. We're from the East, you know. Generations ago my ancestors settled in Pomerania and East Prussia where we had extensive estates. I expect Reineke has told you about lavish and extravagant behaviour: she's quite right, except that they were my family, not hers, she's from Hanover, in fact, and a nice *gemütlich* bourgeois background. But we were great landowners, with serfs, and wolf-hunts, and sleighs, and furs, and all the trappings. I never experienced any of this myself of course: it was all gone when I was an infant. I'm seventy-five this year, you know, though I'm aware I don't look it. Actually, though we continued to live like great princes up to the Great War, we were feeling the strain long before then. All our estates were mortgaged to the hilt, to the Jews of course. And then came disaster, double, treble, oh multiple disaster.' The Baron paused, beamed, puffed at his Romeo y Julietta. 'My poor father, who had the reputation of being the best game-shot in Pomerania, was unfortunately a coward, poor chap. In 1916 he was cashiered for cowardice in face of the enemy, and would have been shot, if his noble blood hadn't saved him. As it was, he was only disgraced. Then, 1917, '18, we lost everything. One estate was left us in East Prussia, but the Jews foreclosed. We were destitute, like millions of other Germans. My father was in despair. He was fit for nothing but playing cards and shooting duck, and those days were over for him. He lay huddled in the single-room apartment we had acquired in the Hallesches Tor district of Berlin – the Wasser-torstrasse to be exact. It was indescribably sordid, and he felt the shame of having reduced his family to that sort of living. Felt it acutely, poor chap. Not that it was entirely his fault. Politics and economics had done for him. They were at least as responsible as his disgrace. Anyway, he had just enough money to kill himself with rotgut brandy, which he did in 1921. My poor mother, a Baroness in her own right, went out charring. Most of the family were dead, and she had too much pride to appeal to the few friends who might have tried to help her. She felt my father's disgrace even more than he did; she had been brought up with an unquestioning sense of honour, you see. Anyway, she soon followed him – malnutrition encouraging cancer, I have always thought – because, dear woman, she always saw to it that when there was any food in the house I got most of it. I was her beacon of hope, you see, the boy who would restore the family honour and fortune. Well, she died when I was fourteen, and I was all alone in the world. What did I do? What could I do in the Berlin of the twenties? I went on the streets, of course. Fortunately I was pretty. Despite our appalling lung hash and potatoes, I had a smooth pearly skin. I was a blond waif, very appealing, I assure you, and within a couple of years, I was as accomplished a whore as you could find on Unter den Linden.'

He chuckled at the memory, and leaned forward and topped up our glasses.

'Are you enjoying this? It's interesting. I've surprised you, haven't I? But you won't guess what happened next. I fell in love. Really. I broke the golden rule of whores. And it did me no harm. Or perhaps it did. Who can tell what my life would have been otherwise?

'He was an Englishman. He called himself a writer. I don't think he was any good but some of his friends were. Isherwood and so on. Ah, you're wondering if Isherwood was my lover too, aren't you? Well, he wasn't. That ought to prove to you that my story is true. It would be so easy to say he was. But no. I told you I was in love with George. I was in love with him, romantically, as only a German boy or perhaps an English boy can be in love. I don't know, perhaps that's nonsense. But that's what we believed then. And he was good to me, and for me. He opened my eyes. He made me see that the world needn't simply be a matter of exploit or be exploited, that there was room for tenderness. Naturally I see now that he was also a father to me. He was a Communist of course, so I became a Communist too. He really believed in a new dawn, and he inspired me with the same belief, so that I was even ready to forgive the Bolsheviks for seizing some of our family estates. He adored me, and it's good to be adored. He called me Bubi. For four years we were together, and those were the years of my first education. We were idealists, I won't bore you with our leather-shorted wanderings in the Schwarz-wald, I'm sure you can imagine it all. But, even now, the memory . . . you know, the memory is lovely.'

He took out a paisley pattern handkerchief and blew his nose.

'And then the Nazis came to power. George was beaten up in the street – he was half-Jewish, you see, as well as being a corrupter of German youth. I was arrested, put in a camp, to be re-educated. The high-minded guards all had their way with me, and, for the first time in my life, something in me said no. But I didn't let on. Then I was picked up, and out, by a captain in the SA, one of Röhm's boys. That didn't last, as you can imagine. But I saw which way the wind was blowing, got myself a girlfriend and joined the Party. Do you blame me? It's scarcely relevant, is it? I did just enough to keep out of trouble, and all the time hated myself. Hated that poor girl eventually too, if it comes to that.

'Then the war. I joined up, still trying to keep out of trouble, and became an officer's servant. I had acquired ways which made me suitable, you see. I knew how to please, and I knew how things should be done. Then, in May 1941, I had my second stroke of luck. I was assigned as servant to one Rupprecht von Hülenberg.'

He smiled at my surprise.

'Which is where you come in, isn't it?' he said. 'Rupert had a photograph, of a girl, standing always by his bedside,' he sighed. 'You've probably guessed it was your mother. "She's the only woman I've ever loved," he said to me, "the only one, Bubi" – for he called me that too, at my suggestion, it made me feel good to be called "Bubi" again – "and she's the wife of my best friend." He talked so much about your father and mother that I came to feel I knew them too. He insisted that your father was the best man, the only altogether honourable man, he had ever met. I thought you would like to know that.'

He sighed again, and looked at me as if he expected some response, but I only shook my head and drank some whisky. I was touched of course by this revelation, by the thought that somehow or other this polished and cynical libertine had carried the memory of my father with him these forty years, as a sort of talisman perhaps. And I was sorry yet again to remember so little of Rupert von Hülenberg, my godfather and the man who had, in a sense, redeemed my father. I had long thought of them like that, as if his involvement in the July plot exculpated Lucien.

'I owe so much to Rupert,' the Baron said. 'Of course he was in love with me, though he could never admit it, and, though by that time I was mad for girls, I suppose I was a little in love with him too and would certainly have let him do whatever he wanted. And taught him a thing or two in the process. But though he wanted me, he didn't want that. Yet in a way he came to rely on me.

'He saved me from being a real Nazi, you know. The temptation was there, in those years of success. Don't believe anyone who tells you the German people weren't mad for Hitler. There were only a few sane ones left among us.

'But Rupert said to me once: "Where were you on Kristallnacht?" And he went on quickly, in case I should answer him. "That night," he said, "I saw a middle-aged Jewish gentleman and his wife, baited by stormtroopers. They made him remove his trousers and even his underpants. Then one of them stripped his wife, slowly, ceremoniously. When the husband protested and struggled, they slashed him across the genitals with a cane. He screamed and they laughed, and, as for me, I fled, into a black alley where I vomited among dustbins. And I looked up at the flames of synagogues and Jewish businesses licking the sky, and around me at the black blind alley, and it was as if all the German people had been driven into that stinking cul-de-sac. That was where Hitler had led us, lured us or driven us, to a place from which even the rats had fled."

'That's what he said, my friend. Those were his exact words, graven on my heart. All I had done myself on Kristallnacht was break a few windows, but I felt ashamed. And Rupert said, "I swore that night it was my life against his. I'm risking my life in

telling you this, Bubi, but it may save your soul." Well, my friend,
I believe it did. There are some – my poor dear wife for instance –
who would assert that I have none to save, that I'm irredeemably
corrupted, but at least I've never failed to recognise evil since
those conversations with Rupert. That was what was wrong with
your father, he said. "Lucien has never felt the attraction of evil,"
he said, "for, you see, Bubi, the horrible thing is that I knew that
night that for a moment I wanted to join in. But Lucien thinks this
is a war like those of history: a war between States, a war of the
Powers; he doesn't realise that it's the infernal powers we are
combating."'

He was wrong, of course. My father was not ignorant of evil.
His dreams showed me that. He was aware of the element of
sadism in him, and frightened of it. It's why he stuck so resolutely
to his desk and writing table.

'I'm hungry,' the Baron said, and enquired of the waiter if he
could bring some smoked-salmon sandwiches. 'Scotch salmon,
to go with the Scotch whisky . . .

'Rupert was wounded,' the Baron said. 'His departure left a
hole in my life. I set myself, like Svejk, simply to survive. I said to
myself, "Any boy who has survived on the streets of Berlin during
the Depression can't let himself be wiped out by a Russian
bullet." So I took care to keep clear, and I came through. When
news reached us of the bomb plot in July '44, I knew Rupert had
had it. It was terrible, I can't say more than that. I deserted later,
Germany was full of deserters, people like me who in their hearts
now said to Hitler and the Nazis, "Well, stuff you." We lived any
old how, thieving, scavenging, looting; working the black market.
It was, I realise now, the beginning of the economic miracle, for in
that terrible last winter of the war we were learning to say not only
"stuff the Nazis" but "stuff ideology". I survived, as you see.
Naturally I turned to the Americans. They were, I at once saw,
my sort of people. I was useful to them, they scratched my back in
turn. I took my opportunities, and here I am, eating smoked-
salmon sandwiches.

'So, that's my story. But bear with me a little longer.'

I sat watching him, nursing my glass of whisky, divided
between the desire to walk out and leave him to his certainty
that all's well that ends well, and a wish to get drunk. But I would
do neither. There was a strength in this big bold man with his
dyed blond hair and his pale fleshy hands and his knowledge that
you can come through if only you don't believe and never doubt.
We had much in common, a certain disdain, a warm distrust of

big words; and yet I was like a parody of him. He wiped his lips with the napkin, poured us each more whisky, took out a maroon leather cigar-case and clipped the end off another Romeo y Julietta. When he had lit it, he removed the band and slipped it, like a ring, over his little finger, smiling as it split.

'I used to be able to do that,' he said, 'without breaking it. But in those days I could hardly even afford cigars. Now that I smoke seven or eight a day, the band breaks every time. Vanity of vanities, eh, my friend . . .

'But we've come through nevertheless,' he said. 'All our life has been distorted by wars: the First War, which, on account of vanity, idleness and stupidity, tore apart what my poor dear wife calls Old Europe, and the Second in which whole legions of madmen made the Four Horsemen of the Apocalypse look like broken-down hacks. Yet at last Europe sees the signs set fair again. We have arrived, somehow or other, at a point when war seems impossible, and a new generation has not even any memory of it. The next century will be as if this crazy twentieth century had never happened. It's enough to make you believe in God. You and I have lived without hope, getting by, scornful, determined only not to be fooled by ideology. You're a rich man and so am I, and my energies have been devoted to seeing that people believe in nothing and so have nothing to fear. And thanks to us, and tens of thousands like us, there are good times just around the corner. It's a truly *belle époque* that's in store for the young. Even the Russians have at last got a glimpse of sanity. For the first time in my life it's good for humankind to be alive. I only wish I was still young.

'But that's only Europe,' he continued. 'You said to me, my friend, that you live in Switzerland because no country on earth is less like South Africa, and I applaud your good sense. But I have interests in South Africa: a newspaper, a string of magazines. I go out for a month every winter, to escape the fogs and look after my affairs there. Now, wherever I go, I take an interest in my young journalists. I dote on them actually, they're my family, you see, they're like my children. So I try, when I can, to see something of them. Now there's a young fellow, name of Niels Nielsen – Danish father and a Scots mother – on one of my papers, that I have had my eye on. I invited him to dinner, and he asked if he could bring his girl along. Well, naturally, yes. She was your daughter. It's an uncommon name, of course, and I was moved to think of her as a link between me and Rupert and Lucien, a new link, new-forged. And I liked her. She's attractive, intelligent, and

more than that; she's vital. You mustn't think that my association
with photo-girls has made me indifferent to true quality. I liked
her, and envied her Niels; but as the evening wore on, and her
first suspicion wore off, I became perturbed. I was hearing music I
had forgotten. I was hearing Rupert again. Do you know what I
mean? The perilous strains of idealism . . .'

For a moment I was revolted. His pale fleshy paw seemed to
hover over the chessboard of our lives, ready perhaps to sacrifice
Sarah to protect his precious Niels.

Then he pressed his hand on mine instead.

'Believe me, my friend, I have your daughter's interest at heart.'

He sat back, the cigar squeezed into the corner of his mouth.
There was no one else in the bar. The waiter flicked crumbs off a
vacated table, and went and stood in the doorway, looking out; it
had started to rain and the sky over the lake was heavy as the past.

'I once did something I've never understood,' he said. 'About
thirty years ago, when I was first rich. I used money and influence
and a bit of bullying, a whiff of blackmail, to get a copy of the print
of those films Hitler gloated over. You know the ones I mean. I
watched Rupert die. It was horrible. Yet I watched it again and
again, and I thought of the Führer's pasty face lighting up as he
watched it. I was ashamed of watching and yet I did it again and
again, like a parson in a porn shop. Finally I destroyed my print; it
was like burning banknotes. The one good feeling I got from the
whole business.'

'I understand you,' I said. 'But though Botha and the Nats are
vile, they're not Hitler and his gang.'

'Get her out,' he said. 'Tell her to make love to young Niels,
have his babies. Tell her your father's story. Tell her how we can
never judge what's right, and how our best intentions are corrupted. Tell her what Europe suffered for ideas. Don't you think
we might have got where we are quicker without them?'

He came close to convincing me, came so close because I
wanted to be convinced, because I sought justification for quiet-
ism. But there is no such thing as absolute justification in this life.
Besides, the story of Rupert and Lucien points in different
directions, doesn't it, even though both failed. Even though both
failed, Rupert in a sense triumphed: the Baron is the consequence
of his victory. He was fashioned by Rupert's death.

My sleep is broken, and last night I thought not of the Baron,
serene in indifference, or of his poor crazy wife, but of a funeral I
attended in England, in Hampshire, ten years ago. It was Jamie

Fernie's, and I had learned of it by chance at the bar of my club; and I went, I suppose, to help bury my youth. It was a sad occasion, as it must always be when you wrap up a wasted life. He had attempted much, succeeded in nothing, consoled himself with that mocker of consolation, the bottle.

It was a raw November afternoon. A rain so thin as to be almost indistinguishable from mist lay like wet fur along the line of the yew trees. There were only about twenty of us in the little country churchyard. Cranmer's words fell soft as the drifting beech leaves. The church (mostly Early English) testified to the comforting continuity of island life. It had been too much for Jamie though.

At first I thought I recognised nobody. There was an old man who might have been his father, for even in antiquity he retained a military bearing. Then, as the coffin was lowered into the quiet earth, a Rolls-Royce drew up at the gate of the churchyard, a thin man, wearing a dark coat with an astrakhan collar, and carrying a wreath, emerged, and, without looking left or right, pranced up the path before weaving his way through the gravestones towards us. He moved with the self-conscious gallantry of an ageing dancer, and I saw that it was Eddie Scrope-Smith.

He detached me quickly from the reception, held in a gloomy library which had the air of having been unoccupied for years, and ushered me to the Rolls.

'I wasn't going to come. I thought I really couldn't bear it. And now I've found you again. Virtue is rewarded.'

He told the chauffeur to drive on.

'It's not my car,' he giggled, 'it belongs to the studios.

'Do you know,' he said, 'all the way down, I've been thinking of that ghastly dinner-party at his parents' house in Paris. Do you remember? In a curious way, Jamie was never the same again, after that holiday. He spoke up for you that evening, he never spoke up satisfactorily for himself.'

Thinking of Eddie now, it seems to me that our friendship resembles that between my father and Marcel Pougier. Like Pougier, Eddie has the fundamental toughness of the Ishmael; he has accepted that he is, in important ways, an outcast. It may seem absurd now to say this, and there are many who would say that, far from being a liability, homosexuality is an asset in his world. Nevertheless it still takes courage and shamelessness to be as blatant as Eddie, to address chauffeurs as darling, for example. And this was even more true when he was young. Perhaps that's wrong: homosexual style has changed after all, and Eddie must seem as out of place in the self-conscious tough gay world as he

used to do in a straight milieu. Looking back at the three of us
who boarded the Golden Arrow, who would have guessed, I
thought that afternoon, that Eddie would be the successful
survivor; that he would see Jamie buried, and me . . . As I am.
And, in the same way, Marcel Pougier came through. He outlived
and surmounted his wartime disgrace. His collaboration was in
fact excused on account of that film of David and Jonathan which
was held to celebrate, in the most subtle fashion, the moral
supremacy of the Resistance. Art saved him.

'Do you remember that extraordinary woman?' Eddie said.
'The one who got drunk and defended your father against that
awful Torrance?'

'Yes,' I said.

'Mathilde something, she had a wonderful beak of a nose.'

Mathilde was dead too. Drink and drugs had done for her, like
poor Jamie. And disappointment, the third 'd'. She had died
forgotten and ignored. I don't know how I had heard of it, or
when; but sometime in the early seventies I got a letter from an
American girl, a poet herself, who had discovered Mathilde's
work, learned of her association with *L'Echo de l'Avenir*, and, with
the extraordinary persistence of Americans, tracked me down.
She proposed to write a memoir of her, attached to a critical
study: could I help with any information, documents? It was
shocking that such a rare talent should be neglected. I didn't
reply.

'Curiously, I met Torrance later,' Eddie said. 'What a shit.'

Mathilde had chosen obscurity. Let her rest there, I thought.
Torrance and Marcel Pougier had been creatures of the limelight.
But with a difference. Both had lived by the Will, but Torrance
had been in thrall to his ego. It had consumed him; he had worn
out such esteem as he had ever won. Pougier, though also self-
centred, had nevertheless subjected himself to the demands of art.
That was how he had suppressed his personality. It comes to me
now that, of all my father's circle, he was the only success:
because he made things, and, in making them, forgot himself,
escaped himself, if only temporarily. When he died half Paris (as
they say) turned out for his funeral. His songs are still sung, and
his best films continually revived. His name is often bracketed
with René Clair's. I suppose he belongs to the same rose period.

'You don't look well,' Eddie said. 'I should say you're drinking
too much, you silly old thing.'

He spread a rug over our knees.

'I've kept my eye on you, you know,' he said. 'I'm a loyal old thing, for all my faults. Don't drive so fast, dearie,' he told the chauffeur. 'A Rolls should move with a certain majesty.'

The untroubled South of England swept past us. Such a neat country of fenced gardens and carports, dahlias and chrysanthemums, of shopping-centres and shopping-trolleys and women pushing what I think are called baby-buggies, of trim industrial units with full carparks. Such a safe country of television, Nescafé and fridge-freezers, of fitted carpets and squares of close-cut lawn, a country where people no longer feel the need to go to church or political meetings, a country criss-crossed by untapped telephone wires, a country all over which sodium street-lamps were coming on in the crepuscular damp.

'Poor Jamie,' Eddie said, 'he hated everything ordinary. It was his little rebellion, and in the end a very little one. He found everything dull, and it made him dull too in the end. I hadn't seen him for years. He was no fun, you see.'

We edged into London. He suggested we have dinner together. I accepted, only demurring at the early hour.

'We'll go to my flat then, and have a drinkie first.'

It was a block behind Harrods. We took the lift to the fourth floor. The second Rachmaninov piano concerto was playing on the gramophone. We shed our overcoats. Eddie rubbed his hands and led me into the drawing room. It ran the whole width of the flat, and there were tall windows looking out on the wet street and the heavy building opposite. A policeman passed by, his helmet glistening. Eddie drew dark-cherry velvet curtains. I admired a Matthew Smith still-life of melons and figs which hung over the chimneypiece. The room was very warm. The music stopped. A Malay boy, wearing only a pair of black swimming-trunks, came in. Eddie kissed him on the cheek.

'I was doing my exercises,' he said.

The upper part of his body glistened with sweat.

'Get us some champagne, lovey, then have a shower and we'll all go out to dinner.'

'Isn't he lovely?' Eddie said. 'We've been together two years. I've never been happier.'

He opened the champagne. I heard doors closing in the flat beyond. Eddie removed his jacket, kicked off his shoes and stretched out on the sofa. He fixed a fat cigarette in a long amber holder.

'Where's the dressing-gown?' I said. 'Who do you think you are, Noël Coward?'

'I'm every bit as good as Noël, in my own line.' He smiled. 'But

it's the French Noël I wanted to speak to you of. Did you know
Marcel Pougier?'

'No.'

'But he was a great friend of your father's.'

'I still didn't know him.'

'Pity, such a dear. Doesn't matter though. I produced one of
his films, his last one. You did know I was a producer now, didn't
you, that I've given up directing? And I got to know him well. I
didn't at first know he was a chum of your father, but you know,
in some mysterious subterranean manner, that dinner-party, of
which we spoke, stayed with me. I was curious about the sort of
man who could rouse such passion, such dislike and such loving
admiration. And one day, when I was dining with Marcel at
Paillard's, we saw a wizened old brute at the next table. I didn't
recognise him. "That's the nastiest man in Paris," Marcel said.
Natch, I was curious. "What's his name?" I asked. It was Philippe
Torrance. His nose was diseased, syph, I should think. "Well," I
said, "he doesn't look nice." "He's even nastier than he looks,"
Marcel said. "He was a protégé of my dearest friend, Lucien de
Balafré, and he ruined him, and has blackguarded his reputation
ever since. What do you say to that?"'

'The last part's true. I don't know how Torrance could be said
to have "ruined" Lucien.'

'Marcel said he had, I don't know more than that. Marcel was
devoted to your father's memory. He wanted to make a film about
him.'

For the next ten minutes Eddie expatiated on the proposed
film. It wasn't really about my father. It was about the
relationship which Marcel supposed had existed between Lucien and Rupert. He had got everything wrong, as people of
his type are inclined to. He was all the more wrong because he
started with what was probably the truth: that Lucien's love for
Rupert was rooted in physical attraction. But surely Marcel
Pougier should have known – and indeed Eddie also – that
that exhausts itself? The intention was to present their love as a
fusion of the Romantic and Classical; it would have ignored, at
least from Eddie's account, what seem to me to have been the
questions that troubled both: how do you confront evil? How
do you accommodate things as they are to the way you would
like them to be? That's to say, it dodged the whole problem of
patriotism.

I said to Eddie: 'You don't want to make a film about two
failures.'

Eddie said: 'Commercially, you are so right. Yet in an odd way that's precisely what I do want. And were they failures?'

We went out to dinner. The Malay boy – 'I'm usually called Charlie' – was amusing and attentive. He was on the make, of course, Eddie represented a way up; but they both knew this and accepted it. It didn't preclude affection. Being with them, thinking of Lucien and Rupert, made me feel even more a mere spectator, but, unlike Jamie Fernie, I was a spectator who had accepted his role.

Eddie reverted to the idea for his film over coffee.

'You underestimate me,' he said, 'because we are old friends who were young and foolish together.'

'No,' I said, 'that's why I trust you. You are for that reason one of my special people. And that, I fancy, is how it was with Marcel Pougier and my father. And maybe it helped Pougier get him wrong, as you think I get you wrong. I don't really know much about my father: what I know has made me believe he was a dull man who tried to do what was right, and failed. No film there, Eddie.'

Looking back on that conversation now, I recognise that I was disingenuous. I simply didn't want a film made, and certainly not by Eddie. But I was right in one sense: a film that simply told the story of Lucien and Rupert was bound to be false, because they were bit-players in the story of Europe.

As we walked back along the lake to our hotel, the Baron said: 'I don't claim originality, you know. My originality has always been confirmed to what is sellable. My dear friend Franz-Josef Strauss said to me a few months ago: "We are moving from the age of Mars, god of war, to the age of Mercury, god of trade and business." He's right, you know. He'll say it in public soon.'

'Mercury was also the god of thieves.'

We walked on in silence. A steamer passed on the lake, offices were emptying in the city.

'He's left out the intervening planet, Venus,' I said.

'Oh, we made a shot at that in the sixties,' the Baron said. 'It didn't work. Make love, not war, remember? But we still made war. Now we are about to try: make money, not war. I think it's on.'

'No love then?'

'Love's a private thing. Where did public assertions of love ever get us?'

Where had love got any of us, even in private? My story seemed a record of tattered affections, broken trust, wounded hearts. Where had love got Eddie – dying – the intolerable and exquisite Bendico Perceval had told me – of AIDS? Or his friend Charlie, already dead? Or Rupert, who, failing in personal life and sublimating his capacity for love of an ideal person in love of an ideal Germany, had died even more horribly than Eddie would? Or my unhappy mother? Or Lucien and Anne? Or Marcel Pougier? Or me? Or my poor adored Freddie?

What was there to put in the other side of the balance? Berthe and Armand? Yes, I conceded that. But what of Guy Fouquet, whose love for his dead wife compelled him to destroy his daughter's love for me?

And my Sarah and her Niels Nielsen? What would love do for them? How would love do for them?

The hours of sleepless nights are disturbed by images of cruelty. There was a girl, blonde and healthy and unquestioning, a pony-club girl, and aching for sex and marriage. She adored me for six months and I never touched her. I adored her too, and dared not touch her. Was that a moral choice, or was it cowardice? At night, in the rank sweat of my dark and solitary bed, what indignities, cruelty and pain my adoration inflicted on her lovely and imaginary body, dwelling on them as long as possible.

Was I right to abstain from action?

She married another, has two children, and, the last time I saw her, had lost youth and beauty; and is only, by my count, thirty. But she has kept her cheerful and confident manner.

What would the Baron say to that story?

There is a Fascism of the soul, and it is because I recognise it that I have abstained from politics and come to live in Switzerland.

Would that answer satisfy him?

He has returned to Germany. Last night, waving his cigar at me (having yet again failed to ring his finger with the band), he said:

'Do you know the secret of my success in life? I believe in nothing, but I don't even do that absolutely. I am the uncommitted observer who will nevertheless gamble everything on a single throw. I find *nihil humanum alienum*, and I have a low opinion of my fellow-humans. Do you remember Chesterton's Father Brown: he said that he was able to solve murders by seeking out the murderer in his heart; sometimes I think I commit them by unmasking the detective in myself.'

I smiled. It was a performance. We can all seek meaning by reversing the apparently axiomatic. Forster began *Howards End* with the words 'only connect', and so put an expression on the lips of two generations of liberals. Haven't I, on the contrary, come through, to the present point, by saying to myself: 'disconnect'?

Yet I'm haunted by what Jacques said to me in the prison at Lyons, quoting Descartes: 'Conquer yourself, not the world.' That, it seems to me, is what Lucien failed to do.

Two letters this morning. I opened Hugh Challefray's first. He is profoundly grateful for all I have done, staggered by the acuity of my psychological insight, even more amazed that I should not wish to publish my 'brilliant' reconstruction myself. It dazzles and overawes him. Nevertheless, he would eagerly begin work, were it not for the fact that he has just been offered a position on the Prime Minister's staff. The opportunity is not one to be lost. Probably the job will not last long. There is an election in the offing, and the public is tired of the governing party, which is of course the Establishment there. If they are defeated he will immediately set to. And so on; I condense four typewritten A4 pages into a paragraph.

The other letter is from Polly. This time it is I, to employ Hugh's hyperbole, who am staggered. She has actually read what I sent. I never believed she would.

'I found it fascinating, darling, and macabre too. It's all so long ago and I'm surprised how right some of your guesses are. That scene between Rup and your father when they discussed me and came back drunk together, what a pair of swine I thought. But you're too kind to your father, you know. As soon as I was out of love with him, and you're right, that happened a long time before we split up, I saw that he was really mean-spirited. He wasn't a real person. He was afraid of living. I hated that magazine of his, it was all so self-important, and he was so wrapped up in it. I remember telling him that Pétain was just an old fart, but he insisted on seeing him as a wise hero. He was so sure of himself he didn't even get angry when I said that, just gave me one of his superior smiles. But I was right, Pétain was an old fart and nothing more. Do you know, when Armand arrived in London in 1940 and told me Lucien had stayed in France and would be in the government, I was so angry I could have scratched his eyes out. God knows, I've never been political, but even I could see that the Nazis were skunks and that you couldn't begin to deal with them without starting to stink yourself. I was glad, you know, when Aurora was shut up in Holloway, serve her right, I thought . . . Rup was right when you made him say that the war was really between decency and indecency, but Lucien didn't understand that you can't be reasonable with indecency, you just have to biff it. It makes me angry still. I still think he stayed because he was a conceited coward, and an ass to be taken in by his precious Marshal. One thing you don't say – maybe it's got nothing to do with your story – but I was so angry that for six months I licked envelopes for the Free French. I knew all along de Gaulle was a hero, and wasn't I right?

'Any chance of you coming home? I'm getting a bit wobbly on the old pins and would like to see you again before I pop off. Have had to put poor old Roddy in a home, he stopped making sense, and started writing cheques all over the place. Too much Cape brandy, poor beast, always told him gin was better for you.

'Sarah came to stay with her boy, a real poppet, such a joy to me since she was a little girl and now it's a comfort to think she has this nice boy.

'Terrible work all this must have been for you, only hope it will do you some good, you've always had a bit of a hang-up about Lucien, haven't you?, maybe you can see him better now. I suppose he was brave in his way and tried to do what was right, but such a prig, prigs always get things wrong, haven't you noticed?

'Do come home and see your old ma. Talking of mas, you are too kind to my ex-ma-in-law, she was a frightful bitch, you know.

'I remember that Torrance, he came to dinner once, Lucien told me he was a wonderful writer, I saw he was a rotter straight away. Shouldn't be surprised if he did have something to do with his death. Mind you, darling, I've never doubted that it was suicide. It's just the sort of way out he would take, typical of him, I said, when they told me. Do you know what was really wrong with him? He didn't like life enough, he was always looking for some sort of substitute for ordinary living.

Look after yourself, all love, Polly.'

The telephone rang. The hotel clerk told me there was a young lady to see me.

It was Sarah. She was huddled in an armchair in the lobby. A young man in a Loden coat sat beside her, perched on the arm. He got up as I approached. I kissed her.

'This is a surprise,' I said. 'You look tired, and cold.'

'I read your book. I took the first flight. This is Niels by the way.'

He smiled and held out his hand.

'It's terrible,' she said.

'You're very dramatic. Besides, it isn't a book, it's not for publication.'

'I didn't mean the quality.'

She looked as if she might cry.

'This isn't the place for talking,' I said. 'We'd better go up to my room. I'm sorry if the book shattered your illusions.'

She shook her head.

It was difficult for either of us to begin. My response was corrupted by the protective love I felt for her. So I occupied myself arranging for coffee and sandwiches to be sent.

'You'll need to eat. Airline food, terrible.'

She shook her head again. Having crossed the world, she had lost the words with which she had embarked. I explained about Mr Challefray, though I'd already done so in the letter which had accompanied her copy of the manuscript.

'You've just missed your boss,' I said to young Niels. 'He thinks very highly of you.'

'My boss? Oh, you mean the old Baron? Is he a friend of yours?'

'He was here till a few days ago. We've just committed his wife to a lunatic asylum.'

The young man sat down.

'He's a strange old bird,' he said.

They were the same physical type. Perhaps the Baron saw in Niels the young man he might himself have been in a different and less complicated world.

'Why did you all lie to me?' Sarah said. 'Why did you let me believe your father was a hero? That he was killed in the Resistance?'

She nursed her coffee-cup in both hands, which were shaking so that the liquid lapped against the rim, and a few drops splashed on to her jeans. I was powerless against her indignation, which recalled her mother, though in her directness she was more like Polly. I could not excuse myself by saying that it was a long time ago, in another life, in another country, when I had devoted months to the elaboration of the story which had so shocked her.

'I've been trying to explain to her the way I see it,' Niels said. There was sunshine in his light flat voice.

'Why did you send it to me if you can't explain?' she said.

'It's not something I've ever wanted to talk about. But when I was driven to write it, I thought you had a right to read the story.

When you were here last,' I said, 'you were so clear and certain about everything that you worried me. Things are never clear and never certain. I hoped Lucien's story might show you that.'

'What it shows me,' she said, 'is why you have made nothing of your life, Daddy.'

The boy Niels had manners better than are found in Europe now. They were so good I even questioned whether he was indeed a journalist. He was anxious that I shouldn't misconstrue the reason for their visit.

'The thing is,' he said to me, when we were alone after dinner, 'that Sarah was so upset by your manuscript, she couldn't stop talking about it, and at last I suggested we come to see you. We both had holidays due, you see. She has liked to believe that she's in some way carrying on where her grandfather left off, she was very proud to think of him as a hero of the Resistance, and now she finds he wasn't, and that life is more complicated than she believed. And she's very fond of you, sir, and worries about you.'

'I worry about her.'

'Can you stay over Christmas?' I asked next morning. 'In that case we'll go to Rome. We'll go to Midnight Mass at the Aracoeli and be serenaded by the pipers who say they are shepherds come down from the Abruzzi. I don't believe it, but I like to believe it.'

Rome is my favourite city – why then have I settled in Geneva? – and especially in winter when the pines on Trinità dei Monti stand black against the dying light, and the travertine stone glows first pink, then red-gold. Stendhal advised visitors to Rome to sacrifice I forget how many francs in order to have a beautiful view; they would keep it for life, he said. But nowadays I prefer to stay in the Inghilterra, which stands on the plain between the Spanish Steps and the Corso in that area of small expensive shops where they put down carpets on the streets at Christmas. And you only have to saunter a hundred yards to have breakfast at the Caffè Greco, or two hundred to eat poached eggs at half-past four in Babington's Tea-rooms. We walked in the morning on the Palatine and lunched at Sabatini's in Trastevere, and strolled and looked, and were happy, in the afternoon. We did not talk of the war or of Lucien, and we dined most evenings in Ranieri's.

Sarah relaxed. I could see her mood easing from day to day. She allowed me to buy her clothes: boots from Gucci and a wide-skirted suit in Scotch cashmere from a shop in Via Borgognona. For the first time since she was a child she looked like a rich man's daughter. Niels was admiring. There was no anger in him, he was at peace with himself. I was almost able to believe that Sarah might be safe.

Then it occurred to me that his peace derived from his moral certainty.

'You don't need to worry about Sarah, sir,' he told me. 'I know our politics seem dangerous to you, but we have the future on our side. Even the Nats know that.'

'And do you see your future still being in South Africa after the blacks take over?'

'Why not?' he said. 'We're all people. But if it doesn't work, then somewhere else. We're not tied anywhere.'

We were sitting outside a wine-shop in Campo dei Fiori. It was a beautiful shining morning with touches of snow on the Alban Hills. Sarah was buying fruit, vegetables and cheese for a picnic lunch we planned to take on the Palatine.

'I used to drink here with a Polish friend,' I said. 'It was when I worked here two years with FAO as one of those speciously high-level consultants that international organisations love to attach to themselves. My Polish friend was a Prince who had lost every-thing he had inherited. And yes, he was in a new way a happy man. He had accommodated himself to things. You could say he was free. He told me once how he had seen a boy shot by the *carabinieri*, just over there, where that orange cat is. The boy had died with a look of surprise on his face. I suppose he had woken up that morning full of life and optimism, the way such boys do.

'Come,' I said, as Sarah approached, 'we'll walk this way.' I led them through a narrow passage, into a little piazza round which tenements ran in a graceful and ancient curve.

'Do you know where we are?'

'Yes,' Niels said, 'I've been here before. It's the Theatre of Pompey, isn't it, where Caesar was killed?'

'They thought they were restoring Liberty. They ran through the streets crying that the Republic and Liberty had been won back. Within eighteen months you had the proscriptions, then more civil war, then the empire, and little by little, even the name of Liberty was forgotten. It's been the same with revolutions ever since. They set out to destroy evil and men release the evil in themselves.'

'But in the long run,' Niels said.

'In the long run?'

'Daddy,' Sarah said, 'history doesn't repeat itself. That's an old lie.'

'No,' I said, 'people repeat history.'

*

People repeat history. I had received a letter. It had arrived circuitously: from my lawyer in Paris, to my bank in Geneva, to the American Express in Rome. Often I don't open letters for several days – some not at all – and some instinct prompted me to neglect this one. It lay on my dressing table for a week, and eventually it was Sarah who, entering to see if I was ready for dinner, picked it up, and said,

'Who's Anne Candice?'

'No idea.'

'Aren't you going to open it? You really should. She might be a beautiful rich widow.'

'Are you so keen to have a stepmother?'

'No,' she said. 'Still, I shall. Oh,' she said, 'I think you will have to read this,' and passed me the single sheet of dove-grey paper.

'I used to be Anne Querouaille,' the first sentence read. There was a Paris address.

We took the Palatino the day after Epiphany. There had been telephone calls, to fix a date. There had been no discussion about whether Sarah and Niels should accompany me. We all took it for granted. It was my decision to travel by train, for that allows a shifting of mood which the aeroplane denies you.

'She must be getting on,' Sarah said.

'Still in her sixties. She was only a girl, you know.'

'It seems incredible.'

'That she should have tracked me down?'

'No, not that. That someone who was then is also now. Do you see what I mean?'

'Yes.'

'I don't know why,' Niels said, 'it's always raining when I come to Paris. I never get Hemingway weather.'

The sky pressed on the mansard roofs. Cars threw up showers of dirty water. There had been snow and now people squelched through grey slush, slipping and splashing. There wasn't a smile anywhere.

'No,' I said. 'Simenon weather.'

We went to our hotel, bathed, changed, reassembled. It was now raining on a sharp diagonal from the north-west. The porter whistled up a taxi.

'Are you nervous?'

In reply I pressed my daughter's hand.

'How do you think she found out about you, where to write and so on? And what can she tell us? She can't want to make excuses.'

It was one of those moments when you talk only to disturb a silence.

We turned off the Boulevard St Germain, and into the narrow Rue du Tournon. The driver searched for the number I had given him, and drew up between a café and an antique shop. There was a concierge, who admitted that Madame Candice had told her to expect us. We mounted to the fifth floor in an ironwork lift of art nouveau design.

I wouldn't have recognised the woman who opened the apartment door to us from the photographs I had found in my father's study at the Château de l'Haye. That was a silly reflection. How many people still resemble their youth? She was medium-sized and thickset with white hair cut straight and hanging loose, as if it had once been long and abundant and then hacked off with an axe. She wore a shaggy sweater and black trousers and the smear of lipstick had been carelessly applied. She had dark glasses on despite the gloom of the apartment.

'I would have known it was you,' she said, 'anywhere. You've got Lucien's eyes. It's like seeing a ghost.'

We drank coffee which she had already prepared. She urged *mille-feuilles* pastries on us, active in hospitality as if to ward off the conversation she had gone to such trouble to invite.

'It's good of you to come,' she said several times.

I had explained Sarah and Niels to her, but she kept glancing at him as if he was an intruder.

'I read everything you wrote for Hugh,' she said. 'You got an awful lot right. I was amazed how much. It was, oddly, comforting. The understanding.'

She now addressed me in English.

'I guess these young people are happier in English,' she said. 'You know Hugh Challefray? I hadn't realised . . .'

'Sure, he's my nephew. Well, my nephew by marriage. He didn't tell you that? Well, he was always a secretive child. Maybe he thought it would put you off. I don't know. He tells me he feels bad about it.'

'It was all your idea? You put him up to it?'

'Not exactly,' she said. 'Or only in a sense. By that I mean that I got Hugh interested in your father. He was looking round for a subject for his thesis, you see.'

'But this is extraordinary,' I said.

'Bob Candice's sister Merrill married Roger Challefray,

Hugh's father. Bob was my husband, you know. So that makes Hugh my nephew. Only in a manner of speaking really, because he was the son of Roger's first wife Betty, who divorced Roger and went to live in Ireland. Then Merrill married him when Rog was working for UNESCO, so Hugh spent a lot of his childhood with Bob and me and I've always thought of him as my nephew. We've always been close and Bob and I had no children of our own, you know.'

'And now?'

'Well, now you've told him I betrayed my lover, which disturbs him somewhat. And it isn't true, or not the way you have it. That's why I had to see you. I don't suppose there's anyone much alive whose good opinion I care for, except Hugh and yourself. Do you mind if I call you Etienne? It's how I think of you. I used to hear so much about you, you know. You were on his mind a lot.'

She pulled out a packet of king-sized Chesterfields and lit one with an old leather-covered lighter. Her fingernails were cut short and not varnished.

'We sometimes dared to talk about after the war, when you would spend holidays with us.' She drew on her cigarette and expelled smoke through her nose. 'I knew this would be difficult. I didn't think it would be this hard to know where to begin.'

Sarah got up and crossed to the window. She stood there a long time looking out at the rain and the wet roofs across the street. We all watched her and didn't speak. Then she turned round and sat down on the sofa beside Anne. She kicked off her shoes, drew her knees up and hugged them.

'Listen,' she said. 'We've come here for the story and we wouldn't have done that if we believed it ended just the way Daddy wrote it. We know it must be tough for you, even if you did offer it yourself. So take your time. We're in no hurry. Why don't you begin at the beginning. Be conventional. When you first met Lucien. Did Daddy get that right?'

Anne smiled, as you might smile leafing through an old photograph album and catching a day when the world was good.

'You're not to worry,' Sarah said. 'It's too long ago for tears. It's a life Niels and me,' she freed her left hand and touched his hair, 'never knew. But we've all now lived with the story a long time. Especially Daddy, and he never wanted to, really. So we would like . . . so you see? Help us to understand.'

'The fact that we've come here,' Niels said, 'that Monsieur de Balafré has come here, proves that it's not a question of blame.

It's maybe for both of you, and for Sarah at one further remove, a matter of letting the dead sleep quiet in the earth.'

'You're bigger than he was,' she said to me, 'and you try to look as if you don't care, which he never could, but you've the same expression in your eyes. And your mouth's the same . . . if I start by saying he was the love of my life does that make it sound like an operetta?'

'No,' Sarah said. 'It sounds right.' She glanced at Niels, and I knew that for the moment at least these two were safe, in love, together.

'But what about Mr Candice?' she said. 'Bob, did you call him? What about him?'

'Oh, he was an American. I married him, and we had a good marriage. He died last year in the fall, too young, he wasn't seventy. We met in '46 – he was a lawyer attached to the Commission – and married in '48. We had a good relationship, but he never set my heart on fire. And I disappointed him too, because – well – he knew there was something missing. Once, when he had an affair with his secretary, he let me know I was like a cracked plate. We made do and mended, but it hurt him that I couldn't be as jealous of his live girls as he was of your dead father. This is off the track,' she said, 'I'm going to fetch a bottle of wine. Sarah, would you care to help me with the glasses?'

There were photographs all over the room, several of Lucien. I wondered if she'd displayed them during the years of her marriage, or whether they'd remained hidden away in a bottom drawer, to be taken out and gazed on when Candice wasn't there. There was one, in a silver frame, of a group at a table with bottles of glasses and coffee-cups and the remains of a meal. Colette was whispering something in a girl's ear while Lucien smiled. I could hardly recall having seen him smile in a photograph before. It was a smile that for the moment accepted things as they were. The girl's face was shaded by Colette's hair. Her head was inclined towards the old lady and she was waving a cigarette in the hand beyond. Her arm had fallen into the sort of line that Ingres might have demanded from a model.

'So long ago,' she said, picking up the photograph, 'like yesterday. When Bob Candice died I came back to Paris. I couldn't have done that twenty years before, it would have been too painful; now it seems it would be painful to live anywhere else. I walk on the *quais* and think what things might have been like. It's my refuge, daydreaming. Moreover, most of the people I think of as my enemies are dead. Certainly the chief of them.'

She handed me a glass of Beaujolais.

'Begin at the beginning, you said? Well, for me, the beginning was an old house in a dull town in Brittany, not even on the sea, about thirty kilometres from Rennes. My father taught at the university there and would stay in the city the night before his lectures and come home in the afternoon in the little train. He was a kind man whose only interest was Celtic archaeology. He died just before the war, and our childhood was passed in a quiet house full of ugly heavy furniture, with a long narrow garden surrounded by a high wall. We spent our time writing stories. I adored Alain, my second brother, and it was because of Alain that I fell in love with your father. For I was in love with him before we met on account of the letters Alain wrote to me from the front. Alain was always honest with me, and the thing you didn't guess in your reconstruction was that he was terrified of showing fear when they went into action. He was so terrified that he could not sleep some nights, he told me, for fear, but lay awake sweating. And then Lucien gave him courage. He thought he was wonderful, and so different from all the other officers in the regiment. So, when Alain was dead and I was in the Ministry of Education, and found myself transferred to Paris, I was desperate to meet your father. His failure to arrive that morning was a Godsend, and I went to collect him, determined to make him fall in love with me. I used to tease him about it later, but he could never believe me. That was the most difficult thing for Lucien, accepting that he could be loved. He had been hurt, you know, by your mother's infidelities.

'One question I've often asked myself: what would Alain have done in 1940? And I'm sure he would have been guided by Lucien, who really had no doubts then that he had done the right thing. He trusted Pétain, and if that was naive, so were 95 per cent of the French people. So was I.'

She lit another cigarette and drank some wine.

'All the same, in one sense Lucien was happy in the winter of 1942 when he was able to leave the government. I think by then he knew there was no future for France that didn't involve terrible suffering. And of course he was shamed by the thing about sending French workers to Germany. If it hadn't been for me, I believe he would have volunteered to go himself.

'You're quite right. His mother didn't like me, though she did once say to me, "At least you're French, at least you understand something of Lucien." But she was jealous because I made him happy, and she couldn't.

'And then Hervé. You assumed too much there. You assumed I loved Hervé as I did Alain. But I always knew Hervé was a little mad. He had such charm but he was a fanatic at heart, and my love for him was protective, not trusting. I even warned Lucien against him, that he couldn't rely on him. Trust. You know that's the word that dominates my memory of the war years. Who you could trust, who you couldn't, how far you could trust anyone. We were living in a world in which the most natural conversation could suddenly open up an abyss. Do you know, even after forty years of America, near enough, I don't believe I have escaped what we learned then: to distrust everything, even love. Perhaps especially love. That's what the war did. It put fear in bed with love. Love has to trust the future and we couldn't . . .'

She paused. The afternoon was darkening.

'Sarah,' she said, 'I've a long way to go and I'm almost out of cigarettes. Stupid of me. No, I really only like these. Would you mind going down to the *tabac* at the corner and getting me a couple of packs? They keep them for me there. Perhaps your young man would go with you.'

'Of course,' Sarah said, 'with pleasure.'

We listened for the clang of the lift door.

Anne said, 'I didn't betray your father, but I do have a confession to make.' She lit a cigarette. 'Actually I have plenty of these,' she said, 'but I couldn't tell you this in front of Sarah. I did betray Lucien once. With Rupert. It was an afternoon in September when the heat dried everything up and made distances short. There was the rattle of crickets outside the window. Lucien had gone into the town, to see the Prefect. We looked at each other. He was drinking coffee and his hand shook and, without speaking, we mounted the stairs to his bedroom. I hadn't even thought of him like that before. Afterwards I lay with my face pressed against his withered arm and heard him say, "I've always wanted to possess everything that was his," and I knew that was true of me too. So, you see, the act of betrayal was in another way a new bond. It made me part of what Rupert shared with Lucien, and him part of what we had.

'I had a miscarriage. You missed that, or didn't guess it. It was while Lucien was in prison and after Hervé had been killed. I knew he was dead, and I was afraid Lucien soon would be also, and then my baby died within me. It might have been Rupert's, I've often wondered, but I don't think it was.

'I left him from sheer misery. I think you were right there. He couldn't speak to me after he had been tortured, could hardly bear to bring himself to look at me. His mother had told him about Rupert – I'm sure of that – she knew everything that happened in the house – she used to know without even spying. But it wasn't on account of that, and not even on account of Hervé, that he couldn't look at me or touch me. It was shame. He thought the torture had degraded him, when it had only proved him human. And my heart was breaking to be with him, and because I was denied by him. But he understood about Rupert, we talked of it later, before the end. You have to believe me.

'I couldn't stay away. It was worse not to be with him. I knew it could never be just the same again. What we keep of the past is always changed by what has happened in between. It can never be three o'clock in the afternoon yesterday, a second time.

'Yet his face, when he came back and saw me sitting on the doorstep . . . it was like a saint's – St Stephen or St John the Baptist . . . glowing with joy. "*Contra mundum*", we said, and *contra mundum* it was. How, when you understand that, could you have been so . . . stupid, if you'll forgive the word, as to believe I could betray him?'

Sarah and Niels returned with the cigarettes.

'Thank you, but I'm sorry,' she said, 'it was foolish of me. I find I had another pack here all the time. Perhaps we should have a second bottle of wine . . . or some tea? No, wine then.

'I urged him to leave Paris and France. But he wouldn't. There were planes that would have taken us to Madrid or Barcelona, and he wasn't Laval – there wouldn't have been international difficulties if they had let him remain – he wasn't important in that way, they wouldn't have surrendered him.

'You were right about Laval, by the way. Lucien actually came to like him and admire him. It was odd, because Laval really had no shame. He was a peasant, that was why Lucien liked him, but it was also what in the end separated them, for Lucien couldn't have been less like a peasant himself . . .

'But he resisted my pleas. He wouldn't go. So there was nothing for it but to stay with him. I wasn't in danger myself, or I didn't think I was, not real danger.

'We talked. How everybody talked those last days, round and round, like people lost in a maze, beating our thoughts against facts like the sea surging on the rocks . . .

'He laughed when he told me of how Drieu had spoken to that little girl in the Ritz bar advising her to wait there for an American. It was almost what I did myself eighteen months later.

'But I'm rambling, as if I was still in the maze. It's because I don't want to arrive at my destination. You understand that, don't you Sarah?'

'Yes,' Sarah said, 'I think I do.'

Someone in the street below began to play a trumpet. It was the *St Louis Blues*: 'I hate to see that evening sun go down.' The notes, melancholy as the cry of gulls, rose through the failing light.

'It's a friend of mine,' Anne said. 'We've become friends. He really does come from St Louis, but he doesn't want to go home. He plays in the street every afternoon, for the last two months now, since his lover shot himself. We sometimes have a drink together in the little bar on the corner. He used to be a professional, but he's not very good, is he?'

The trumpet's bray cut through the noise of the traffic, filling the apartment with the sense of things – time, lovers, chances, afternoons – drifting beyond hope.

'We got on the train at 11.37,' Anne said. 'I had at last persuaded him to come to my mother's home. It was weariness made him agree. The train moved slowly and uncertainly because the line was damaged in places, and we scarcely dared to talk. Lucien sat with his back to the engine, as the suburbs ran away from us. Into the past.

'They boarded the train on the outskirts of Orléans. Young men, with rifles slung across their backs, cheerful and confident. They asked for him by name. He stood up, and the other people in the compartment seemed to shrink away. It was a boy with tousled black curly hair who took him by the arm. "Are you his girl?" he said to me. "We want you too."

'I was pushed into a little cell in the police station, and left alone. I threw myself down on the pallet bed, shaking and weeping. We had had papers, I'd seen to that myself. I had told no one of our plans. When they brought me a hunk of bread and some soup, I asked, "Who informed on us?" Naturally I got no answer. The girl spat in my soup. She called me "a collaborator's whore".

'Lucien had talked so often of his determination to stand trial. When I looked at that spittle curling in my soup, I knew he had no chance. I began to cry, and the girl smacked me on the cheek and then hit me on the side of the head with the bunch of keys she was carrying. Look.'

She pushed back the lock of hair that hung over her left temple and thrust her face forward so that the light fell on a little criss-cross cicatrice.

'It's not much, is it. Yet that's the only physical damage I suffered in the whole war. But it was the first time in my life anyone had hit me.

'They left me in the dark. It was cold and damp and there was no blanket. I curled up, hugging myself for warmth, and gnawed the bread. In the morning the blood had formed a thick crust over the wound. I begged to be allowed to see Lucien. No good. That went on for two days. They didn't hit me again, but each time the girl brought me the soup, she spat in it. Once she threw the bread on to the floor, and told me to get down on my knees and pick it up with my teeth. I looked at her, in a battle of wills, which I lost. The cell stank. The chamberpot was overflowing, and I didn't dare ask for another in case the girl threw its contents in my face. That night two other women – one a girl of sixteen – were thrown in to join me. They'd both had their heads shaved. The older one looked at me as if she couldn't credit the hair on my head. The young one crouched in the corner of the cell covering her bald head with her arms. When she fell asleep her arms dropped away, and a band of moonlight lay like pale shiny wax on her skull.'

She stopped.

'I'm not sure that I can go on,' she said. 'I've brought you here, and I don't know that I can.'

There was nothing I could say. All my life there has never been anything I could say at moments which demanded speech. I have never known how to encourage others, or strengthen them or comfort them. I have remained locked up in my iron mask, and self-pity has persuaded me that my father turned the key. So now, as Anne shed her Americanised assurance, and as I could see her features reform themselves into those of an old French peasant woman, whose only response to adversity must be endurance, I was held dumb. But Sarah leaned over and kissed her. She held her a moment, and said:

'It's terrible for you, reliving this, but you yourself said it's not the same, the past is past. And don't think, whatever you have to tell us, that it's a question of blame. Not now, not ever. And as for the horror, which I'm sure you've never spoken of, maybe it will grow less, diminish, if you can only bring yourself to tell us.'

Anne said, 'It was that image of the girl's skull, gleaming like dirty tallow. I've always carried that with me, and of course, as I've said, many worse things were done by others, by the Nazis, and, yes, by the French Fascists too.

'I don't remember now if I slept that night. But we didn't speak. And in the morning the same girl, who was our warder, came again, and she stood outside the cell, and threw her head back, and laughed. Then she told me I was wanted. Her mood changed abruptly, it had been the other girls she was laughing at, with their shaven heads, and now she was angry. "You bitch," she said, "you've cheated us." I didn't know what she meant. She pushed me into a room where there was a man sitting behind a desk, and two others lounging by the window, with their backs to me. "Has he spoken of killing himself?" the man at the desk said. "No," I answered truthfully. "He wants to stand trial," I said. "Then why were you running away?" "Because I persuaded him." "He's escaped us." One of the men at the window turned round and I knew from the expression on his face what the words meant. "I don't believe it," I said, "this is some sort of trick." Yet I knew it wasn't that, but a lie. They made me see his body, still dangling. "For identification," one said. Then the two men went away, and I was taken back to the little room and left there with Guy Fouquet. He gave me some brandy. I wanted to be sick but I forced it down. I wanted to sob, but dared not. He made me sit.

'"I hated him," he said, "till we talked the other night. And I don't believe he killed himself either." "Then," I said, "you must order an investigation." He only smiled. He told me that when I had recovered I would understand the absurdity of what I was asking. What was the death of one collaborator more or less? "Nevertheless, I don't like it," he said. "And I will tell you one thing. I have no evidence, and I'm not going to exhaust myself trying to find it, but I have no doubt there were people he could have compromised, people who would rather he had no opportunity to speak, and perhaps whoever let us know he was on that train also contrived, I don't know how, to hasten his death . . . we won't keep you. You were going to your mother's. I suggest you continue your journey." "What happens to the body?" I asked. "Can I have it?" "What would you do with it? No, it will have to be buried here."'

'He saw me on to the train,' she said. 'Guy Fouquet did. And gave me a pass. And the last thing he said was: "I hate myself so much that I can never forgive or forget, but I almost liked him, that last talk we had . . ."'

She stopped again. She was crying. We sat without speaking. Children shouted and laughed in the street below.

'I've brought you a long way, perhaps to tell you nothing of value. But I had to. I couldn't let you think or believe that I had betrayed him. Do you believe me?'

'Yes,' I said.

'I've thought about it so often. I've never stopped, it seems to me. And I don't know who did. There were two old friends he met the day before we left Paris, who had written for his magazine. One was that Torrance, the other Léon-Paul Cebran. He thought they were friends, he might have told them of our plans.'

'I know of Torrance. What happened to Cebran?'

'He died, years ago, of cirrhosis, I think. You remember he was a Fascist in 1940. He converted, or recanted, in time. Certainly he denounced others. But how either could have arranged Lucien's murder – for that's what it was – I don't know.'

'So even in the end, we have a mystery.'

'Do you know the worst thing? I have never been able to recall his last words to me. He must have said something just before we were separated, but I have never been able to remember what.'

'Why don't you come back to South Africa?' Sarah said. 'Come home now this is over.'

We were standing at the window of the airport lounge, watching the snow. It was falling in small flakes from an iron sky. Despite the snow their flight would take off in twenty minutes. They would soar over the mountains and deserts to Africa. As from an aeroplane, but an old two-seater one, I looked down on a red road descending like a scar into a wide hollow where a white farmhouse stood surrounded by gum trees. There was a dam with waterfowl and spirals of milk-blue smoke rose from the house and the nearby kraal. A hawk hung above the trees and there was silence but for the chug-chug of the four-stroke engine and the buzz of insects. At ground level the air would be sharp and aromatic. When the aeroplane passed over, the land would relapse into an ancient peace.

But of course they wouldn't fly over Africa; politics forbade it, commanded them to take the route over the ocean.

'I know what you've been thinking ever since we left Anne.' Sarah placed her arm on mine. 'You've been thinking about her conversation with Guy Fouquet and wondering whether Berthe and Armand weren't completely wrong when they warned you off Freddie. Haven't you?'

'Daughter,' I said. 'You're Rose's daughter, and mine.'

The intercom crackled, calling them to Africa.

'Well, won't you?' she said.

'I'll see out winter in Europe.'

Niels shook my hand. I kissed Sarah, holding her close to give me strength.

'Take care of her,' I said.

I stood at the window and watched the plane slide along the runway, out of sight. Then it returned faster, its nose lifted, and I gazed after it till it was swallowed up in cloud. I lit a cigar and turned away, shrugging myself into my overcoat.

Of course Sarah was right. These thoughts had indeed occupied my mind. If things were not what they have been, they would not be as they are. My uncle and aunt's intentions had been of the best, brought about the worst. And yet there was Sarah calling me back to Africa, my daughter who was one consequence of their intervention in my life. If only, if only . . . but then, also, if only, for example, Rupert had laughed at Lucien in that casino where they had discussed his love for Polly, if only he had played the man, instead of the man of honour, and gone off with her, mightn't Lucien himself have behaved differently in 1940? Things are as they have been made, and not as we might wish to rearrange them in the past. Life takes its shape undeflected by imponderables, and my residence in the city of Calvin comes close to persuading me that shape is determined irrespective of our will.

The young taxi-driver was incredulous, sceptical. To look for a tree in a forest? That was madness. And in this weather, in this snow? He would need chains for his car.

'Very well, then,' I said, 'I'll pay to have them fixed.'

It wasn't, his look said, a question of money, but of my sanity.

His mood lifted as we set out. This was after all an adventure, in a small way, something to talk about in his favourite bar. This old lunatic who sought a single tree in a forest.

'Do you know where we should begin to look?'

'No,' I said, 'there may be foresters who would help.'

We stopped at an inn on the outskirts of the forest. I explained my business as we ate charcuterie, and an omelette, and drank *vin gris* followed by *marc* with our coffee.

The innkeeper expressed ignorance. He was too young, he said, to remember the war. Besides, such things were better forgotten. France was different now; all that had been put behind us. At last, however, he bethought him of an old forester who might remember, 'But it's a long time ago, and the young men, you know, were absent then, or so I've heard.' He sent someone to fetch the ancient. Meanwhile we should all have another glass of *marc*, on the house, this time. He was intrigued by my curiosity. And so on.

At last the old man appeared, grumbling. He cheered up on being offered a drink, and then became voluble.

Of course he remembered it all. Why, he had selected the tree himself. As he said this, his face took on the ingratiating expression of a peasant who sees the chance of a reward. He remembered the Marshal standing there at the ceremony. It had been a fine thing, though everyone thereabouts had now forgotten all about it. He could see his blue gaze to this day. Ah, there was a man. They didn't make men like old Papa Pétain now, a good man, whatever lies were later told about him.

But there was nothing to see now. Didn't I know? They had cut it down after the war. That's what they had done. They'd revenged themselves on a tree. It had been chopped up for firewood. Why, he'd burned some himself.

The gentleman wished to see where it had stood? In a clearing not a kilometre from here. Those had been his instructions. The Marshal was an old man, you know, well over a hundred, they said, and it stood to reason he couldn't walk far from his car. There had been a cavalcade of cars, a regular cavalcade. And a Bishop. He spat on the floor. Certainly, he would guide the gentleman. But it was a cold day and he felt the cold at his age. Yes, perhaps another drop would be wise.

Of course there was nothing to see. Other great oaks thrust their naked arms to the sky. The clearing was still. There were footprints of animals, rabbits, deer, perhaps a weasel, in the snow. Scrub and saplings had grown over and around the toppled oak. 'The National Revolution is also a Natural Revolution.'

The old forester tugged the cap off his head and wiped it across his eyes.

'For years,' he said, 'someone used to lay a wreath of lilies on the stump, on his birthday in April. But that was a long time ago. It all stopped a long time ago.'

I write this back in Geneva. I have written a letter to Anne, thanking her, and saying I hope to see her when next in Paris. I have written too to my dear cousin, Jeanne-Marie, to tell her everything, to ask her also to pray for me, to the God of Forgiveness in whom she believes, or used to believe.

The night before Sarah and Niels flew back to Africa we sat for a long time drinking brandy after dinner. The weight of Lucien's collaboration hung over us, swinging like a pendulum that threatened to descend. The equation seemed so obvious to them.

'In the end,' Sarah said, 'he must have been glad to die.'

'I have an uncle,' Niels said, 'my mother's brother, who used to be a disciple of Smuts. When he was a young man he worked in

his private office. He stayed with the United Party as it disin-
tegrated. Last year he was admitted to a clinic suffering from
chronic alcoholism. Do you see what I mean?'

'What was his name?' I said.

'Piet Doorktrievor, he was a lawyer.'

'It's a small country, South Africa,' I said. 'I used to know him
well. I hadn't heard that about him.'

'It's not a small country, Daddy. It's a big black country.'

'No, Sarah,' Niels said, 'it's very small for the blacks. It's a prison.'

'It's a lunatic asylum . . .'

'A concentration camp . . .'

'Poor Piet,' I said, 'I hope he recovers.'

'He doesn't want to recover, he wants to die.'

I didn't say: 'People who seek death, find it.' Instead I tilted the
bottle and poured us each another drink.

'I understand what you are urging,' I said, 'and I appreciate
that you are too kind to say it outright.'

'Believe me,' Niels said, 'people like you who don't belong to the
torturable classes can have more influence than you can imagine.'

'Is there any class that can't be tortured? Can you believe that
after what we have learned?'

There was a news bulletin today. Three young white South
Africans have been arrested; they are charged with collaboration
with a banned organisation. Two are lawyers, the third a doctor of
philosophy. I don't recognise their names, but I wonder if they are
friends of Niels and Sarah.

And in what way they will be tortured.

I tried to telephone the Johannesburg number Sarah left me.
The line was dead. I called my lawyer in Cape Town. He was
unavailable, in conference, they said. I was reluctant to speak to a
partner whom I did not know. I left a message, opaque save to the
initiated.

Then, in fulfilment of a promise I had made the Baron, I went
to see his 'poor dear wife' in her asylum. She wore a rose pinned
to her hair, and told me she expected good news, any day now.

'Old Europe is resurgent,' she said, 'resurgent. I expect my
estates in the east to be restored to me.'

'Conquer yourself, not the world': so Jacques quoted Descartes to
me in the prison visiting room.

That advice had done for the *garagiste* Simon.

★

Did you know that Pétain's middle name was Benoni? It is Hebrew, meaning 'son of sorrow'. It was the name Rachel gave her newborn son, whom we know better as Benjamin, as she died (*Genesis* xxxv: 18).

It would be a pleasant irony to think that the chief of the most anti-Semitic regime France has ever shamefully known had Jewish blood, but this is not so: the name was often given to children born into Royalist families, to remind them, as they grew, of what had been lost and destroyed. Benoni.

Benoni: it is a universal name, one that wings its way through the cold night, across mountains, deserts and seas, reaching even unto Africa.

Benoni.

And this afternoon, restless, I played chess again. My Ukrainian friend beat me twice, first with black, then with white.

He said, 'You don't win because you don't care enough.'

'Is that true of life as of chess?'

'Who can tell?' he said. 'Sometimes I think I win at chess because I no longer care about life. But then sometimes I think the opposite. Ignorant people call this a mere game, not realising that life unfolds as a game of another sort, in which we are the pieces. Now I am only a pawn. I used to be more ambitious. I used to think I was a knight. I fought, you know, in the Free Ukrainian Army. I was lucky to survive. It was a miracle. We fought for Hitler, and almost all my colleagues were sent back by the British to be murdered by Stalin or to perish in his filthy Gulag. I used to think my survival was a meaningless miracle, in the early years after the war when I was scraping a living and dodging up side-streets at the sight of a policeman. But now I know miracles are no more meaningless than anything else. Man has an instinct to survive. We must live for the moment, that's all.'

He sipped his lemon tea. I ordered another brandy and gave him a cigar and lit one myself.

'Do you still believe in a free Ukraine?'

'I don't know,' he said. 'It was a Cause, a reason for action, and I'm still a Ukrainian and I'm free. Why shouldn't I still believe if I choose? After all, I could believe in something still less substantial, like the Trinity. No doubt I did great wrong, but then I suffered great wrong myself. That's the story of History, isn't it? That's what History is, and we are bound to it. It's a wheel that turns, and sometimes we are at the bottom of the revolution. If the weight on the cart is sufficient then we are crushed. But at other periods we are clear of the ground, and then we have the illusion of being free. Meanwhile I have a daughter and grand-children. She's married to a Swiss engineer. When I was in the prison camp, I would have given a lot to be a Swiss engineer and to come home every night to a dish of fondue and a bottle of wine. But there it is. She looks after her old father, and I win at chess. I'm too old for other causes. On the other hand, she won't be pleased when I come home stinking of this very good cigar.'

'Do you miss the Ukraine?'

'The mornings, the smell of the river, of horses by the river, and also that horizon you can never hope to reach, that lures you on. All that. But again, there it is. I sometimes think, my friend, that exile is a foretaste of the hereafter, even of Paradise. We won't value this life till we have lost it and are confronted by God. Then we shall realise it was good. What is exile? The knowledge that we have lost what we did not deserve to have. It is easier for us who know we are exiles to know we are sons of Adam. I can tell you are an exile too. From where are you exiled, my friend?'

I puffed my cigar. I sipped my brandy.

'I'm not sure,' I said, 'that I can claim the honour.'

At the next table four businessmen, buttoned into dark suits, were discussing money over coffee and chocolate cake.

'On the other hand I can't claim to belong here like these gentlemen,' I said, 'and, like you, I have no country except in memory.'

He began to set up the pieces.

'Let us have another game,' he said, 'while we enjoy our cigars. There's neither guilt nor fear in chess.'

He smiled.

'You asked about the free Ukraine. Not long ago I was approached by some young men who wished me to lend my name to an enterprise in that connection. I have, you see, despite everything, a certain reputation still in some quarters. I listened to their argument, and I admit I felt a tremor of excitement. But do you know what I said? "Thank you, gentlemen, but I would rather play chess." They thought I had gone soft, that I was a renegade. I could see that. But I know these people now, because I was such myself. I know how noble ideals bring misery to the poor and weak. It's your move,' he said.

I hesitated.

'No,' he said, 'my daughter won't be pleased to smell the smoke, even of this excellent cigar. She's afraid of cancer, you see.

Even in Switzerland, my friend, people must find something to fear – cancer, bankruptcy, the dark, it doesn't matter.'

I advanced a pawn to K4.

'Let me bring a knight into play,' he said. 'These days I am too timid in my use of that daring piece.'

It was snowing as I walked back to my hotel. The flakes fell as they did in childhood, changing the world. In the night and for a few hours of the early morning the city would be another place.

At the hotel desk, I asked if there was a telex for me.

'From Africa,' I said, as if the information might make it more likely to materialise.

The clerk shook his head.

'No, sir,' he said, 'there is nothing new, even from Africa.'